Flora Annie Webster Steel

Tales of the Punjab - Told by the People

Flora Annie Webster Steel

Tales of the Punjab - Told by the People

ISBN/EAN: 9783337023935

Printed in Europe, USA, Canada, Australia, Japan

Cover: Foto ©Andreas Hilbeck / pixelio.de

More available books at **www.hansebooks.com**

TALES OF THE PUNJAB

TALES OF THE PUNJAB

TOLD BY THE PEOPLE

BY

FLORA-ANNIE STEEL

WITH ILLUSTRATIONS

BY J. LOCKWOOD KIPLING, C.I.E.

AND

NOTES BY R. C. TEMPLE

London

MACMILLAN AND CO.

AND NEW YORK

1894

First Edition November 1894
Reprinted December 1894

PREFACE

MANY of the tales in this collection appeared either in the *Indian Antiquary*, the *Calcutta Review*, or the *Legends of the Punjab.* They were then in the form of literal translations, in many cases uncouth or even unpresentable to ears polite, in all scarcely intelligible to the untravelled English reader; for it must be remembered that, with the exception of the Adventures of Raja Rasâlu, all these stories are strictly folk-tales passing current among a people who can neither read nor write, and whose diction is full of colloquialisms, and, if we choose to call them so, vulgarisms. It would be manifestly unfair, for instance, to compare the literary standard of such tales with that of the *Arabian Nights*, the *Tales of a Parrot*, or similar works. The manner in which these stories were collected is in itself sufficient to show how misleading it would be, if, with the intention of giving the conventional Eastern flavour to the text, it were to be manipulated into a flowery dignity; and as a description of the procedure will serve the double purpose of credential and excuse, the authors give it,

—premising that all the stories but three have been collected by Mrs. F. A. Steel during winter tours through the various districts of which her husband has been Chief Magistrate.

A carpet is spread under a tree in the vicinity of the spot which the Magistrate has chosen for his *darbâr*, but far enough away from bureaucracy to let the village idlers approach it should they feel so inclined. In a very few minutes, as a rule, some of them begin to edge up to it, and as they are generally small boys, they commence nudging each other, whispering, and sniggering. The fancied approach of a *chuprâsî*, the 'corrupt lictor' of India, who attends at every *darbâr*, will however cause a sudden stampede; but after a time these become less and less frequent, the wild beasts, as it were, becoming tamer. By and by a group of women stop to gaze, and then the question 'What do you want?' invariably brings the answer 'To see your honour' (*âp ke darshan âe*). Once the ice is broken, the only difficulties are, first, to understand your visitors, and secondly, to get them to go away. When the general conversation is fairly started, inquiries are made by degrees as to how many witches there are in the village, or what cures they know for fever and the evil eye, etc. At first these are met by denials expressed in set terms, but a little patient talk will generally lead to some remarks which point the villagers' minds in the direction required, till at last, after many persuasions, some child begins a story, others correct the details, emulation conquers shyness, and finally the story-teller is brought to the front with acclamations : for there is always a story-teller *par excellence* in every village—generally a boy.

Then comes the need for patience, since in all probability the first story is one you have heard a hundred times, or else some pointless and disconnected jumble.   At the conclusion of either, however, the teller must be profusely complimented, in the hopes of eliciting something more valuable.   But it is possible to waste many hours, and in the end find yourself possessed of nothing save some feeble variant of a well-known legend, or, what is worse, a compilation of oddments which have lingered in a faulty memory from half a dozen distinct stories. After a time, however, the attentive collector is rewarded by finding that a coherent whole is growing up in his or her mind out of the shreds and patches heard here and there, and it is delight indeed when your own dim suspicion that this part of the puzzle fits into that is confirmed by finding the two incidents preserved side by side in the mouth of some perfectly unconscious witness.   Some of the tales in this volume have thus been a year or more on the stocks before they had been heard sufficiently often to make their form conclusive.

And this accounts for what may be called the greater literary sequence of these tales over those to be found in many similar collections.   They have been selected carefully with the object of securing a good story in what appears to be its best form ; but they have not been doctored in any way, not even in the language. That is neither a transliteration— which would have needed a whole dictionary to be intelligible—nor a version orientalised to suit English tastes. It is an attempt to translate one colloquialism by another, and thus to preserve the aroma of rough ready wit existing side by side with that perfume of pure poesy which every now and again contrasts so strangely with the other. Nothing would have been easier than to alter the style ; but to do so would, in the collector's opinion, have robbed the stories of all human value.

That such has been the deliberate choice may be seen at a glance through the only story which has a different origin. The Adventures of Raja Rasâlu was translated from the rough manuscript of a village accountant ; and, being current in a more or less classical form, it approaches more nearly to the conventional standards of an Indian tale.

The work has been apportioned between the authors in this way. Mrs. F. A. Steel is responsible for the text, and Major R. C. Temple for the annotations and the appendices on Analysis and Survey of Incidents. The latter conforms strictly to the method adopted by the Folklore Society and is intended to form part of their scheme of investigations into the general machinery of folk-tales.

It is therefore hoped that the form of the book may fulfil the double intention with which it was written; namely, that the text should interest children, and at the same time the notes should render it valuable to those who study Folklore on its scientific side.

F. A. STEEL.

R. C. TEMPLE.

TO THE LITTLE READER

WOULD you like to know how these stories are told? Come with me, and you shall see. There! take my hand and do not be afraid, for Prince Hassan's carpet is beneath your feet. So now!—'Hey presto! Abracadabra!' Here we are in a Punjabi village.

*　　*　　*　　*　　*

It is sunset. Over the limitless plain, vast and unbroken as the heaven above, the hot cloudless sky cools slowly into shadow. The men leave their labour amid the fields, which, like an oasis in the desert, surround the mud-built village, and, plough on shoulder, drive their bullocks homewards. The women set aside their spinning-wheels, and prepare the simple evening meal. The little girls troop, basket on head, from the outskirts of the village, where all day long they have been at work, kneading, drying, and stacking the fuel-cakes so necessary in that woodless country. The boys, half hidden in clouds of dust, drive the herds of gaunt cattle and ponderous buffaloes to the thorn-hedged yards. The day is over,—the day which has been so hard and toilful even for the children,—and with the night comes rest and play. The village, so deserted before, is alive with voices ; the elders cluster round the courtyard doors, the little ones whoop through the narrow alleys. But as the short-lived Indian twilight dies into darkness, the voices one by one are hushed, and as the stars come out the children disappear. But not to sleep : it is too hot, for the sun which has beaten so fiercely all day on the mud walls, and floors, and roofs, has left a legacy of warmth behind it, and not till midnight will the cool breeze spring up, bringing with it refreshment and repose. How then are the long dark hours to be passed ? In all the village not a lamp or candle is to be found ; the only light—and that too used but sparingly and of necessity—being the dim smoky flame of an oil-fed wick. Yet, in spite of this, the hours, though dark, are not dreary, for this, in an Indian village, is *story-telling time ;* not only from choice, but from obedience to the well-known precept which forbids such idle amusement between sunrise and sunset. Ask little Kaniyâ, yonder, why it is that he, the best story-teller in the village, never opens his lips till after sunset, and he will grin from ear to ear, and with a flash of dark eyes and white teeth, answer that travellers lose their way when idle boys and girls tell tales by daylight. And Narainî, the herd-girl, will hang her head and cover her dusky face with her rag of a veil, if you put the question to her; or little Râm Jas shake his bald shaven poll in denial; but not one of the dark-skinned, bare-limbed village children will yield to your request for a story.

No, no!—from sunrise to sunset, when even the little ones must labour, not a word; but from sunset to sunrise, when no man can work, the tongues chatter glibly enough, for that is story-telling time. Then, after the scanty meal is over, the bairns drag their wooden-legged, string-woven bedsteads into the open, and settle themselves down like young birds in a nest, three or four to a bed, while others coil up on mats upon the ground, and some, stealing in for an hour from distant alleys, beg a place here or there.

The stars twinkle overhead, the mosquito sings through the hot air, the village dogs bark at imaginary foes, and from one crowded nest after another rises a childish voice telling some tale, old yet ever new,—tales that were told in the sunrise of the world, and will be told in its sunset. The little audience listens, dozes, dreams, and still the wily Jackal meets his match, or Bopolûchî brave and bold returns rich and victorious from the robber's den. Hark!—that is Kaniyâ's voice, and there is an expectant stir amongst the drowsy listeners as he begins the old old formula—

'Once upon a time——'

CONTENTS

NCE upon a time a soldier died, leaving a widow and one son. They were dreadfully poor, and at last matters became so bad that they had nothing left in the house to eat.

'Mother,' said the son, 'give me four shillings, and I will go seek my fortune in the wide world.'

'Alas!' answered the mother, 'and where am I, who haven't a farthing wherewith to buy bread, to find four shillings?'

'There is that old coat of my father's,' returned the lad; 'look in the pocket—perchance there is something there.'

So she looked, and behold! there were six shillings hidden away at the very bottom of the pocket!

'More than I bargained for,' quoth the lad, laughing. 'See, mother, these two shillings are for you; you can live on that till I return, the rest will pay my way until I find my fortune.'

So he set off to find his fortune, and on the way
he saw a tigress, licking her paw, and moaning mournfully. He was just about to run away from the
terrible creature, when she called to him faintly,
saying, 'Good lad, if you will take out this thorn for
me, I shall be for ever grateful.'

'Not I!' answered the lad. 'Why, if I begin to

pull it out, and it pains you, you will kill me with a
pat of your paw.'

'No, no!' cried the tigress, 'I will turn my face
to this tree, and when the pain comes I will pat *it*.'

To this the soldier's son agreed; so he pulled out
the thorn, and when the pain came the tigress gave
the tree such a blow that the trunk split all to pieces.
Then she turned towards the soldier's son, and said
gratefully, 'Take this box as a reward, my son, but
do not open it until you have travelled nine miles.'

So the soldier's son thanked the tigress, and set off with the box to find his fortune. Now when he had gone five miles, he felt certain that the box weighed more than it had at first, and every step he took it seemed to grow heavier and heavier. He tried to struggle on—though it was all he could do to carry the box—until he had gone about eight miles and a quarter, when his patience gave way. 'I believe that tigress was a witch, and is playing off her tricks upon me,' he cried, 'but I will stand this nonsense no longer. Lie there, you wretched old box!—heaven knows what is in you, and I don't care.'

So saying, he flung the box down on the ground: it burst open with the shock, and out stepped a little old man. He was only one span high, but his beard was a span and a quarter long, and trailed upon the ground.

The little mannikin immediately began to stamp about and scold the lad roundly for letting the box down so violently.

'Upon my word!' quoth the soldier's son, scarcely able to restrain a smile at the ridiculous little figure, 'but you are weighty for your size, old gentleman! And what may your name be?'

'Sir Buzz!' snapped the one-span mannikin, still stamping about in a great rage.

'Upon my word!' quoth the soldier's son once more, 'if *you* are all the box contained, I am glad I didn't trouble to carry it farther.'

'That's not polite,' snarled the mannikin; 'perhaps if you had carried it the full nine miles you might have found something better; but that's neither

here nor there. I'm good enough for you, at any
rate, and will serve you faithfully according to my
mistress's orders.'

'Serve me!—then I wish to goodness you'd serve
me with some dinner, for I am mighty hungry!
Here are four shillings to pay for it.'

No sooner had the soldier's son said this and
given the money, than with a *whiz! boom! bing!*
like a big bee, Sir Buzz flew through the air to a
confectioner's shop in the nearest town. There he
stood, the one-span mannikin, with the span and a
quarter beard trailing on the ground, just by the big
preserving pan, and cried in ever so loud a voice,
'Ho! ho! Sir Confectioner, bring me sweets!'

The confectioner looked round the shop, and out
of the door, and down the street, but could see no
one, for tiny Sir Buzz was quite hidden by the preserving pan. Then the mannikin called out louder
still, 'Ho! ho! Sir Confectioner, bring me sweets!'
And when the confectioner looked in vain for his
customer, Sir Buzz grew angry, and ran and pinched
him on the legs, and kicked him on the foot, saying,
'Impudent knave! do you mean to say you can't
see *me?* Why, I was standing by the preserving
pan all the time!'

The confectioner apologised humbly, and hurried
away to bring out his best sweets for his irritable
little customer. Then Sir Buzz chose about a
hundredweight of them, and said, 'Quick, tie them
up in something and give them into my hand; I'll
carry them home.'

'They will be a good weight, sir,' smiled the
confectioner.

'What business is that of yours, I should like to know?' snapped Sir Buzz. 'Just you do as you're told, and here is your money.' So saying he jingled the four shillings in his pocket.

'As you please, sir,' replied the man cheerfully, as he tied up the sweets into a huge bundle and placed it on the little mannikin's outstretched hand, fully expecting him to sink under the weight; when lo! with a *boom! bing!* he whizzed off with the money still in his pocket.

He alighted at a corn-chandler's shop, and, standing behind a basket of flour, called out at the top of his voice, 'Ho! ho! Sir Chandler, bring me flour!'

And when the corn-chandler looked round the shop, and out of the window, and down the street, without seeing anybody, the one-span mannikin, with his beard trailing on the ground, cried again louder than before, 'Ho! ho! Sir Chandler, bring me flour!'

Then on receiving no answer, he flew into a violent rage, and ran and bit the unfortunate corn-chandler on the leg, pinched him, and kicked him, saying, 'Impudent varlet! don't pretend you couldn't see *me!* Why, I was standing close beside you behind that basket!'

So the corn-chandler apologised humbly for his mistake, and asked Sir Buzz how much flour he wanted.

'Two hundredweight,' replied the mannikin, 'two hundredweight, neither more nor less. Tie it up in a bundle, and I'll take it with me.'

'Your honour has a cart or beast of burden with you, doubtless?' said the chandler, 'for two hundredweight is a heavy load.'

'What's that to you?' shrieked Sir Buzz, stamping his foot, 'isn't it enough if I pay for it?' And then he jingled the money in his pocket again.

So the corn-chandler tied up the flour in a bundle, and placed it in the mannikin's outstretched hand, fully expecting it would crush him, when, with a whiz! Sir Buzz flew off, with the shillings still in his pocket. *Boom! bing! boom!*

The soldier's son was just wondering what had become of his one-span servant, when, with a whir! the little fellow alighted beside him, and wiping his face with his handkerchief, as if he were dreadfully hot and tired, said thoughtfully, 'Now I do hope I've brought enough, but you men have such terrible appetites!'

'More than enough, I should say,' laughed the lad, looking at the huge bundles.

Then Sir Buzz cooked the girdle-cakes, and the soldier's son ate three of them and a handful of sweets; but the one-span mannikin gobbled up all the rest, saying at each mouthful, 'You men have such terrible appetites—such terrible appetites!'

After that, the soldier's son and his servant Sir Buzz travelled ever so far, until they came to the King's city. Now the King had a daughter called Princess Blossom, who was so lovely, and tender, and slim, and fair, that she only weighed five flowers. Every morning she was weighed in golden scales, and the scale always turned when the fifth flower was put in, neither less nor more.

Now it so happened that the soldier's son by chance caught a glimpse of the lovely, tender, slim, and fair Princess Blossom, and, of course, he fell desperately

in love with her. He would neither sleep nor eat
his dinner, and did nothing all day long but say to
his faithful mannikin, 'Oh, dearest Sir Buzz! oh,
kind Sir Buzz!—carry me to the Princess Blossom,
that I may see and speak to her.'

'Carry you!' snapped the little fellow scornfully,
'that's a likely story! Why, you're ten times as big
as I am. You should carry *me*!'

Nevertheless, when the soldier's son begged and
prayed, growing pale and pining away with thinking
of the Princess Blossom, Sir Buzz, who had a kind
heart, was moved, and bade the lad sit on his hand.
Then with a tremendous *boom! bing! boom!* they
whizzed away and were in the palace in a second.
Being night-time, the Princess was asleep; nevertheless the booming wakened her and she was quite
frightened to see a handsome young man kneeling
beside her. She began of course to scream, but
stopped at once when the soldier's son with the
greatest politeness, and in the most elegant of
language, begged her not to be alarmed. And after
that they talked together about everything delightful,
while Sir Buzz stood at the door and did sentry;
but he stood a brick up on end first, so that he might
not seem to pry upon the young people.

Now when the dawn was just breaking, the
soldier's son and Princess Blossom, wearied of talking,
fell asleep; whereupon Sir Buzz, being a faithful
servant, said to himself, 'Now what is to be done?
If my master remains here asleep, some one will
discover him, and he will be killed as sure as my
name is Buzz; but if I wake him, ten to one he
will refuse to go.'

So without more ado he put his hand under the bed, and *bing! boom!* carried it into a large garden outside the town. There he set it down in the shade of the biggest tree, and pulling up the next biggest one by the roots, threw it over his shoulder, and marched up and down keeping guard.

Before long the whole town was in a commotion, because the Princess Blossom had been carried off, and all the world and his wife turned out to look for her. By and by the one-eyed Chief Constable came to the garden gate.

'What do you want here?' cried valiant Sir Buzz, making passes at him with the tree.

The Chief Constable with his one eye could see nothing save the branches, but he replied sturdily, 'I want the Princess Blossom!'

'I'll blossom you! Get out of *my* garden, will you?' shrieked the one-span mannikin, with his one and quarter span beard trailing on the ground; and with that he belaboured the Constable's pony so hard with the tree that it bolted away, nearly throwing its rider.

The poor man went straight to the King, saying, 'Your Majesty! I am convinced your Majesty's daughter, the Princess Blossom, is in your Majesty's garden, just outside the town, as there is a tree there which fights terribly.'

Upon this the King summoned all his horses and men, and going to the garden tried to get in; but Sir Buzz behind the tree routed them all, for half were killed, and the rest ran away. The noise of the battle, however, awoke the young couple, and as they were now convinced they could no longer exist apart, they determined to fly together. So when the fight was over, the soldier's son, the Princess Blossom, and Sir Buzz set out to see the world.

Now the soldier's son was so enchanted with his good luck in winning the Princess, that he said to Sir Buzz, 'My fortune is made already ; so I shan't want you any more, and you can go back to your mistress.'

'Pooh!' said Sir Buzz. 'Young people always think so ; however, have it your own way, only take this hair out of my beard, and if you *should* get into trouble, just burn it in the fire. I'll come to your aid.'

So Sir Buzz boomed off, and the soldier's son and the Princess Blossom lived and travelled together very happily, until at last they lost their way in a forest, and wandered about for some time without any food. When they were nearly starving, a Brahman found them, and hearing their story said, 'Alas! you poor children!—come home with me, and I will give you something to eat.'

Now had he said 'I will eat you,' it would have been much nearer the mark, for he was no Brahman, but a dreadful vampire, who loved to devour handsome young men and slender girls. But, knowing nothing of all this, the couple went home with him quite cheerfully. He was most polite, and when they arrived at his house, said, 'Please get ready whatever you want to eat, for I have no cook. Here are my keys ; open all my cupboards save the one with the golden key. Meanwhile I will go and gather firewood.'

Then the Princess Blossom began to prepare the

food, while the soldier's son opened all the cupboards. In them he saw lovely jewels, and dresses, and cups and platters, such bags of gold and silver, that his curiosity got the better of his discretion, and, regardless of the Brahman's warning, he said, 'I *will* see what wonderful thing is hidden in the cupboard with the golden key.' So he opened it, and lo! it was full of human skulls, picked quite clean, and beautifully polished. At this dreadful sight the soldier's son flew back to the Princess Blossom, and said, 'We are lost! we are lost!—this is no Brahman, but a horrid vampire!'

At that moment they heard him at the door, and the Princess, who was very brave and kept her wits about her, had barely time to thrust the magic hair into the fire, before the vampire, with sharp teeth and fierce eyes, appeared. But at the selfsame moment a *boom! boom! binging* noise was heard in the air, coming nearer and nearer. Whereupon the vampire, who knew very well who his enemy was, changed into a heavy rain pouring down in torrents, hoping thus to drown Sir Buzz, but *he* changed into the storm wind beating back the rain. Then the vampire changed to a dove, but Sir Buzz, pursuing it as a hawk, pressed it so hard that it had barely time to change into a rose, and drop into King Indra's lap as he sat in his celestial court listening to the singing of some dancing girls. Then Sir Buzz, quick as thought, changed into an old musician, and standing beside the bard who was thrumming the guitar, said, 'Brother, you are tired; let *me* play.'

And he played so wonderfully, and sang with such piercing sweetness, that King Indra said, 'What shall I give you as a reward? Name what you please, and it shall be yours.'

Then Sir Buzz said, 'I only ask the rose that is in your Majesty's lap.'

'I had rather you asked more, or less,' replied King Indra; 'it is but a rose, yet it fell from heaven; nevertheless it is yours.'

So saying, he threw the rose towards the musician, and lo! the petals fell in a shower on the ground. Sir Buzz went down on his knees and instantly gathered them up; but one petal escaping, changed into a mouse. Whereupon Sir Buzz, with the speed of lightning, turned into a cat, which caught and gobbled up the mouse.

Now all this time the Princess Blossom and the soldier's son, shivering and shaking, were awaiting the issue of the combat in the vampire's hut; when suddenly, with a *bing! boom!* Sir Buzz arrived victorious, shook his head, and said, 'You two had better go home, for you are not fit to take care of yourselves.'

Then he gathered together all the jewels and gold in one hand, placed the Princess and the soldier's son in the other, and whizzed away home, to where the poor mother—who all this time had been living on the two shillings—was delighted to see them.

Then with a louder *boom! bing! boom!* than usual, Sir Buzz, without even waiting for thanks, whizzed out of sight, and was never seen or heard of again.

But the soldier's son and the Princess Blossom lived happily ever after.

THE RAT'S WEDDING

ONCE upon a time a fat sleek Rat was caught in a shower of rain, and being far from shelter he set to work and soon dug a nice hole in the ground, in which he sat as dry as a bone while the rain-drops splashed outside, making little puddles on the road.

Now in the course of his digging he came upon a fine bit of root, quite dry and fit for fuel, which he set aside carefully—for the Rat is an economical creature—in order to take it home with him. So when the shower was over, he set off with the dry root in his mouth. As he went along, daintily picking his way through the puddles, he saw a poor man vainly trying to light a fire, while a little circle of children stood by, and cried piteously.

'Goodness gracious!' exclaimed the Rat, who was both soft-hearted and curious, 'what a dreadful noise to make! What *is* the matter?'

'The bairns are hungry,' answered the man; 'they are crying for their breakfast, but the sticks are damp, the fire won't burn, and so I can't bake the cakes.'

'If that is all your trouble, perhaps I can help you,' said the good-natured Rat; 'you are welcome to this dry root, and I'll warrant it will soon make a fine blaze.'

The poor man, with a thousand thanks, took the dry root, and in his turn presented the Rat with a morsel of dough, as a reward for his kindness and generosity.

'What a remarkably lucky fellow I am!' thought the Rat, as he trotted off gaily with his prize, 'and clever too! Fancy making a bargain like that— food enough to last me five days in return for a rotten old stick! *Wah! wah! wah!* what it is to have brains!'

Going along, hugging his good fortune in this way, he came presently to a potter's yard, where the potter, leaving his wheel to spin round by itself, was trying to pacify his three little children, who were scream-ing and crying as if they would burst.

'My gracious!' cried the Rat, stopping his ears, 'what a noise!—do tell me what it is all about.'

'I suppose they are hungry,' replied the potter ruefully; 'their mother has gone to get flour in the bazaar, for there is none in the house. In the mean-time I can neither work nor rest because of them.'

'Is that all!' answered the officious Rat; 'then I can help you. Take this dough, cook it quickly, and stop their mouths with food.'

The potter overwhelmed the Rat with thanks for his obliging kindness, and choosing out a nice well-burnt pipkin, insisted on his accepting it as a remem-brance.

The Rat was delighted at the exchange, and though

the pipkin was just a trifle awkward for him to manage, he succeeded after infinite trouble in balancing it on his head, and went away gingerly, *tink-a-tink, tink-a-tink*, down the road, with his tail over his arm for fear he should trip on it. And all the time he kept saying to himself, 'What a lucky fellow I am! and clever too! Such a hand at a bargain!'

By and by he came to where some neatherds were herding their cattle. One of them was milking a buffalo, and having no pail he used his shoes instead.

'Oh fie! oh fie!' cried the cleanly Rat, quite shocked at the sight. 'What a nasty dirty trick!—why don't you use a pail?'

'For the best of all reasons—we haven't got one!' growled the neatherd, who did not see why the Rat should put his finger in the pie.

'If that is all,' replied the dainty Rat, 'oblige me by using this pipkin, for I cannot bear dirt!'

The neatherd, nothing loath, took the pipkin, and milked away until it was brimming over; then turning to the Rat, who stood looking on, said, 'Here, little fellow, you may have a drink, in payment.'

But if the Rat was good-natured he was also shrewd. 'No, no, my friend,' said he, 'that will not do! As if I could drink the worth of my pipkin at a draught! My dear sir, *I couldn't hold it!* Besides, I never make a bad bargain, so I expect you at least to give me the buffalo that gave the milk.'

'Nonsense!' cried the neatherd; 'a buffalo for a pipkin! Who ever heard of such a price? And what on earth could *you* do with a buffalo when you got it? Why, the pipkin was about as much as you could manage.'

At this the Rat drew himself up with dignity, for he did not like allusions to his size.

'That is my affair, not yours,' he retorted ; 'your business is to hand over the buffalo.'

So just for the fun of the thing, and to amuse themselves at the Rat's expense, the neatherds loosed the buffalo's halter and began to tie it to the little animal's tail.

'No! no!' he called, in a great hurry ; 'if the beast pulled, the skin of my tail would come off, and then where should I be ? Tie it round my neck, if you please.'

So with much laughter the neatherds tied the halter round the Rat's neck, and he, after a polite leave-taking, set off gaily towards home with his prize ; that is to say, he set off with the *rope*, for no sooner did he come to the end of the tether than he was brought up with a round turn ; the buffalo, nose down grazing away, would not budge until it had finished its tuft of grass, and then seeing another in a different direction marched off towards it, while the Rat, to avoid being dragged, had to trot humbly behind, willy-nilly.

He was too proud to confess the truth, of course, and, nodding his head knowingly to the neatherds, said, 'Ta-ta, good people ! I am going home this way. It may be a little longer, but it's much shadier.'

And when the neatherds roared with laughter he took no notice, but trotted on, looking as dignified as possible.

'After all,' he reasoned to himself, 'when one keeps a buffalo one has to look after its grazing.

A beast must get a good bellyful of grass if it is to give any milk, and I have plenty of time at my disposal.'

So all day long he trotted about after the buffalo, making believe; but by evening he was dead tired, and felt truly thankful when the great big beast, having eaten enough, lay down under a tree to chew the cud.

Just then a bridal party came by. The bridegroom and his friends had evidently gone on to the next village, leaving the bride's palanquin to follow; so the palanquin bearers, being lazy fellows and seeing a nice shady tree, put down their burden, and began to cook some food.

'What detestable meanness!' grumbled one; 'a grand wedding, and nothing but plain rice pottage to eat! Not a scrap of meat in it, neither sweet nor salt! It would serve the skinflints right if we upset the bride into a ditch!'

'Dear me!' cried the Rat at once, seeing a way out of his difficulty, 'that *is* a shame! I sympathise with your feelings so entirely that if you will allow me I'll give you my buffalo. You can kill it, and cook it.'

'*Your* buffalo!' returned the discontented bearers, 'what rubbish! Whoever heard of a rat owning a buffalo?'

'Not often, I admit,' replied the Rat with conscious pride; 'but look for yourselves. Can you not see that I am leading the beast by a string?'

'Oh, never mind the string!' cried a great big hungry bearer; 'master or no master, I mean to have meat to my dinner!'

Whereupon they killed the buffalo, and, cooking its flesh, ate their dinner with relish ; then, offering the remains to the Rat, said carelessly, ' Here, little Rat-skin, that is for you ! '

' Now look here ! ' cried the Rat hotly ; ' I'll have none of your pottage, nor your sauce either.   You don't suppose I am going to give my best buffalo, that gave quarts and quarts of milk—the buffalo I have been feeding all day—for a wee bit of rice ? No !—I got a loaf for a bit of stick ; I got a pipkin for a little loaf ; I got a buffalo for a pipkin ; and now I'll have the bride for my buffalo—the bride, and nothing else ! '

By this time the servants, having satisfied their hunger, began to reflect on what they had done, and becoming alarmed at the consequences, arrived at the conclusion it would be wisest to make their escape whilst they could.   So, leaving the bride in her palanquin, they took to their heels in various directions.

The Rat, being as it were left in possession, advanced to the palanquin, and drawing aside the curtain, with the sweetest of voices and best of bows begged the bride to descend.   She hardly knew whether to laugh or to cry, but as any company, even a Rat's, was better than being quite alone in the wilderness, she did as she was bidden, and followed the lead of her guide, who set off as fast as he could for his hole.

As he trotted along beside the lovely young bride, who, by her rich dress and glittering jewels, seemed to be some king's daughter, he kept saying to himself, ' How clever I am !   What bargains I do make, to be sure ! '

When they arrived at his hole, the Rat stepped forward with the greatest politeness, and said, 'Welcome, madam, to my humble abode! Pray step in, or if you will allow me, and as the passage is somewhat dark, I will show you the way.'

Whereupon he ran in first, but after a time, finding the bride did not follow, he put his nose out again,

saying testily, 'Well, madam, why don't you follow? Don't you know it's rude to keep your husband waiting?'

'My good sir,' laughed the handsome young bride, 'I can't squeeze into that little hole!'

The Rat coughed; then after a moment's thought he replied, 'There is some truth in your remark— you *are* overgrown, and I suppose I shall have to build you a thatch somewhere. For to-night you can rest under that wild plum-tree.'

'But I am so hungry!' said the bride ruefully.

'Dear, dear! everybody seems hungry to-day!' returned the Rat pettishly; 'however, that's easily settled—I'll fetch you some supper in a trice.'

So he ran into his hole, returning immediately with an ear of millet and a dry pea.

'There!' said he, triumphantly, 'isn't that a fine meal?'

'I can't eat that!' whimpered the bride; 'it isn't a mouthful; and I want rice pottage, and cakes, and sweet eggs, and sugar-drops. I shall die if I don't get them!'

'Oh dear me!' cried the Rat in a rage, 'what a nuisance a bride is, to be sure! Why don't you eat the wild plums?'

'I can't live on wild plums!' retorted the weeping bride; 'nobody could; besides, they are only half ripe, and I can't reach them.'

'Rubbish!' cried the Rat; 'ripe or unripe, they must do you for to-night, and to-morrow you can gather a basketful, sell them in the city, and buy sugar-drops and sweet eggs to your heart's content!'

So the next morning the Rat climbed up into the plum-tree, and nibbled away at the stalks till the fruit fell down into the bride's veil. Then, unripe as they were, she carried them into the city, calling out through the streets—

'Green plums I sell! green plums I sell!
Princess am I, Rat's bride as well!'

As she passed by the palace, her mother the Queen heard her voice, and, running out, recognised her daughter. Great were the rejoicings, for every one thought the poor bride had been eaten by wild beasts. In the midst of the feasting and merriment, the Rat, who had followed the Princess at a distance, and had become alarmed at her long absence, arrived at the door, against which he beat with a big knobby stick, calling out fiercely, 'Give me my wife! give me my wife! She is mine by fair bargain. I gave a stick and I got a loaf; I gave a loaf and I got a pipkin; I gave a pipkin and I got a buffalo; I gave a buffalo and I got a bride. Give me my wife! give me my wife!'

'La! son-in-law! what a fuss you do make!' said the wily old Queen, through the door, 'and all about nothing! Who wants to run away with your wife? On the contrary, we are proud to see you, and I only keep you waiting at the door till we can spread the carpets, and receive you in style.'

Hearing this, the Rat was mollified, and waited patiently outside whilst the cunning old Queen prepared for his reception, which she did by cutting a hole in the very middle of a stool, putting a red-hot stone underneath, covering it over with a stew-pan-lid, and then spreading a beautiful embroidered cloth over all.

Then she went to the door, and receiving the Rat with the greatest respect, led him to the stool, praying him to be seated.

'Dear! dear! how clever I am! What bargains I do make, to be sure!' said he to himself as he climbed on to the stool. 'Here I am, son-in-law to a real live Queen! What will the neighbours say?'

At first he sat down on the edge of the stool, but even there it was warm, and after a while he began to fidget, saying, 'Dear me, mother-in-law!

how hot your house is! Everything I touch seems burning!'

'You are out of 'the wind there, my son,' replied the cunning old Queen ; 'sit more in the middle of the stool, and then you will feel the breeze and get cooler.'

But he didn't! for the stewpan-lid by this time had become so hot, that the Rat fairly frizzled when he sat down on it ; and it was not until he had left all his tail, half his hair, and a large piece of his skin behind him, that he managed to escape, howling with pain, and vowing that never, never, never again would he make a bargain!

ONG ago there lived a King who had an only son, by name Prince Bahrâmgor, who was as splendid as the noonday sun, and as beautiful as the midnight moon. Now one day the Prince went a-hunting, and he hunted to the north, but found no game; he hunted to the south, yet no quarry arose ; he hunted to the east, and still found nothing. Then he turned towards the setting sun, when suddenly from a thicket flashed a golden deer. Burnished gold were its hoofs and horns, rich gold its body. Dazzled by the wonderful sight, the astonished Prince bade his retainers form a circle round the beautiful strange creature, and so gradually enclose and secure it.

'Remember,' said the Prince, 'I hold him towards whom the deer may run to be responsible for its escape, or capture.'

Closer and closer drew the glittering circle of horsemen, while in the centre stood the golden deer, until, with marvellous speed, it fled straight towards the Prince. But he was swifter still, and caught it by the golden horns. Then the creature found human voice, and cried, 'Let me go, oh! Prince Bahrâmgor, and I will give you countless treasures!'

But the Prince laughed, saying, 'Not so! I have gold and jewels galore, but never a golden deer.'

'Let me go,' pleaded the deer, 'and I will give you more than treasures!'

'And what may that be?' asked the Prince, still laughing.

'I will give you a ride on my back such as never mortal man rode before,' replied the deer.

'Done!' cried the gay Prince, vaulting lightly to the deer's back; and immediately, like a bird from a thicket, the strange glittering creature rose through the air till it was lost to sight. For seven days and seven nights it carried the Prince over all the world, so that he could see everything like a picture passing below, and on the evening of the seventh day it touched the earth once more, and instantly vanished. Prince Bahrâmgor rubbed his eyes in bewilderment, for he had never been in such a strange country before. Everything seemed new and unfamiliar. He wandered about for some time looking for the trace of a house or a footprint, when suddenly from the ground at his feet popped a wee old man.

'How did you come here? and what are you looking for, my son?' quoth he politely.

So Prince Bahrâmgor told him how he had ridden thither on a golden deer, which had disappeared, and how he was now quite lost and bewildered in this strange country.

'Do not be alarmed, my son,' returned the wee old man; 'it is true you are in Demonsland, but

no one shall hurt you, for I am the demon Jasdrûl
whose life you saved when I was on the earth in the
shape of a golden deer.'

Then the demon Jasdrûl took Prince Bahrâmgor
to his house, and treated him right royally, giving him
a hundred keys, and saying, ' These are the keys of
my palaces and gardens.   Amuse yourself by looking
at them, and mayhap somewhere you may find a
treasure worth having.'

So every day Prince Bahrâmgor opened a new
garden, and examined a new palace, and in one he
found rooms full of gold, and in another jewels, and
in a third rich stuffs, in fact everything the heart
could desire, until he came to the hundredth palace,
and that he found was a mere hovel, full of all
poisonous things, herbs, stones, snakes, and insects.
But the garden in which it stood was by far the most
magnificent of all.   It was seven miles this way, and
seven miles that, full of tall trees and bright flowers,
lakes, streams, fountains, and summer-houses.   Gay
butterflies flitted about, and birds sang in it all day
and all night.   The Prince, enchanted, wandered
seven miles this way, and seven miles that, until he
was so tired that he lay down to rest in a marble
summer-house, where he found a golden bed, all
spread with silken shawls.   Now while he slept, the
Fairy Princess Shâhpasand, who was taking the air,
fairy-fashion, in the shape of a pigeon, happened
to fly over the garden, and catching sight of the
beautiful, splendid, handsome young Prince, she
sank to earth in sheer astonishment at beholding
such a lovely sight, and, resuming her natural shape
—as fairies always do when they touch the ground

—she stooped over the young man and gave him a kiss.

He woke up in a hurry, and what was his astonishment on seeing the most beautiful Princess in the world kneeling gracefully beside him !

' Dearest Prince! ' cried the maiden, clasping her hands, ' I have been looking for you everywhere ! '

Now the very same thing befell Prince Bahrâmgor that had happened to the Princess Shâhpasand—that is to say, no sooner did he set eyes on her than he fell desperately in love, and so, of course, they agreed to get married without any delay.   Nevertheless, the Prince thought it best first to consult his host, the demon Jasdrûl,seeing how powerful he was in Demonsland.   To the young man's delight, the demon not only gave his consent, but appeared greatly pleased, rubbing his hands and saying, ' Now you will remain with me and be so happy that you will never think of returning to your own country any more.'

So Prince Bahrâmgor and the Fairy Princess Shâhpasand were married, and lived ever so happily, for ever so long a time.

At last the thought of the home he had left came back to the Prince, and he began to think longingly of his father the King, his mother the Queen, and of his favourite horse and hound.   Then from thinking of them he fell to speaking of them to the Princess, his wife, and then from speaking he took to sighing and sighing and refusing his dinner, until he became quite pale and thin.   Now the demon Jasdrûl used to sit every night in a little echoing room below the Prince and Princess's chamber, and listen to what they said, so as to be sure they were happy ; and when he heard the Prince talking of his far-away home on the earth, he sighed too, for he was a kind-hearted demon, and loved his handsome young Prince.

At last he asked Prince Bahrâmgor what was the cause of his growing so pale and sighing so often—for so amiable was the young man that he would rather have died of grief than have committed the rudeness of telling his host he was longing to get away ; but when he was asked he said piteously, ' Oh, good demon ! let me go home and see my father the King, my mother the Queen, my horse and my hound, for I am very weary. Let me and my Princess go, or assuredly I shall die ! '

At first the demon refused, but at last he took pity on the Prince, and said, ' Be it so ; nevertheless you will soon repent and long to be back in Demons-land ; for the world has changed since you left it, and you will have trouble. Take this hair with you, and when you need help, burn it, then I will come immediately to your assistance.'

Then the demon Jasdrûl said a regretful good-bye, and, Hey presto !—Prince Bahrâmgor found himself standing outside his native city, with his beautiful bride beside him.

But, alas ! as the good-natured demon had fore-told, everything was changed. His father and mother were both dead, a usurper sat on the throne, and had put a price on Bahrâmgor's head should he ever return from his mysterious journey. Luckily no one recognised the young · Prince (so much had he changed during his residence in Demonsland) save his old huntsman, who, though overjoyed to see his master once more, said it was as much as his life was worth to give the Prince shelter; still, being a faithful servant, he agreed to let the young couple live in the garret of his house.

'My old mother, who is blind,' he said, 'will never see you coming and going; and as you used to be fond of sport, you can help me to hunt, as I used to help you.'

So the splendid Prince Bahrâmgor and his lovely Princess hid in the garret of the huntsman's house, and no one knew they were there. Now one fine day, when the Prince had gone out to hunt, as servant to the huntsman, Princess Shâhpasand took the opportunity of washing her beautiful golden hair, which hung round her ivory neck and down to her pretty ankles like a shower of sunshine, and when she had washed it she combed it, and set the window ajar so that the breeze might blow in and dry her hair.

Just at this moment the Chief Constable of the town happened to pass by, and hearing the window open, looked up and saw the lovely Shâhpasand, with her glittering golden hair. He was so overcome at the sight that he fell right off his horse into the gutter. His servants, thinking he had a fit, picked him up and carried him back to his house, where he never ceased raving about a beautiful fairy with golden hair in the huntsman's garret. This set everybody wondering whether he had been bewitched, and the story meeting the King's ear, he sent down some soldiers to make inquiries at the huntsman's house.

'No one lives here!' said the huntsman's cross old mother, 'no beautiful lady, nor ugly one either, nor any person at all, save me and my son. However, go to the garret and look for yourselves.'

Hearing these words of the old woman, Princess Shâhpasand bolted the door, and, seizing a knife, cut a hole in the wooden roof. Then, taking the form of a pigeon, she flew out, so that when the soldiers burst open the door they found no one in the garret.

The poor Princess was greatly distressed at having to leave her beautiful young Prince in this hurried way, and as she flew past the blind old crone she whispered in her ear, 'I go to my father's house in the Emerald Mountain.'

In the evening when Prince Bahrâmgor returned from hunting, great was his grief at finding the garret empty! Nor could the blind old crone tell him much of what had occurred; still, when he heard of the mysterious voice which whispered, 'I go to my father's house in the Emerald Mountain,' he was at first somewhat comforted. Afterwards, when he reflected that he had not the remotest idea where the Emerald Mountain was to be found, he fell into a very sad state, and casting himself on the ground he sobbed and sighed; he refused his dinner, and never ceased crying, 'Oh, my dearest Princess! my dearest Princess!'

At last he remembered the magic hair, and taking it from its hiding-place threw it into the fire. It had scarcely begun to burn when, Hey presto!— the demon Jasdrûl appeared, and asked him what he wanted.

'Show me the way to the Emerald Mountain,' cried the Prince.

Then the kind-hearted demon shook his head sorrowfully, saying, 'You would never reach it alive, my son. Be guided by me,—forget all that has passed, and begin a new life.'

'I have but one life,' answered the faithful Prince, 'and that is gone if I lose my dearest Princess! As I must die, let me die seeking her.'

Then the demon Jasdrûl was touched by the constancy of the splendid young Prince, and promised to aid him as far as possible. So he carried the young man back to Demonsland, and giving him a magic wand, bade him travel over the country until he came to the demon Nânak Chand's house.

'You will meet with many dangers by the way,' said his old friend, 'but keep the magic wand in your hand day and night, and nothing will harm you. That is all I can do for you, but Nânak Chand, who is my elder brother, can help you farther on your way.'

So Prince Bahrâmgor travelled through Demonsland, and because he held the magic wand in his hand day and night, no harm came to him. At last he arrived at the demon Nânak Chand's house, just as the demon had awakened from sleep, which, according to the habit of demons, had lasted for twelve years. Naturally he was desperately hungry, and on catching sight of the Prince, thought what a dainty morsel he would be for breakfast; nevertheless, though his mouth watered, the demon restrained his appetite when he saw the wand, and asked the Prince politely what he wanted. But when the demon Nânak Chand had heard the whole story, he shook his head, saying, 'You will never reach the Emerald

Mountain, my son. Be guided by me,—forget all that has passed, and begin a new life.'

Then the splendid young Prince answered as before, 'I have but one life, and that is gone if I lose my dearest Princess! If I must die, let me die seeking her.'

This answer touched the demon Nânak Chand, and he gave the faithful Prince a box of powdered antimony, and bade him travel on through Demonsland till he came to the house of the great demon Safed. 'For,' said he, 'Safed is my eldest brother, and if anybody can do what you want, he will. If you are in need, rub the powder on your eyes, and whatever you wish near will be near, but whatever you wish far will be far.'

So the constant Prince travelled on through all the dangers and difficulties of Demonsland, till he reached the demon Safed's house, to whom he told his story, showing the powder and the magic wand, which had brought him so far in safety.

But the great demon Safed shook his head, saying, 'You will never reach the Emerald Mountain alive, my son. Be guided by me,—forget all that has passed, and begin a new life.'

Still the faithful Prince gave the same answer, 'I have but one life, and that is gone if I lose my dearest Princess! If I must die, let me die seeking her.'

Then the great demon nodded his head approvingly, and said, 'You are a brave lad, and I must do my best for you. Take this *yech*-cap: whenever you put it on you will become invisible. Journey to the north, and after a while in the far distance you will see the Emerald Mountain. Then put the powder on your eyes and wish the mountain near, for it is an enchanted hill, and the farther you climb the higher it grows. On the summit lies the Emerald City : enter it by means of your invisible cap, and find the Princess—if you can.'

So the Prince journeyed joyfully to the north, until in the far far distance he saw the glittering Emerald Mountain. Then he rubbed the powder on his eyes, and behold! what he desired was near, and the Emerald City lay before him, looking as if it had been cut out of a single jewel. But the Prince thought of nothing save his dearest Princess, and wandered up and down the gleaming city protected by his invisible cap. Still he could not find her. The fact was, the Princess Shâhpasand's father had locked her up inside seven prisons, for fear she should fly away again, for he doated on her, and was in terror lest she should escape back to earth and her handsome young Prince, of whom she never ceased talking.

'If your husband comes to you, well and good,' said the old man, 'but you shall never go back to him.'

So the poor Princess wept all day long inside her seven prisons, for how could mortal man ever reach the Emerald Mountain ?

Now the Prince, whilst roaming disconsolately about the city, noticed a servant woman who every day at a certain hour entered a certain door with a tray of sweet dishes on her head. Being curious, he took advantage of his invisible cap, and when she opened the door he slipped in behind her. Nothing was to be seen but a large door, which, after shutting and locking the outer one, the servant opened. Again Prince Bahrâmgor slipped in behind her, and again saw nothing but a huge door. And so on he went through all the seven doors, till he came to the seventh prison, and there sat the beautiful Princess Shâhpasand, weeping salt tears. At the sight of her he could scarcely refrain from flinging himself at her feet, but remembering that he was invisible, he waited till the servant after putting down the tray retired, locking all the seven prisons one by one. Then he sat down by the Princess and began to eat out of the same dish with her.

She, poor thing, had not the appetite of a sparrow, and scarcely ate anything, so when she saw the contents of the dish disappearing, she thought she must be dreaming. But when the whole had vanished, she became convinced some one was in the room with her, and cried out faintly, 'Who eats in the same dish with me?'

Then Prince Bahrâmgor lifted the *yech*-cap from his forehead, so that he was no longer quite invisible, but showed like a figure seen in early dawn. At this the Princess wept bitterly, calling him by name, thinking she had seen his ghost, but as he lifted the *yech*-cap more and more, and, growing from a shadow to real flesh and blood, clasped her in his arms, her tears changed to radiant smiles.

Great was the astonishment of the servant next day when she found the handsome young Prince seated beside his dearest Princess. She ran to tell the King, who, on hearing the whole story from his daughter's lips, was very much pleased at the courage

D

and constancy of Prince Bahrâmgor, and ordered
Princess Shâhpasand to be released at once; 'For,'
he said, 'now her husband has found his way to her,
my daughter will not want to go to him.'

Then he appointed the Prince to be his heir, and
the faithful Prince Bahrâmgor and his beautiful
bride lived happily ever afterwards in the Emerald
kingdom.

THE BEAR'S BAD BARGAIN

NCE upon a time, a very old woodman lived with his very old wife in a tiny hut close to the orchard of a rich man,— so close that the boughs of a pear-tree hung right over the cottage yard. Now it was agreed between the rich man and the woodman, that if any of the fruit fell into the yard, the old couple were to be allowed to eat it ; so you may imagine with what hungry eyes they watched the pears ripening, and prayed for a storm of wind, or a flock of flying foxes, or anything which would cause the fruit to fall. But nothing came, and the old wife, who was a grumbling, scolding old thing, declared they would infallibly become beggars. So she took to giving her husband nothing but dry bread to eat, and insisted on his working harder than ever, till the poor old soul got quite thin; and all because the pears would not fall down! At last, the woodman turned round and declared he would not work any more unless his wife gave him *khichrî* to his dinner; so with a very bad grace the old woman took some rice and pulse, some butter and spices, and began to cook a savoury *khichrî*. What an appetising smell it had, to be sure! The woodman was for gobbling it up as soon as ever it was ready. 'No, no,' cried the greedy old wife, 'not till you have brought me in another load of wood; and mind it is a good one. You must work for your dinner.'

So the old man set off to the forest and began to hack and to hew with such a will that he soon had quite a large bundle, and with every faggot he cut he seemed to smell the savoury *khichrî*, and think of the feast that was coming.

Just then a bear came swinging by, with its great black nose tilted in the air, and its little keen eyes peering about; for bears, though good enough fellows on the whole, are just dreadfully inquisitive.

'Peace be with you, friend!' said the bear, 'and what may you be going to do with that remarkably large bundle of wood?'

'It is for my wife,' returned the woodman. 'The fact is,' he added confidentially, smacking his lips, 'she has made *such* a *khichrî* for dinner! and if I bring in a good bundle of wood she is pretty sure to give me a plentiful portion. Oh, my dear fellow, you should just smell that *khichrî*!'

At this the bear's mouth began to water, for, like all bears, he was a dreadful glutton.

'Do you think your wife would give me some too, if I brought her a bundle of wood?' he asked anxiously.

'Perhaps; if it was a very big load,' answered the woodman craftily.

'Would—would four hundredweight be enough?' asked the bear.

'I'm afraid not,' returned the woodman, shaking his head; 'you see *khichrî* is an expensive dish to make,—there is rice in it, and plenty of butter, and pulse, and——'

'Would—would eight hundredweight do?'

'Say half a ton, and it's a bargain!' quoth the woodman.

'Half a ton is a large quantity!' sighed the bear.

'There is saffron in the *khichrî*,' remarked the woodman casually.

The bear licked his lips, and his little eyes twinkled with greed and delight.

'Well, it's a bargain! Go home sharp and tell your wife to keep the *khichrî* hot; I'll be with you in a trice.'

Away went the woodman in great glee to tell his wife how the bear had agreed to bring half a ton of wood in return for a share of the *khichrî*.

Now the wife could not help allowing that her husband had made a good bargain, but being by nature a grumbler, she was determined not to be pleased, so she began to scold the old man for not having settled exactly the share the bear was to have; 'For,' said she, 'he will gobble up the potful before we have finished our first helping.'

On this the woodman became quite pale. 'In

that case,' he said, 'we had better begin now, and
have a fair start.'   So without more ado they squatted
down on the floor, with the brass pot full of *khichrî*
between them, and began to eat as fast as they could.

'Remember to leave some for the bear, wife,' said
the woodman, speaking with his mouth crammed
full.

'Certainly, certainly,' she replied, helping herself
to another handful.

'My dear,' cried the old woman in her turn, with
her mouth so full that she could hardly speak,
'remember the poor bear!'

'Certainly, certainly, my love!' returned the old
man, taking another mouthful.

So it went on, till there was not a single grain
left in the pot.

'What's to be done now?' said the woodman; 'it
is all your fault, wife, for eating so much.'

'My fault!' retorted his wife scornfully, 'why, you
ate twice as much as I did!'

'No, I didn't!'

'Yes, you did!—men always eat more than
women.'

'No, they don't!'

'Yes, they do!'

'Well, it's no use quarrelling about it now,' said
the woodman, 'the *khichrî's* gone, and the bear will
be furious.'

'That wouldn't matter much if we could get the
wood,' said the greedy old woman.   'I'll tell you
what we must do,—we must lock up everything there
is to eat in the house, leave the *khichrî* pot by the fire,
and hide in the garret.   When the bear comes he will

think we have gone out and left his dinner for him. Then he will throw down his bundle and come in. Of course he will rampage a little when he finds the pot is empty, but he can't do much mischief, and I don't think he will take the trouble of carrying the wood away.'

So they made haste to lock up all the food and hide themselves in the garret.

Meanwhile the bear had been toiling and moiling away at his bundle of wood, which took him much longer to collect than he expected ; however, at last he arrived quite exhausted at the woodcutter's cottage. Seeing the brass *khichrî* pot by the fire, he threw down his load and went in. And then—mercy ! wasn't he angry when he found nothing in it—not even a grain of rice, nor a tiny wee bit of pulse, but only a smell that was so uncommonly nice that he actually cried with rage and disappointment. He flew into the most dreadful temper, but though he turned the house topsy-turvy, he could not find a morsel of food. Finally, he declared he would take the wood away again, but, as the crafty old woman had imagined, when he came to the task, he did not care, even for the sake of revenge, to carry so heavy a burden.

' I won't go away empty-handed,' said he to himself, seizing the *khichrî* pot ; 'if I can't get the taste I'll have the smell ! '

Now, as he left the cottage, he caught sight of the beautiful golden pears hanging over into the yard. His mouth began to water at once, for he was desperately hungry, and the pears were the first of the season ; in a trice he was on the wall, up the tree, and, gathering the biggest and ripest one he could find, was just putting it into his mouth, when a thought struck him.

'If I take these pears home I shall be able to sell them for ever so much to the other bears, and then with the money I shall be able to buy some *khichrî*. Ha, ha! I shall have the best of the bargain after all!'

So saying, he began to gather the ripe pears as fast as he could and put them into the *khichrî* pot, but whenever he came to an unripe one he would shake his head and say, 'No one would buy that, yet it is a pity to waste it.' So he would pop it into his mouth and eat it, making wry faces if it was very sour.

Now all this time the woodman's wife had been watching the bear through a crevice, and holding her breath for fear of discovery; but, at last, what with being asthmatic, and having a cold in her head, she could hold it no longer, and just as the *khichrî* pot was quite full of golden ripe pears, out she came with the most tremendous sneeze you ever heard— '*A-h-che-u!*'

The bear, thinking some one had fired a gun at him, dropped the *khichrî* pot into the cottage yard, and fled into the forest as fast as his legs would carry him.

So the woodman and his wife got the *khichrî*, the wood, and the coveted pears, but the poor bear got nothing but a very bad stomach-ache from eating unripe fruit.

PRINCE LIONHEART AND HIS THREE FRIENDS

NCE upon a time there lived a King and Queen who would have been as happy as the day was long had it not been for this one circumstance,—they had no children.

At last an old *fakîr*, or devotee, coming to the palace, asked to see the Queen, and giving her some barleycorns, told her to eat them and cease weeping, for in nine months she would have a beautiful little son. The Queen ate the barleycorns, and sure enough after nine months she bore the most charming, lovely, splendid Prince that ever was seen, who was called Lionheart, because he was so brave and so strong.

Now when he grew up to man's estate, Prince Lionheart grew restless also, and was for ever begging his father the King to allow him to travel in the wide world and seek adventures. Then the King would shake his head, saying *only* sons were too precious to be turned adrift ; but at last, seeing the young Prince could think of nothing else, he gave his consent, and

Prince Lionheart set off on his travels, taking no one
with him but his three companions, the Knifegrinder,
the Blacksmith, and the Carpenter.

Now when these four valiant young men had gone
a short distance, they came upon a magnificent city,
lying deserted and desolate in the wilderness. Passing through it they saw tall houses, broad bazaars,
shops still full of goods, everything pointing to a
large and wealthy population ; but neither in street
nor house was a human being to be seen. This
astonished them very much, until the Knifegrinder,
clapping his hand to his forehead, said, 'I remember!
This must be the city I have heard about, where a
demon lives who will let no one dwell in peace. We
had best be off!'

'Not a bit of it!' cried Prince Lionheart. 'At any
rate not until I've had my dinner, for I am just
desperately hungry!'

So they went to the shops, and bought all they
required, laying the proper price for each thing on
the counters just as if the shopkeepers had been
there. Then going to the palace, which stood in the
middle of the town, Prince Lionheart bade the Knifegrinder prepare the dinner, while he and his other
companions took a further look at the city.

No sooner had they set off, than the Knifegrinder,
going to the kitchen, began to cook the food. It
sent up a savoury smell, and the Knifegrinder was
just thinking how nice it would taste, when he saw
a little figure beside him, clad in armour, with sword
and lance, riding on a gaily-caparisoned mouse.

'Give me my dinner!' cried the mannikin, angrily
shaking his lance.

'*Your* dinner! Come, that is a joke!' quoth the Knifegrinder, laughing.

'Give it me at once!' cried the little warrior in a louder voice, 'or I'll hang you to the nearest *pípal* tree!'

'Wah! whipper-snapper!' replied the valiant Knife-grinder, 'come a little nearer, and let me squash you between finger and thumb!'

At these words the mannikin suddenly shot up into a terribly tall demon, whereupon the Knife-grinder's courage disappeared, and, falling on his knees, he begged for mercy. But his piteous cries were of no use, for in a trice he was hung to the top-most branch of the *pípal* tree.

'I'll teach 'em to cook in my kitchen!' growled the demon, as he gobbled up all the cakes and savoury stew. When he had finished every morsel he disappeared.

Now the Knifegrinder wriggled so desperately that the *pípal* branch broke, and he came crashing through the tree to the ground, without much hurt beyond a great fright and a few bruises. However, he was so dreadfully alarmed that he rushed into the sleeping-room, and rolling himself up in his quilt, shook from head to foot as if he had the ague.

By and by in came Prince Lionheart and his companions, all three as hungry as hunters, crying, 'Well, jolly Knifegrinder! where's the dinner?'

Whereupon he groaned out from under his quilt, 'Don't be angry, for it's nobody's fault ; only just as it was ready I got a fit of ague, and as I lay shiver-ing and shaking a dog came in and walked off with everything.'

He was afraid that if he told the truth his companions would think him a coward for not fighting
the demon.

'What a pity!' cried the Prince, 'but we must
just cook some more.   Here! you Blacksmith! do
you prepare the dinner, while the Carpenter and I
have another look at the city.'

Now, no sooner had the Blacksmith begun to sniff
the savoury smell, and think how nice the cakes and
stew would taste, than the little warrior appeared to
him also.   And he was quite as brave at first as the
Knifegrinder had been, and afterwards he too fell on
his knees and prayed for mercy.   In fact everything
happened to him as it had happened to the Knifegrinder, and when he fell from the tree he too fled
into the sleeping-room, and rolling himself in his quilt
began to shiver and shake; so that when Prince
Lionheart and the Carpenter came back, hungry as
hunters, there was no dinner.

Then the Carpenter stayed behind to cook, but he
fared no better than the two others, so that when
hungry Prince Lionheart returned there were three
sick men, shivering and shaking under their quilts,
and no dinner.   Whereupon the Prince set to work
to cook his food himself.

No sooner had it begun to give off a savoury
smell than the tiny mouse-warrior appeared, very
fierce and valiant.

'Upon my word, you are really a very pretty
little fellow!' said the Prince in a patronising way;
'and what may you want?'

'Give me my dinner!' shrieked the mannikin.

'It is not *your* dinner, my dear sir, it is *my*

dinner !' quoth the Prince ; 'but to avoid disputes let's fight it out.'

Upon this the mouse-warrior began to stretch and grow till he became a terribly tall demon. But instead of falling on his knees and begging for mercy, the Prince only burst into a fit of laughter, and said, 'My good sir ! there is a medium in all things ! Just now you were ridiculously small, at present you are absurdly big ; but, as you seem to be able to alter your size without much trouble, suppose for once in a way you show some spirit, and become just my size, neither less nor more ; then we can settle whose dinner it really is.'

The demon could not withstand the Prince's reasoning, so he shrank to an ordinary size, and setting to work with a will, began to tilt at the Prince in fine style. But valiant Lionheart never yielded an inch, and finally, after a terrific battle, slew the demon with his sharp sword.

Then guessing at the truth he roused his three sick friends, saying with a smile, 'O ye valiant ones ! arise, for I have killed the ague !'

And they got up sheepishly, and fell to praising their leader for his incomparable valour.

After this, Prince Lionheart sent messages to all the inhabitants of the town who had been driven away by the wicked demon, telling them they could return and dwell in safety, on condition of their taking the Knifegrinder as their king, and giving him their richest and most beautiful maiden as a bride.

This they did with great joy, but when the wedding was over, and Prince Lionheart prepared to set out once more on his adventures, the Knifegrinder

threw himself before his master, begging to be
allowed to accompany him.   Prince Lionheart, however, refused the request, bidding him remain to
govern his kingdom, and at the same time gave him
a barley plant, bidding him tend it very carefully ;
since so long as it flourished he might be assured
his master was alive and well.   If, on the contrary,
it drooped, then he might know that misfortune was
at hand, and set off to help if he chose.

So the Knifegrinder king remained behind with
his bride and his barley plant, but Prince Lionheart,
the Blacksmith, and the Carpenter set forth on their
travels.

By and by they came to another desolate city,
lying deserted in the wilderness, and as before they
wandered through it, wondering at the tall palaces,
the empty streets, and the vacant shops where never
a human being was to be seen, until the Blacksmith,
suddenly recollecting, said, ' I remember now ! This
must be the city where the dreadful ghost lives
which kills every one.   We had best be off ! '

' After we have had our dinners ! ' quoth hungry
Lionheart.

So having bought all they required from a vacant
shop, putting the proper price of everything on the
counter, since there was no shopkeeper, they repaired
to the palace, where the Blacksmith was installed
as cook, whilst the others looked through the town.

No sooner had the dinner begun to give off an
appetising smell than the ghost appeared in the
form of an old woman, awful and forbidding, with
black wrinkled skin, and feet turned backwards.

At this sight the valiant Blacksmith never stopped

to parley, but fled into another room and bolted the door. Whereupon the ghost ate up the dinner in no time, and disappeared ; so that when Prince Lionheart and the Carpenter returned, as hungry as hunters, there was no dinner to be found, and no Blacksmith.

Then the Prince bade the Carpenter do the cooking while he went abroad to see the town. But the Carpenter fared no better, for the ghost appeared to him also, so that he fled and locked himself up in another room.

' This is really too bad ! ' quoth Prince Lionheart, when he returned to find no dinner, no Blacksmith, no Carpenter. So he began to cook the food himself, and no sooner had it given out a savoury smell than the ghost arrived ; this time, however, seeing so handsome a young man before her she would not assume her own hag-like shape, but appeared instead as a beautiful young woman.

However, the Prince was not in the least bit deceived, for he looked down at her feet, and when he saw they were set on hind side before, he knew at once what she was ; so drawing his sharp strong sword, he said, ' I must trouble you to take your own shape again, as I don't like killing beautiful young women ! '

At this the ghost shrieked with rage, and changed into her own loathsome form once more ; but at the same moment Prince Lionheart gave one stroke of his sword, and the horrible, awful thing lay dead at his feet.

Then the Blacksmith and the Carpenter crept out of their hiding-places, and the Prince sent messages to all the townsfolk, bidding them come back and dwell in peace, on condition of their making the Blacksmith king, and giving him to wife the prettiest, the richest, and the best-born maiden in the city.

To this they consented with one accord, and after the wedding was over, Prince Lionheart and the Carpenter set forth once more on their travels. The Blacksmith king was loath to let them go without him, but his master gave him also a barley plant, saying, 'Water and tend it carefully; for so long as it flourishes you may rest assured I am well and happy; but if it droops, know that I am in trouble, and come to help me.'

Prince Lionheart and the Carpenter had not journeyed far ere they came to a big town, where they halted to rest; and as luck would have it the Carpenter fell in love with the fairest maiden in the city, who was as beautiful as the moon and all the stars. He began to sigh and grumble over the good fortune of the Knifegrinder and the Blacksmith, and wish that he too could find a kingdom and a lovely bride, until his master took pity on him, and sending for the chief inhabitants, told them who he was, and ordered them to make the Carpenter king, and marry him to the maiden of his choice.

This order they obeyed, for Prince Lionheart's fame had been noised abroad, and they feared his displeasure; so when the marriage was over, and the Carpenter duly established as king, Prince Lionheart went forth on his journey alone, after giving a barley plant, as he had done before, by which his prosperity or misfortune might be known.

Having journeyed for a long time, he came at last

E

to a river, and as he sat resting on the bank, what was his astonishment to see a ruby of enormous size floating down the stream! Then another, and another drifted past him, each of huge size and glowing hue! Wonderstruck, he determined to find out whence they came. So he travelled up stream for two days and two nights, watching the rubies sweep by in the current, until he came to a beautiful marble palace built close to the water's edge. Gay gardens surrounded it, marble steps led down to the river, where, on a magnificent tree which stretched its branches over the stream, hung a golden basket. Now if Prince Lionheart had been wonderstruck before, what was his astonishment when he saw that the basket contained the head of the most lovely, the most beautiful, the most perfect young Princess that ever was seen! The eyes were closed, the golden hair fluttered in the breeze, and every minute from the slender throat a drop of crimson blood fell into the water, and changing into a ruby, drifted down the stream!

Prince Lionheart was overcome with pity at this heartrending sight; tears rose to his eyes, and he determined to search through the palace for some explanation of the beautiful mysterious head.

So he wandered through richly-decorated marble halls, through carved galleries and spacious corridors, without seeing a living creature, until he came to a sleeping-room hung with silver tissue, and there, on a white satin bed, lay the headless body of a young and beautiful girl! One glance convinced him that it belonged to the exquisite head he had seen swinging in the golden basket by the river-side, and, urged by the desire to see the two lovely portions united, he set off swiftly to the tree, soon returning with the basket in his hand. He placed the head gently on the severed throat, when, lo and behold! they joined together in a trice and the beautiful maiden started up to life once more. The Prince was overjoyed, and, falling on his knees, begged the lovely girl to tell him who she was, and how she came to be alone in the mysterious palace. She informed him that she was a king's daughter, with whom a wicked Jinn had fallen in love, in consequence of which passion he had carried her off by his magical arts: and being desperately jealous, never left her without first cutting off her head, and hanging it up in the golden basket until his return.

Prince Lionheart, hearing this cruel story, besought the beautiful Princess to fly with him without delay, but she assured him they must first kill the Jinn, or they would never succeed in making their escape. So she promised to coax the Jinn into telling her the secret of his life, and in the meantime bade the Prince cut off her head once more, and replace it in the golden basket, so that her cruel gaoler might not suspect anything.

The poor Prince could hardly bring himself to perform so dreadful a task, but seeing it was absolutely necessary, he shut his eyes from the heartrending sight, and with one blow of his sharp bright sword cut off his dear Princess's head, and after returning the golden basket to its place, hid himself in a closet hard by the sleeping-room.

By and by the Jinn arrived, and, putting on the Princess's head once more, cried angrily, 'Fee! fa! fum! This room smells of man's flesh!'

Then the Princess pretended to weep, saying, 'Do not be angry with me, good Jinn, for how can I know aught? Am I not dead whilst you are away? Eat me if you like, but do not be angry with me!'

Whereupon the Jinn, who loved her to distraction, swore he would rather die himself than kill her.

'That would be worse for me!' answered the girl, 'for if you were to die while you are away from here, it would be very awkward for me: I should be neither dead nor alive.'

'Don't distress yourself!' returned the Jinn; 'I am not likely to be killed, for my life lies in something very safe.'

'I hope so, I am sure!' replied the Princess, 'but I believe you only say that to comfort me. I shall never be content until you tell me where it lies, then I can judge for myself if it is safe.'

At first the Jinn refused, but the Princess coaxed and wheedled so prettily, and he began to get so very sleepy, that at last he replied, 'I shall never be killed except by a Prince called Lionheart; nor by him unless he can find the solitary tree, where a dog and a horse keep sentinel day and night. Even then he must pass these warders unhurt, climb the tree, kill the starling which sits singing in a golden cage on the topmost branch, tear open its crop, and destroy the bumble bee it contains. So I am safe; for it would need a lion's heart, or great wisdom, to reach the tree and overcome its guardians.'

'How are they to be overcome?' pleaded the Princess; 'tell me that, and I shall be satisfied.'

The Jinn, who was more than half asleep, and quite tired of being cross-questioned, answered drowsily,

'In front of the horse lies a heap of bones, and in front of the dog a heap of grass. Whoever takes a long stick and changes the heaps, so that the horse has grass, and the dog bones, will have no difficulty in passing.'

The Prince, overhearing this, set off at once to find the solitary tree, and ere long discovered it, with a savage horse and furious dog keeping watch and ward over it. They, however, became quite mild and meek when they received their proper food, and the Prince without any difficulty climbed the tree, seized the starling, and began to twist its neck. At this moment the Jinn, awakening from sleep, became aware of what was passing, and flew through the air to do battle for his life. The Prince, however, seeing him approach, hastily cut open the bird's crop, seized the bumble bee, and just as the Jinn was alighting on the tree, tore off the insect's wings. The Jinn instantly fell to the ground with a crash, but, determined to kill his enemy, began to climb. Then the Prince twisted off the bee's legs, and lo! the Jinn became legless, also; and when the bee's head was torn off, the Jinn's life went out entirely.

So Prince Lionheart returned in triumph to the Princess, who was overjoyed to hear of her tyrant's death. He would have started at once with her to his father's kingdom, but she begged for a little rest, so they stayed in the palace, examining all the riches it contained.

Now one day the Princess went down to the river to bathe, and wash her beautiful golden hair, and as she combed it, one or two long strands came out in the comb, shining and glittering like burnished gold.

She was proud of her beautiful hair, and said to herself, 'I will not throw these hairs into the river, to sink in the nasty dirty mud,' so she made a green cup out of a *pîpal* leaf, coiled the golden hairs inside, and set it afloat on the stream.

It so happened that the river, farther down, flowed past a royal city, and the King was sailing in his pleasure-boat, when he espied something sparkling like sunlight on the water, and bidding his boatmen row towards it, found the *pîpal* leaf cup and the glittering golden hairs.

He thought he had never before seen anything half so beautiful, and determined not to rest day or night until he had found the owner. Therefore he sent for the wisest women in his kingdom, in order to find out where the owner of the glistening golden hair dwelt.

The first wise woman said, 'If she is on Earth I promise to find her.'

The second said, 'If she is in Heaven I will tear open the sky and bring her to you.'

But the third laughed, saying, 'Pooh! if you tear open the sky I will put a patch in it, so that none will be able to tell the new piece from the old.'

The King, considering the last wise woman had proved herself to be the cleverest, engaged her to seek for the beautiful owner of the glistening golden hair.

Now as the hairs had been found in the river, the wise woman guessed they must have floated down stream from some place higher up, so she set off in a grand royal boat, and the boatmen rowed and rowed until at last they came in sight of the Jinn's magical marble palace.

Then the cunning wise woman went alone to the steps of the palace, and began to weep and to wail. It so happened that as Prince Lionheart had that day gone out hunting, the Princess was all alone, and having a tender heart, she no sooner heard the old woman weeping than she came out to see what was the matter.

'Mother,' said she kindly, 'why do you weep?'

'My daughter,' cried the wise woman, 'I weep to think what will become of you if the handsome Prince is slain by any mischance, and you are left here in the wilderness alone.' For the witch knew by her arts all about the Prince.

'Very true!' replied the Princess, wringing her hands; 'what a dreadful thing it would be! I never thought of it before!'

All day long she wept over the idea, and at night, when the Prince returned, she told him of her fears; but he laughed at them, saying his life lay in safety, and it was very unlikely any mischance should befall him.

Then the Princess was comforted; only she begged him to tell her wherein it lay, so that she might help to preserve it.

'It lies,' returned the Prince, 'in my sharp sword, which never fails. If harm were to come to it I should die; nevertheless, by fair means naught can prevail against it, so do not fret, sweetheart!'

'It would be wiser to leave it safe at home when you go hunting,' pleaded the Princess, and though Prince Lionheart told her again there was no cause to be alarmed, she made up her mind to have her own way, and the very next morning, when the Prince went a-hunting, she hid his strong sharp sword, and put another in the scabbard, so that he was none the wiser.

Thus when the wise woman came once more and wept on the marble stairs, the Princess called to her joyfully, 'Don't cry, mother!—the Prince's life is safe to-day. It lies in his sword, and that is hidden away in my cupboard.'

Then the wicked old hag waited until the Princess took her noonday sleep, and when everything was quiet she stole to the cupboard, took the sword, made a fierce fire, and placed the sharp shining blade in the glowing embers. As it grew hotter and hotter, Prince Lionheart felt a burning fever creep over his body, and knowing the magical property of his sword, drew it out to see if aught had befallen it, and lo! it was not his own sword but a changeling! He cried aloud, 'I am undone! I am undone!' and galloped homewards. But the wise woman blew up the fire so quickly that the sword became red-hot ere Prince Lionheart could arrive, and just as he appeared on the other side of the stream, a rivet came out of the sword hilt, which rolled off, and so did the Prince's head.

Then the wise woman, going to the Princess, said, 'Daughter! see how tangled your beautiful hair is after your sleep! Let me wash and dress it against your husband's return.' So they went down the marble steps to the river; but the wise woman said, 'Step into my boat, sweetheart; the water is clearer on the farther side.'

And then, whilst the Princess's long golden hair was all over her eyes like a veil, so that she could not see, the wicked old hag loosed the boat, which went drifting down stream.

In vain the Princess wept and wailed ; all she could do was to make a great vow, saying, 'O you shameless old thing! You are taking me away to some king's palace, I know ; but no matter who he may be, I swear not to look on his face for twelve years!'

At last they arrived at the royal city, greatly to the King's delight ; but when he found how solemn an oath the Princess had taken, he built her a high tower, where she lived all alone. No one save the hewers of wood and drawers of water were allowed even to enter the courtyard surrounding it, so there she lived and wept over her lost Lionheart.

Now when the Prince's head had rolled off in that shocking manner, the barley plant he had given to the Knifegrinder king suddenly snapped right in two, so that the ear fell to the ground.

This greatly troubled the faithful Knifegrinder, who immediately guessed some terrible disaster had overtaken his dear Prince. He gathered an army without delay, and set off in aid, meeting on the way with the Blacksmith and the Carpenter kings, who were both on the same errand. When it became evident that the three barley plants had fallen at the selfsame moment, the three friends feared the worst, and were not surprised when, after long journeying, they found the Prince's body, all burnt and blistered, lying by the river-side, and his head close to it. Knowing the magical properties of the sword, they looked for it at once, and when they found a change-ling in its place their hearts sank indeed! They lifted the body, and carried it to the palace, intending to weep and wail over it, when, lo! they found the real sword, all blistered and burnt, in a heap of ashes, the rivet gone, the hilt lying beside it.

'That is soon mended!' cried the Blacksmith king; so he blew up the fire, forged a rivet, and fastened the hilt to the blade. No sooner had he done so than the Prince's head grew to his shoulders as firm as ever.

'My turn now!' quoth the Knifegrinder king; and he spun his wheel so deftly that the blisters and stains disappeared like magic, and the sword was soon as bright as ever. And as he spun his wheel, the burns and scars disappeared likewise from Prince Lionheart's body, until at last the Prince sat up alive, as handsome as before.

'Where is my Princess?' he cried, the very first thing, and then told his friends of all that had passed.

'It is my turn now!' quoth the Carpenter king gleefully; 'give me your sword, and I will fetch the Princess back in no time.'

So he set off with the bright strong sword in his hand to find the lost Princess. Ere long he came to the royal city, and noticing a tall new-built tower, inquired who dwelt within. When the townspeople told him it was a strange Princess, who was kept in such close imprisonment that no one but hewers of wood and drawers of water were allowed even to enter the courtyard, he was certain it must be she whom he sought. However, to make sure, he disguised himself as a woodman, and going beneath the windows, cried, 'Wood! wood! Fifteen gold pieces for this bundle of wood!'

The Princess, who was sitting on the roof, taking

the air, bade her servant ask what sort of wood it was to make it so expensive.

'It is only firewood,' answered the disguised Carpenter, 'but it was cut with this sharp bright sword!'

Hearing these words, the Princess, with a beating heart, peered through the parapet, and recognised Prince Lionheart's sword. So she bade her servant inquire if the woodman had anything else to sell, and he replied that he had a wonderful flying palanquin, which he would show to the Princess, if she wished it, when she walked in the garden at evening.

She agreed to the proposal, and the Carpenter spent all the day in fashioning a marvellous palanquin. This he took with him to the tower garden, saying, 'Seat yourself in it, my Princess, and try how well it flies.'

But the King's sister, who was there, said the Princess must not go alone, so she got in also, and so did the wicked wise woman. Then the Carpenter king jumped up outside, and immediately the palanquin began to fly higher and higher, like a bird.

'I have had enough!—let us go down,' said the King's sister after a time.

Whereupon the Carpenter seized her by the waist, and threw her overboard, just as they were sailing above the river, so that she was drowned; but he waited until they were just above the high tower before he threw down the wicked wise woman, so that she got finely smashed on the stones.

Then the palanquin flew straight to the Jinn's magical marble palace, where Prince Lionheart, who had been awaiting the Carpenter king's arrival with

the greatest impatience, was overjoyed to see his
Princess once more, and set off, escorted by his three
companion kings, to his father's dominions.   But
when the poor old King, who had very much aged
since his son's departure, saw the three armies coming,
he made sure they were an invading force, so he
went out to meet them, and said, ' Take all my riches,
but leave my poor people in peace, for I am old, and
cannot fight.   Had my dear brave son Lionheart
been with me, it would have been a different affair,
but he left us years ago, and no one has heard aught
of him since.'

On this, the Prince flung himself on his father's
neck, and told him all that had occurred, and how
these were his three old friends—the Knifegrinder,
the Blacksmith, and the Carpenter.   This greatly
delighted the old man ; but when he saw the golden-
haired bride his son had brought home, his joy knew
no bounds.

So everybody was pleased, and lived happily ever
after.

THE LAMBIKIN.

NCE upon a time there was a wee wee Lambikin, who frolicked about on his little tottery legs, and enjoyed himself amazingly.

Now one day he set off to visit his Granny, and was jumping with joy to think of all the good things he should get from her, when whom should he meet but a Jackal, who looked at the tender young morsel and said—'Lambikin! Lambikin! I'll EAT YOU!'

But Lambikin only gave a little frisk, and said—

'To Granny's house I go,
Where I shall fatter grow,
Then you can eat me so.'

The Jackal thought this reasonable, and let Lambikin pass.

By and by he met a Vulture, and the Vulture,

looking hungrily at the tender morsel before him, said—'Lambikin! Lambikin! I'll EAT YOU!'

But Lambikin only gave a little frisk, and said—

> 'To Granny's house I go,
> Where I shall fatter grow,
> Then you can eat me so.'

The Vulture thought this reasonable, and let Lambikin pass.

And by and by he met a Tiger, and then a Wolf, and a Dog, and an Eagle, and all these, when they saw the tender little morsel, said—'Lambikin! Lambikin! I'll EAT YOU!'

But to all of them Lambikin replied, with a little frisk—

> 'To Granny's house I go,
> Where I shall fatter grow,
> Then you can eat me so.'

At last he reached his Granny's house, and said, all in a great hurry, 'Granny, dear, I've promised to get very fat; so, as people ought to keep their promises, please put me into the corn-bin *at once.*'

So his Granny said he was a good boy, and put him into the corn-bin, and there the greedy little Lambikin stayed for seven days, and ate, and ate, and ate, until he could scarcely waddle, and his Granny said he was fat enough for anything, and must go home. But cunning little Lambikin said that would never do, for some animal would be sure to eat him on the way back, he was so plump and tender.

'I'll tell you what you must do,' said Master Lambikin, 'you must make a little drumikin out of the skin of my little brother who died, and then I can sit inside and trundle along nicely, for I'm as tight as a drum myself.'

So his Granny made a nice little drumikin out of his brother's skin, with the wool inside, and Lambikin curled himself up snug and warm in the middle, and trundled away gaily. Soon he met with the Eagle, who called out—

'Drumikin ! Drumikin !
Have you seen Lambikin ? '

And Mr. Lambikin, curled up in his soft warm nest, replied—

'Lost in the forest, and so are you,
On, little Drumikin ! Tum-pa, tum-too ! '

'How very annoying!' sighed the Eagle, thinking regretfully of the tender morsel he had let slip.

Meanwhile Lambikin trundled along, laughing to himself, and singing—

'Tum-pa, tum-too ;
Tum-pa, tum-too ! '

Every animal and bird he met asked him the same question—

'Drumikin ! Drumikin !
Have you seen Lambikin ? '

And to each of them the little sly-boots replied—

'Lost in the forest, and so are you,
On, little Drumikin ! Tum-pa, tum-too ;
Tum-pa, tum-too ; Tum-pa, tum-too ! '

Then they all sighed to think of the tender little morsel they had let slip.

At last the Jackal came limping along, for all his sorry looks as sharp as a needle, and he too called out—

'Drumikin ! Drumikin !
Have you seen Lambikin ? '

And Lambikin, curled up in his snug little nest, replied gaily—

'Lost in the forest, and so are you,
   On, little Drumikin ! Tum-pa——'

But he never got any further, for the Jackal recognised his voice at once, and cried, ' Hullo ! you've turned yourself inside out, have you ? Just you come out of that !'

Whereupon he tore open Drumikin and gobbled up Lambikin.

NCE upon a time a number of young girls went to draw water at the village well, and while they were filling their jars, fell a-talking of their betrothals and weddings.

Said one—'My uncle will soon be coming with the bridal presents, and he is to bring the finest clothes imaginable.'

Said a second—'And my uncle-in-law is coming, I know, bringing the most delicious sweetmeats you could think of.'

Said a third—'Oh, my uncle will be here in no time, with the rarest jewels in the world.'

But Bopolûchî, the prettiest girl of them all, looked sad, for she was an orphan, and had no one to arrange a marriage for her. Nevertheless she was too proud to remain silent, so she said gaily—'And my uncle is coming also, bringing me fine dresses, fine food, and fine jewels.'

Now a wandering pedlar, who sold sweet scents and cosmetics of all sorts to the country women, happened to be sitting near the well, and heard what

Bopolûchî said. Being much struck by her beauty and spirit, he determined to marry her himself, and the very next day, disguised as a well-to-do farmer, he came to Bopolûchî's house laden with trays upon trays full of fine dresses, fine food, and fine jewels ; for he was not a real pedlar, but a wicked robber, ever so rich.

Bopolûchî could hardly believe her eyes, for everything was just as she had foretold, and the robber said he was her father's brother, who had been away in the world for years, and had now come back to arrange her marriage with one of his sons, her cousin.

Hearing this, Bopolûchî of course believed it all, and was ever so much pleased ; so she packed up the few things she possessed in a bundle, and set off with the robber in high spirits.

But as they went along the road, a crow sitting on a branch croaked—

'Bopolûchî, 'tis a pity !
You have lost your wits, my pretty !
'Tis no uncle that relieves you,
But a robber who deceives you !'

'Uncle !' said Bopolûchî, 'that crow croaks funnily. What does it say ?'

'Pooh !' returned the robber, 'all the crows in this country croak like that.'

A little farther on they met a peacock, which, as soon as it caught sight of the pretty little maiden, began to scream—

'Bopolûchî, 'tis a pity !
You have lost your wits, my pretty !
'Tis no uncle that relieves you,
But a robber who deceives you !'

'Uncle!' said the girl, 'that peacock screams funnily. What does it say?'

'Pooh!' returned the robber, 'all peacocks scream like that in this country.'

By and by a jackal slunk across the road; the moment it saw poor pretty Bopolûchî it began to howl—

'Bopolûchî, 'tis a pity!
You have lost your wits, my pretty!
'Tis no uncle that relieves you,
But a robber who deceives you!'

'Uncle!' said the maiden, 'that jackal howls funnily. What does it say?'

'Pooh!' returned the robber, 'all jackals howl like that in this country.'

So poor pretty Bopolûchî journeyed on till they reached the robber's house. Then he told her who he was, and how he intended to marry her himself. She wept and cried bitterly, but the robber had no pity, and left her in charge of his old, oh! ever so old mother, while he went out to make arrangements for the marriage feast.

Now Bopolûchî had such beautiful hair that it reached right down to her ankles, but the old mother hadn't a hair on her old bald head.

'Daughter!' said the old, ever so old mother, as she was putting the bridal dress on Bopolûchî, 'how did you manage to get such beautiful hair?'

'Well,' replied Bopolûchî, 'my mother made it grow by pounding my head in the big mortar for husking rice. At every stroke of the pestle my hair grew longer and longer. I assure you it is a plan that never fails.'

'Perhaps it would make *my* hair grow!' said the old woman eagerly.

'Perhaps it would!' quoth cunning Bopolûchî.

So the old, ever so old mother put her head in the mortar, and Bopolûchî pounded away with such a will that the old lady died.

Then Bopolûchî dressed the dead body in the scarlet bridal dress, seated it on the low bridal chair, drew the veil well over the face, and put the spinning-wheel in front of it, so that when the robber came home he might think it was the bride. Then she put on the old mother's clothes, and seizing her own bundle, stepped out of the house as quickly as possible.

On her way home she met the robber, who was returning with a stolen millstone, to grind the corn for the wedding feast, on his head. She was dread-fully frightened, and slipped behind the hedge, so as not to be seen. But the robber, not recognising her in the old mother's dress, thought she was some strange woman from a neighbouring village, and so to avoid being seen he slipped behind the other hedge. Thus Bopolûchî reached home in safety.

Meanwhile, the robber, having come to his house, saw the figure in bridal scarlet sitting on the bridal chair, spinning, and of course thought it was Bopolûchî. So he called to her to help him down with the mill-stone, but she didn't answer. He called again, but still she didn't answer. Then he fell into a rage, and threw the millstone at her head. The figure toppled over, and lo and behold! it was not Bopolûchî at all, but his old, ever so old mother! Whereupon the robber wept, and beat his breast, thinking he had killed her; but when he discovered

pretty Bopolûchî had run away, he became wild with
rage, and determined to bring her back somehow.

Now Bopolûchî was convinced that the robber
would try to carry her off, so every night she begged
a new lodging in some friend's house, leaving her
own little bed in her own little house quite empty ;
but after a month or so she had come to the end of

her friends, and did not like to ask any of them to
give her shelter a second time.   So she determined
to brave it out and sleep at home, whatever happened ;
but she took a bill-hook to bed with her.   Sure
enough, in the very middle of the night four men
crept in, and each seizing a leg of the bed, lifted it
up and walked off, the robber himself having hold of
the leg close behind her head.   Bopolûchî was wide
awake, but pretended to be fast asleep, until she

came to a wild deserted spot, where the thieves were
off their guard ; then she whipped out the bill-hook,
and in a twinkling cut off the heads of the two
thieves at the foot of the bed.   Turning round
quickly, she did the same to the other thief at the
head, but the robber himself ran away in a terrible
fright, and scrambled like a wild cat up a tree close
by before she could reach him.

'Come down!' cried brave Bopolûchî, brandishing
the bill-hook, 'and fight it out!'

But the robber would not come down ; so
Bopolûchî gathered all the sticks she could find, piled
them round the tree, and set fire to them.   Of course
the tree caught fire also, and the robber, half stifled
with the smoke, tried to jump down, and was killed.

After that, Bopolûchî went to the robber's house
and carried off all the gold and silver, jewels and
clothes, that were hidden there, coming back to the
village so rich that she could marry any one she
pleased.   And that was the end of Bopolûchî's
adventures.

PRINCESS AUBERGINE

NCE upon a time there lived a poor Brahman and his wife, so poor, that often they did not know whither to turn for a meal, and were reduced to wild herbs and roots for their dinner.

Now one day, as the Brahman was gathering such herbs as he could find in the wilderness, he came upon an Aubergine, or egg-plant. Thinking it might prove useful by and by, he dug it up, took it home, and planted it by his cottage door. Every day he watered and tended it, so that it grew wonderfully, and at last bore one large fruit as big as a pear, purple and white and glossy,—such a handsome fruit, that the good couple thought it a pity to pick it, and let it hang on the plant day after day, until one fine morning when there was absolutely nothing to eat in the house. Then the Brahman said to his wife, 'We must eat the egg-fruit ; go and cut it, and prepare it for dinner.'

So the Brahman's wife took a knife, and cut the beautiful purple and white fruit off the plant, and as she did so she thought she heard a low moan. But when she sat down and began to peel the egg-fruit, she heard a tiny voice say quite distinctly, 'Take care!—oh, please take care! Peel more gently, or I am sure the knife will run into me!'

The good woman was terribly perplexed, but went on peeling as gently as she could, wondering all the time what had bewitched the egg-fruit, until she had cut quite through the rind, when—what do you think happened? Why, out stepped the most beautiful little maiden imaginable, dressed in purple and white satin!

The poor Brahman and his wife were mightily astonished, but still more delighted; for, having no children of their own, they looked on the tiny maiden as a godsend, and determined to adopt her. So they took the greatest care of her, petting and spoiling her, and always calling her the Princess Aubergine; for, said the worthy couple, if she was not a Princess *really*, she was dainty and delicate enough to be any king's daughter.

Now not far from the Brahman's hut lived a King, who had a beautiful wife, and seven stalwart young sons. One day, a slave-girl from the palace, happening to pass by the Brahman's cottage, went in to ask for a light, and there she saw the beautiful Aubergine. She went straight home to the palace, and told her mistress how in a hovel close by there lived a Princess so lovely and charming, that were the King once to set eyes on her, he would straightway forget, not only his Queen, but every other woman in the world.

Now the Queen, who was of a very jealous disposition, could not bear the idea of any one being

more beautiful than she was herself, so she cast about
in her mind how she could destroy the lovely Aubergine. If she could only inveigle the girl into the
palace, she could easily do the rest, for she was a
sorceress, and learned in all sorts of magic. So she
sent a message to the Princess Aubergine, to say that
the fame of her great beauty had reached the palace,
and the Queen would like to see with her own eyes
if report said true.

Now lovely Aubergine was vain of her beauty,
and fell into the trap. She went to the palace, and
the Queen, pretending to be wonderstruck, said, ' You
were born to live in kings' houses! From this time
you must never leave me ; henceforth you are my
sister.'

This flattered Princess Aubergine's vanity, so,
nothing loath, she remained in the palace, and exchanged veils with the Queen, and drank milk out of
the same cup with her, as is the custom when two
people say they will be sisters.

But the Queen, from the very first moment she set
eyes on her, had seen that Princess Aubergine was
no human being, but a fairy, and knew she must be
very careful how she set about her magic. Therefore
she laid strong spells upon her while she slept, and
said—

    ' Beautiful Aubergine ! tell me true—
    In what thing does your life lie ? '

And the Princess answered—' In the life of your
eldest son. Kill him, and I will die also.'

So the very next morning the wicked Queen went
to where her eldest son lay sleeping, and killed him
with her own hands. Then she sent the slave-girl

to the Princess's apartments, hoping to hear she was
dead too, but the girl returned saying the Princess
was alive and well.

Then the Queen wept tears of rage, for she knew
her spells had not been strong enough, and she had
killed her son for naught.   Nevertheless, the next
night she laid stronger spells upon the Princess
Aubergine, saying—

  ' Princess Aubergine! tell me true—
  In what thing does your life lie ? '

And the sleeping Princess answered—' In the
life of your second son.   Kill him, and I too will
die.'

So the wicked Queen killed her second son with
her own hands, but when she sent the slave-girl to see
whether Aubergine was dead also, the girl returned
again saying the Princess was alive and well.

Then the sorceress-queen cried with rage and
spite, for she had killed her second son for naught.
Nevertheless, she would not give up her wicked project,
and the next night laid still stronger spells on the
sleeping Princess, asking her—

  ' Princess Aubergine! tell me true—
  In what thing does your life lie ? '

And the Princess replied—' In the life of your
third son.   Kill him, and I must die also ! '

But the same thing happened.   Though the young
Prince was killed by his wicked mother, Aubergine
remained alive and well ; and so it went on day after
day, until all the seven young Princes were slain, and
their cruel mother still wept tears of rage and spite,
at having killed her seven sons for naught.

Then the sorceress-queen summoned up all her

art, and laid such strong spells on the Princess Aubergine that she could no longer resist them, and was
obliged to answer truly ; so when the wicked Queen
asked—

     'Princess Aubergine ! tell me true—
     In what thing does your life lie ?'
the poor Princess was obliged to answer—' In a river
far away there lives a red and green fish. Inside the
fish there is a bumble bee, inside the bee a tiny box,
and inside the box is the wonderful nine-lakh necklace. Put it on, and I shall die.'

Then the Queen was satisfied, and set about finding
the red and green fish. Therefore, when her husband
the King came to see her, she began to sob and to
cry, until he asked her what was the matter. Then
she told him she had set her heart on procuring the
wonderful nine-lakh necklace.

'But where is it to be found ?' asked the King.

And the Queen answered in the words of the Princess Aubergine,—' In a river far away there lives a
red and green fish. Inside the fish there is a bumble
bee, inside the bee a tiny box, and in the box is the
nine-lakh necklace.'

Now the King was a very kind man, and had
grieved sincerely for the loss of his seven young sons,
who, the Queen said, had died suddenly of an in-
fectious disease. Seeing his wife so distressed, and
being anxious to comfort her, he gave orders that
every fisherman in his kingdom was to fish all day
until the red and green fish was found. So all the
fishermen set to work, and ere long the Queen's desire
was fulfilled—the red and green fish was caught, and
when the wicked sorceress opened it, there was the

bumble bee, and inside the bee was the box, and inside the box the wonderful nine-lakh necklace, which the Queen put on at once.

Now no sooner had the Princess Aubergine been forced to tell the secret of her life by the Queen's magic, than she knew she must die; so she returned sadly to her foster-parents' hut, and telling them of her approaching death, begged them neither to burn nor bury her body. 'This is what I wish you to do,' she said; 'dress me in my finest clothes, lay me on my bed, scatter flowers over me, and carry me to the wildest wilderness. There you must place the bed on the ground, and build a high mud wall around it, so that no one will be able to see over.'

The poor foster-parents, weeping bitterly, promised to do as she wished; so when the Princess died (which happened at the very moment the wicked Queen put on the nine-lakh necklace), they dressed her in her best clothes, scattered flowers over the bed, and carried her out to the wildest wilderness.

Now when the Queen sent the slave-girl to the Brahman's hut to inquire if the Princess Aubergine was really dead, the girl returned saying, 'She is dead, but neither burnt nor buried; she lies out in the wilderness to the north, covered with flowers, as beautiful as the moon!'

The Queen was not satisfied with this reply, but as she could do no more, had to be content.

Now the King grieved bitterly for his seven young sons, and to try to forget his grief he went out hunting every day; so the Queen, who feared lest in his wanderings he might find the dead Princess Aubergine, made him promise never to hunt towards

the north, for, she said, 'some evil will surely befall
you if you do.'

But one day, having hunted to the east, and the
south, and the west, without finding game, he forgot
his promise, and hunted towards the north. In his
wanderings he lost his way, and came upon a high
enclosure, with no door ; being curious to know what
it contained, he climbed over the wall. He could
scarcely believe his eyes when he saw a lovely Princess
lying on a flower-strewn bed, looking as if she had
just fallen asleep. It seemed impossible she could be
dead, so, kneeling down beside her, he spent the whole
day praying and beseeching her to open her eyes. At
nightfall he returned to his palace, but with the dawn-
ing he took his bow, and, dismissing all his attendants
on the pretext of hunting alone, flew to his beautiful
Princess. So he passed day after day, kneeling distractedly beside the lovely Aubergine, beseeching her
to rise ; but she never stirred.

Now at the end of a year he, one day, found the
most beautiful little boy imaginable lying beside the
Princess. He was greatly astonished, but taking the
child in his arms, cared for it tenderly all day, and at
night laid it down beside its dead mother. After
some time the child learnt to talk, and when the
King asked it if its mother was always dead, it replied,
' No ! at night she is alive, and cares for me as you
do during the day.'

Hearing this, the King bade the boy ask his mother
what made her die, and the next day the boy replied,
' My mother says it is the nine-lakh necklace your
Queen wears. At night, when the Queen takes
it off, my mother becomes alive again, but every

morning, when the Queen puts it on, my mother dies.'

This greatly puzzled the King, who could not imagine what his Queen could have to do with the mysterious Princess, so he told the boy to ask his mother whose son he was.

The next morning the boy replied, 'Mother bade me say I am your son, sent to console you for the loss of the seven fair sons your wicked Queen murdered out of jealousy of my mother, the lovely Princess Aubergine.'

Then the King grew very wroth at the thought of his dead sons, and bade the boy ask his mother how the wicked Queen was to be punished, and by what means the necklace could be recovered.

The next morning the boy replied, 'Mother says I am the only person who can recover the necklace, so to-night, when you return to the palace, you are to take me with you.' So the King carried the boy back to the palace, and told all his ministers and courtiers that the child was his heir. On this, the sorceress-queen, thinking of her own dead sons, became mad with jealousy, and determined to poison the boy. To this end she prepared some tempting sweetmeats, and, caressing the child, gave him a handful, bidding him eat them ; but the child refused, saying he would not do so until she gave him the glittering necklace she wore round her throat, to play with.

Determined to poison the boy, and seeing no other way of inducing him to eat the sweetmeats, the sorceress-queen slipped off the nine-lakh necklace, and gave it to the child. No sooner had he touched it than he fled away so fast that none of the servants or guards could stop him, and never drew breath till he reached the place where the beautiful Princess Aubergine lay dead. He threw the necklace over her head, and immediately she rose up lovelier than ever. Then the King came, and besought her to return to the palace as his bride, but she replied, ' I will never be your wife till that wicked sorceress is dead, for she would only murder me and my boy, as she murdered your seven young sons. If you will dig a deep ditch at the threshold of the palace, fill it with scorpions and snakes, throw the wicked Queen into it, and bury her alive, I will walk over her grave to be your wife.'

So the King ordered a deep ditch to be dug, and had it filled with scorpions and snakes. Then he went to the sorceress-queen, and bade her come to see something very wonderful. But she refused, suspecting a trick. Then the guards seized her, bound her, flung her into the ditch amongst the scorpions and snakes, and buried her alive with them. As for the Princess Aubergine, she and her son walked over the grave, and lived happily in the palace ever after.

VALIANT VICKY, THE BRAVE WEAVER

 NCE upon a time there lived a little weaver, by name Victor Prince, but because his head was big, his legs thin, and he was altogether small, and weak, and ridiculous, his neighbours called him Vicky—Little Vicky the Weaver.

But despite his size, his thin legs, and his ridiculous appearance, Vicky was very valiant, and loved to *talk* for hours of his bravery, and the heroic acts he would perform if Fate gave him an opportunity. Only Fate did not, and in consequence Vicky remained little Vicky the valiant weaver, who was laughed at by all for his boasting.

Now one day, as Vicky was sitting at his loom, weaving, a mosquito settled on his left hand just as he was throwing the shuttle from his right hand, and by chance, after gliding swiftly through the warp, the shuttle came flying into his left hand on the very spot where the mosquito had settled, and squashed it. Seeing this, Vicky became desperately excited : ' It is as I have always said,' he cried ; ' if I only had the chance I knew I could show my mettle! Now, I'd like to know how many people could have done that? Killing a mosquito is easy, and throwing a shuttle is easy, but to do both at one time is a mighty different affair! It is easy enough to shoot a great hulking man—there is something to see, something to aim at ; then guns and crossbows are made for shooting; but to shoot a *mosquito* with a *shuttle* is quite another thing. That requires a man!'

The more he thought over the matter, the more elated he became over his skill and bravery, until he determined that he would no longer suffer himself to be called 'Vicky.' No! now that he had shown his mettle he would be called 'Victor'—'Victor Prince' —or better still, 'Prince Victor'; that was a name worthy his merits. But when he announced this determination to the neighbours, they roared with laughter, and though some did call him Prince Victor, it was with such sniggering and giggling and mock reverence that the little man flew home in a rage. Here he met with no better reception, for his wife, a fine handsome young woman, who was tired to death by her ridiculous little husband's whims and fancies, sharply bade him hold his tongue and not make a fool of himself. Upon this, beside himself with pride and mortification, he seized her by the hair, and beat her most unmercifully. Then, resolving to stay no longer in a town where his merits were unrecognised, he bade her prepare some bread for a journey, and set about packing his bundle.

'I will go into the world!' he said to himself. 'The man who can shoot a mosquito dead with a shuttle ought not to hide his light under a bushel.'

G

So off he set, with his bundle, his shuttle, and a loaf of bread tied up in a kerchief.

Now as he journeyed he came to a city where a dreadful elephant came daily to make a meal off the inhabitants. Many mighty warriors had gone against it, . but none had returned. On hearing this the valiant little weaver thought to himself, 'Now is my chance! A great haystack of an elephant will be a fine mark to a man who has shot a mosquito with a shuttle!' So he went to the King, and announced that he proposed single-handed to meet and slay the elephant. At first the King thought the little man was mad, but as he persisted in his words, he told him that he was free to try his luck if he chose to run the risk; adding that many better men than he had failed.

Nevertheless, our brave weaver was nothing daunted; he even refused to take either sword or bow, but strutted out to meet the elephant armed only with his shuttle.

'It is a weapon I thoroughly understand, good people,' he replied boastfully to those who urged him to choose some more deadly arm, 'and it has done its work in its time, I can tell you!'

It was a beautiful sight to see little Vicky swaggering out to meet his enemy, while the townsfolk flocked to the walls to witness the fight. Never was such a valiant weaver till the elephant, descrying its tiny antagonist, trumpeted fiercely, and charged right at him, and then, alas! all the little man's courage disappeared, and forgetting his new name of Prince Victor he dropped his bundle, his shuttle, and his bread, and bolted away as fast as Vicky's legs could carry him.

Now it so happened that his wife had made the bread ever so sweet, and had put all sorts of tasty spices in it, because she wanted to hide the flavour of the poison she had put in it also; for she was a wicked, revengeful woman, who wanted to be rid of her tiresome, whimsical little husband. And so, as the elephant charged past, it smelt the delicious spices, and catching up the bread with its long trunk, gobbled it up without stopping an instant. Meanwhile fear lent speed to Vicky's short legs, but though he ran like a hare, the elephant soon overtook him. In vain he doubled and doubled, and the beast's hot breath was on him, when in sheer desperation he turned, hoping to bolt through the enormous creature's legs ; being half blind with fear, however, he ran full tilt against them instead. Now, as luck would have it, at that very moment the poison took effect, and the elephant fell to the ground stone dead.

When the spectators saw the monster fall they could scarcely believe their eyes, but their astonishment was greater still when, running up to the scene of action, they found Valiant Vicky seated in triumph on the elephant's head, calmly mopping his face with his handkerchief.

'I had to pretend to run away,' he explained, 'or the coward would never have engaged me. Then I gave him a little push, and he fell down, as you see. Elephants are big beasts, but they have no strength to speak of.'

The good folks were amazed at the careless way in which Valiant Vicky spoke of his achievement, and as they had been too far off to see very distinctly what had occurred, they went and told the King that the little weaver was just a fearful wee man, and had knocked over the elephant like a ninepin. Then the King said to himself, 'None of my warriors and wrestlers, no, not even the heroes of old, could have done this. I must secure this little man's services if I can.' So he asked Vicky why he was wandering about the world.

'For pleasure, for service, or for conquest!' returned Valiant Vicky, laying such stress on the last word that the King, in a great hurry, made him Commander-in-Chief of his whole army, for fear he should take service elsewhere.

So there was Valiant Vicky a mighty fine warrior, and as proud as a peacock of having fulfilled his own predictions.

'I knew it!' he would say to himself when he was dressed out in full fig, with shining armour and waving plumes, and spears, swords, and shields ; 'I *felt* I had it in me!'

Now after some time a terribly savage tiger came ravaging the country, and at last the city-folk petitioned that the mighty Prince Victor might be sent out to destroy it. So out he went at the head of his army,—for he was a great man now, and had quite forgotten all about looms and shuttles. But first he made the King promise his daughter in marriage as a reward. 'Nothing for nothing!' said the astute little weaver to himself, and when the promise was given he went out as gay as a lark.

'Do not distress yourselves, good people,' he said to those who flocked round him praying for his successful return ; 'it is ridiculous to suppose the tiger will have a chance. Why, I knocked over an elephant with my little finger! I am really invincible!

But, alas for our Valiant Vicky! No sooner did he see the tiger lashing its tail and charging down on him, than he ran for the nearest tree, and scrambled into the branches. There he sat like a monkey, while the tiger glowered at him from below. Of course when the army saw their Commander-in-Chief bolt like a mouse, they followed his example, and never stopped until they reached the city, where they spread the news that the little hero had fled up a tree.

'There let him stay!' said the King, secretly relieved, for he was jealous of the little weaver's prowess, and did not want him for a son-in-law.

Meanwhile, Valiant Vicky sat cowering in the tree, while the tiger occupied itself below with sharpening its teeth and claws, and curling its whiskers, till poor Vicky nearly tumbled into its jaws with fright. So one day, two days, three days, six days passed by; on the seventh the tiger was fiercer, hungrier, and more watchful than ever. As for the poor little weaver, he was so hungry that his hunger made him brave, and he determined to try and slip past his enemy during its mid-day snooze. He crept stealthily down inch by inch, till his foot was within a yard of the ground, and then? Why then the tiger, which had had one eye open all the time, jumped up with a roar!

Valiant Vicky shrieked with fear, and making a tremendous effort, swung himself into a branch, cocking his little bandy legs over it to keep them out of reach, for the tiger's red panting mouth and gleaming white teeth were within half an inch of his toes. In doing so, his dagger fell out of its sheath, and went pop into the tiger's wide-open mouth, and thus point foremost down into its stomach, so that it died!

Valiant Vicky could scarcely believe his good fortune, but, after prodding at the body with a branch, and finding it did not move, he concluded the tiger really was dead, and ventured down. Then he cut off its head, and went home in triumph to the King.

'You and your warriors are a nice set of cowards!' said he, wrathfully. 'Here have I been fighting that tiger for seven days and seven nights, without bite or sup, whilst you have been guzzling and snoozing at home. Pah! it's disgusting!

but I suppose every one is not a hero as I am!'
So Prince Victor married the King's daughter, and
was a greater man than ever.

But by and by a neighbouring prince, who bore a
grudge against the King, came with a huge army, and
encamped outside the city, swearing to put every man,
woman, and child within it to the sword. Hearing
this, the inhabitants of course cried with one accord,
'Prince Victor! Prince Victor to the rescue!' so the
valiant little weaver was ordered by the King to
go out and destroy the invading army, after which
he was to receive half the kingdom as a reward.
Now Valiant Vicky, with all his boasting, was no
fool, and he said to himself, 'This is a very different
affair from the others. A man may kill a mosquito,
an elephant, and a tiger; yet another man may kill
him. And here is not one man, but thousands!
No, no!—what is the use of half a kingdom if you
haven't a head on your shoulders? Under the
circumstances I prefer *not* to be a hero!'

So in the dead of night he bade his wife rise, pack
up her golden dishes, and follow him—'Not that you
will want the golden dishes at my house,' he explained
boastfully, 'for I have heaps and heaps, but on the
journey these will be useful.' Then he crept outside
the city, followed by his wife carrying the bundle, and
began to steal through the enemy's camp.

Just as they were in the very middle of it, a big
cockchafer flew into Valiant Vicky's face. 'Run!
run!' he shrieked to his wife, in a terrible taking,
and setting off as fast as he could, never stopped till
he had reached his room again and hidden under the
bed. His wife set off at a run likewise, dropping

her bundle of golden dishes with a clang. The noise roused the enemy, who, thinking they were attacked, flew to arms ; but being half asleep, and the night being pitch-dark, they could not distinguish friend from foe, and falling on each other, fought with such fury that by next morning not one was left alive ! And then, as may be imagined, great were the rejoicings at Prince Victor's prowess. 'It was a mere trifle !' remarked that valiant little gentleman modestly ; 'when a man can shoot a mosquito with a shuttle, everything else is child's play.'

So he received half the kingdom, and ruled it with great dignity, refusing ever afterwards to fight, saying truly that kings never fought themselves, but paid others to fight for them.

Thus he lived in peace, and when he died every one said Valiant Vicky was the greatest hero the world had ever seen.

THE SON OF SEVEN MOTHERS

NCE upon a time there lived a King who had seven wives, but no children. This was a great grief to him, especially when he remembered that on his death there would be no heir to inherit the kingdom.

Now, one day, a poor old *fakír*, or religious devotee, came to the King and said, 'Your prayers are heard, your desire shall be accomplished, and each of your seven queens shall bear a son.'

The King's delight at this promise knew no bounds, and he gave orders for appropriate festivities to be prepared against the coming event throughout the length and breadth of the land.

Meanwhile the seven Queens lived luxuriously in a splendid palace, attended by hundreds of female slaves, and fed to their hearts' content on sweetmeats and confectionery.

Now the King was very fond of hunting, and one day, before he started, the seven Queens sent him a message saying, 'May it please our dearest lord not to hunt towards the north to-day, for we have dreamt bad dreams, and fear lest evil should befall you.'

The King, to allay their anxiety, promised regard for their wishes, and set out towards the south ; but as luck would have it, although he hunted diligently, he found no game. Nor had he greater success to the east or west, so that, being a keen sportsman, and determined not to go home empty-handed, he forgot all about his promise, and turned to the north. Here also he met at first with no reward, but just as he had made up his mind to give up for that day, a white hind with golden horns and silver hoofs flashed past him into a thicket. So quickly did it pass, that he scarcely saw it ; nevertheless a burning desire to capture and possess the beautiful strange creature filled his breast. He instantly ordered his attendants to form a ring round the thicket, and so encircle the hind ; then, gradually narrowing the circle, he pressed forward till he could distinctly see the white hind panting in the midst. Nearer and nearer he advanced, when, just as he thought to lay hold of the beautiful strange creature, it gave one mighty bound, leapt clean over the King's head, and fled towards the mountains. Forgetful of all else, the King, setting spurs to his horse, followed at full speed. On, on he galloped, leaving his retinue far behind, but keeping the white hind in view, and never drawing bridle, until, finding himself in a narrow ravine with no outlet, he reined in his steed. Before him stood a miserable hovel, into which, being tired after his long unsuccessful chase, he entered to ask for a drink of water. An old woman, seated in the hut at a spinning-wheel, answered his request by call-

ing to her daughter, and immediately from an inner
room came a maiden so lovely and charming, so
white-skinned and golden-haired, that the King was
transfixed by astonishment at seeing so beautiful a
sight in the wretched hovel.

She held the vessel of water to the King's lips, and
as he drank he looked into her eyes, and then it became clear to him that the girl was no other than the
white hind with the golden horns and silver feet he
had chased so far.

Her beauty bewitched him completely, and he fell
on his knees, begging her to return with him as his
bride ; but she only laughed, saying seven Queens
were quite enough even for a King to manage.   However, when he would take no refusal, but implored
her to have pity on him, and promised her everything
she could desire, she replied, 'Give me the eyes of
your seven wives, and then perhaps I may believe
that you mean what you say.'

The King was so carried away by the glamour of
the white hind's magical beauty, that he went home
at once, had the eyes of his seven Queens taken out,
and, after throwing the poor blind creatures into a
noisome dungeon whence they could not escape, set
off once more for the hovel in the ravine, bearing
with him his loathsome offering.   But the white hind
only laughed cruelly when she saw the fourteen eyes,
and threading them as a necklace, flung it round her
mother's neck, saying, ' Wear that, little mother, as a
keepsake, whilst I am away in the King's palace.'

Then she went back with the bewitched monarch
as his bride, and he gave her the seven Queens' rich
clothes and jewels to wear, the seven Queens' palace

to live in, and the seven Queens' slaves to wait upon
her ; so that she really had everything even a witch
could desire.

Now, very soon after the seven wretched, hapless
Queens were cast into prison, the first Queen's baby
was born. It was a handsome boy, but the Queens
were so desperately hungry that they killed the child
at once, and, dividing it into seven portions, ate it.
All except the youngest Queen, who saved her portion
secretly.

The next day the second Queen's baby was born,
and they did the same with it, and with all the babies
in turn, one after the other, until the seventh and
youngest Queen's baby was born on the seventh day.
But when the other six Queens came to the young
mother, and wanted to take it away, saying, ' Give
us your child to eat, as you have eaten ours ! ' she
produced the six pieces of the other babies untouched,
and answered, ' Not so ! here are six pieces for you ;
eat them, and leave my child alone. You cannot
complain, for you have each your fair share, neither
more nor less.'

Now, though the other Queens were very jealous
that the youngest amongst them should by forethought and self-denial have saved her baby's life,
they could say nothing ; for, as the young mother
had told them, they received their full share. And
though at first they disliked the handsome little boy,
he soon proved so useful to them, that ere long they
all looked on him as their son. Almost as soon as
he was born he began scraping at the mud wall of
their dungeon, and in an incredibly short space of
time had made a hole big enough for him to crawl

through. Through this he disappeared, returning in an hour or so laden with sweetmeats, which he divided equally amongst the seven blind Queens.

As he grew older he enlarged the hole, and slipped out two or three times every day to play with the little nobles in the town. No one knew who the tiny boy was, but everybody liked him, and he was so full of funny tricks and antics, so merry and bright, that he was sure to be rewarded by some girdle-cakes, a handful of parched grain, or some sweetmeats. All these things he brought home to his seven mothers, as he loved to call the seven blind Queens, who by his help lived on in their dungeon when all the world thought they had starved to death ages before.

At last, when he was quite a big lad, he one day took his bow and arrow, and went out to seek for game. Coming by chance upon the palace where the white hind lived in wicked splendour and magnificence, he saw some pigeons fluttering round the white marble turrets, and, taking good aim, shot one dead. It came tumbling past the very window where the white Queen was sitting; she rose to see what was the matter, and looked out. At the first glance at the handsome young lad standing there bow in hand, she knew by witchcraft that it was the King's son.

She nearly died of envy and spite, determining to destroy the lad without delay; therefore, sending a servant to bring him to her presence, she asked him if he would sell her the pigeon he had just shot.

'No,' replied the sturdy lad, 'the pigeon is for my seven blind mothers, who live in the noisome dungeon, and who would die if I did not bring them food.'

'Poor souls!' cried the cunning white witch; 'would you not like to bring them their eyes again? Give me the pigeon, my dear, and I faithfully promise to show you where to find them.'

Hearing this, the lad was delighted beyond measure, and gave up the pigeon at once. Whereupon the white Queen told him to seek her mother without delay, and ask for the eyes which she wore as a necklace.

'She will not fail to give them,' said the cruel Queen, 'if you show her this token on which I have written what I want done.'

So saying, she gave the lad a piece of broken potsherd, with these words inscribed on it—'Kill the bearer at once, and sprinkle his blood like water!'

Now, as the son of seven mothers could not read, he took the fatal message cheerfully, and set off to find the white Queen's mother.

But while he was journeying he passed through a town, where every one of the inhabitants looked so sad that he could not help asking what was the matter. They told him it was because the King's only daughter refused to marry; so when her father died there would be no heir to the throne. They greatly feared she must be out of her mind, for though every good-looking young man in the kingdom had been shown to her, she declared she would only marry one who was the son of seven mothers, and of course no one had ever heard of such a thing. Still the King, in despair, had ordered every man who entered the city gates to be led before the Princess in case she might relent. So, much to the lad's impatience, for he was in an immense hurry to find his mothers' eyes, he was dragged into the presence-chamber.

No sooner did the Princess catch sight of him than she blushed, and, turning to the King, said, ' Dear father, this is my choice ! '

Never were such rejoicings as these few words produced. The inhabitants nearly went wild with joy, but the son of seven mothers said he would not marry the Princess unless they first let him recover his mothers' eyes. Now when the beautiful bride heard his story, she asked to see the potsherd, for she was very learned and clever ; so much so that on seeing the treacherous words, she said nothing, but taking another similarly-shaped bit of potsherd, wrote on it these words—' Take care of this lad, give him all he desires,' and returned it to the son of seven mothers, who, none the wiser, set off on his quest.

Ere long, he arrived at the hovel in the ravine, where the white witch's mother, a hideous old creature, grumbled dreadfully on reading the message, especially when the lad asked for the necklace of eyes. Nevertheless she took it off, and gave it him, saying, ' There are only thirteen of 'em now, for I ate one last week, when I was hungry.'

The lad, however, was only too glad to get any at all, so he hurried home as fast as he could to his seven mothers, and gave two eyes apiece to the six elder Queens ; but to the youngest he gave one, say-ing, ' Dearest little mother !—I will be your other eye always ! '

After this he set off to marry the Princess, as he had promised, but when passing by the white Queen's

palace he again saw some pigeons on the roof.
Drawing his bow, he shot one, and again it came
fluttering past the window. Then the white hind
looked out, and lo! there was the King's son alive
and well.

She cried with hatred and disgust, but sending
for the lad, asked him how he had returned so soon,
and when she heard how he had brought home the
thirteen eyes, and given them to the seven blind
Queens, she could hardly restrain her rage. Nevertheless she pretended to be charmed with his success,
and told him that if he would give her this pigeon
also, she would reward him with the Jôgi's wonderful
cow, whose milk flows all day long, and makes a
pond as big as a kingdom. The lad, nothing loath,
gave her the pigeon ; whereupon, as before, she bade
him go ask her mother for the cow, and gave him a
potsherd whereon was written—' Kill this lad without
fail, and sprinkle his blood like water ! '

But on the way, the son of seven mothers looked
in on the Princess, just to tell her how he came to be
delayed, and she, after reading the message on the
potsherd, gave him another in its stead ; so that
when the lad reached the old hag's hut and asked
her for the Jôgi's cow, she could not refuse, but told
the boy how to find it ; and, bidding him of all things
not to be afraid of the eighteen thousand demons
who kept watch and ward over the treasure, told
him to be off before she became too angry at her
daughter's foolishness in thus giving away so many
good things.

Then the lad did as he had been told bravely.
He journeyed on and on till he came to a milk-white

pond, guarded by the eighteen thousand demons. They were really frightful to behold, but, plucking up courage, he whistled a tune as he walked through them, looking neither to the right nor the left. By and by he came upon the Jôgi's cow, tall, white, and beautiful, while the Jôgi himself, who was king of all the demons, sat milking her day and night, and the milk streamed from her udder, filling the milk-white tank.

The Jôgi, seeing the lad, called out fiercely, ' What do you want here ? '

Then the lad answered, according to the old hag's bidding, ' I want your skin, for King Indra is making a new kettledrum, and says your skin is nice and tough.'

Upon this the Jôgi began to shiver and shake (for no Jinn or Jôgi dares disobey King Indra's command), and, falling at the lad's feet, cried, ' If you will spare me I will give you anything I possess, even my beautiful white cow ! '

To this, the son of seven mothers, after a little pretended hesitation, agreed, saying that after all it would not be difficult to find a nice tough skin like the Jôgi's elsewhere ; so, driving the wonderful cow before him, he set off homewards. The seven Queens were delighted to possess so marvellous an animal, and though they toiled from morning till night making curds and whey, besides selling milk to the confectioners, they could not use half the cow gave, and became richer and richer day by day.

Seeing them so comfortably off, the son of seven mothers started with a light heart to marry the Princess ; but when passing the white hind's palace he

H

could not resist sending a bolt at some pigeons which were cooing on the parapet, and for the third time one fell dead just beneath the window where the white Queen was sitting. Looking out, she saw the lad hale and hearty standing before her, and grew whiter than ever with rage and spite.

She sent for him to ask how he had returned so soon, and when she heard how kindly her mother had received him, she very nearly had a fit ; however, she dissembled her feelings as well as she could, and, smiling sweetly, said she was glad to have been able to fulfil her promise, and that if he would give her this third pigeon, she would do yet more for him than she had done before, by giving him the million-fold rice, which ripens in one night.

The lad was of course delighted at the very idea, and, giving up the pigeon, set off on his quest, armed as before with a potsherd, on which was written, ' Do not fail this time. Kill the lad, and sprinkle his blood like water ! '

But when he looked in on his Princess, just to prevent her becoming anxious about him, she asked to see the potsherd as usual, and substituted another, on which was written, ' Yet again give this lad all he requires, for his blood shall be as your blood ! '

Now when the old hag saw this, and heard how the lad wanted the million-fold rice which ripens in a single night, she fell into the most furious rage, but being terribly afraid of her daughter, she controlled herself, and bade the boy go and find the field guarded by eighteen millions of demons, warning him on no account to look back after having plucked the tallest spike of rice, which grew in the centre.

So the son of seven mothers set off, and soon came to the field where, guarded by eighteen millions of demons, the million-fold rice grew. He walked on bravely, looking neither to the right nor left, till he reached the centre and plucked the tallest ear ; but as he turned homewards a thousand sweet voices rose behind him, crying in tenderest accents, ' Pluck me too ! oh, please pluck me too ! ' He looked back, and lo ! there was nothing left of him but a little heap of ashes !

Now as time passed by and the lad did not return, the old hag grew uneasy, remembering the message ' his blood shall be as your blood ' ; so she set off to see what had happened.

Soon she came to the heap of ashes, and knowing by her arts what it was, she took a little water, and kneading the ashes into a paste, formed it into the likeness of a man ; then, putting a drop of blood from her little finger into its mouth, she blew on it, and instantly the son of seven mothers started up as well as ever.

' Don't you disobey orders again ! ' grumbled the old hag, ' or next time I'll leave you alone. Now be off, before I repent of my kindness ! '

So the son of seven mothers returned joyfully to the seven Queens, who, by the aid of the million-fold rice, soon became the richest people in the kingdom. Then they celebrated their son's marriage to the clever Princess with all imaginable pomp ; but the bride was so clever, she would not rest until she had made known her husband to his father, and punished the wicked white witch. So she made her husband build a palace exactly like the one in which the seven

Queens had lived, and in which the white witch now dwelt in splendour. Then, when all was prepared, she bade her husband give a grand feast to the King. Now the King had heard much of the mysterious son of seven mothers, and his marvellous wealth, so he gladly accepted the invitation ; but what was his astonishment when on entering the palace he found it was a facsimile of his own in every particular ! And when his host, richly attired, led him straight to the private hall, where on royal thrones sat the seven Queens, dressed as he had last seen them, he was speechless with surprise, until the Princess, coming forward, threw herself at his feet, and told him the whole story. Then the King awoke from his enchantment, and his anger rose against the wicked white hind who had bewitched him so long, until he could not contain himself. So she was put to death, and her grave ploughed over, and after that the seven Queens returned to their own splendid palace, and everybody lived happily.

THE SPARROW AND THE CROW

 SPARROW AND A CROW once agreed to have *khichrî* for dinner. So the Sparrow brought rice, and the Crow brought lentils, and the Sparrow was cook, and when the *khichrî* was ready, the Crow stood by to claim his share.

'Who ever heard of any one sitting down to dinner so dirty as you are?' quoth the Sparrow scornfully. 'Your body is quite black, and your head looks as if it were covered with ashes. For goodness gracious sake, go and wash in the Pond first.'

The Crow, though a little huffy at being called dirty, deemed it best to comply, for he knew what a determined little person the Sparrow was; so he went to the Pond, and said—

'Your name, sir, is Pond,
    But my name is Crow.
Please give me some water,
    For if you do so
I can wash beak and feet
And the nice *khichrî* eat;

Though I really don't know
  What the Sparrow can
    mean,
For I'm sure, as Crows go,
  I'm remarkably clean!'
  But the Pond said,
'Certainly I will give you
water; but first you must
go to the Deer, and beg him
to lend you a horn. Then
with it you can dig a nice
little rill for the water to
flow in clean and fresh.' .

  So the Crow flew to the
Deer, and said—
'Your name, sir, is Deer,
  But my name is Crow.
Oh, give me a horn, please,
  For if you do so
I can dig a clean rill
For the water to fill;
Then I'll wash beak and
    feet
And the nice *khichrî* eat;
Though I really don't know
  What the Sparrow can
    mean,
For I'm sure, as Crows go,
  I'm remarkably clean!'
  But the Deer said,
'Certainly I will give you
a horn; but first you must
go to the Cow, and ask her

to give you some milk for me to drink. Then I shall grow fat, and not mind the pain of breaking my horn.'

So the Crow flew off to the Cow, and said—

'Your name, ma'am, is Cow,
    But my name is Crow.
Oh, give me some milk, please,
    For if you do so
The pain will be borne,
Deer will give me his horn,
And I'll dig a clean rill
For the water to fill ;
Then I'll wash beak and feet
And the nice *khichrî* eat ;
Though I really don't know
    What the Sparrow can mean,
For I'm sure, as Crows go,
    I'm remarkably clean !'

But the Cow said, 'Certainly I will give you milk, only first you must bring me some Grass ; for who ever heard of a cow giving milk without grass ?

So the Crow flew to some Grass, and said—

'Your name, sir, is Grass,
    But my name is Crow.
Oh, give me some blades, please,
    For if you do so
Madam Cow will give milk
To the Deer sleek as silk ;
The pain will be borne,
He will give me his horn,
And I'll dig a clean rill
For the water to fill ;

Then I'll wash beak and feet
And the nice *khichrî* eat ;
Though I really don't know
    What the Sparrow can mean,
For I'm sure, as Crows go,
    I'm remarkably clean !'

But the Grass said, 'Certainly I will give you Grass ; but first you must go to the Blacksmith, and ask him to make you a sickle.   Then you can cut me, for who ever heard of Grass cutting itself?'

So the Crow went to the Blacksmith, and said—

'Your name, sir, is Smith,
    But my name is Crow.
Please give me a sickle,
    ·For if you do so
The Grass I can mow
As food for the Cow ;
Madam Cow will give milk
To the Deer sleek as silk ;
The pain will be borne,
He will give me his horn,
And I'll dig a clean rill
For the water to fill ;
Then I'll wash beak·and feet
And the nice *khichrî* eat ;
Though I really don't know
    What the Sparrow can mean,
For I'm sure, as Crows go,
    I'm remarkably clean !'

'With pleasure,' said the Blacksmith, 'if you will light the fire and blow the bellows.'

So the Crow began to light the fire, and blow the bellows, but in so doing he fell right in—to—the—very—middle—of—the—FIRE, and was burnt !

So that was the end of him, and the Sparrow ate all the *khichrî*.

THE TIGER, THE BRÂHMAN, AND THE JACKAL

ONCE upon a time a tiger was caught in a trap. He tried in vain to get out through the bars, and rolled and bit with rage and grief when he failed.

By chance a poor Brâhman came by. 'Let me out of this cage, O pious one!' cried the tiger.

'Nay, my friend,' replied the Brâhman mildly, 'you would probably eat me if I did.'

'Not at all!' swore the tiger with many oaths; 'on the contrary, I should be for ever grateful, and serve you as a slave!'

Now when the tiger sobbed and sighed and wept and swore, the pious Brâhman's heart softened, and at last he consented to open the door of the cage. Out popped the tiger, and, seizing the poor man, cried, 'What a fool you are! What is to prevent my eating you now, for after being cooped up so long I am just terribly hungry!'

In vain the Brâhman pleaded for his life; the most he could gain was a promise to abide by the decision of the first three things he chose to question as to the justice of the tiger's action.

So the Brâhman first asked a *pîpal* tree what it thought of the matter, but the *pîpal* tree replied coldly,

'What have you to complain about? Don't I give shade and shelter to every one who passes by, and don't they in return tear down my branches to feed their cattle? Don't whimper—be a man!'

Then the Brâhman, sad at heart, went farther afield till he saw a buffalo turning a well-wheel; but he fared no better from it, for it answered, 'You are a fool to expect gratitude! Look at me! While I gave milk they fed me on cotton-seed and oil-cake,

but now I am dry they yoke me here, and give me refuse as fodder!'

The Brâhman, still more sad, asked the road to give him its opinion.

'My dear sir,' said the road, 'how foolish you are to expect anything else! Here am I, useful to everybody, yet all, rich and poor, great and small, trample on me as they go past, giving me nothing but the ashes of their pipes and the husks of their grain!'

On this the Brâhman turned back sorrowfully, and on the way he met a jackal, who called out, 'Why, what's the matter, Mr. Brâhman? You look as miserable as a fish out of water!'

Then the Brâhman told him all that had occurred. 'How very confusing!' said the jackal, when the recital was ended; 'would you mind telling me over again? for everything seems so mixed up!'

The Brâhman told it all over again, but the jackal shook his head in a distracted sort of way, and still could not understand.

'It's very odd,' said he sadly, 'but it all seems to go in at one ear and out at the other! I will go to the place where it all happened, and then perhaps I shall be able to give a judgment.'

So they returned to the cage, by which the tiger was waiting for the Brâhman, and sharpening his teeth and claws.

'You've been away a long time!' growled the savage beast, 'but now let us begin our dinner.'

'*Our* dinner!' thought the wretched Brâhman, as his knees knocked together with fright; 'what a remarkably delicate way of putting it!'

'Give me five minutes, my lord!' he pleaded, 'in order that I may explain matters to the jackal here, who is somewhat slow in his wits.'

The tiger consented, and the Brâhman began the whole story over again, not missing a single detail, and spinning as long a yarn as possible.

'Oh, my poor brain! oh, my poor brain!' cried the jackal, wringing his paws. 'Let me see! how did it all begin? You were in the cage, and the tiger came walking by——'

'Pooh!' interrupted the tiger, 'what a fool you are! *I* was in the cage.'

'Of course!' cried the jackal, pretending to tremble with fright; 'yes! I was in the cage—no, I wasn't —dear! dear! where are my wits?   Let me see— the tiger was in the Brâhman, and the cage came walking by——no, that's not it either!   Well, don't mind me, but begin your dinner, for I shall never understand!'

'Yes, you shall!' returned the tiger, in a rage at the jackal's stupidity; 'I'll *make* you understand! Look here—I am the tiger——'

'Yes, my lord!'

'And that is the Brâhman——'

'Yes, my lord!'

'And that is the cage——'

'Yes, my lord!'

'And I was in the cage—do you understand?'

'Yes—no—   Please, my lord——'

'Well?' cried the tiger, impatiently.

'Please, my lord!—how did you get in?'

'How!—why, in the usual way, of course!'

'Oh dear me!—my head is beginning to whirl again!   Please don't be angry, my lord, but what is the usual way?'

At this the tiger lost patience, and, jumping into the cage, cried, 'This way!   Now do you understand how it was?'

'Perfectly!' grinned the jackal, as he dexterously shut the door; 'and if you will permit me to say so, I think matters will remain as they were!'

THE KING OF THE CROCODILES

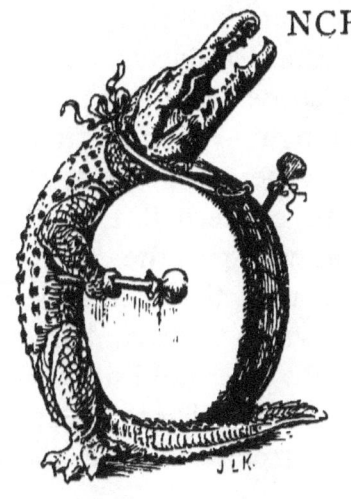

ONCE upon a time a farmer went out to look at his fields by the side of the river, and found to his dismay that all his young green wheat had been trodden down, and nearly destroyed, by a number of crocodiles, which were lying lazily amid the crops like great logs of wood. He flew into a great rage, bidding them go back to the water, but they only laughed at him.

Every day the same thing occurred,—every day the farmer found the crocodiles lying in his young wheat, until one morning he completely lost his temper, and, when they refused to budge, began throwing stones at them. At this they rushed on him fiercely, and he, quaking with fear, fell on his knees, begging them not to hurt him.

'We will hurt neither you nor your young wheat,' said the biggest crocodile, 'if you will give us your daughter in marriage ; but if not, we will eat you for throwing stones at us.'

The farmer, thinking of nothing but saving his own life, promised what the crocodiles required of him ; but when, on his return home, he told his wife what he had done, she was very much vexed, for their daughter was as beautiful as the moon, and her betrothal into a very rich family had already taken place. So his wife persuaded the farmer to disregard the promise made to the crocodiles, and proceed with his daughter's marriage as if nothing had happened ; but when the wedding-day drew near the bridegroom died, and there was an end to that business. The farmer's daughter, however, was so beautiful that she was very soon asked in marriage again, but this time her suitor fell sick of a lingering illness ; in short, so many misfortunes occurred to all concerned, that at last even the farmer's wife acknowledged the crocodiles must have something to do with the bad luck. By her advice the farmer went down to the river bank to try to induce the crocodiles to release him from his promise, but they would hear of no excuse, threatening fearful punishments if the agreement were not fulfilled at once.

So the farmer returned home to his wife very sorrowful ; she, however, was determined to resist to the uttermost, and refused to give up her daughter.

The very next day the poor girl fell down and broke her leg. Then the mother said, 'These demons of crocodiles will certainly kill us all !—better to marry our daughter to a strange house than see her die.'

Accordingly, the farmer went down to the river and informed the crocodiles they might send the bridal procession to fetch the bride as soon as they chose.

The next day a number of female crocodiles came to the bride's house with trays full of beautiful clothes, and *henna* for staining the bride's hands. They behaved with the utmost politeness, and carried out all the proper ceremonies with the greatest precision. Nevertheless the beautiful bride wept, saying, ' Oh, mother ! are you marrying me into the river ? I shall be drowned ! '

In due course the bridal procession arrived, and all the village was wonderstruck at the magnificence of the arrangements. Never was there such a retinue of crocodiles, some playing instruments of music, others bearing trays upon trays full of sweetmeats, garments, and jewels, and all dressed in the richest of stuffs. In the middle, a perfect blaze of gold and gems, sat the King of the Crocodiles.

The sight of so much magnificence somewhat comforted the beautiful bride, nevertheless she wept bitterly when she was put into the gorgeous bride's palanquin and borne off to the river bank. Arrived at the edge of the stream, the crocodiles dragged the poor girl out, and forced her into the water, despite her struggles, for, thinking she was going to be drowned, she screamed with terror ; but lo and behold ! no sooner had her feet touched the water than it divided before her, and, rising up on either side, showed a path leading to the bottom of the river, down which the bridal party disappeared, leaving the bride's father, who had accompanied her so far, upon the bank, very much astonished at the marvellous sight.

Some months passed by without further news of the crocodiles. The farmer's wife wept because she had lost her daughter, declaring that the girl was really drowned, and her husband's fine story about the stream dividing was a mere invention.

Now when the King of the Crocodiles was on the point of leaving with his bride, he had given a piece of brick to her father, with these words: 'If ever you want to see your daughter, go down to the river, throw this brick as far as you can into the stream, and you will see what you will see!'

Remembering this, the farmer said to his wife, 'Since you are so distressed, I will go myself and see if my daughter be alive or dead.'

Then he went to the river bank, taking the brick, and threw it ever so far into the stream. Immediately the waters rolled back from before his feet, leaving a dry path to the bottom of the river. It looked so inviting, spread with clean sand, and bordered by flowers, that the farmer hastened along it without the least hesitation, until he came to a magnificent palace, with a golden roof, and shining, glittering diamond walls. Lofty trees and gay gardens surrounded it, and a sentry paced up and down before the gateway.

'Whose palace is this?' asked the farmer of the sentry, who replied that it belonged to the King of the Crocodiles.

'My daughter has at least a splendid house to live in!' thought the farmer; 'I only wish her husband were half as handsome!'

Then, turning to the sentry, he asked if his daughter were within.

'Your daughter!' returned the sentry, 'what should she do here?'

'She married the King of the Crocodiles, and I want to see her.'

At this the sentry burst out laughing. 'A likely story, indeed!' he cried; 'what! *my* master married to *your* daughter! Ha! ha! ha!'

Now the farmer's daughter was sitting beside an open window in the palace, waiting for her husband to return from hunting. She was as happy as the day was long, for you must know that in his own river-kingdom the King of the Crocodiles was the handsomest young Prince anybody ever set eyes upon; it was only when he went on shore that he assumed the form of a crocodile. So what with her magnificent palace and splendid young Prince, the farmer's daughter had been too happy even to think of her old home; but now, hearing a strange voice speaking to the sentry, her memory awakened, and she recognised her father's tones. Looking out, she saw him there, standing in his poor clothes, in the glittering court; she longed to run and fling her arms round his neck, but dared not disobey her husband, who had forbidden her to go out of, or to let any one into the palace without his permission. So all she could do was to lean out of the window, and call to him, saying, 'Oh, dearest father! I am here! Only wait till my husband, the King of the Crocodiles, returns, and I will ask him to let you in. I dare not without his leave.'

The father, though overjoyed to find his daughter

alive, did not wonder she was afraid of her terrible husband, so he waited patiently.

In a short time a troop of horsemen entered the court. Every man was dressed from head to foot in armour made of glittering silver plates, but in the centre of all rode a Prince clad in gold—bright burnished gold, from the crown of his head to the soles of his feet,—the handsomest, most gallant young Prince that ever was seen.

Then the poor farmer fell at the gold-clad horseman's feet, and cried, 'O King! cherish me! for I am a poor man whose daughter was carried off by the dreadful King of the Crocodiles!'

Then the gold-clad horseman smiled, saying, '*I* am the King of the Crocodiles! Your daughter is a good, obedient wife, and will be very glad to see you.'

After this there were great rejoicings and merry-makings, but when a few days had passed away in feasting, the farmer became restless, and begged to be allowed to take his daughter home with him for a short visit, in order to convince his wife the girl was well and happy. But the Crocodile King refused, saying, 'Not so! but if you like I will give you a house and land here; then you can dwell with us.'

The farmer said he must first ask his wife, and returned home, taking several bricks with him, to throw into the river and make the stream divide.

His wife would not at first agree to live in the Crocodile Kingdom, but she consented to go there on a visit, and afterwards became so fond of the

beautiful river country that she was constantly going
to see her daughter the Queen ; till at length the old
couple never returned to shore, but lived altogether
in Crocodile Kingdom with their son-in-law, the King
of the Crocodiles.

NCE upon a time there was a little boy who lost his parents; so he went to live with his Auntie, and she set him to herd sheep. All day long the little fellow wandered barefoot through the pathless plain, tending his flock, and playing his tiny shepherd's pipe from morn till eve.

But one day came a great big wolf, and looked hungrily at the small shepherd and his fat sheep, saying, 'Little boy! shall I eat you, or your sheep?'

Then the little boy answered politely, 'I don't know, Mr. Wolf; I must ask my Auntie.'

So all day long he piped away on his tiny pipe, and in the evening, when he brought the flock home, he went to his Auntie and said, 'Auntie dear, a great big wolf asked me to-day if he should eat me, or your sheep. Which shall it be?'

Then his Auntie looked at the wee little shepherd, and at the fat flock, and said sharply, 'Which shall it be?—why, *you*, of course!'

So next morning the little boy drove his flock out into the pathless plain, and blew away cheerfully

on his shepherd's pipe until the great big wolf appeared.   Then he laid aside his pipe, and, going up
to the savage beast, said, 'Oh, if you please, Mr.
Wolf, I asked my Auntie, and she says you are to
eat *me.*'

Now-the wolf, savage as wolves always are, could
not help having just a spark of pity for the tiny
barefoot shepherd who played his pipe so sweetly,
therefore he said kindly, ' Could I do anything for
you, little boy, after I've eaten you ? '

' Thank you ! ' returned the tiny shepherd.   ' If
you would be so kind, after you've picked the bones,
as to thread my anklebone on a string and hang, it
on the tree that weeps over the pond yonder, I shall
be much obliged.'

So the wolf ate the little shepherd, picked the
bones, and afterwards hung the anklebone by a
string to the branches of the tree, where it danced
and swung in the sunlight.

Now, one day, three robbers, who had just robbed
a palace, happening to pass that way, sat down
under the tree and began to divide the spoil.   Just
as they had arranged all the golden dishes and
precious jewels and costly stuffs into three heaps, a
jackal howled.   Now you must know that thieves
always use the jackal's cry as a note of warning, so
that when at the very same moment Little Anklebone's thread snapped, and he fell plump on the
head of the chief robber, the man imagined some
one had thrown a pebble at him, and, shouting
' Run ! run !—we are discovered ! ' he bolted away
as hard as he could, followed by his companions,
leaving all the treasure behind them.

'Now,' said Little Anklebone to himself, 'I shall lead a fine life!'

So he gathered the treasure together, and sat under the tree that drooped over the pond, and played so sweetly on a new shepherd's pipe, that all the beasts of the forest, and the birds of the air, and the fishes of the pond came to listen to him. Then Little Anklebone put marble basins round the pond for the animals to drink out of, and in the evening the does, and the tigresses, and the she-wolves gathered round him to be milked, and when he had drunk his fill he milked the rest into the pond, till at last it became a pond of milk. And Little Anklebone sat by the milken pond and piped away on his shepherd's pipe.

Now, one day, an old woman, passing by with her jar for water, heard the sweet strains of Little Anklebone's pipe, and following the sound, came upon the pond of milk, and saw the animals, and the birds, and the fishes, listening to the music. She was wonderstruck, especially when Little Anklebone, from his seat under the tree, called out, 'Fill your jar, mother! All drink who come hither!'

Then the old woman filled her jar with milk, and went on her way rejoicing at her good fortune. But as she journeyed she met with the King of that country, who, having been a-hunting, had lost his way in the pathless plain.

'Give me a drink of water, good mother,' he cried, seeing the jar; 'I am half dead with thirst!'

'It is milk, my son,' replied the old woman; 'I got it yonder from a milken pond.' Then she told the King of the wonders she had seen, so that he

resolved to have a peep at them himself. And when
he saw the milken pond, and all the animals and
birds and fishes gathered round, while Little Anklebone played ever so sweetly on his shepherd's pipe,
he said, ' I must have the tiny piper, if I die for it ! '

No sooner did Little Anklebone hear these words
than he set off at a run, and the King after him.
Never was there such a chase before or since, for
Little Anklebone hid himself amid the thickest briars
and thorns, and the King was so determined to have
the tiny piper, that he did not care for scratches.
At last the King was successful, but no sooner did
he take hold of Little Anklebone than the clouds
above began to thunder and lighten horribly, and
from below came the lowing of many does, and louder
than all came the voice of the little piper himself
singing these words—

> ' O clouds ! why should you storm and flare ?
> Poor Anklebone is forced to roam.
> O does ! why wait the milker's care ?
> Poor Anklebone must leave his home.'

And he sang so piercingly sweet that pity filled the
King's heart, especially when he saw it was nothing
but a bone after all. So he let it go again, and the
little piper went back to his seat under the tree by
the pond ; and there he sits still, and plays his
shepherd's pipe, while all the beasts of the forest,
and birds of the air, and fishes of the pond, gather
round and listen to his music. And sometimes,
people wandering through the pathless plain hear the
pipe, and then they say, ' That is Little Anklebone,
who was eaten by a wolf ages ago !

THE CLOSE ALLIANCE

A TALE OF WOE

NE day a farmer went with his bullocks to plough his field. He had just turned the first furrow, when a tiger walked up to him and said, 'Peace be with you, friend! How are you this fine morning?'

'The same to you, my lord, and I am pretty well, thank you!' returned the farmer, quaking with fear, but thinking it wisest to be polite.

'I am glad to hear it,' replied the tiger cheerfully, 'because Providence has sent me to eat your two bullocks. You are a God-fearing man, I know, so make haste and unyoke them.'

'My friend, are you sure you are not making a mistake?' asked the farmer, whose courage had returned now that he knew it was merely a question of gobbling up bullocks; 'because Providence sent me to plough this field, and, in order to plough, one must have oxen. Had you not better go and make further inquiries?'

'There is no occasion for delay, and I should be sorry to keep you waiting,' returned the tiger. 'If you'll unyoke the bullocks I'll be ready in a moment.' With that the savage creature fell to sharpening his teeth and claws in a very significant manner.

But the farmer begged and prayed that his oxen might not be eaten, and promised that if the tiger would spare them, he would give in exchange a fine fat young milch cow, which his wife had tied up in the yard at home.

To this the tiger agreed, and, taking the oxen with him, the farmer went sadly homewards. Seeing him return so early from the fields, his wife, who was a stirring, busy woman, called out, 'What! lazy-bones!—back already, and *my* work just beginning!'

Then the farmer explained how he had met the tiger, and how to save the bullocks he had promised the milch cow in exchange. At this the wife began to cry, saying, 'A likely story, indeed!—saving your stupid old bullocks at the expense of my beautiful cow! Where will the children get milk? and how can I cook my pottage and collops without butter?'

'All very fine, wife,' retorted the farmer, 'but

how can we make bread without corn ? and how can you have corn without bullocks to plough the fields ? Pottage and collops are very nice, but it is better to do without milk and butter than without bread, so make haste and untie the cow.'

'You great gaby!' wept the wife, 'if you had an ounce of sense in your brain you'd think of some plan to get out of the scrape!'

'Think yourself!' cried the husband, in a rage.

'Very well!' returned the wife ; 'but if I do the thinking you must obey orders ; I can't do both. Go back to the tiger, and tell him the cow wouldn't come along with you, but that your wife is bringing it.'

The farmer, who was a great coward, didn't half like the idea of going back empty-handed to the tiger, but as he could think of no other plan he did as he was bid, and found the beast still sharpening his teeth and claws for very hunger ; and when he heard he had to wait still longer for his dinner, he began to prowl about, and lash his tail, and curl his whiskers, in a most terrible manner, causing the poor farmer's knees to knock together with terror.

Now, when the farmer had left the house, his wife went to the stable and saddled the pony ; then she put on her husband's best clothes, tied the turban very high, so as to make her look as tall as possible, bestrode the pony, and set off to the field where the tiger was.

She rode along, swaggering and blustering, till she came to where the lane turned into the field, and then she called out, as bold as brass, 'Now, please the powers! I may find a tiger in this place ; for I

haven't tasted tiger's meat since yesterday, when, as
luck would have it, I ate three for breakfast.'

Hearing these words, and seeing the speaker ride
boldly at him, the tiger became so alarmed that he
turned tail, and bolted into the forest, going away at
such a headlong pace that he nearly overturned his

own jackal ; for tigers always have a jackal of their own, who, as it were, waits at table and clears away the bones.

'My lord ! my lord !' cried the jackal, 'whither away so fast ?'

'Run ! run !' panted the tiger ; 'there's the very devil of a horseman in yonder fields, who thinks nothing of eating three tigers for breakfast !'

At this the jackal sniggered in his sleeve. 'My dear lord,' said he, 'the sun has dazzled your eyes ! That was no horseman, but only the farmer's wife dressed up as a man !'

'Are you quite sure ?' asked the tiger, pausing.

'Quite sure, my lord,' repeated the jackal ; 'and if your lordship's eyes had not been dazzled by— ahem !—the sun, your lordship would have seen her pigtail hanging down behind.'

'But you may be mistaken !' persisted the cowardly tiger ; 'it was the very devil of a horse- man to look at !'

'Who's afraid ?' replied the brave jackal. 'Come ! don't give up your dinner because of a woman !'

'But you may be bribed to betray me !' argued the tiger, who, like all cowards, was suspicious.

'Let us go together, then !' returned the gallant jackal.

'Nay ! but you may take me there and then run away !' insisted the tiger cunningly.

'In that case, let us tie our tails together, and then I can't !' The jackal, you see, was determined not to be done out of his bones.

To this the tiger agreed, and having tied their

tails together in a reef-knot, the pair set off arm-in-arm.

Now the farmer and his wife had remained in the field, laughing over the trick she had played on the tiger, when, lo and behold! what should they see but the gallant pair coming back ever so bravely, with their tails tied together.

'Run!' cried the farmer; 'we are lost! we are lost!'

'Nothing of the kind, you great gaby!' answered his wife coolly, 'if you will only stop that noise and be quiet. I can't hear myself speak!'

Then she waited till the pair were within hail, when she called out politely, 'How very kind of you, dear Mr. Jackal, to bring me such a nice fat tiger! I shan't be a moment finishing my share of him, and then you can have the bones.'

At these words the tiger became wild with fright, and, quite forgetting the jackal, and that reef-knot in their tails, he bolted away full tilt, dragging the jackal behind him. Bumpety, bump, bump, over the stones!—crash, scratch, patch, through the briars!

In vain the poor jackal howled and shrieked to the tiger to stop,—the noise behind him only frightened the coward more; and away he went, helter-skelter, hurry-scurry, over hill and dale, till he was *nearly* dead with fatigue, and the jackal was *quite* dead from bumps and bruises.

Moral—Don't tie your tail to a coward's.

THE TWO BROTHERS

NCE upon a time there lived a King who had two young sons ; they were good boys, and sat in school learning all that kings' sons ought to know. But while they were still learning, the Queen their mother died, and their father the King shortly after married again. Of course the new wife was jealous of the two young Princes, and, as stepmothers usually do, she soon began to ill-use the poor boys. First she gave them barley-meal instead of wheaten cakes to eat, and then even these were made without salt. After a time, the meal of which the cakes were made was sour and full of weevils ; so matters went on from bad to worse, until at last she took to beating the poor young Princes, and when they cried, she complained to the King of their disobedience and peevishness, so that he too was angry, and beat them again.

At length the lads agreed it was high time to seek some remedy.

'Let us go into the world,' said the younger, 'and earn our own living.'

K

'Yes,' cried the elder, 'let us go at once, and
never again eat bread under this roof.'

'Not so, brother,' replied the younger, who was
wise beyond his years, 'don't you remember the
saying—

'"With empty stomachs don't venture away,
     Be it December, or be it May"?'

So they ate their bread, bad as it was, and afterwards, both mounting on one pony, they set out to
seek their fortune.

Having journeyed for some time through a barren
country, they dismounted under a large tree, and sat
down to rest. By chance a starling and a parrot,
flying past, settled on the branches of the tree, and
began to dispute as to who should have the best
place.

'I never heard of such impertinence!' cried the
starling, pushing and striving to get to the topmost
branch ; 'why, I am so important a bird, that if any
man eats me he will without doubt become Prime
Minister!'

'Make room for your betters!' returned the parrot,
hustling the starling away ; 'why, if any man eats
me, he will without doubt become a King!'

Hearing these words, the brothers instantly drew
out their crossbows, and aiming at the same time,
both the birds fell dead at the selfsame moment.
Now these two brothers were so fond of each other
that neither would allow he had shot the parrot, for
each wanted the other to be the King, and even when
the birds had been cooked and were ready to eat, the
two lads were still disputing over the matter. But
at last the younger said, 'Dearest brother, we are

only wasting time. You are the elder, and must take your right, since it was your fate to be born first.'

So the elder Prince ate the parrot, and the younger Prince ate the starling; then they mounted their pony and rode away. They had gone but a little way, however, when the elder brother missed his whip, and thinking he had perhaps left it under the tree, proposed to go back and find it.

'Not so,' said the younger Prince, 'you are King, I am only Minister; therefore it is my place to go and fetch the whip.'

'Be it as you wish,' replied the elder, 'only take the pony, which will enable you to return quicker. In the meantime I will go on foot to yonder town.'

The younger Prince accordingly rode back to the tree, but the Snake-demon, to whom it belonged, had returned during the interval, and no sooner did the poor Prince set foot within its shade than the horrid serpent flew at him and killed him.

Meanwhile, the elder Prince, loitering along the road, arrived at last at the town, which he found in a state of great commotion. The King had recently died, and though all the inhabitants had marched past the sacred elephant in file, the animal had not chosen to elect any one of them to the vacant throne by kneeling down and saluting the favoured individual as he passed by, for in this manner Kings were elected in that country. Therefore the people were in great consternation, and orders had been issued that every stranger entering the gates of the city was forthwith to be led before the sacred elephant. No sooner, therefore, had the elder Prince set foot

in the town than he was dragged unceremoniously —for there had been many disappointments—before the over-particular animal. This time, however, it had found what it wanted, for the very instant it caught sight of the Prince it went down on its knees and began in a great hurry to salute him with its trunk. So the Prince was immediately elected to the throne, amid general rejoicings.

All this time the younger Prince lay dead under the tree, so that the King his brother, after waiting and searching for him in vain, gave him up for lost, and appointed another Prime Minister.

But it so happened that a magician and his wife, who, being wise folk, were not afraid of the serpents which dwelt in the tree, came to draw water at the spring which flowed from the roots ; and when the magician's wife saw the dead Prince lying there, so handsome and young, she thought she had never seen anything so beautiful before, and, taking pity on him, said to her husband, ' You are for ever talking of your wisdom and power: prove it by bringing this dead lad to life ! '

At first the magician refused, but when his wife began to jeer at him, saying his vaunted power was all pretence, he replied angrily, ' Very well ; you shall see that although I myself have no power to bring the dead back to life, I can force others to do the deed.'

Whereupon he bade his wife fill her brass drinking bowl at the spring, when, lo and behold ! every drop of the water flowed into the little vessel, and the fountain was dry !

' Now,' said the magician, ' come away home, and you shall see what you will see.'

When the serpents found their spring had dried up, they were terribly put out, for serpents are thirsty creatures, and love water. They bore the drought for three days, but after that they went in a body to the magician, and told him they would do whatever he desired if he would only restore the water of their spring. This he promised to do, if they in their turn restored the dead Prince to life ; and when they gladly performed this task, the magician emptied the brass bowl, all the water flowed back into the spring, and the serpents drank and were happy.

The young Prince, on coming back to life, fancied he had awakened from sleep, and fearing lest his brother should be vexed at his delay, seized the whip, mounted the pony—which all this time had been quietly grazing beside its master—and rode off. But in his hurry and confusion he took the wrong road, and so arrived at last at a different city from the one wherein his brother was king.

It was growing late in the evening, and having no money in his pocket, the young Prince was at a loss how to procure anything to eat ; but seeing a good-natured-looking old woman herding goats, he said to her, 'Mother, if you will give me something to eat you may herd this pony of mine also, for it will be yours.'

To this the old woman agreed, and the Prince went to live in her house, finding her very kind and good-natured. But in the course of a day or two he noticed that his hostess looked very sad, so he asked her what was the matter.

'The matter is this, my son,' replied the old woman, tearfully ; 'in this kingdom there lives an ogre, which every day devours a young man, a goat, and a wheaten cake—in consideration of receiving which meal punctually, he leaves the other inhabitants in peace. Therefore every day this meal has to be provided, and it falls to the lot of every inhabitant in turn to prepare it, under pain of death. It is my turn to-day. The cake I can make, the goat I have, but where is the young man?'

'Why does not some one kill the ogre?' asked the brave young Prince.

'Many have tried, but all have failed, though the King has gone so far as to promise his daughter in marriage, and half his kingdom, to a successful champion. And now it is my turn, and I must die, for where shall I find a young man?' said the poor old woman, weeping bitterly.

'Don't cry, Goody,' returned the good-natured Prince; 'you have been very kind to me, and I will do my best for you by making part of the ogre's dinner.'

And though the old woman at first refused flatly to allow so handsome a young man to sacrifice himself, he laughed at her fears, and cheered her up so that she gave in.

'Only one thing I ask of you, Goody,' quoth the Prince; 'make the wheaten cake as big as you can, and give me the finest and fattest goat in your flock.'

This she promised to do, and when everything was prepared, the Prince, leading the goat and carrying the cake, went to the tree where the ogre came every evening to receive and devour his accustomed meal. Having tied the goat to the tree, and laid the cake on the ground, the Prince stepped outside the trench that was dug round the ogre's dining-room, and waited.   Presently the ogre, a very frightful monster indeed, appeared.   Now he generally ate the young man first, for as a rule the cakes and goats brought to him were not appetising ; but this evening, seeing the biggest cake and the fattest goat he ever set eyes upon, he just went straight at them and began to gobble them up.   As he was finishing the last mouthful, and was looking about for his man's flesh, the Prince sprang at him, sword in hand.   Then ensued a terrible contest.   The ogre fought like an ogre, but in consequence of having eaten the cake and the goat, one the biggest and the other the fattest that ever was seen, he was not nearly so active as usual, and after a tremendous battle the brave Prince was victorious, and laid his enemy at his feet. Rejoicing at his success, the young man cut off the ogre's head, tied it up in a handkerchief as a trophy, and then, being quite wearied out by the combat, lay down to rest and fell fast asleep.

Now, every morning, a scavenger came to the ogre's dining-room to clear away the remains of the last night's feast, for the ogre was mighty fastidious, and could not bear the smell of old bones ; and this particular morning, when the scavenger saw only half the quantity of bones, he was much astonished, and beginning to search for more, found the young Prince hard by, fast asleep, with the ogre's head by his side.

'Ho! ho!' thought the scavenger, 'this is a fine chance for me!'

So, lifting the Prince, who, being dead tired, did not awake, he put him gently into a clay-pit close by, and covered him up with clay. Then he took the ogre's head, and going to the King, claimed half the kingdom and the Princess in marriage, as his reward for slaying the ogre.

Although the King had his suspicions that all was not fair, he was obliged to fulfil his promise as far as giving up part of his kingdom was concerned, but for the present he managed to evade the dreadful necessity of giving his daughter in marriage to a scavenger, by the excuse that the Princess was desirous of a year's delay. So the Scavenger-king reigned over half the kingdom, and made great preparations for his future marriage.

Meanwhile, some potters coming to get clay from their pit were mightily astonished to find a handsome young man, insensible, but still breathing, hidden away under the clay. Taking him home, they handed him over to the care of their women, who soon brought him round. On coming to himself, he learnt with surprise of the scavenger's victory over the ogre, with which all the town was ringing. He understood how the wicked wretch had stepped in and defrauded him, and having no witness but his own word, saw it would be useless to dispute the point ; therefore he gladly accepted the potters' offer of teaching him their trade.

Thus the Prince sat at the potters' wheel, and proved so clever, that ere long they became famous for the beautiful patterns and excellent workmanship of their wares ; so much so, that the story of the handsome young potter who had been found in a clay-pit soon became noised abroad ; and although the Prince had wisely never breathed a word of his adventures to any one, yet, when the news of his existence reached the Scavenger-king's ears, he determined in some way or another to get rid of the young man, lest the truth should leak out.

Now, just at this time, the fleet of merchant vessels which annually came to the city with merchandise and spices was detained in harbour by calms and contrary winds. So long were they detained that the merchants feared lest they should be unable to return within the

year; and as this was a serious matter, the auguries were consulted. They declared that until a human sacrifice was made the vessels would never leave port. When this was reported to the Scavenger-king he seized his opportunity, and said, 'Be it so; but do not sacrifice a citizen. Give the merchants that good-for-nothing potter-lad, who comes no one knows whence.'

The courtiers of course lauded the kindness of the Scavenger-king to the skies, and the Prince was handed over to the merchants, who, taking him on board their ships, prepared to kill him. However, he begged and prayed them so hard to wait till evening, on the chance of a breeze coming up, that they consented to wait till sunset. Then, when none came, the Prince took a knife and made a tiny cut on his little finger. As the first drop of blood flowed forth, the sails of the first ship filled with wind, and she glided swiftly out of harbour; at the second drop, the second ship did likewise, and so on till the whole fleet were sailing before a strong breeze.

The merchants were enchanted at having such a valuable possession as the Prince, who could thus compel the winds, and took the very greatest care of him; before long he was a great favourite with them all, for he was really an amiable young man. At length they arrived at another city, which happened to be the very one where the Prince's brother had been elected King by the elephant, and while the merchants went into the town to transact business, they left the Prince to watch over the vessels. Now, growing weary of watching, the Prince, to amuse himself, began, with the clay on the shore beside him, to make a model from memory of his father's palace. Growing interested in his work, he worked away till he had made the most beautiful thing imaginable. There was the garden full of flowers, the King on his throne, the courtiers sitting round,—even the Princes learning in school, and the pigeons fluttering about the tower. When it was quite finished, the poor young Prince could not help the tears coming into his eyes, as he looked at it, and he sighed to think of past days.

Just at that very moment the Prime Minister's

daughter, surrounded by her women, happened to pass that way. She looked at the beautiful model, and was wonderstruck, but when she saw the handsome, sad young man who sat sighing beside it, she went straight home, locked the doors, and refused to eat anything at all. Her father, fearing she was ill, sent to inquire what was wrong, whereupon she sent him this reply: 'Tell my father I will neither eat nor drink until he marries me to the young man who sits sighing on the sea-shore beside a king's palace made of clay.'

At first the Prime Minister was very angry, but seeing his daughter was determined to starve herself to death if she did not gain her point, he outwardly gave his consent; privately, however, arranging with the merchants that immediately after the marriage the bride and bridegroom were to go on board the ships, which were at once to set sail, and that on the first opportunity the Prince was to be thrown overboard, and the Princess brought back to her father.

So the marriage took place, the ships sailed away, and a day or two afterwards the merchants pushed the young man overboard as he was sitting on the prow. But it so happened that a rope was hanging from the bride's window in the stern, and as the Prince drifted by, he caught it and climbed up into her cabin unseen. She hid him in her box, where he lay concealed, and when they brought her food, she refused to eat, pretending grief, and saying, 'Leave it here; perhaps I may be hungry by and by.' Then she shared the meal with her husband.

The merchants, thinking they had managed everything beautifully, turned their ships round, and brought the bride and her box back to her father, who, being much pleased, rewarded them handsomely.

His daughter also was quite content, and having reached her own apartments, let her husband out of the box and dressed him as a woman-servant, so that he could go about the palace quite securely.

Now the Prince had of course told his wife the whole story of his life, and when she in return had related how the King of that country had been elected by the elephant, her husband began to feel sure he had found his long-lost brother at last. Then he laid a plan to make sure. Every day a bouquet of flowers was sent to the King from the Minister's garden, so one evening the Prince, in his disguise, went up to the gardener's daughter, who was cutting flowers, and said, ' I will teach you a new fashion of arranging them, if you like.' Then, taking the flowers, he tied them together just as his father's gardener used to do.

The next morning, when the King saw the bouquet, he became quite pale, and turning to the gardener, asked him who had arranged the flowers.

' I did, sire,' replied the gardener, trembling with fear.

' You lie, knave ! ' cried the King ; ' but go, bring me just such another bouquet to-morrow, or your head shall be the forfeit ! '

That day the gardener's daughter came weeping to the disguised Prince, and, telling him all, besought him to make her another bouquet to save her father's life. The Prince willingly consented, for he was now certain the King was his long-lost brother ; and, making a still more beautiful bouquet, concealed a paper, on which his name was written, amidst the flowers.

When the King discovered the paper he turned quite pale, and said to the gardener, 'I am now convinced you never made this nosegay ; but tell me the truth, and I will forgive you.'

Whereupon the gardener fell on his knees and confessed that one of the women-servants in the Prime Minister's palace had made it for his daughter. This surprised the King immensely, and he determined to disguise himself and go with the gardener's daughter to cut flowers in the Minister's garden, which he accordingly did; but no sooner did the disguised young Prince behold his brother than he recognised him, and wishing to see if power and wealth had made his brother forget their youthful affection, he parried all questions as to where he had learnt to arrange flowers, and replied by telling the story of his adventures, as far as the eating of the starling and the parrot. Then he declared he was too tired to proceed further that day, but would continue his story on the next. The King, though greatly excited, was accordingly obliged to wait till the next evening, when the Prince told of his fight with the demon and delivery by the potters. Then once more he declared he was tired, and the King, who was on pins and needles to hear more, had to wait yet another day ; and so on until the seventh day, when the Prince concluded his tale by relating his marriage with the Prime Minister's daughter, and disguise as a woman.

Then the King fell on his brother's neck and rejoiced greatly ; the Minister also, when he heard what an excellent marriage his daughter had made, was so pleased that he voluntarily resigned his office in favour of his son-in-law. So what the parrot and the starling had said came true, for the one brother was King, and the other Prime Minister.

The very first thing the King did was to send ambassadors to the court of the king who owned the country where the ogre had been killed, telling him the truth of the story, and saying that his brother, being quite satisfied as Prime Minister, did not intend to claim half the kingdom. At this, the king of that country was so delighted that he begged the Minister Prince to accept of his daughter as a bride, to which the Prince replied that he was already married, but that his brother the King would gladly make her his wife.

So there were immense rejoicings, but the Scavenger-king was put to death, as he very well deserved.

THE JACKAL AND THE IGUANA

NE moonlight night, a miserable, half-starved jackal, skulking through the village, found a worn-out pair of shoes in the gutter. They were too tough for him to eat, so, determined to make some use of them, he strung them to his ears like earrings, and, going down to the edge of the pond, gathered all the old bones he could find together, and built a platform with them, plastering it over with mud.

On this he sat in a dignified attitude, and when any animal came to the pond to drink, he cried out in a loud voice, 'Hi! stop! You must not taste a drop till you have done homage to me. So repeat these verses, which I have composed in honour of the occasion :—

'Silver is his days, plastered o'er with gold ;
In his ears are jewels,—some prince I must behold !'

Now, as most of the animals were very thirsty,

and in a great hurry to drink, they did not care
to dispute the matter, but gabbled off the words
without a second thought. Even the royal tiger,
treating it as a jest, repeated the jackal's rhyme, in
consequence of which the latter became quite cock-a-

hoop, and really began to believe he was a personage
of great importance.

By and by an iguana, or big lizard, came wadd-
ling and wheezing down to the water, looking for all
the world like a baby alligator.

'Hi! you there!' sang out the jackal; 'you
mustn't drink until you have said—

'Silver is his daïs, plastered o'er with gold ;
In his ears are jewels,—some prince I must behold !'

'Pouf! pouf! pouf!' gasped the iguana. 'Mercy on us, how dry my throat is! Mightn't I have just a wee sip of water first? and then I could do justice to your admirable lines; at present I am as hoarse as a crow!'

'By all means!' replied the jackal, with a grati-fied smirk. 'I flatter myself the verses *are* good, especially when well recited.'

So the iguana, nose down into the water, drank away, until the jackal began to think he would never leave off, and was quite taken aback when he finally came to an end of his draught, and began to move away.

'Hi! hi!' cried the jackal, recovering his presence of mind; 'stop a bit, and say—

'Silver is his daïs, plastered o'er with gold;
  In his ears are jewels,—some prince I must behold!'

'Dear me!' replied the iguana, politely, 'I was very nearly forgetting! Let me see—I must try my voice first—Do, re, me, fa, sol, la, si,—that is right! Now, how does it run?'

'Silver is his daïs, plastered o'er with gold;
  In his ears are jewels,—some prince I must behold!'

repeated the jackal, not observing that the lizard was carefully edging farther and farther away.

'Exactly so,' returned the iguana; 'I think I could say that!' Whereupon he sang out at the top of his voice—

'Bones make up his daïs, with mud it's plastered o'er,
  Old shoes are his ear-drops : a jackal, nothing more!'

And turning round, he bolted-for his hole as hard as he could.

The jackal could scarcely believe his ears, and sat dumb with astonishment. Then, rage lending him wings, he flew after the lizard, who, despite his short legs and scanty breath, put his best foot foremost, and scuttled away at a great rate.

It was a near race, however, for just as he popped into his hole, the jackal caught him by the tail, and held on. Then it was a case of 'pull butcher, pull baker,' until the lizard made certain his tail must come off, and the jackal felt as if his front teeth would come out. Still not an inch did either budge, one way or the other, and there they might have remained till the present day, had not the iguana called out, in his sweetest tones, 'Friend, I give in! Just leave hold of my tail, will you? then I can turn round and come out.'

Whereupon the jackal let go, and the tail disappeared up the hole in a twinkling; while all the reward the jackal got for digging away until his nails were nearly worn out, was hearing the iguana sing softly—

'Bones make up his daïs, with mud it's plastered o'er,
 Old shoes are his ear-drops : a jackal, nothing more!'

THE DEATH AND BURIAL OF POOR HEN-SPARROW

ONCE upon a time there lived a cock-sparrow and his wife, who were both growing old. But despite his years the cock-sparrow was a gay, festive old bird, who plumed himself upon his appearance, and was quite a ladies' man. So he cast his eyes on a lively young hen, and determined to marry her, for he was tired of his sober old wife. The wedding was a mighty grand affair, and everybody as jolly and merry as could be, except of course the poor old wife, who crept away from all the noise and fun to sit disconsolately on a quiet branch just under a crow's nest, where she could be as melancholy as she liked without anybody poking fun at her.

Now while she sat there it began to rain, and after a while the drops, soaking through the crow's nest, came drip-dripping on to her feathers ; she, however, was far too miserable to care, and sat there all huddled up and peepy till the shower was over. Now it so happened that the crow had used some scraps of dyed cloth in lining its nest, and as these became wet the colours ran, and dripping down on to the poor old hen-sparrow beneath, dyed her feathers until she was as gay as a peacock.

Fine feathers make fine birds, we all know, and she really looked quite spruce ; so much so, that when she flew home, the new wife nearly burst with envy, and asked her at once where she had found such a lovely dress.

'Easily enough,' replied the old wife ; 'I just went into the dyer's vat.'

The bride instantly determined to go there also. She could not endure the notion of the old thing being better dressed than she was, so she flew off at once to the dyer's, and being in a great hurry, went pop into the middle of the vat, without waiting to see if it was hot or cold. It turned out to be just scalding ; consequently the poor thing was half boiled before she managed to scramble out. Meanwhile, the gay old cock, not finding his bride at home, flew about distractedly in search of her, and you may imagine what bitter tears he wept when he found her, half drowned and half boiled, with her feathers all awry, lying by the dyer's vat.

'What has happened ?' quoth he.

But the poor bedraggled thing could only gasp out feebly—

> 'The old wife was dyed—
> The nasty old cat !
> And I, the gay bride,
> Fell into the vat !'

Whereupon the cock-sparrow took her up tenderly in his bill, and flew away home with his precious burden. Now, just as he was crossing the big river in front of his house, the old hen-sparrow, in her gay dress, looked out of the window, and when she saw her old husband bringing home his young bride in such a sorry plight, she burst out laughing shrilly, and called aloud, 'That is right! that is right! Remember what the song says——

'Old wives must scramble through water and mud,
  But young wives are carried dry-shod o'er the flood.'

This allusion so enraged her husband that he could not contain himself, but cried out, 'Hold your tongue, you shameless old cat!'

Of course, when he opened his mouth to speak, the poor draggled bride fell out, and going plump into the river, was drowned. Whereupon the cock-sparrow was so distracted with grief that he picked off all his feathers until he was as bare as a ploughed field. Then, going to a *pîpal* tree, he sat all naked and forlorn on the branches, sobbing and sighing.

'What has happened?' cried the *pîpal* tree, aghast at the sight.

'Don't ask me!' wailed the cock-sparrow; 'it isn't manners to ask questions when a body is in deep mourning.'

But the *pîpal* would not be satisfied without an answer, so at last poor bereaved cock-sparrow replied——

'The ugly hen painted.
By jealousy tainted,
The pretty hen dyed.
Lamenting his bride,
The cock, bald and bare,
Sobs loud in despair!'

On hearing this sad tale, the *pîpal* became overwhelmed with grief, and declaring it must mourn also, shed all its leaves on the spot.

By and by a buffalo, coming in the heat of the day
to rest in the shade of the *pîpal* tree, was astonished
to find nothing but bare twigs.

'What has happened?' cried the buffalo; 'you
were as green as possible yesterday!'

'Don't ask me!' whimpered the *pîpal*. 'Where
are your manners? Don't you know it isn't decent
to ask questions when people are in mourning?'

But the buffalo insisted on having an answer, so at
last, with many sobs and sighs, the *pîpal* replied—

> 'The ugly hen painted.
> By jealousy tainted,
> The pretty hen dyed.
> Bewailing his bride,
> The cock, bald and bare,
> Sobs loud in despair;
> The *pîpal* tree grieves
> By shedding its leaves!'

'Oh dear me!' cried the buffalo, 'how very sad!
I really must mourn too!' So she immediately cast
her horns, and began to weep and wail. After a while,
becoming thirsty, she went to drink at the river-side.

'Goodness gracious!' cried the river, 'what is the
matter? and what have you done with your horns?'

'How rude you are!' wept the buffalo. 'Can't
you see I am in deep mourning? and it isn't polite
to ask questions.'

But the river persisted, until the buffalo, with
many groans, replied—

> 'The ugly hen painted.
> By jealousy tainted,
> The pretty hen dyed.

Lamenting his bride,
The cock, bald and bare,
Sobs loud in despair ;
The *pípal* tree grieves
By shedding its leaves ;
The buffalo mourns
By casting her horns ! '

'Dreadful ! ' cried the river, and wept so fast that its water became quite salt.

By and by a cuckoo, coming to bathe in the stream, called out, 'Why, river ! what has happened ? You are as salt as tears ! '

'Don't ask me ! ' mourned the stream ; 'it is too dreadful for words ! '

Nevertheless, when the cuckoo would take no denial, the river replied—

'The ugly hen painted.
By jealousy tainted,
The pretty hen dyed.
Lamenting his bride,
The cock, bald and bare,
Sobs loud in despair ;
The *pípal* tree grieves
By shedding its leaves ;
The buffalo mourns
By casting her horns ;
The stream, weeping fast,
Grows briny at last ! '

'Oh dear ! oh dear me ! ' cried the cuckoo, 'how very very sad ! I must mourn too ! ' So it plucked out an eye, and going to a corn-merchant's shop, sat on the doorstep and wept.

'Why, little cuckoo! what's the matter?' cried Bhagtu the shopkeeper. 'You are generally the pertest of birds, and to-day you are as dull as ditch-water!'

'Don't ask me!' snivelled the cuckoo; 'it is such terrible grief! such dreadful sorrow! such—such horrible pain!'

However, when Bhagtu persisted, the cuckoo, wiping its one eye on its wing, replied—

> 'The ugly hen painted.
> By jealousy tainted,
> The pretty hen dyed.
> Lamenting his bride,
> The cock, bald and bare,
> Sobs loud in despair;
> The *pípal* tree grieves
> By shedding its leaves;
> The buffalo mourns
> By casting her horns;
> The stream, weeping fast,
> Grows briny at last;
> The cuckoo with sighs
> Blinds one of its eyes!'

'Bless my heart!' cried Bhagtu, 'but that is simply the most heartrending tale I ever heard in my life! I must really mourn likewise!' Whereupon he wept, and wailed, and beat his breast, until he went completely out of his mind; and when the Queen's maidservant came to buy of him, he gave her pepper instead of turmeric, onion instead of garlic, and wheat instead of pulse.

'Dear me, friend Bhagtu!' quoth the maidservant, 'your wits are wool-gathering! What's the matter?'

'Don't! please don't!' cried Bhagtu; 'I wish you wouldn't ask me, for I am trying to forget all about it. It is too dreadful—too too terrible!'

At last, however, yielding to the maid's entreaties, he replied, with many sobs and tears—

> 'The ugly hen painted.
> By jealousy tainted,
> The pretty hen dyed.
> Lamenting his bride,
> The cock, bald and bare,
> Sobs loud in despair;
> The *pípal* tree grieves
> By shedding its leaves;
> The buffalo mourns
> By casting her horns;
> The stream, weeping fast,
> Grows briny at last;
> The cuckoo with sighs
> Blinds one of its eyes;
> Bhagtu's grief so intense is,
> He loses his senses!'

'How very sad!' exclaimed the maidservant. 'I don't wonder at your distress; but it is always so in this miserable world!—everything goes wrong!'

Whereupon she fell to railing at everybody and everything in the world, until the Queen said to her, 'What is the matter, my child? What distresses you?'

'Oh!' replied the maidservant, 'the old story! every one is miserable, and I most of all! Such dreadful news!—

'The ugly hen painted.
By jealousy tainted,
The pretty hen dyed.
Lamenting his bride,
The cock, bald and bare,
Sobs loud in despair ;
The *pîpal* tree grieves
By shedding its leaves ;
The buffalo mourns
By casting her horns ;
The stream, weeping fast,
Grows briny at last ;
The cuckoo with sighs
Blinds one of its eyes ;
Bhagtu's grief so intense is,
He loses his senses ;
The maidservant wailing
Has taken to railing ! '

'Too true !' wept the Queen, 'too true ! The world is a vale of tears ! There is nothing for it but to try and forget !' Whereupon she set to work dancing away as hard as she could.

By and by in came the Prince, who, seeing her twirling about, said, 'Why, mother ! what is the matter ? '

The Queen, without stopping, gasped out—

'The ugly hen painted.
By jealousy tainted,
The pretty hen dyed.
Lamenting his bride,
The' cock, bald and bare,
Sobs loud in despair ;

The *pípal* tree grieves
By shedding its leaves ;
The buffalo mourns
By casting her horns ;
The stream, weeping fast,
Grows briny at last ;
The cuckoo with sighs
Blinds one of its eyes ;
Bhagtu's grief so intense is,
He loses his senses ;
The maidservant wailing
Has taken to railing ;
The Queen, joy enhancing,
Takes refuge in dancing ! '

'If that is your mourning, I'll mourn too ! ' cried
the Prince, and seizing his tambourine, he began to
thump on it with a will.　Hearing the noise, the King
came in, and asked what was the matter.

'This is the matter ! ' cried the Prince, drumming
away with all his might—

'The ugly hen painted.
By jealousy tainted,
The pretty hen dyed.
Lamenting his bride,
The cock, bald and bare,
Sobs loud in despair ;
The *pípal* tree grieves
By shedding its leaves ;
The buffalo mourns
By casting her horns ;
The stream, weeping fast,
Grows briny at last ;

The cuckoo with sighs
Blinds one of its eyes ;
Bhagtu's grief so intense is,
He loses his senses ;
The maidservant wailing
Has taken to railing ;
The Queen, joy enhancing,
Takes refuge in dancing ;
To aid the mirth coming,
The Prince begins drumming ! '

'Capital ! capital ! ' cried the King, ' that's the
way to do it ! ' so, seizing his zither, he began to
thrum away like one possessed.

And as they danced, the Queen, the King, the
Prince, and the maidservant sang—

' The ugly hen painted.
By jealousy tainted,
The pretty hen dyed.
Bewailing his bride, ·
The cock, bald and bare,
Sobs loud in despair ;
The *pípal* tree grieves
By shedding its leaves ;
The buffalo mourns
By casting her horns ;
The stream, weeping fast,
Grows briny at last ;
The cuckoo with sighs
Blinds one of its eyes ;
Bhagtu's grief so intense is,
He loses his senses ;
The maidservant wailing

Has taken to railing ;
The Queen, joy enhancing,
Takes refuge in dancing ;
To aid the mirth coming,
The Prince begins drumming ;
To join in it with her
The King strums the zither ! '

So they danced and sang till they were tired, and that was how every one mourned poor cock-sparrow's pretty bride.

BULBUL once lived in a forest, and sang all day to her mate, till one morning she said, ' Oh, dearest husband ! you sing beautifully, but I should so like some nice green pepper to eat ! '

The obedient bulbul at once flew off to find some, but though he flew for miles, peeping into every garden by the way, he could not discover a single green pepper. Either there was no fruit at all on the bushes, but only tiny white star-flowers, or the peppers were all ripe, and crimson red.

At last, right out in the wilderness, he came upon a high-walled garden. Tall mango-trees shaded it on all sides, shutting out fierce sunshine and rough winds, and within grew innumerable flowers and fruits. But there was no sign of life within its walls —no birds, no butterflies, only silence and a perfume of flowers.

The bulbul alighted in the middle of the garden, and, lo ! there grew a solitary pepper plant, and amid the polished leaves shone a single green fruit of immense size, gleaming like an emerald.

Greatly delighted, the bird flew home to his mate, and telling her he had found the most beautiful green pepper in the world, brought her back with him to the garden, where she at once began to eat the delicious morsel.

Now the Jinn to whom the garden belonged had all this time been asleep in a summer-house ; and as he generally kept awake for twelve whole years, and then slept for another twelve years, he was of course very sound asleep, and knew nothing of the bulbul's coming and going.   Nevertheless, as the time of his awaking was not far off, he had dreadful nightmares whilst the green pepper was being pecked to pieces, and, becoming restless, awoke just when the bulbul's wife, after laying one glittering emerald-green egg beneath the pepper plant, flew away with her husband.

As usual, the Jinn, after yawning and stretching, went to see how his pet pepper was getting on. Great was his sorrow and rage at finding it pecked to pieces.   He could not imagine what had done the mischief, knowing as he did that neither bird, beast, nor insect lived in the garden.

'Some dreadful creeping thing from that horrid world outside must have stolen in, whilst I slept,' said the Jinn to himself, and immediately began to search for the intruder.   He found nothing, however, but the glittering green egg, with which he was so much astonished that he took it to his summer-house, wrapped it up in cotton-wool, and put it away carefully in a carved niche in the wall.   Every day he went and looked at it, sighing over the thought of his lost pepper, until one morning, lo and behold ! the egg had disappeared, and in its place sat the loveliest little maiden, dressed from head to foot in emerald-green, while round her neck hung a single emerald of great size, shaped just like the green pepper.

The Jinn, who was a quiet, inoffensive creature, was delighted, for he loved children, and this one was the daintiest little morsel ever beheld. So he made it the business of his life to tend Princess Pepperina, for such the maiden informed him was her name.

Now, when twelve years had passed by in the flowery garden, it became time for the good-natured Jinn to go to sleep again ; and it puzzled him very much to think what would become of his Princess when he was no longer able to take care of her. But it so happened that a great King and his Minister, while hunting in the forest, came upon the high-walled garden, and being curious to see what was inside, they climbed over the wall, and found the lovely Princess Pepperina seated by the pepper plant.

The King immediately fell in love with her, and in the most elegant language begged her to be his wife. But the Princess hung down her head modestly, saying, ' Not so !—you must ask the Jinn who owns this garden ; only he has an unfortunate habit of eating men sometimes.'

Nevertheless, when she saw the young King kneeling before her, she could not help thinking him the handsomest and most splendid young man in the world, so her heart softened, and when she heard the Jinn's footstep, she cried, ' Hide yourself in the garden, and I will see if I can persuade my guardian to listen to you.'

M

Now, no sooner had the Jinn appeared, than he began to sniff about, and cry 'Fee! fa! fum! I smell the blood of a man!'

Then the Princess Pepperina soothed him, saying, 'Dear Jinn! you may eat *me* if you like, for there is no one else here.'

And the Jinn replied, kissing and caressing her the while, 'My dearest life! I would sooner eat bricks and mortar!'

After that the Princess cunningly led the conversation to the Jinn's approaching slumbers, and wondered tearfully what she should do alone in the walled garden. At this the good-hearted Jinn became greatly troubled, until at last he declared that the best plan would be to marry her to some young nobleman, but, he added, a worthy husband was hard to find, especially as it was necessary he should be as handsome, as a man, as Princess Pepperina was beautiful amongst women. Hearing this, the Princess seized her opportunity, and asked the Jinn if he would promise to let her marry any one who was as beautiful as she was. The Jinn promised faithfully, little thinking the Princess already had her eye on such a one, and was immensely astonished when she clapped her hands, and the splendid young King appeared from a thicket. Nevertheless, when the young couple stood together hand in hand, even the Jinn was obliged to own that such a handsome pair had never before been seen; so he gave his consent to their marriage, which was performed in ever so great a hurry, for already the Jinn had begun to nod and yawn. Still, when it came to saying good-bye to his dear little Princess, he wept so

much that the tears kept him awake, and he followed
her in his thoughts, until the desire to see her face
once more became so strong that he changed himself into a dove, which flying after her, fluttered
above her head. She seemed quite happy, talking
and whispering to her handsome husband, so he flew
home again to sleep. But the green mantle of his
dear little Princess kept floating before his eyes,
so that he could not rest, and changing himself
into a hawk, he sped after her, circling far above
her head. She was smiling by her husband's side,
so the Jinn flew home to his garden, yawning terribly.
But the soft eyes of his dear little Pepperina seemed
to look into his, driving sleep far from them ; so he
changed into an eagle, and soaring far up into the
blue sky, saw with his bright piercing gaze the
Princess entering a King's palace far away on the
horizon. Then the good Jinn was satisfied, and fell
fast asleep.

Now during the years which followed, the young
King remained passionately in love with his beautiful
bride, but the other women in the palace were very
jealous of her, especially after she gave birth to
the most lovely young Prince imaginable. They
determined to compass her ruin, and spent hours
in thinking how they might kill her, or lay a snare
for her.

Every night they would come to the door of the
Queen's room, and whisper, to see if she was awake,
' The Princess Pepperina is awake, but all the world
is fast asleep.'

Now the emerald, which the young Queen still
wore round her neck, was a real talisman, and always

told the truth; if any one even whispered a story, it just up and out with the truth *at once*, and shamed the culprit without remorse. So the emerald on these occasions would answer, ' Not so! the Princess Pepperina is asleep. It is the world that wakes.'

Then the wicked women would shrink away, for they knew they had no power to harm the Princess while the talisman was round her neck.

At last it so happened that when the young Queen was bathing she took off the emerald talisman, and left it by mistake in the bathing-place. So that night, when the jealous women as usual came whispering round the door, ' The Princess Pepperina is awake, but all the world sleeps,' the truthful talisman called out from the bathing-place, ' Not so! the Princess Pepperina sleeps. It is the world that wakes.'

Knowing by the sound of the talisman's voice that it was not in its usual place, these wicked creatures stole into the room gently, killed the infant Prince, who was peacefully sleeping in his little crib, cut him into little bits, laid them in his mother's bed, and gently stained her lips with the blood.

Early next morning they flew to the King, weeping and wailing, bidding him come and see the horrible sight.

' Look!' said they, ' the beautiful wife you loved so much is an ogress! We warned you against her, and now she has killed her child in order to eat its flesh!'

The King was terribly grieved and wroth, for he loved his wife, and yet could not deny she was an ogress; so he ordered her to be whipped out of his kingdom and then slain.

So the lovely tender fair young Queen was scourged out of the land, and then cruelly murdered, whilst the wicked jealous women rejoiced at their evil success.

But when Princess Pepperina died, her body became a high white marble wall, her eyes turned into liquid pools of water, her green mantle changed into stretches of verdant grass, her long curling hair into lovely creepers and tendrils, while her scarlet mouth and white teeth became a beautiful bed of roses and narcissus. Then her soul took the form of a sheldrake and its mate,—those loving birds which, like the turtle-dove, are always constant,—and floating on the liquid pools, they mourned all day long the sad fate of the Princess Pepperina.

Now, after many days, the young King, who, despite her supposed-crime, could not help bewailing his beautiful bride, went out a-hunting, and finding no game, wandered far afield, until he came to the high white marble wall. Curious to see what it enclosed, he climbed over on to the verdant grass, where the tendrils waved softly, the roses and narcissus blossomed, and the loving birds floated on the liquid pools mourning all day long.

The King, weary and sad, lay down to rest in the lovely spot, and listened to the cry of the birds, and as he listened, the meaning seemed to grow plain, so that he heard them tell the whole story of the wicked women's treachery.

Then the one bird said, weeping, to the other, ' Can she never become alive again ? ' And the other answered, ' If the King were to catch us, and hold us close, heart to heart, while he severed our heads from our bodies with one blow of his sword, so that neither

of us should die before the other, the Princess Pepperina would become alive once more. But if one
dies before the other, she will always remain as she is!'

Then the King, with a beating heart, called the
birds to him, and they came quite readily, standing
heart to heart while he cut off their heads with one
blow of his sword, so that they fell dead at the selfsame moment.

At the very same instant the Princess Pepperina
appeared, smiling, more beautiful than ever ; but,
strange to say, the liquid pools, the grass, the climb-
ing tendrils, and the flowers remained as they were.

Then the King besought her to return home with
him, vowing he would never again distrust her, and
would put all the wicked traitors to death ; but she
refused, saying she would prefer to live always within
the high white marble walls, where no one could
molest her.

'Just so!' cried the Jinn, who, having but that
moment awakened from his twelve years' sleep, had
flown straight to his dearest Princess. 'Here you
shall live, and I will live with you!'

Then he built the King and Queen a magnificent
palace, where they lived very happily ever after ; and
as no one knew anything about it, no one was jealous
of the beautiful Princess Pepperina.

PEASIE AND BEANSIE

ONCE upon a time there were two sisters, who lived together; but while the elder, Beansie by name, was a hard quarrelsome creature, apt to disagree with everybody, Peasie, the younger, was soft and most agreeable.

Now, one day, Peasie, who was for ever trying to please somebody, said to her sister, 'Beansie, my dear! don't you think we ought to pay a visit to our poor old father? He must be dull now—it is harvest time, and he is left alone in the house.'

'I don't care if he is!' replied Beansie. 'Go yourself! I'm not going to walk about in the heat to please any old man!'

So kind Peasie set off alone, and on the way she met a plum-tree. 'Oh, Peasie!' cried the tree, 'stop a bit, there's a good soul, and tidy up my thorns a little; they are scattered about so that I feel quite uncomfortable!'

'So they are, I declare!' returned Peasie, and forthwith set to work with such a will that ere long the tree was as neat as a new pin.

A little farther on she met a fire, and the fire cried out, 'Oh, sweet Peasie! tidy up my hearth a bit, for I am half choked in the ashes!'

'So you are, I declare!' returned good-natured Peasie, setting herself to clear them away, until the fire crackled and flamed with pleasure.

Farther on she met a *pipal* tree, and the *pipal* called out, 'Oh, kind Peasie! bind up this broken branch for me, or it will die, and I shall lose it!'

'Poor thing! poor thing!' cried soft-hearted Peasie; and tearing a bandage from her veil, she bound up the wounded limb carefully.

After a while she met a stream, and the stream cried out, 'Pretty Peasie! clear away the sand and dead leaves from my mouth, for I cannot run when I am stifled!'

'No more you can!' quoth obliging Peasie; and in a trice she made the channel so clear and clean that the water flowed on swiftly.

At last she arrived, rather tired, at her old father's house, but his delight at seeing her was so great that he would scarcely let her away in the evening, and insisted on giving her a spinning-wheel, a buffalo, some brass pots, a bed, and all sorts of things, just as if she had been a bride going to her husband. These she put on the buffalo's back, and set off homewards.

Now, as she passed the stream, she saw a web of fine cloth floating down.

'Take it, Peasie, take it!' tinkled the stream; 'I have carried it far, as a reward for your kindness.'

So she gathered up the cloth, laid it on the buffalo, and went on her way.

By and by she passed the *pípal* tree, and lo! on the branch she had tied up hung a string of pearls.

'Take it, Peasie, take it!' rustled the *pípal;* 'I caught it from a Prince's turban as a reward for your kindness.'

Then she took the pearls, fastened them round her pretty slender throat, and went on her way rejoicing.

Farther on she came to the fire, burning brightly, and on it was a girdle with a nice hot sweet-cake.

'Take it, Peasie, take it!' crackled the fire; 'I have cooked it to a turn, in reward for your kindness.'

So lucky Peasie took the nice hot cake, and, dividing it into two pieces, put one aside for her sister, and ate the other while she went on her way.

Now when she reached the plum-tree, the topmost branches were bending down, covered with ripe yellow fruit.

'Take some, Peasie, take some!' groaned the laden tree; 'I have ripened these as a reward for your kindness.'

So she gathered her veil full, and eating some, set the rest aside for her sister; but when she arrived at home, instead of being pleased at her little sister's good fortune and thoughtfulness, disagreeable Beansie nearly cried with spite and envy, and was so cross, that poor little sweet Peasie became quite remorseful over her own luck, and suggested that her sister might be equally fortunate if she also went to visit her father.

So, next morning, greedy Beansie set off to see what she could get from the old man. But when she came to the plum-tree, and it cried out, 'Oh, Beansie! stop a bit and tidy up my thorns a little, there's a good soul!' the disobliging Beansie tossed her head, and replied, 'A likely story! Why, I could travel three miles in the time it would take me to settle up your stupid old thorns! Do it yourself!'

And when she met the *pípal* tree, and it asked her to tie up its broken branch, she only laughed, saying, 'It doesn't hurt *me*, and I should have walked three miles in the time it would take to set it right; so ask somebody else!'

Then when the fire said to her, 'Oh, sweet Beansie! tidy up my hearth a bit, for I am half choked by my ashes,' the unkind girl replied, 'The more fool you for having ashes! You don't suppose I am going to dawdle about helping people who won't help themselves? Not a bit of it!'

So when she met the stream, and it asked her to clear away the sand and the dead leaves which choked it, she replied, 'Do you imagine I'm going to stop my walk that you may run? No, no!—every one for himself!'

At last she reached her father's house, full of determination not to go away without a heavy load for at least two buffaloes, when, just as she was entering the courtyard, her brother and his wife fell upon her, and whacked her most unmercifully, crying, 'So this is your plan, is it? Yesterday comes Peasie, while we were hard at work, and wheedles her doting old father out of his best buffalo, and goodness knows what else besides, and to-day *you* come to rob us! Out of the house, you baggage!'

With that they hounded her away, hot, tired, bruised, and hungry.

'Never mind!' said she, to console herself, 'I shall get the web of cloth yet!'

Sure enough, when she crossed the stream, there was a web, three times as fine as Peasie's, floating close to the shore, and greedy Beansie went straight to get it; but, alas! the water was so deep that she was very nearly drowned, while the beautiful cloth floated past her very fingers. Thus all she got for her pains was a ducking.

'Never mind!' thought she, 'I'll have the string of pearls!'

Yes, there it hung on the broken branch; but when Beansie jumped to catch it, branch and all fell right on her head, so that she was stunned. When she came to herself, some one else had walked off with the pearls, and she had only a bump on her head as big as an egg.

All these misfortunes had quite wearied her out;

she was starving with hunger, and hurried on to the fire, hoping for a nice hot sweet girdle-cake.

Yes, there it was, smelling most deliciously, and Beansie snatched at it so hastily that she burnt her fingers horribly and the cake rolled away. Before she had done blowing at her fingers and hopping about in pain, a crow had carried off the cake, and she was left lamenting.

'At any rate, I'll have the plums!' cried miserable Beansie, setting off at a run, her mouth watering at the sight of the luscious yellow fruit on the topmost branches. First she held on to a lower branch with her left hand, and reached for the fruit with the right; then, when that was all scratched and torn by the thorns, she held on with her right, and tried to get the fruit with the left, but all to no avail; and when face and hands were all bleeding and full of prickles, she gave up the useless quest, and went home, bruised, beaten, wet, sore, hungry, and scratched all over, where I have no doubt her kind sister Peasie put her to bed, and gave her gruel and posset.

THE JACKAL AND THE PARTRIDGE

 JACKAL and a Partridge swore eternal friendship ; but the Jackal was very exacting and jealous. 'You don't do half as much for me as I do for you,' he used to say, 'and yet you talk a great deal of your friendship. Now my idea of a friend is one who is able to make me laugh or cry, give me a good meal, or save my life if need be. You couldn't do that !'

'Let us see,' answered the Partridge ; 'follow me at a little distance, and if I don't make you laugh soon you may eat me !'

So she flew on till she met two travellers trudging along, one behind the other. They were both footsore and weary, and the first carried his bundle on a stick over his shoulder, while the second had his shoes in his hand.

Lightly as a feather the Partridge settled on the first traveller's stick. He, none the wiser, trudged on, but the second traveller, seeing the bird sitting so tamely just in front of his nose, said to himself,

'What a chance for a supper!' and immediately flung his shoes at it, they being ready to hand. Whereupon the Partridge flew away, and the shoes knocked off the first traveller's turban.

'What a plague do you mean?' cried he, angrily turning on his companion. 'Why did you throw your shoes at my head?'

'Brother!' replied the other mildly, 'do not be vexed. I didn't throw them at you, but at a Partridge that was sitting on your stick.'

'On my stick! Do you take me for a fool?' shouted the injured man, in a great rage. 'Don't tell me such cock-and-bull stories. First you insult me, and then you lie like a coward; but I'll teach you manners!'

Then he fell upon his fellow-traveller without
more ado, and they fought until they could not see
out of their eyes, till their noses were bleeding, their
clothes in rags, and the Jackal had nearly died of
laughing.

'Are you satisfied?' asked the Partridge of her
friend.

'Well,' answered the Jackal, 'you have certainly
made me laugh, but I doubt if you could make me
cry. It is easy enough to be a buffoon; it is more
difficult to excite the higher emotions.'

'Let us see,' retorted the Partridge, somewhat
piqued; 'there is a huntsman with his dogs coming
along the road. Just creep into that hollow tree
and watch me: if you don't weep scalding tears, you
must have no feeling in you!'

The Jackal did as he was bid, and watched the
Partridge, who began fluttering about the bushes till
the dogs caught sight of her, when she flew to the
hollow tree where the Jackal was hidden. Of course
the dogs smelt him at once, and set up such a yelp-
ing and scratching that the huntsman came up, and
seeing what it was, dragged the Jackal out by the
tail. Whereupon the dogs worried him to their
hearts' content, and finally left him for dead.

By and by he opened his eyes—for he was only
foxing—and saw the Partridge sitting on a branch
above him.

'Did you cry?' she asked anxiously. 'Did I
rouse your higher emo——'

'Be quiet, will you!' snarled the Jackal; 'I'm
half dead with fear!'

So there the Jackal lay for some time, getting

the better of his bruises, and meanwhile he became hungry.

'Now is the time for friendship!' said he to the Partridge. 'Get me a good dinner, and I will acknowledge you are a true friend.' ·

'Very well!' replied the Partridge; 'only watch me, and help yourself when the time comes.'

Just then a troop of women came by, carrying their husbands' dinners to the harvest-field.

The Partridge gave a little plaintive cry, and began fluttering along from bush to bush as if she were wounded.

'A wounded bird!—a wounded bird!' cried the women; 'we can easily catch it!'

Whereupon they set off in pursuit, but the cunning Partridge played a thousand tricks, till they became so excited over the chase that they put their bundles on the ground in order to pursue it more nimbly. The Jackal, meanwhile, seizing his opportunity, crept up, and made off with a good dinner.

'Are you satisfied now?' asked the Partridge.

'Well,' returned the Jackal, 'I confess you have given me a very good dinner; you have also made me laugh—and cry—ahem! But, after all, the great test of friendship is beyond you—you couldn't save my life!'

'Perhaps not,' acquiesced the Partridge mournfully, 'I am so small and weak. But it grows late—we should be going home; and as it is a long way round by the ford, let us go across the river. My friend the crocodile will carry us over.'

Accordingly, they set off for the river, and the crocodile kindly consented to carry them across, so they sat on his broad back and he ferried them over. But just as they were in the middle of the stream the Partridge remarked, ' I believe the crocodile intends to play us a trick.   How awkward if he were to drop you into the water ! '

' Awkward for you too ! ' replied the Jackal, turning pale.

' Not at all! not at all !   I have wings, you haven't.'

On this the Jackal shivered and shook with fear, and when the crocodile, in a gruesome growl, remarked that he was hungry and wanted a good meal, the wretched creature hadn't a word to say.

' Pooh ! ' cried the Partridge airily, ' don't try tricks on *us*,—I should fly away, and as for my friend the Jackal, you couldn't hurt *him*.   He is not such a fool as to take his life with him on these little excursions ; he leaves it at home, locked up in the cupboard.'

' Is that a fact ? ' asked the crocodile, surprised.

' Certainly ! ' retorted the Partridge.   ' Try to eat him if you like, but you will only tire yourself to no purpose.'

' Dear me ! how very odd ! ' gasped the crocodile ; and he was so taken aback that he carried the Jackal safe to shore.

' Well, are you satisfied now?' asked the Partridge..

' My dear madam ! ' quoth the Jackal, ' you have made me laugh, you have made me cry, you have given me a good dinner, and you have saved my life ; but upon my honour I think you are too clever for a friend ; so, good-bye ! '

And the Jackal never went near the Partridge again.

N

THE SNAKE-WOMAN AND KING
ALI MARDAN

NCE upon a time King Ali. Mardan went out a-hunting, and as he hunted in the forest above the beautiful Dal lake, which stretches clear and placid between the mountains and the royal town of Srinagar, he came suddenly on a maiden, lovely as a flower, who, seated beneath a tree, was weeping bitterly. Bidding his followers remain at a distance, he went up to the damsel, and asked her who she was, and how she came to be alone in the wild forest.

'O great King,' she answered, looking up in his face, 'I am the Emperor of China's handmaiden, and as I wandered about in the pleasure-grounds of his palace I lost my way. I know not how far I have come since, but now I must surely die, for I am weary and hungry!'

'So fair a maiden must not die while Ali Mardan can deliver her,' quoth the monarch, gazing ardently on the beautiful girl. So he bade his servants convey her with the greatest care to his summer palace in the Shalimar gardens, where the fountains scatter dewdrops over the beds of flowers, and laden fruit-trees bend over the marble colonnades. And there, amid the flowers and sunshine, she lived with the King, who speedily became so enamoured of her that he forgot everything else in the world.

So the days passed until it chanced that a Jôgi's servant, coming back from the holy lake Gangabal, which lies on the snowy peak of Haramukh, whither he went every year to draw water for his master, passed by the gardens; and over the high garden wall he saw the tops of the fountains, leaping and splashing like silver sunshine. He was so astonished at the sight that he put his vessel of water on the ground, and climbed over the wall, determined to see the wonderful things inside. Once in the garden amid the fountains and flowers, he wandered hither and thither, bewildered by beauty, until, wearied out by excitement, he lay down under a tree and fell asleep.

Now the King, coming to walk in the garden, found the man lying there, and noticed that he held something fast in his closed right hand. Stooping down, Ali Mardan gently loosed the fingers, and discovered a tiny box filled with a sweet-smelling ointment. While he was examining this more closely, the sleeper awoke, and missing his box, began to weep and wail; whereupon the King bade him be comforted, and showing him the box, promised to return it if he would faithfully tell why it was so precious to him.

'O great King,' replied the Jôgi's servant, 'the box belongs to my master, and it contains a holy ointment of many virtues. By its power I am preserved from all harm, and am able to go to Gangabal and return with my jar full of water in so short a time that my master is never without the sacred element.'

Then the King was astonished, and, looking at the man keenly, said, 'Tell me the truth! Is your master indeed such a holy saint? Is he indeed such a wonderful man?'

'O King,' replied the servant, 'he is indeed such a man, and there is nothing in the world he does not know!'

This reply aroused the King's curiosity, and putting the box in his vest, he said to the servant, 'Go home to your master, and tell him King Ali Mardan has his box, and means to keep it until he comes to fetch it himself.' In this way he hoped to entice the holy Jôgi into his presence.

So the servant, seeing there was nothing else to be done, set off to his master, but he was two years and a half in reaching home, because he had not the precious box with the magical ointment; and all this time Ali Mardan lived with the beautiful stranger in the Shalimar palace, and forgot everything in the wide world except her loveliness. Yet he was not happy, and a strange look came over his face, and a stony stare into his eyes.

Now, when the servant reached home at last, and told his master what had occurred, the Jôgi was very angry, but as he could not get on without the box which enabled him to procure the water from Ganga-bal, he set off at once to the court of King Ali Mardan. On his arrival, the King treated him with the greatest honour, and faithfully fulfilled the promise of returning the box.

Now the Jôgi was indeed a learned man, and

when he saw the King he knew at once all was not right, so he said, ' O King, you have been gracious unto me, and I in my turn desire to do you a kind action ; so tell me truly,—have you always had that white scared face and those stony eyes ? '

The King hung his head.

' Tell me truly,' continued the holy Jôgi, ' have you any strange woman in your palace ? '

Then Ali Mardan, feeling a strange relief in speaking, told the Jôgi about the finding of the maiden, so lovely and forlorn, in the forest.

' She is no handmaiden of the Emperor of China —she is no woman ! ' quoth the Jôgi fearlessly ; ' she is nothing but a Lamia—the dreadful two-hundred-years-old snake which has the power of taking woman's shape ! '

Hearing this, King Ali Mardan was at first indignant, for he was madly in love with the stranger ; but when the Jôgi insisted, he became alarmed, and at last promised to obey the holy man's orders, and so discover the truth or falsehood of his words.

Therefore, that same evening he ordered two kinds of *khichrî* to be made ready for supper, and placed in one dish, so that one half was sweet *khichrî*, and the other half salt.

Now, when as usual the King sat down to eat out of the same dish with the Snake-woman, he turned the salt side towards her and the sweet side towards himself.

She found her portion very salt, but, seeing the King eat his with relish and without remark, finished hers in silence. But when they had retired to rest, and the King, obeying the Jôgi's orders, had feigned sleep, the Snake-woman became so dreadfully thirsty, in consequence of all the salt food she had eaten, that she longed for a drink of water ; and as there was none in the room, she was obliged to go outside to get some.

Now, if a Snake-woman goes out at night, she must resume her own loathsome form ; so, as King Ali Mardan lay feigning sleep, he saw the beautiful form in his arms change to a deadly slimy snake, that slid from the bed out of the door into the garden. He followed it softly, watching it drink of every fountain by the way, until it reached the Dal lake, where it drank and bathed for hours.

Fully satisfied of the truth of the Jôgi's story, King Ali Mardan begged him for aid in getting rid of the beautiful horror. This the Jôgi promised to do, if the King would faithfully obey orders. So they made an oven of a hundred different kinds of metal melted together, and closed by a strong lid and a heavy padlock. This they placed in a shady corner of the garden, fastening it securely to the ground by strong chains. When all was ready, the King said to the Snake-woman, ' My heart's beloved ! let us wander in the gardens alone to-day, and amuse ourselves by cooking our own food.'

She, nothing loath, consented, and so they wandered about in the garden ; and when dinner-time came, set to work, with laughter and mirth, to cook their own food.

The King heated the oven very hot, and kneaded the bread, but being clumsy at it, he told the Snake-woman he could do no more, and that she must bake the bread. This she at first refused to do, saying

that she disliked ovens, but when the King pretended
to be vexed, averring she could not love him since
she refused to help, she gave in, and set to work
with a very bad grace to tend the baking.

Then, just as she stooped over the oven's mouth,
to turn the loaves, the King, seizing his opportunity,
pushed her in, and clapping down the cover, locked
and double-locked it.

Now, when the Snake-woman found herself caught
in the scorching oven, she bounded so, that had it
not been for the strong chains, she would have
bounded out of the garden, oven and all! But as
it was, all she could do was to bound up and down,
whilst the King and the Jôgi piled fuel on to the
fire, and the oven grew hotter and hotter. So it
went on from four o'clock one afternoon to four
o'clock the next, when the Snake-woman ceased to
bound, and all was quiet.

They waited until the oven grew cold, and then opened it, when not a trace of the Snake-woman was to be seen, only a tiny heap of ashes, out of which the Jôgi took a small round stone, and gave it to the King, saying, 'This is the real essence of the Snake-woman, and whatever you touch with it will turn to gold.'

But King Ali Mardan said such a treasure was more than any man's life was worth, since it must bring envy and battle and murder to its possessor; so when he went to Attock he threw the magical Snake-stone into the river, lest it should bring strife into the world.

NCE upon a time there lived a King who had two sons, and when he died he left them all his treasures ; but the younger brother began to squander it all so lavishly that the elder said, 'Let us divide what there is, and do you take your own share, and do what you please with it.'

So the younger took his portion, and spent every farthing of it in no time.

When he had literally nothing left, he asked his wife to give him what she had. Then she wept, saying, 'I have nothing left but one small piece of jewellery ; however, take that also if you want it.'

So he took the jewel, sold it for four pounds, and taking the money with him, set off to make his fortune in the world.

As he went on his way he met a man with a cat. 'How much for your cat ?' asked the spendthrift Prince.

'Nothing less than a golden pound,' replied the man.

'A bargain indeed!' cried the spendthrift, and immediately bought the cat for a golden sovereign.

By and by he met a man with a dog, and called out as before, 'How much for your dog?' And when the man said not less than a golden pound, the Prince again declared it was a bargain indeed, and bought it cheerfully.

Then he met a man carrying a parrot, and called out as before, 'How much for the parrot?' And when he heard it was only a golden sovereign he was delighted, saying once more that was a bargain indeed.

He had only one pound left. Yet even then, when he met a Jôgi carrying a serpent, he cried out at once, 'O Jôgi, how much for the snake?'

'Not a farthing less than a golden sovereign,' quoth the Jôgi.

'And very little, too!' cried the spendthrift, handing over his last coin.

So there he was, possessed of a cat, a dog, a parrot, and a snake, but not a single penny in his pocket. However, he set to work bravely to earn his living; but the hard labour wearied him dreadfully, for being a Prince he was not used to it. Now when his serpent saw this, it pitied its kind master, and said, 'Prince, if you are not afraid to come to my father's house, he will perhaps give you something for saving me from the Jôgi.' The spendthrift Prince was not a bit afraid of anything, so he and the serpent set off together, but when they arrived at the house, the snake bade the Prince wait outside, while it went in alone and prepared the snake-father for a visitor. When the snake-father heard what the serpent had to say, he was much pleased, declaring he would reward the Prince by giving him anything he desired. So the serpent went out to fetch the Prince into the snake-father's presence, and when doing so, it whispered in his ear, 'My father will give you anything you desire. Remember only to ask for his little ring as a keepsake.'

This rather astonished the Prince, who naturally thought a ring would be of little use to a man who was half starving ; however, he did as he was bid, and when the snake-father asked him what he desired, he replied, 'Thank you ; I have everything, and want for nothing.'

Then the snake-father asked him once more what he would take as a reward, but again he answered that he wanted nothing, having all that heart could desire.

Nevertheless, when the snake-father asked him the third time, he replied, 'Since you wish me to take something, let it be the ring you wear on your finger, as a keepsake.'

Then the snake-father frowned, and looked displeased, saying, 'Were it not for my promise, I would have turned you into ashes on the spot, for daring to ask for my greatest treasure. But as I have said, it must be. Take the ring, and go !'

So the Prince, taking the ring, set off homewards with his servant the serpent, to whom he said regretfully, 'This old ring is a mistake ; I have only made the snake-father angry by asking for it, and much good it will do me ! It would have been wiser to say a sack of gold.'

'Not so, my Prince !' replied the serpent ; 'that

ring is a wonderful ring! You have only to make a clean square place on the ground, plaster it over according to the custom of holy places, put the ring in the centre, sprinkle it with buttermilk, and then whatever you wish for will be granted immediately.'

Vastly delighted at possessing so great a treasure as this magic ring, the Prince went on his way rejoicing, but by and by, as he trudged along the road, he began to feel hungry, and thought he would put his ring to the test. So, making a holy place, he put the ring in the centre, sprinkled it with buttermilk, and cried, 'O ring, I want some sweetmeats for dinner!'

No sooner had he uttered the words, than a dishful of most delicious sweets appeared on the holy place. These he ate, and then set off to a city he saw in the distance.

As he entered the gate a proclamation was being made that any one who would build a palace of gold, with golden stairs, in the middle of the sea, in the course of one night, should have half the kingdom, and the King's daughter in marriage; but if he failed, instant death should be his portion.

Hearing this, the spendthrift Prince went at once to the Court and declared his readiness to fulfil the conditions.

The King was much surprised at his temerity, and bade him consider well what he was doing, telling him that many princes had tried to perform the task before, and showing him a necklace of their heads, in hopes that the dreadful sight might deter him from his purpose.

But the Prince merely replied that he was not afraid, and that he was certain he should succeed.

Whereupon the King ordered him to build the palace that very night, and setting a guard over him, bade the sentries be careful the young boaster did not run away. Now when evening came, the Prince lay down calmly to sleep, whereat the guard whispered amongst themselves that he must be a madman to fling away his life so uselessly. Nevertheless, with the first streak of dawn the Prince arose, and making a holy place, laid the ring in the centre, sprinkled it with buttermilk, and cried, 'O ring, I want a palace of gold, with golden stairs, in the midst of the sea!'

And lo! there in the sea it stood, all glittering in the sunshine. Seeing this, the guard ran to tell the King, who could scarcely believe his eyes when he and all his Court came to the spot and beheld the golden palace.

Nevertheless, as the Prince had fulfilled his promise, the King performed his, and gave his daughter in marriage, and half his kingdom, to the spendthrift.

'I don't want your kingdom, or your daughter either!' said the Prince. 'I will take the palace I have built in the sea as my reward.'

So he went to dwell there, but when they sent the Princess to him, he relented, seeing her beauty; and so they were married and lived very happily together.

Now, when the Prince went out a-hunting he took his dog with him, but he left the cat and the parrot in the palace, to amuse the Princess; nevertheless, one day, when he returned, he found her very sad and sorrowful, and when he begged her to tell him what was the matter, she said, 'O dear Prince, I wish to be turned into gold by the power of the magic ring by which you built this glittering golden palace.'

So, to please her, he made a holy place, put the ring in the centre, sprinkled it with buttermilk, and cried, 'O ring, turn my wife into gold!'

No sooner had he said the words than his wish was accomplished, and his wife became a golden Princess.

Now, when the golden Princess was washing her beautiful golden hair one day, two long glittering hairs came out in the comb. She looked at them, regretting that there were no poor people near to whom she might have given the golden strands; then, determining they should not be lost, she made a cup of green leaves, and curling the hairs inside it, set it afloat upon the sea.

As luck would have it, after drifting hither and thither, it reached a distant shore where a washerman was at work. The poor man, seeing the wonderful gold hairs, took them to the King, hoping for a reward; and the King in his turn showed them to his son, who was so much struck by the sight that he lay down on a dirty old bed, to mark his extreme grief and despair, and, refusing to eat or drink anything, swore he must marry the owner of the beautiful golden hair, or die.

The King, greatly distressed at his son's state, cast about how he should find the golden-haired Princess, and after calling his ministers and nobles to help him, came to the conclusion that it would be best to employ a wise woman. So he called the

wisest woman in the land to him, and she promised
to find the Princess, on condition of the King, in his
turn, promising to give her anything she desired as a
reward.

Then the wise woman caused a golden barge to
be made, and in the barge a silken cradle swinging
from silken ropes. When all was ready, she set off in
the direction whence the leafy cup had come, taking
with her four boatmen, whom she trained carefully
always to stop rowing when she put up her finger,
and go on as long as she kept it down.

After a long while they came in sight of the golden
palace, which the wise woman guessed at once must
belong to the golden Princess ; so, putting up her
finger, the boatmen ceased rowing, and the wise
woman, stepping out of the boat, went swiftly into
the palace. There she saw the golden Princess,
sitting on a golden throne ; and going up to her, she
laid her hands upon the Princess's head, as is the
custom when relatives visit each other ; afterwards
she kissed her and petted her, saying, ' Dearest niece !
do you not know me ?   I am your aunt.'

But the Princess at first drew back, and said she
had never seen or heard of such an aunt.   Then the
wise woman explained how she had left home years
before, and made up such a cunning, plausible story
that the Princess, who was only too glad to get a
companion, really believed what she said, and invited
her to stop a few days in the palace.

Now, as they sat talking together, the wise woman
asked the Princess if she did not find it dull alone in
the palace in the midst of the sea, and inquired how
they managed to live there without servants, and how

the Prince her husband came and went. Then the
Princess told her about the wonderful ring the Prince
wore day and night, and how by its help they had
everything heart could desire.

On this, the pretended aunt looked very grave,
and suggested the terrible plight in which the Princess
would be left should the Prince come to harm while
away from her. She spoke so earnestly that the
Princess became quite alarmed, and the same evening,
when her husband returned, she said to him, 'Husband,
I wish you would give me the ring to keep while you
are away a-hunting, for if you were to come to harm,
what would become of me alone in this sea-girt
palace ? '

So, next morning, when the Prince went a-hunting,
he left the magical ring in his wife's keeping.

As soon as the wicked wise woman knew that
the ring was really in the possession of the Princess,
she persuaded her to go down the golden stairs to
the sea, and look at the golden boat with the silken
cradle ; so, by coaxing words and cunning arts the
golden Princess was inveigled into the boat, in order
to have a tiny sail on the sea ; but no sooner was
her prize safe in the silken cradle, than the pretended
aunt turned down her finger, and the boatmen
immediately began to row swiftly away.

Soon the Princess begged to be taken back, but
the wise woman only laughed, and answered all the
poor girl's tears and prayers with slaps and harsh
words. At last they arrived at the royal city, where
great rejoicings arose when the news was noised
abroad that the wise woman had returned with the
golden bride for the love-sick Prince. Nevertheless,

despite all entreaties, the Princess refused even to look at the Prince for six months ; if in that time, she said, her husband did not claim her, she might think of marriage, but until then she would not hear of it.

To this the Prince agreed, seeing that six months was not a very long time to wait ; besides, he knew that even should her husband or any other guardian turn up, nothing was easier than to kill them, and so get rid both of them and their claims.

Meanwhile, the spendthrift Prince having returned from hunting, called out as usual to his wife on reaching the golden stairs, but received no answer ; then, entering the palace, he found no one there save the parrot, which flew towards him and said, 'O master, the Princess's aunt came here, and has carried her off in a golden boat.'

Hearing this, the poor Prince fell to the ground in a fit, and would not be consoled. At last, however, he recovered a little, when the parrot, to comfort him, bade him wait there while it flew away over the sea to gather news of the lost bride.

So the faithful parrot flew from land to land, from city to city, from house to house, until it saw the glitter of the Princess's golden hair. Then it fluttered down beside her and bidding her be of good courage, for it had come to help her, asked for the magic ring. Whereupon the golden Princess wept more than ever, for she knew the wise woman kept the ring in her mouth day and night, and that none could take it from her.

However, when the parrot consulted the cat, which had accompanied the faithful bird, the crafty creature declared nothing could be easier.

O

'All the Princess has to do,' said the cat, 'is to ask the wise woman to give her rice for supper to-night, and instead of eating it all, she must scatter some in front of the rat-hole in her room. The rest is my business, and yours.'

So that night the Princess had rice for supper, and instead of eating it all, she scattered some before the rat-hole. Then she went to bed, and slept soundly, and the wise woman snored beside her. By and by, when all was quiet, the rats came out to eat up the rice, when the cat, with one bound, pounced on the one which had the longest tail, and carrying it to where the wise woman lay snoring with her mouth open, thrust the tail up her nose. She woke with a most terrific sneeze, and the ring flew out of her mouth on to the floor. Before she could turn, the parrot seized it in his beak, and, without pausing a moment, flew back with it to his master the spend-thrift Prince, who had nothing to do but make a holy place, lay the ring in the centre, sprinkle it with buttermilk, and say, 'O ring, I want my wife!' and there she was, as beautiful as ever, and overjoyed at seeing the golden palace and her dear husband once more.

THE JACKAL AND THE PEA-HEN

ONCE upon a time a Jackal and a Pea-hen swore eternal friendship. Every day they had their meals together, and spent hours in pleasant conversation.

Now, one day, the Pea-hen had juicy plums for dinner, and the Jackal, for his part, had as juicy a young kid ; so they enjoyed themselves immensely. But when the feast was over, the Pea-hen rose gravely, and, after scratching up the ground, carefully sowed all the plum-stones in a row.

'It is my custom to do so when I eat plums,' she said, with quite an aggravating air of complacent virtue ; 'my mother, good creature, brought me up in excellent habits, and with her dying breath bade me never be wasteful. Now these stones will grow into trees, the fruit of which, even if I do not live to see the day, will afford a meal to many a hungry peacock.'

These words made the Jackal feel rather mean, so he answered loftily, 'Exactly so ! I always plant my bones for the same reason.' And he carefully dug up a piece of ground, and sowed the bones of the kid at intervals.

After this, the pair used to come every day and look at their gardens ; by and by the plum-stones shot into tender green stems, but the bones made never a sign.

'Bones do take a long time germinating,' remarked the Jackal, pretending to be quite at his ease; 'I have known them remain unchanged in the ground for months.'

'My dear sir,' answered the Pea-hen, with ill-concealed irony, '*I* have known them remain so for *years !*'

So time passed on, and every day, when they visited the garden, the self-complacent Pea-hen became more and more sarcastic, the Jackal more and more savage.

At last the plum-trees blossomed and bore fruit, and the Pea-hen sat down to a perfect feast of ripe juicy plums.

'He! he!' sniggered she to the Jackal, who, having been unsuccessful in hunting that day, stood by dinnerless, hungry, and in consequence very cross; 'what a time those old bones of yours do take in coming up! But when they do, my! what a crop you'll have !'

The Jackal was bursting with rage, but she wouldn't take warning, and went on: 'Poor dear! you do look hungry! There seems some chance of your starving before harvest. What a pity it is you can't eat plums in the meantime !'

'If I can't eat plums, I can eat the plum-eater !' quoth the Jackal; and with that he pounced on the Pea-hen, and gobbled her up.

Moral—It is never safe to be wiser than one's friends.

It is never safe
to be wiser than
one's friends.

THE GRAIN OF CORN

ONCE upon a time a farmer's wife was winnowing corn, when a crow, flying past, swooped off with a grain from the winnowing basket and perched on a tree close by to eat it. The farmer's wife, greatly enraged, flung a clod at the bird with so good an aim that the crow fell to the ground, dropping the grain of corn, which rolled into a crack in the tree. The farmer's wife, seeing the crow fall, ran up to it, and seizing it by the tail, cried, 'Give me back my grain of corn, or I will kill you!'

The wretched bird, in fear of death, promised to do so, but, lo and behold! when he came to search for the grain, it had rolled so far into the crack that neither by beak nor claw could he reach it.

So he flew off to a woodman, and said—

> 'Man! man! cut tree;
> I can't get the grain of corn
> To save my life from the farmer's wife!'

But the woodman refused to cut the tree; so the crow flew on to the King's palace, and said—

> 'King! king! kill man;
> Man won't cut tree;

I can't get the grain of corn
To save my life from the farmer's wife!'

But the King refused to kill the man; so the
crow flew on to the Queen, and said—

'Queen! Queen! coax King;
King won't kill man;
Man won't cut tree;
I can't get the grain of corn
To save my life from the farmer's wife!'

But the Queen refused to coax the King; so the
crow flew on till he met a snake, and said—

'Snake! snake! bite Queen;
Queen won't coax King;
King won't kill man;
Man won't cut tree;
I can't get the grain of corn
To save my life from the farmer's wife!'

But the snake refused to bite the Queen; so the
crow flew on till he met a stick, and said—

'Stick! stick! beat snake;
Snake won't bite Queen;
Queen won't coax King;
King won't kill man;
Man won't cut tree;
I can't get the grain of corn
To save my life from the farmer's wife!'

But the stick refused to beat the snake; so the
crow flew on till he saw a fire, and said—

'Fire! fire! burn stick;
Stick won't beat snake;
Snake won't bite Queen;

Queen won't coax King ;
King won't kill man ;
Man won't cut tree ;
I can't get the grain of corn
To save my life from the farmer's wife ! '

But the fire refused to burn the stick ; so the crow flew on till he met some water, and said—

'Water ! water ! quench fire ;
Fire won't burn stick ;
Stick won't beat snake ;
Snake won't bite Queen ;
Queen won't coax King ;
King won't kill man ;
Man won't cut tree ;
I can't get the grain of corn
To save my life from the farmer's wife !'

But the water refused to quench the fire ; so the crow flew on till he met an ox, and said—

'Ox ! ox ! drink water ;
Water won't quench fire ;
Fire won't burn stick ;
Stick won't beat snake ;
Snake won't bite Queen ;
Queen won't coax King ;
King won't kill man ;
Man won't cut tree ;
I can't get the grain of corn
To save my life from the farmer's wife !'

But the ox refused to drink the water ; so the crow flew on till he met a rope, and said—

'Rope ! rope ! bind ox ;

Ox won't drink water ;
Water won't quench fire ;
Fire won't burn stick ;
Stick won't beat snake ;
Snake won't bite Queen ;
Queen won't coax King ;
King won't kill man ;
Man won't cut tree ;
I can't get the grain of corn
To save my life from the farmer's wife ! '

But the rope wouldn't bind the ox ; so the crow
flew on till he met a mouse, and said—

'Mouse ! mouse ! gnaw rope ;
Rope won't bind ox ;
Ox won't drink water ;
Water won't quench fire ;
Fire won't burn stick ;
Stick won't beat snake ;
Snake won't bite Queen ;
Queen won't coax King ;
King won't kill man ;
Man won't cut tree ;
I can't get the grain of corn
To save my life from the farmer's wife ! '

But the mouse wouldn't gnaw the rope ; so the
crow flew on until he met a cat, and said—

'Cat ! cat ! catch mouse ;
Mouse won't gnaw rope ;
Rope won't bind ox ;
Ox won't drink water ;
Water won't quench fire ;
Fire won't burn stick ;

Stick won't beat snake ;
Snake won't bite Queen ;
Queen won't coax King ;
King won't kill man ;
Man won't cut tree ;
And I can't get the grain of corn
To save my life from the farmer's wife !'

The moment the cat heard the name of mouse, she was after it ; for the world will come to an end before a cat will leave a mouse alone.

'So the cat began to catch the mouse,
The mouse began to gnaw the rope,
The rope began to bind the ox,
The ox began to drink the water,
The water began to quench the fire,
The fire began to burn the stick,
The stick began to beat the snake,
The snake began to bite the Queen,
The Queen began to coax the King,
The King began to kill the man,
The man began to cut the tree ;
So the crow got the grain of corn,
And saved his life from the farmer's wife !'

HERE was once a farmer who suffered much at the hands of a money-lender. Good harvests, or bad, the farmer was always poor, the money-lender rich. At last, when he hadn't a farthing left, the farmer went to the money-lender's house, and said, 'You can't squeeze water from a stone, and as you have nothing to get by me now, you might tell me the secret of becoming rich.'

'My friend,' returned the money-lender piously, 'riches come from Ram—ask *him*.'

'Thank you, I will!' replied the simple farmer; so he prepared three girdle-cakes to last him on the journey, and set out to find Ram.

First he met a Brâhman, and to him he gave a cake, asking him to point out the road to Ram; but the Brâhman only took the cake and went on his way without a word. Next the farmer met a Jôgi or devotee, and to him he gave a cake, without receiving any help in return. At last, he came upon a poor man sitting under a tree, and finding out he was hungry, the kindly farmer gave him his last cake, and sitting down to rest beside him, entered into conversation.

'And where are you going?' asked the poor man at length.

'Oh, I have a long journey before me, for I am going to find Ram!' replied the farmer. 'I don't suppose you could tell me which way to go?'

'Perhaps I can,' said the poor man, smiling, 'for *I* am Ram! What do you want of me?'

Then the farmer told the whole story, and Ram, taking pity on him, gave him a conch shell, and showed him how to blow it in a particular way, saying, 'Remember! whatever you wish for, you have only to blow the conch that way, and your wish will be fulfilled. Only have a care of that money-lender, for even magic is not proof against their wiles!'

The farmer went back to his village rejoicing. In fact the money-lender noticed his high spirits at once, and said to himself, 'Some good fortune must have befallen the stupid fellow, to make him hold his head so jauntily.' Therefore he went over to the simple farmer's house, and congratulated him on his good fortune, in such cunning words, pretending to have heard all about it, that before long the farmer found himself telling the whole story—all except the secret of blowing the conch, for, with all his simplicity, the farmer was not quite such a fool as to tell that.

Nevertheless, the money-lender determined to have the conch by hook or by crook, and as he was villain enough not to stick at trifles, he waited for a favourable opportunity and stole it.

But, after nearly bursting himself with blowing the thing in every conceivable way, he was obliged to give up the secret as a bad job.   However, being determined to succeed, he went back to the farmer, and said, ' Now, my friend! I've got your conch, but I can't use it ; you haven't got it, so it's clear you can't use it either.   The matter is at a standstill unless we make a bargain.   Now, I promise to give you back your conch, and never to interfere with your using it, on one condition, which is this,—whatever you get from it, I am to get double.'

' Never !' cried the farmer ; ' that would be the old business all over again ! '

' Not at all ! ' replied the wily money-lender ; ' you will have your share !   Now, don't be a dog in the manger, for if *you* get all you want, what can it matter to you if *I* am rich or poor ? '

At last, though it went sorely against the grain to be of any benefit to a money-lender, the farmer was forced to yield, and from that time, no matter what he gained by the power of the conch, the money-lender gained double.   And the knowledge that this was so preyed upon the farmer's mind day and night, until he had no satisfaction out of anything he did get.

At last there came a very dry season,—so dry that the farmer's crops withered for want of rain. Then he blew his conch, and wished for a well to water them, and, lo ! there was the well.   *But the money-lender had two !*—two beautiful new wells ! This was too much for any farmer to stand ; and our friend brooded over it, and brooded over it, till at last a bright idea came into his head.   He seized the conch, blew it loudly, and cried out, 'O Ram, I wish to be blind of one eye!' And so he was, in a twinkling, but the money-lender, of course, was blind of both eyes, and in trying to steer his way between the two new wells, he fell into one and was drowned.

Now this true story shows that a farmer once got the better of a money-lender ; but only by losing one of his eyes!

THE LORD OF DEATH

NCE upon a time there was a road, and every one who travelled along it died. Some folk said they were killed by a snake, others said by a scorpion, but certain it is they all died.

Now a very old man was travelling along the road, and being tired, sat down on a stone to rest; when suddenly, close beside him, he saw a scorpion as big as a cock, which, while he looked at it, changed into a horrible snake. He was wonderstruck, and as the creature glided away, he determined to follow it at a little distance, and so find out what it really was.

So the snake sped on day and night, and behind it followed the old man like a shadow. Once it went into an inn, and killed several travellers; another time it slid into the King's house and killed him. Then it crept up the waterspout to the Queen's palace, and killed the King's youngest daughter. So it passed on, and wherever it went the sound of weeping and wailing arose, and the old man followed it, silent· as a shadow.

Suddenly the road became a broad, deep, swift

river, on the banks of which sat some poor travellers who longed to cross over, but had no money to pay the ferry. Then the snake changed into a handsome buffalo, with a brass necklace and bells round its neck, and stood by the brink of the stream. When the poor travellers saw this, they said, ' This beast is going to swim to its home across the river ; let us get on its back, and hold on to its tail, so that we too shall get over the stream.'

Then they climbed on its back and held by its tail, and the buffalo swam away with them bravely ; but when it reached the middle, it began to kick, until they tumbled off, or let go, and were all drowned.

When the old man, who had crossed the river in a boat, reached the other side, the buffalo had disappeared, and in its stead stood a beautiful ox. Seeing this handsome creature wandering about, a peasant, struck with covetousness, lured it to his home. It was very gentle, suffering itself to be tied up with the other cattle ; but in the dead of night it changed into a snake, bit all the flocks and herds, and then, creeping into the house, killed all the sleeping folk, and crept away. But behind it the old man still followed, as silent as a shadow.

Presently they came to another river, where the snake changed itself into the likeness of a beautiful young girl, fair to see, and covered with costly jewels. After a while, two brothers, soldiers, came by, and as they approached the girl, she began to weep bitterly.

' What is the matter ? ' asked the brothers ; ' and why do you, so young and beautiful, sit by the river alone ? '

Then the snake-girl answered, ' My husband was

even now taking me home ; and going down to the
stream to look for the ferry-boat, fell to washing his
face, when he slipped in, and was drowned. So I
have neither husband nor relations ! '

' Do not fear ! ' cried the elder of the two brothers,
who had become enamoured of her beauty ; ' come
with me, and I will marry you.'

' On one condition,' answered the girl : ' you must
never ask me to do any household work ; and no
matter for what I ask, you must give it me.'

' I will obey you like a slave ! ' promised the young
man.

' Then go at once to the well, and fetch me a cup
of water. Your brother can stay with me,' quoth the
girl.

But when the elder brother had gone, the snake-
girl turned to the younger, saying, ' Fly with me, for
I love you ! My promise to your brother was a trick
to get him away ! '

' Not so ! ' returned the young man ; ' you are his
promised wife, and I look on you as my sister.'

On this the girl became angry, weeping and wailing, until the elder brother returned, when she called
out, ' O husband, what a villain is here ! Your
brother asked me to fly with him, and leave you ! '

Then bitter wrath at this treachery arose in the
elder brother's heart, so that he drew his sword and
challenged the younger to battle. Then they fought
all day long, until by evening they both lay dead upon
the field, and then the girl took the form of a snake
once more, and behind it followed the old man silent
as a shadow. But at last it changed into the likeness of an old white-bearded man, and when he who

P

had followed so long saw one like himself, he took courage, and laying hold of the white beard, asked, 'Who and what are you?'

Then the old man smiled and answered, 'Some call me the Lord of Death, because I go about bringing death to the world.'

'Give me death!' pleaded the other, 'for I have followed you far, silent as a shadow, and I am aweary.'

But the Lord of Death shook his head, saying, 'Not so! I only give to those whose years are full, and you have sixty years of life to come!'

Then the old white-bearded man vanished, but whether he really was the Lord of Death, or a devil, who can tell?

THE WRESTLERS

A STORY OF HEROES

THERE was, once upon a time, long ago, a wrestler living in a far country, who, hearing there was a mighty man in India, determined to have a fall with him; so, tying up ten thousand pounds weight of flour in his blanket, he put the bundle on his head and set off jauntily. Towards evening he came to a little pond in the middle of the desert, and sat down to eat his dinner. First, he stooped down and took a good long drink of the water; then, emptying his flour into the remainder of the pond, stirred it into good thick brose, off which he made a hearty meal, and lying down under a tree, soon fell fast asleep.

Now, for many years an elephant had drunk daily at the pond, and, coming as usual that evening for its draught, was surprised to find nothing but a little mud and flour at the bottom.

'What shall I do?' it said to itself, 'for there is no more water to be found for twenty miles!'

Going away disconsolate, it espied the wrestler sleeping placidly under the tree, and at once made sure he was the author of the mischief; so, galloping up to the sleeping man, it stamped on his head in a furious rage, determined to crush him.

But, to his astonishment, the wrestler only stirred a little, and said sleepily, 'What is the matter? what is the matter? If you want to shampoo my head, why the plague don't you do it properly? What's worth doing at all is worth doing well; so put a little of your weight into it, my friend!'

The elephant stared, and left off stamping; but, nothing daunted, seized the wrestler round the waist with its trunk, intending to heave him up and dash him to pieces on the ground. 'Ho! ho! my little friend!—that is your plan, is it?' quoth the wrestler, with a yawn; and catching hold of the elephant's tail, and swinging the monster over his shoulder, he continued his journey jauntily.

By and by he reached his destination, and, standing outside the Indian wrestler's house, cried out, 'Ho! my friend! Come out and try a fall!'

'My husband's not at home to-day,' answered the wrestler's wife from inside; 'he has gone into the wood to cut pea-sticks.'

'Well, well! when he returns give him this, with my compliments, and tell him the owner has come from far to challenge him.'

So saying, he chucked the elephant clean over the courtyard wall.

'Oh, mamma! mamma!' cried a treble voice from within, 'I declare that nasty man has thrown a mouse over the wall into my lap! What shall I do to him?'

'Never mind, little daughter!' answered the wrestler's wife; 'papa will teach him better manners. Take the grass broom and sweep the mouse away.'

Then there was a sound of sweeping, and immediately the dead elephant came flying over the wall.

'Ahem!' thought the wrestler outside, 'if the little daughter can do this, the father will be a worthy foe!'

So he set off to the wood to meet the Indian wrestler, whom he soon saw coming along the road, dragging a hundred and sixty carts laden with brushwood.

'Now we shall see!' quoth the stranger, with a wink; and stealing behind the carts, he laid hold of the last, and began to pull.

'That's a deep rut! thought the Indian wrestler, and pulled a little harder. So it went on for an hour, but not an inch one way or the other did the carts budge.

'I believe there is some one hanging on behind!' quoth the Indian wrestler at last, and walked back to see who it was. Whereupon the stranger, coming to meet him, said, 'We seem pretty well matched; let us have a fall together.'

'With all my heart!' answered the other, 'but not here alone in the wilds; it is no fun fighting without applause.'

'But I haven't time to wait!' said the stranger; 'I have to be off at once, so it must be here or nowhere.'

Just then an old woman came hurrying by with big strides.

'Here's an audience!' cried the wrestler, and called aloud, 'Mother! mother! stop and see fair play!'

'I can't, my sons, I can't!' she replied, 'for my daughter is going to steal my camels, and I am off to stop her; but if you like, you can jump on to the palm of my hand, and wrestle there as I go along.'

So the wrestlers jumped on to the old woman's palm, and wrestled away as she strode over hill and dale.

Now when the old woman's daughter saw her mother, with the wrestlers wrestling on her hand, she said to herself, ' Here she comes, with the soldiers she spoke about!   It is time for me to be off!'

So she picked up the hundred and sixty camels, tied them in her blanket, and swinging it over her shoulder, set off at a run.

But one of the camels put its head out of the blanket and began groaning and hubble-bubble-ubbling, after the manner of camels ; so, to quiet it, the girl tore down a tree or two, and stuffed them into the bundle also.   On this, the farmer to whom the trees belonged came running up, and calling, ' Stop thief! stop thief!'

' Thief, indeed!' quoth the girl angrily ; and with that she bundled farmer, fields, crops, oxen, house, and all into the blanket.

Soon she came to a town, and being hungry, asked a pastry-cook to give her some sweets ; but he re-fused, so she caught up the town bodily ; and so on with everything she met, until her blanket was quite full.

At last she came to a big water-melon, and being thirsty, she sat down to eat it ; and afterwards, feeling sleepy, she determined to rest a while.   But the camels in her bundle made such a hubble-bubble-ubbling that they disturbed her, so she just packed everything into the lower half of the water-melon rind, and popping on the upper half as a lid, she rolled herself in the blanket and used the melon as a pillow.

Now, while she slept, a big flood arose, and carried off the water-melon, which, after floating down stream ever so far, stuck on a mud-bank. The top fell off, and out hopped the camels, the trees, the farmer, the oxen, the house, the town, and all the other things, until there was quite a new world on the mud-bank in the middle of the river.

THE LEGEND OF GWÂSHBRÂRI, THE GLACIER-HEARTED QUEEN

ONCE upon a time, ever so long ago, when this old world was young, and everything was very different from what it is nowadays, the mighty Westarwân was King of all the mountains. High above all other hills he reared his lofty head, so lofty, that when the summer clouds closed in upon his broad shoulders he was alone under the blue sky. And thus, being so far above the world, and so lonely in his dignity, he became proud, and even when the mists cleared away, leaving the fair new world stretched smiling at his feet, he never turned his eyes upon it, but gazed day and night upon the sun and stars.

Now Harâmukh, and Nangâ Parbat, and all the other hills that stood in a vast circle round great Westarwân, as courtiers waiting on their king, grew vexed because he treated them as nought; and when the summer cloud that soared above their heads hung on his shoulders like a royal robe, they would say bitter, wrathful words of spite and envy.

Only the beautiful Gwâshbrâri, cold and glistening amid her glaciers, would keep silence. Self-satisfied, serene, her beauty was enough for her; others might rise farther through the mists, but there was none so fair as she in all the land.

Yet once, when the cloud-veil wrapped Westarwân from sight, and the wrath rose loud and fierce, she flashed a contemptuous smile upon the rest, bidding them hold their peace.

'What need to wrangle?' she said, in calm superiority; 'great Westarwân is proud; but though the stars seem to crown his head, his feet are of the earth, earthy. He is made of the same stuff as we are; there is more of it, that is all.'

'The more reason to resent his pride!' retorted the grumblers. 'Who made him a King over us?'

Gwâshbrâri smiled an evil smile. 'O fools! poor fools and blind! giving him a majesty he has not in my sight. I tell you mighty Westarwân, for all his star-crowned loftiness, is no King to me. 'Tis I who am his Queen!'

Then the mighty hills laughed aloud, for Gwâsh-brâri was the lowliest of them all.

'Wait and see!' answered the cold passionless voice. 'Before to-morrow's sunrise great Westarwân shall be my slave!'

Once more the mighty hills echoed with scornful laughter, yet the icy-hearted beauty took no heed. Lovely, serene, she smiled on all through the long summer's day; only once or twice from her snowy sides would rise a white puff of smoke, showing where some avalanche had swept the sure-footed ibex to destruction.

But with the setting sun a rosy radiance fell over the whole world. Then Gwâshbrâri's pale face flushed into life, her chill beauty glowed into passion. Transfigured, glorified, she shone on the fast-darkening horizon like a star.

And mighty Westarwân, noting the rosy radiance in the east, turned his proud eyes towards it; and, lo! the perfection of her beauty smote upon his senses with a sharp, wistful wonder that such loveliness could be—that such worthiness could exist in the world which he despised. The setting sun sank lower, reflecting a ruddier glow on Gwâshbrâri's face; it seemed as if she blushed beneath the great King's gaze. A mighty longing filled his soul, bursting from his lips in one passionate cry—'O Gwâshbrâri! kiss me, or I die!'

The sound echoed through the valleys, while the startled peaks stood round expectant.

Beneath her borrowed blush Gwâshbrâri smiled triumphant, as she answered back, 'How can that be, great King, and I so lowly? Even if I *would*, how could I reach your star-crowned head?—I who on tip-toe cannot touch your cloud-robed shoulder?'

Yet again the passionate cry rang out—'I love you! kiss me, or I die!'

Then the glacier-hearted beauty whispered soft and low, the sweet music of her voice weaving a magical spell round the great Westarwân—'You love me? Know you not that those who love must stoop? Bend your proud head to my lips, and seek the kiss I cannot choose but give!'

Slowly, surely, as one under a charm, the monarch of the mountains stooped—nearer and nearer to her radiant beauty, forgetful of all else in earth or sky.

The sun set. The rosy blush faded from Gwâshbrâri's fair false face, leaving it cold as ice, pitiless as death. The stars began to gleam in the pale heavens, but the King lay at Gwâshbrâri's feet, discrowned for ever !

And that is why great Westarwân stretches his long length across the valley of Kashmîr, resting his once lofty head upon the glacier heart of Queen Gwâshbrâri.

And every night the star crown hangs in the heavens as of yore.

THE BARBER'S CLEVER WIFE

ONCE upon a time there lived a barber, who was such a poor silly creature that he couldn't even ply his trade decently, but snipped off his customers' ears instead of their hair, and cut their throats instead of shaving them. So of course he grew poorer every day, till at last he found himself with nothing left in his house but his wife and his razor, both of whom were as sharp as sharp could be.

For his wife was an exceedingly clever person, who was continually rating her husband for his stupidity; and when she saw they hadn't a farthing left, she fell as usual to scolding.

But the barber took it very calmly. 'What is the use of making such a fuss, my dear?' said he; 'you've told me all this before, and I quite agree with you. I never *did* work, I never *could* work, and I never *will* work. That is the fact!'

'Then you must beg!' returned his wife, 'for *I* will not starve to please you! Go to the palace, and beg something of the King. There is a wedding feast going on, and he is sure to give alms to the poor.'

'Very well, my dear!' said the barber submissively. He was rather afraid of his clever wife, so he did as

he was bid, and going to the palace, begged of the
King to give him something.

'Something?' asked the King; 'what thing?'

Now the barber's wife had not mentioned anything
in particular, and the barber was far too addle-pated
to think of anything by himself, so he answered
cautiously, 'Oh, something!'

'Will a piece of land do?' said the King.

Whereupon the lazy barber, glad to be helped out
of the difficulty, remarked that perhaps a piece of land
would do as well as anything else.

Then the King ordered a piece of waste, outside
the city, should be given to the barber, who went
home quite satisfied.

'Well! what did you get?' asked the clever wife,
who was waiting impatiently for his return. 'Give it
me quick, that I may go and buy bread!'

And you may imagine how she scolded when she
found he had only got a piece of waste land.

'But land is land!' remonstrated the barber; 'it
can't run away, so we must always have something
now!'

'Was there ever such a dunderhead?' raged the
clever wife. 'What good is ground unless we can
till it? and where are we to get bullocks and
ploughs?'

But being, as we have said, an exceedingly clever
person, she set her wits to work, and soon thought of
a plan whereby to make the best of a bad bargain.

She took her husband with her, and set off to
the piece of waste land; then, bidding her husband
imitate her, she began walking about the field, and
peering anxiously into the ground. But when any-

body came that way, she would sit down, and pretend to be doing nothing at all.

Now it so happened that seven thieves were hiding in a thicket hard by, and they watched the barber and his wife all day, until they became convinced something mysterious was going on. So at sunset they sent one of their number to try and find out what it was.

'Well, the fact is,' said the barber's wife, after beating about the bush for some time, and with many injunctions to strict secrecy, 'this field belonged to my grandfather, who buried five pots full of gold in it, and we were just trying to discover the exact spot before beginning to dig. You won't tell any one, will you?'

The thief promised he wouldn't, of course, but the moment the barber and his wife went home, he called his companions, and telling them of the hidden treasure, set them to work. All night long they dug and delved, till the field looked as if it had been ploughed seven times over, and they were as tired as tired could be; but never a gold piece, nor a silver piece, nor a farthing did they find, so when dawn came they went away disgusted.

The barber's wife, when she found the field so beautifully ploughed, laughed heartily at the success of her stratagem, and going to the corn-dealer's shop, borrowed some rice to sow in the field. This the corn-dealer willingly gave her, for he reckoned he would get it back threefold at harvest time. And so he did, for never was there such a crop!—the barber's wife paid her debts, kept enough for the house, and sold the rest for a great crock of gold pieces.

Now, when the thieves saw this, they were very angry indeed, and going to the barber's house, said, 'Give us our share of the harvest, for we tilled the ground, as you very well know.'

'I told you there was gold in the ground,' laughed the barber's wife, 'but you didn't find it. I have, and there's a crock full of it in the house, only you rascals shall never have a farthing of it!'

'Very well!' said the thieves; 'look out for yourself to-night. If you won't give us our share we'll take it!'

So that night one of the thieves hid himself in the house, intending to open the door to his comrades when the housefolk were asleep; but the barber's wife saw him with the corner of her eye, and determined to lead him a dance. Therefore, when her husband, who was in a dreadful state of alarm, asked her what she had done with the gold pieces, she replied, 'Put them where no one will find them, —under the sweetmeats, in the crock that stands in the niche by the door.'

The thief chuckled at hearing this, and after waiting till all was quiet, he crept out, and feeling about for the crock, made off with it, whispering to his comrades that he had got the prize. Fearing pursuit, they fled to a thicket, where they sat down to divide the spoil.

'She said there were sweetmeats on the top,' said the thief; 'I will divide them first, and then we can eat them, for it is hungry work, this waiting and watching.'

So he divided what he thought were the sweetmeats as well as he could in the dark. Now in reality the crock was full of all sorts of horrible things that the barber's wife had put there on purpose, and so when the thieves crammed its contents into their mouths, you may imagine what faces they made and how they vowed revenge.

But when they returned next day to threaten and repeat their claim to a share of the crop, the barber's wife only laughed at them.

'Have a care!' they cried; 'twice you have fooled us—once by making us dig all night, and next by feeding us on filth and breaking our caste. It will be our turn to-night!'

Then another thief hid himself in the house, but the barber's wife saw him with half an eye, and when her husband asked, 'What have you done with the gold, my dear? I hope you haven't put it under the pillow?' she answered, 'Don't be alarmed; it is out of the house. I have hung it in the branches of the *nîm* tree outside. No one will think of looking for it there!'

The hidden thief chuckled, and when the house-folk were asleep he slipped out and told his companions.

'Sure enough, there it is!' cried the captain of the band, peering up into the branches. 'One of you go up and fetch it down.' Now what he saw was really a hornets' nest, full of great big brown and yellow hornets.

So one of the thieves climbed up the tree; but when he came close to the nest, and was just reaching up to take hold of it, a hornet flew out and stung him on the thigh. He immediately clapped his hand to the spot.

'Oh, you thief!' cried out the rest from below, 'you're pocketing the gold pieces, are you? Oh! shabby! shabby!'—For you see it was very dark, and when the poor man clapped his hand to the place where he had been stung, they thought he was putting his hand in his pocket.

'I assure you I'm not doing anything of the kind!' retorted the thief; 'but there is something that bites in this tree!'

Just at that moment another hornet stung him on the breast, and he clapped his hand there.

'Fie! fie for shame! We saw you do it that time!' cried the rest. 'Just you stop that at once, or we will make you!'

So they sent up another thief, but he fared no better, for by this time the hornets were thoroughly roused, and they stung the poor man all over, so that he kept clapping his hands here, there, and everywhere.

'Shame! Shabby! Ssh-sh!' bawled the rest; and then one after another they climbed into the tree, determined to share the booty, and one after another began clapping their hands about their bodies, till it came to the captain's turn. Then he, intent on having the prize, seized hold of the hornets' nest, and as the branch on which they were all standing broke at the selfsame moment, they all came tumbling down with the hornets' nest on top of them. And then, in spite of bumps and bruises, you can imagine what a stampede there was!

After this the barber's wife had some peace, for every one of the seven thieves was in hospital. In fact, they were laid up for so long a time that she

began to think that they were never coming back
again, and ceased to be on the look-out. But she
was wrong, for one night, when she had left the
window open, she was awakened by whisperings outside, and at once recognised the thieves' voices. She
gave herself up for lost ; but, determined not to yield
without a struggle, she seized her husband's razor,
crept to the side of the window, and stood quite still.
By and by the first thief began to creep through
cautiously. She just waited till the tip of his nose
was visible, and then, flash !—she sliced it off with
the razor as clean as a whistle.

'Confound it !' yelled the thief, drawing back
mighty quick ; 'I've cut my nose on something !'

'Hush-sh-sh-sh !' whispered the others, 'you'll
wake some one. Go on !'

'Not I !' said the thief ; 'I'm bleeding like a pig !'

'Pooh !—knocked your nose against the shutter,
I suppose,' returned the second thief. 'I'll go !'

But, swish !—off went the tip of his nose too.

'Dear me !' said he ruefully, 'there certainly is
something sharp inside !'

'A bit of bamboo in the lattice, most likely,' remarked the third thief. 'I'll go !'

And, flick !—off went his nose too.

'It is most extraordinary !' he exclaimed, hurriedly
retiring ; 'I feel exactly as if some one had cut the
tip of my nose off !'

'Rubbish !' said the fourth thief. 'What cowards
you all are ! Let *me* go !'

But he fared no better, nor the fifth thief, nor the
sixth.

'My friends !' said the captain, when it came to

his turn, 'you are all disabled. One man must remain unhurt to protect the wounded. Let us return another night.'—He was a cautious man, you see, and valued his nose.

So they crept away sulkily, and the barber's wife lit a lamp, and gathering up all the nose tips, put them away safely in a little box.

Now before the robbers' noses were healed over, the hot weather set in, and the barber and his wife, finding it warm sleeping in the house, put their beds outside ; for they made sure the thieves would not return. But they did, and seizing such a good opportunity for revenge, they lifted up the wife's bed, and carried her off fast asleep. She woke to find herself borne along on the heads of four of the thieves, whilst the other three ran beside her. She gave herself up for lost, and though she thought, and thought, and thought, she could find no way of escape ; till, as luck would have it, the robbers paused to take breath under a banyan tree. Quick as lightning, she seized hold of a branch that was within reach, and swung herself into the tree, leaving her quilt on the bed just as if she were still in it.

'Let us rest a bit here,' said the thieves who were carrying the bed ; 'there is plenty of time, and we are tired. She is dreadfully heavy !'

The barber's wife could hardly help laughing, but she had to keep very still, for it was a bright moonlight night ; and the robbers, after setting down their burden, began to squabble as to who should take first watch. At last they determined that it should be the captain, for the others had really barely recovered from the shock of having their noses sliced off; so they lay down to sleep, while the captain walked up and down, watching the bed, and the barber's wife sat perched up in the tree like a great bird.

Suddenly an idea came into her head, and drawing her white veil becomingly over her face, she began to sing softly. The robber captain looked up, and saw the veiled figure of a woman in the tree. Of course he was a little surprised, but being a good-looking young fellow, and rather vain of his appearance, he jumped at once to the conclusion that it was a fairy who had fallen in love with his handsome face. For fairies do such things sometimes, especially on moonlight nights. So he twirled his moustaches, and strutted about, waiting for her to speak. But when she went on singing, and took no notice of him, he stopped and called out, 'Come down, my beauty! I won't hurt you!'

But still she went on singing; so he climbed up into the tree, determined to attract her attention. When he came quite close, she turned away her head and sighed.

'What is the matter, my beauty?' he asked tenderly. 'Of course you are a fairy, and have fallen in love with me, but there is nothing to sigh at in that, surely?'

'Ah—ah—ah!' said the barber's wife, with another sigh, 'I believe you're fickle! Men with long-pointed noses always are!'

But the robber captain swore he was the most constant of men; yet still the fairy sighed and sighed, until he almost wished his nose had been shortened too.

'You are telling stories, I am sure!' said the pretended fairy. 'Just let me touch your tongue with the tip of mine, and then I shall be able to taste if there are fibs about!'

So the robber captain put out his tongue, and, snip!—the barber's wife bit the tip off clean!

What with the fright and the pain, he tumbled off the branch, and fell bump on the ground, where he sat with his legs very wide apart, looking as if he had come from the skies.

'What is the matter?' cried his comrades, awakened by the noise of his fall.

'*Bul-ul-a-bul-ul-ul!*' answered he, pointing up into the tree; for of course he could not speak plainly without the tip of his tongue.

'What—is—the—matter?' they bawled in his ear, as if that would do any good.

'*Bul-ul-a-bul-ul-ul!*' said he, still pointing upwards.

'The man is bewitched!' cried one; 'there must be a ghost in the tree!'

Just then the barber's wife began flapping her veil and howling; whereupon, without waiting to look, the thieves in a terrible fright set off at a run, dragging their leader with them; and the barber's wife, coming down from the tree, put her bed on her head, and walked quietly home.

After this, the thieves came to the conclusion that it was no use trying to gain their point by force, so they went to law to claim their share. But the barber's wife pleaded her own cause so well, bringing out the nose and tongue tips as witnesses, that the King made the barber his Wazîr, saying, 'He will never do a foolish thing as long as his wife is alive!'

THE JACKAL AND THE CROCODILE

ONCE upon a time, Mr. Jackal was trotting along gaily, when he caught sight of a wild plum-tree laden with fruit on the other side of a broad deep stream. He could not get across anyhow, so he just sat down on the bank, and looked at the ripe luscious fruit until his mouth watered with desire.

Now it so happened that, just then, Miss Crocodile came floating down stream with her nose in the air.

'Good morning, my dear!' said Mr. Jackal politely; 'how beautiful you look to-day, and how charmingly you swim! Now, if I could only swim too, what a fine feast of plums we two friends might have over there together!" And Mr. Jackal laid his paw on his heart, and sighed.

Now Miss Crocodile had a very inflammable heart, and when Mr. Jackal looked at her so admiringly, and spoke so sentimentally, she simpered and blushed, saying, 'Oh! Mr. Jackal! how can you talk so? I could never dream of going out to dinner with you, unless—unless——'

'Unless what?' asked the Jackal persuasively.

'Unless we were going to be married!' simpered Miss Crocodile.

'And why shouldn't we be married, my charmer?' returned the Jackal eagerly. 'I would go and fetch the barber to begin the betrothals at once, but I am so faint with hunger just at present that I should never reach the village. Now, if the most adorable of her sex would only take pity on her slave, and carry me over the stream, I might refresh myself with those plums, and so gain strength to accomplish the ardent desire of my heart!'

Here the Jackal sighed so piteously, and cast such sheep's-eyes at Miss Crocodile, that she was unable to withstand him. So she carried him across to the plum-tree, and then sat on the water's edge to think over her wedding dress, while Mr. Jackal feasted on the plums, and enjoyed himself.

'Now for the barber, my beauty!' cried the gay Jackal, when he had eaten as much as he could. Then the blushing Miss Crocodile carried him back again, and bade him be quick about his business, like a dear good creature, for really she felt so flustered at the very idea that she didn't know what mightn't happen.

'Now, don't distress yourself, my dear!' quoth the deceitful Mr. Jackal, springing to the bank, 'because it's not impossible that I may not find the barber, and then, you know, you may have to wait some time, a considerable time in fact, before I return. So don't injure your health for my sake, if you please.'

With that he blew her a kiss, and trotted away with his tail up.

Of course he never came back, though trusting Miss Crocodile waited patiently for him ; at last she understood what a gay deceitful fellow he was, and determined to have her revenge on him one way or another.

So she hid herself in the water, under the roots of a tree, close to a ford where Mr. Jackal always came to drink.   By and by, sure enough, he came lilting along in a self-satisfied way, and went right into the water for a good long draught.   Whereupon Miss Crocodile seized him by the right leg, and held on.   He guessed at once what had happened, and called out, ' Oh ! my heart's adored ! I'm drowning ! I'm drowning !   If you love me, leave hold of that old root and get a good grip of my leg—it is just next door ! '

Hearing this, Miss Crocodile thought she must have made a mistake, and, letting go the Jackal's leg in a hurry, seized an old root close by, and held on. Whereupon Mr. Jackal jumped nimbly to shore, and ran off with his tail up, calling out, ' Have a little patience, my beauty !   The barber will come some day ! '

But this time Miss Crocodile knew better than to wait, and being now dreadfully angry, she crawled away to the Jackal's hole, and slipping inside, lay quiet.

By and by Mr. Jackal came lilting along with his tail up.

' Ho ! ho !   That is your game, is it ? ' said he to himself, when he saw the trail of the crocodile in the sandy soil.   So he stood outside, and said aloud, ' Bless my stars ! what has happened ?   I don't half

like to go in, for whenever I come home my wife
always calls out,

'"Oh, dearest hubby hub!
What have you brought for grub
To me and the darling cub?"

and to-day she doesn't say anything!'
Hearing this, Miss Crocodile sang out from inside,

'Oh, dearest hubby hub!
What have you brought for grub
To me and the darling cub?'

The Jackal winked a very big wink, and stealing
in softly, stood at the doorway. Meanwhile Miss
Crocodile, hearing him coming, held her breath, and
lay, shamming dead, like a big log.

'Bless my stars!' cried Mr. Jackal, taking out his
pocket-handkerchief, 'how very very sad! Here's
poor Miss Crocodile stone dead, and all for love of
me! Dear! dear! Yet it is very odd, and I don't
think she can be quite dead, you know—for dead
folks always wag their tails!'

On this, Miss Crocodile began to wag her tail
very gently, and Mr. Jackal ran off, roaring with
laughter, and saying, 'Oho!—oho! so dead folk
always wag their tails!'

HOW RAJA RASÂLU WAS BORN

 NCE there lived a great Raja, whose name was Sâlbâhan, and he had two Queens. Now the elder, by name Queen Achhrâ, had a fair young son called Prince Pûran ; but the younger, by name Lonâ, though she wept and prayed at many a shrine, had never a child to gladden her eyes. So, being a bad, deceitful woman, envy and rage took possession of her heart, and she so poisoned Raja Sâlbâhan's mind against his son, young Pûran, that just as the Prince was growing to manhood, his father became madly jealous of him, and in a fit of anger ordered his hands and feet to be cut off. Not content even with this cruelty, Raja Sâlbâhan had the poor young man thrown into a deep well. Nevertheless, Pûran did not die, as no doubt the enraged father hoped and expected ; for God preserved the innocent Prince, so that he lived on, miraculously, at the bottom of the well, until, years after, the great and holy Guru Goraknâth came to the place, and finding Prince Pûran still alive, not only released him from his dreadful prison, but, by the power of magic, restored his hands and feet. Then Pûran, in gratitude for this great boon, became a *faqîr*, and placing the sacred earrings in his ears, followed Goraknâth as a disciple, and was called Pûran Bhagat.

But as time went by, his heart yearned to see his mother's face, so Guru Goraknâth gave him leave to visit his native town, and Pûran Bhagat journeyed thither and took up his abode in a large walled garden, where he had often played as a child. And, lo! he found it neglected and barren, so that his heart became sad when he saw the broken water-courses and the withered trees. Then he sprinkled the dry ground with water from his drinking vessel, and prayed that all might become green again. And, lo! even as he prayed, the trees shot forth leaves, the grass grew, the flowers bloomed, and all was as it had once been.

The news of this marvellous thing spread fast through the city, and all the world went out to see the holy man who had performed the wonder. Even the Raja Sâlbâhan and his two Queens heard of it in the palace, and they too went to the garden to see it with their own eyes. But Pûran Bhagat's mother, Queen Achhrâ, had wept so long for her darling, that the tears had blinded her eyes, and so she went, not to see, but to ask the wonder-working *faqîr* to restore her sight. Therefore, little knowing from whom she asked the boon, she fell on the ground before Pûran Bhagat, begging him to cure her; and, lo! almost before she asked, it was done, and she saw plainly.

Then deceitful Queen Lonâ, who all these years

had been longing vainly for a son, when she saw what mighty power the unknown *faqîr* possessed, fell on the ground also, and begged for an heir to gladden the heart of Raja Sâlbâhan.

Then Pûran Bhagat spoke, and his voice was stern,—'Raja Sâlbâhan already has a son. Where is he? What have you done with him? Speak truth, Queen Lonâ, if you would find favour with God!'

Then the woman's great longing for a son conquered her pride, and though her husband stood by, she humbled herself before the *faqîr* and told the truth,—how she had deceived the father and destroyed the son.

Then Pûran Bhagat rose to his feet, stretched out his hands towards her, and a smile was on his face, as he said softly, 'Even so, Queen Lonâ! even so! And behold! *I* am Prince Pûran, whom you destroyed and God delivered! I have a message for you. Your fault is forgiven, but not forgotten; you shall indeed bear a son, who shall be brave and good, yet will he cause you to weep tears as bitter as those my mother wept for me. So! take this grain of rice; eat it, and you shall bear a son that will be no son to you, for even as I was reft from my mother's eyes, so will he be reft from yours. Go in peace; your fault is forgiven, but not forgotten!'

Queen Lonâ returned to the palace, and when the time for the birth of the promised son drew nigh, she inquired of three Jôgis who came begging to her gate, what the child's fate would be, and the youngest of them answered and said, 'O Queen, the child will be a boy, and he will live to be a great

man.   But for twelve years you must not look upon
his face, for if either you or his father see it before
the twelve years are past, you will surely die!   This
is what you must do,—as soon as the child is born
you must send him away to a cellar underneath the
ground, and never let him see the light of day for
twelve years.   After they are over, he may come
forth, bathe in the river, put on new clothes, and visit
you.   His name shall be Raja Rasâlu, and he shall
be known far and wide. '

So, when a fair young Prince was in due time
born into the world, his parents hid him away in an
underground palace, with nurses, and servants, and
everything else a King's son might desire.   And
with him they sent a young colt, born the same day,
and a sword, a spear, and a shield, against the day
when Raja Rasâlu should go forth into the world.

So there the child lived, playing with his colt, and
talking to his parrot, while the nurses taught him all
things needful for a King's son to know.

HOW RAJA RASÂLU WENT OUT INTO THE WORLD

OUNG Rasâlu lived on, far from the light of day, for eleven long years, growing tall and strong, yet contented to remain playing with his colt and talking to his parrot; but when the twelfth year began, the lad's heart leapt up with desire for change, and he loved to listen to the sounds of life which came to him in his palace-prison from the outside world.

'I must go and see where the voices come from!' he said; and when his nurses told him he must not go for one year more, he only laughed aloud, saying, 'Nay! I stay no longer here for any man!'

Then he saddled his horse Bhaunr Irâqi, put on his shining armour, and rode forth into the world; but—mindful of what his nurses had often told him—when he came to the river, he dismounted, and going into the water, washed himself and his clothes.

Then, clean of raiment, fair of face, and brave of heart, he rode on his way until he reached his father's city. There he sat down to rest a while by a well, where the women were drawing water in earthen pitchers. Now, as they passed him, their full pitchers poised upon their heads, the gay young Prince flung stones at the earthen vessels, and broke them all. Then the women, drenched with water, went weeping and wailing to the palace, complaining to the King that a mighty young Prince in shining armour, with a parrot on his wrist and a gallant steed beside him, sat by the well, and broke their pitchers.

Now, as soon as Raja Sâlbâhan heard this, he guessed at once that it was Prince Rasâlu come forth before the time, and, mindful of the Jôgis' words that he would die if he looked on his son's face before twelve years were past, he did not dare to send his guards to seize the offender and bring him to be judged. So he bade the women be comforted, and for the future take pitchers of iron and brass, and gave new ones from his treasury to those who did not possess any of their own.

But when Prince Rasâlu saw the women returning to the well with pitchers of iron and brass, he laughed to himself, and drew his mighty bow till the sharp-pointed arrows pierced the metal vessels as though they had been clay.

Yet still the King did not send for him, and so he mounted his steed and set off in the pride of his youth and strength to the palace. He strode into the audience hall, where his father sat trembling, and saluted him with all reverence ; but Raja Sâlbâhan, in fear of his life, turned his back hastily and said never a word in reply.

Then Prince Rasâlu called scornfully to him across the hall—

'I came to greet thee, King, and not to harm thee!
    What have I done that thou shouldst turn away?
Sceptre and empire have no power to charm me—
    I go to seek a worthier prize than they!'

Then he strode out of the hall, full of bitterness
and anger; but, as he passed under the palace
windows, he heard his mother weeping, and the
sound softened his heart, so that his wrath died
down, and a great loneliness fell upon him, because
he was spurned by both father and mother. So he
cried sorrowfully—

'O heart crown'd with grief, hast thou naught
    But tears for thy son?
Art mother of mine?   Give one thought
    To my life just begun!'

And Queen Lonâ answered through her tears—

'Yea! mother am I, though I weep,
    So hold this word sure,—
Go, reign king of all men, but keep
    Thy heart good and pure!'

So Raja Rasâlu was comforted, and began to
make ready for fortune. He took with him his
horse Bhaunr Irâqi, and his parrot, both of whom
had lived with him since he was born; and besides
these tried and trusted friends he had two others—
a carpenter lad, and a goldsmith lad, who were
determined to follow the Prince till death.

So they made a goodly company, and Queen
Lonâ, when she saw them going, watched them from
her window till she saw nothing but a cloud of dust

on the horizon ; then she bowed her head on her hands and wept, saying—

> 'O son who ne'er gladdened mine eyes,
> Let the cloud of thy going arise,
> Dim the sunlight and darken the day ;
> For the mother whose son is away
>   Is as dust !'

HOW RAJA RASÂLU'S FRIENDS FORSOOK HIM

NOW, on the first day, Raja Rasâlu journeyed far,
until he came to a lonely forest, where he halted for
the night. And seeing it was a desolate place, and
the night dark, he determined to set a watch. So
he divided the time into three watches, and the
carpenter took the first, the goldsmith the second,
and Raja Rasâlu the third.

Then the goldsmith lad spread a couch of clean
grass for his master, and fearing lest the Prince's heart
should sink at the change from his former luxurious
life, he said these words of encouragement—

> ‘Cradled till now on softest down,
>   Grass is thy couch to-night ;
> Yet grieve not thou if Fortune frown—
>   Brave hearts heed not her slight !’

Now, when Raja Rasâlu and the goldsmith's son
slept, a snake came out of a thicket hard by, and
crept towards the sleepers.

‘Who are you?’ quoth the carpenter lad, ‘and
why do you come hither?’

‘I have destroyed all things within twelve miles !’
returned the serpent. ‘Who are *you* that have dared
to come hither?

Then the snake attacked the carpenter, and they fought until the snake was killed, when the carpenter hid the dead body under his shield, and said nothing of the adventure to his comrades, lest he should alarm them, for, like the goldsmith, he thought the Prince might be discouraged.

Now, when it came to Raja Rasâlu's turn to keep watch, a dreadful unspeakable horror came out of the thicket. Nevertheless, Rasâlu went up to it boldly, and cried aloud, 'Who are you? and what brings you here?'

Then the awful unspeakable horror replied, 'I have killed everything for thrice twelve miles around! Who are *you* that dare come hither?'

Whereupon Rasâlu drew his mighty bow, and pierced the horror with an arrow, so that it fled into a cave, whither the Prince followed it. And they fought long and fiercely, till at last the horror died, and Rasâlu returned to watch in peace.

Now, when morning broke, Raja Rasâlu called his sleeping servants, and the carpenter showed with pride the body of the serpent he had killed.

''Tis but a small snake!' quoth the Raja. 'Come and see what I killed in the cave!'

And, behold! when the goldsmith lad and the carpenter lad saw the awful, dreadful, unspeakable horror Raja Rasâlu had slain, they were exceedingly afraid, and falling on their knees, begged to be allowed to return to the city, saying, 'O mighty Rasâlu, you are a Raja and a hero! You can fight such horrors; we are but ordinary folk, and if we follow you we shall surely be killed. Such things are nought to you, but they are death to us. Let us go!'

Then Rasâlu looked at them sorrowfully, and bade them do as they wished, saying—

'Aloes linger long before they flower :
   Gracious rain too soon is overpast :
  Youth and strength are with us but an hour :
   All glad life must end in death at last !
But king reigns king without consent of courtier ;
  Rulers may rule, though none heed their command.
Heaven-crown'd heads stoop not, but rise the haughtier,
  Alone and houseless in a stranger's land !'

So his friends forsook him, and Rasâlu journeyed on alone.

HOW RAJA RASÂLU KILLED THE GIANTS

Now, after a time, Raja Rasâlu arrived at Nîlâ city, and as he entered the town he saw an old woman making unleavened bread, and as she made it she sometimes wept, and sometimes laughed ; so Rasâlu asked her why she wept and laughed, but she answered sadly, as she kneaded her cakes, 'Why do you ask ?   What will you gain by it ?'

'Nay, mother !' replied Rasâlu, 'if you tell me. the truth, one of us must benefit by it.'

And when the old woman looked in Rasâlu's face she saw that it was kind, so she opened her heart to

him, saying, with tears, 'O stranger, I had seven
fair sons, and now I have but one left, for six of them
have been killed by a dreadful giant who comes
every day to this city to receive tribute from us,—
every day a fair young man, a buffalo, and a basket
of cakes! Six of my sons have gone, and now
to-day it has once more fallen to my lot to provide
the tribute ; and my boy, my darling, my youngest,
must meet the fate of his brothers. Therefore I
weep!'

Then Rasâlu was moved to pity, and said—

'Fond, foolish mother! cease these tears—
  Keep thou thy son. I fear nor death nor life,
  Seeking my fortune everywhere in strife.
My head for his I give!—so calm your fears.'

Still the old woman shook her head doubtfully,
saying, 'Fair words, fair words! but who will really
risk his life for another?'

Then Rasâlu smiled at her, and dismounting from
his gallant steed, Bhaunr Irâqi, he sat down carelessly to rest, as if indeed he were a son of the house,
and said, 'Fear not, mother! I give you my word
of honour that I will risk my life to save your son.'

Just then the high officials of the city, whose duty
it was to claim the giant's tribute, appeared in
sight, and the old woman fell a-weeping once more,
saying—

'O Prince, with the gallant gray steed and the
    turban bound high
  O'er thy fair bearded face ; keep thy word, my
    oppressor draws nigh!'

Then Raja Rasâlu rose in his shining armour, and haughtily bade the guards stand aside.

'Fair words!' replied the chief officer; 'but if this woman does not send the tribute at once, the giants will come and disturb the whole city. Her son must go!'

'I go in his stead!' quoth Rasâlu more haughtily still. 'Stand back, and let me pass!'

Then, despite their denials, he mounted his horse, and taking the basket of cakes and the buffalo, he set off to find the giant, bidding the buffalo show him the shortest road.

Now, as he came near the giants' house, he met one of them carrying a huge skinful of water. No sooner did the water-carrier giant see Raja Rasâlu riding along on his horse Bhaunr Irâqi and leading the buffalo, than he said to himself, 'Oho! we have a horse extra to-day! I think I will eat it myself, before my brothers see it!'

Then he reached out his hand, but Rasâlu drew his sharp sword and smote the giant's hand off at a blow, so that he fled from him in great fear.

Now, as he fled, he met his sister the giantess, who called out to him, 'Brother, whither away so fast?'

And the giant answered in haste, 'Raja Rasâlu has come at last, and see!—he has cut off my hand with one blow of his sword!'

Then the giantess, overcome with fear, fled with her brother, and as they fled they called aloud—

'Fly! brethren, fly!
Take the path that is nearest;
The fire burns high
That will scorch up our dearest!'

Life's joys we have seen :
East and west we must wander !
What has been, has been ;
Quick ! some remedy ponder.'

Then all the giants turned and fled to their astrologer brother, and bade him look in his books to see if Raja Rasâlu were really born into the world. And when they heard that he was, they prepared to fly east and west ; but even as they turned, Raja Rasâlu rode up on Bhaunr Irâqi, and challenged them to fight, saying, 'Come forth, for I am Rasâlu, son of Raja Sâlbâhan, and born enemy of the giants !'

Then one of the giants tried to brazen it out, saying, 'I have eaten many Rasâlus like you ! When the real man comes, his horse's heel-ropes will bind us and his sword cut us up of their own accord !'

Then Raja Rasâlu loosed his heel-ropes, and dropped his sword upon the ground, and, lo ! the heel-ropes bound the giants, and the sword cut them in pieces.

Still, seven giants who were left tried to brazen it out, saying, 'Aha ! We have eaten many Rasâlus like you ! When the real man comes, his arrow will pierce seven girdles placed one behind the other.'

So they took seven iron girdles for baking bread, and placed them one behind the other, as a shield, and behind them stood the seven giants, who were own brothers, and, lo ! when Raja Rasâlu twanged his mighty bow, the arrow pierced through the seven girdles, and spitted the seven giants in a row !

But the giantess, their sister, escaped, and fled to a cave in the Gandgari mountains. Then Raja Rasâlu had a statue made in his likeness, and clad it in

shining armour, with sword and spear and shield.
And he placed it as a sentinel at the entrance of the
cave, so that the giantess dared not come forth, but
starved to death inside.

So this is how he killed the giants.

HOW RAJA RASÂLU BECAME A JÔGI

HEN, after a time, Rasâlu went to Hodinagari. And when he reached the house of the beautiful far-famed Queen Sundrân, he saw an old Jôgi sitting at the gate, by the side of his sacred fire.

'Wherefore do you sit there, father?' asked Raja Rasâlu.

'My son,' returned the Jôgi, 'for two-and-twenty years have I waited thus to see the beautiful Sundrân, yet have I never seen her!'

'Make me your pupil,' quoth Rasâlu, 'and I will wait too.'

'You work miracles already, my son,' said the Jôgi; 'so where is the use of your becoming one of us?'

Nevertheless, Raja Rasâlu would not be denied, so the Jôgi bored his ears and put in the sacred ear-rings. Then the new disciple put aside his shining armour, and sat by the fire in a Jôgi's loin-cloth, waiting to see Queen Sundrân.

Then, at night, the old Jôgi went and begged alms

from four houses, and half of what he got he gave to
Rasâlu and half he ate himself. Now Raja Rasâlu,
being a very holy man, and a hero besides, did not
care for food, and was well content with his half
share, but the Jôgi felt starved.

The next day the same thing happened, and still
Rasâlu sat by the fire waiting to see the beautiful
Queen Sundrân.

Then the Jôgi lost patience, and said, 'O my
disciple, I made you a pupil in order that you
might beg, and feed me, and behold, it is I who have
to starve to feed you!'

'You gave no orders!' quoth Rasâlu, laughing.
'How can a disciple beg without his master's leave?'

'I order you now!' returned the Jôgi. 'Go and
beg enough for you and for me.'

So Raja Rasâlu rose up, and stood at the gate of
Queen Sundrân's palace, in his Jôgi's dress, and sang,

'*Alakh!* at thy threshold I stand,
    Drawn from far by the name of thy charms;
Fair Sundrân, with generous hand,   ·
    Give the earring-decked Jôgi an alms!'

Now when Queen Sundrân, from within, heard
Rasâlu's voice, its sweetness pierced her heart, so
that she immediately sent out alms by the hand of
her maid-servant. But when the maiden came to the
gate, and saw the exceeding beauty of Rasâlu, standing outside, fair in face and form, she fainted away,
dropping the alms upon the ground.

Then once more Rasâlu sang, and again his voice
fell sweetly on Queen Sundrân's ears, so that she sent
out more alms by the hand of another maiden. But

she also fainted away at the sight of Rasâlu's marvellous beauty.

Then Queen Sundrân rose, and came forth herself,
fair and stately.   She chid the maidens, gathered up
the broken alms, and setting the food aside, filled the
plate with jewels and put it herself into Rasâlu's hands,
saying proudly—

'Since when have the earrings been thine?
　　Since when wert thou made a *faqîr*?
What arrow from Love's bow has struck thee?
　　What seekest thou here?
Do you beg of all women you see,
　　Or only, fair Jôgi, of me?'

And Rasâlu, in his Jôgi's habit, bent his head
towards her, saying softly—

'A day since the earrings were mine,
　　A day since I turned a *faqîr;*
But yesterday Love's arrow struck me;
　　I seek nothing here!
I beg nought of others I see,
　　But only, fair Sundrân, of thee!'

Now, when Rasâlu returned to his master with the
plate full of jewels, the old Jôgi was sorely astonished,
and bade him take them back, and ask for food instead.   So Rasâlu returned to the gate, and sang—

'*Alakh!* at thy threshold I stand,
　　Drawn from far by the fame of thy charms;
Fair Sundrân, with generous hand,
　　Give the earring-decked beggar an alms!'

Then Queen Sundrân rose up, proud and beautiful,
and coming to the gate, said softly—

'No beggar thou!   The quiver of thy mouth
    Is set with pearly shafts; its bow is red
As rubies rare.   Though ashes hide thy youth,
    Thine eyes, thy colour, herald it instead!
Deceive me not—pretend no false desire—
But ask the secret alms thou dost require.'

But Rasâlu smiled a scornful smile, saying—

'Fair Queen! what though the quiver of my mouth
    Be set with glistening pearls and rubies red?
I trade not jewels, east, west, north, or south;
    Take back thy gems, and give me food instead.
Thy gifts are rich and rare, but costly charms
Scarce find fit placing in a Jôgi's alms!'   .

Then Queen Sundrân took back the jewels, and
bade the beautiful Jôgi wait an hour till the food was
cooked.   Nevertheless, she learnt no more of him,
for he sat by the gate and said never a word.   Only
when Queen Sundrân gave him a plate piled up with
sweets, and looked at him sadly, saying—

'What King's son art thou? and whence dost thou
    come?
What name hast thou, Jôgi, and where is thy home?'

then Raja Rasâlu, taking the alms, replied—

'I am fair Lonâ's son; my father's name
    Great Sâlbâhan, who reigns at Siâlkot.
I am Rasâlu; for thy beauty's fame
    These ashes, and the Jôgi's begging note,
To see if thou wert fair as all men say;
Lo! I have seen it, and I go my way!'

Then Rasâlu returned to his master with the
sweets, and after that he went away from the place,

for he feared lest the Queen, knowing who he was, might try to keep him prisoner.

And beautiful Sundrân waited for the Jôgi's cry, and when none came, she went forth, proud and stately, to ask the old Jôgi whither his pupil had gone.

Now he, vexed that she should come forth to ask for a stranger, when he had sat at her gates for two-and-twenty years with never a word or sign, answered back, 'My pupil? I was hungry, and I ate him, because he did not bring me alms enough.'

'Oh, monster!' cried Queen Sundrân. 'Did I not send thee jewels and sweets? Did not these satisfy thee, that thou must feast on beauty also?'

'I know not,' quoth the Jôgi; 'only this I know —I put the youth on a spit, roasted him, and ate him up. He tasted well!'

'Then roast and eat me too!' cried poor Queen Sundrân; and with the words she threw herself into the sacred fire and became *sati* for the love of the beautiful Jôgi Rasâlu.

And he, going thence, thought not of her, but fancying he would like to be king a while, he snatched the throne from Raja Hari Chand, and reigned in his stead.

HOW RAJA RASÂLU JOURNEYED TO THE CITY OF KING SARKAP

Now, after he had reigned a while in Hodinagari, Rasâlu gave up his kingdom, and started off to play *chaupur* with King Sarkap. And as he journeyed there came a fierce storm of thunder and lightning, so that he sought shelter, and found none save an old graveyard, where a headless corpse lay upon the ground. So lonesome was it that even the corpse seemed company, and Rasâlu, sitting down beside it, said—

'There is no one here, nor far nor near,
    Save this breathless corpse so cold and grim ;
Would God he might come to life again,
    'Twould be less lonely to talk to him.'

And immediately the headless corpse arose and sat beside Raja Rasâlu. And he, nothing astonished, said to it—

'The storm beats fierce and loud,
    The clouds rise thick in the west ;
What ails thy grave and thy shroud,
    O corpse, that thou canst not rest ?'

Then the headless corpse replied—

'On earth I was even as thou,
My turban awry like a king,
My head with the highest, I trow,
Having my fun and my fling,
Fighting my foes like a brave,
Living my life with a swing.
And, now I am dead,
Sins, heavy as lead,
Will give me no rest in my grave!'

So the night passed on, dark and dreary, while Rasâlu sat in the graveyard and talked to the headless corpse. Now when morning broke and Rasâlu said he must continue his journey, the headless corpse asked him whither he was going; and when he said, 'to play *chaupur* with King Sarkap,' the corpse begged him to give up the idea, saying, 'I am King Sarkap's brother, and I know his ways. Every day, before breakfast, he cuts off the heads of two or three men, just to amuse himself. One day no one else was at hand, so he cut off mine, and he will surely cut off yours on some pretence or another. However, if you are determined to go and play *chaupur* with him, take some of the bones from this graveyard, and make your dice out of them, and then the enchanted dice with which my brother plays will lose their virtue. Otherwise he will always win.'

So Rasâlu took some of the bones lying about, and fashioned them into dice, and these he put into his pocket. Then, bidding adieu to the headless corpse, he went on his way to play *chaupur* with the King.

HOW RAJA RASÂLU SWUNG THE SEVENTY FAIR MAIDENS, DAUGHTERS OF THE KING

Now, as Raja Rasâlu, tender-hearted and strong, journeyed along to play *chaupur* with the King, he came to a burning forest, and a voice rose from the fire saying, 'O traveller, for God's sake save me from the fire!'

Then the Prince turned towards the burning forest, and, lo! the voice was the voice of a tiny cricket. Nevertheless, Rasâlu, tender-hearted and strong, snatched it from the fire and set it at liberty. Then the little creature, full of gratitude, pulled out one of its feelers, and giving it to its preserver, said, 'Keep this, and should you ever be in trouble, put it into the fire, and instantly I will come to your aid.'

The Prince smiled, saying, 'What help could *you* give *me*?' Nevertheless, he kept the hair and went on his way.

Now, when he reached the city of King Sarkap, seventy maidens, daughters of the King, came out to meet him—seventy fair maidens, merry and careless, full of smiles and laughter; but one, the youngest of them all, when she saw the gallant young Prince

S

riding on Bhaunr Irâqi, going gaily to his doom, was filled with pity, and called to him, saying—

    'Fair Prince, on the charger so gray,
        Turn thee back! turn thee back!
    Or lower thy lance for the fray;
    Thy head will be forfeit to-day!
    Dost love life? then, stranger, I pray,
        Turn thee back! turn thee back!'

But he, smiling at the maiden, answered lightly—

    'Fair maiden, I come from afar,
    Sworn conqueror in love and in war!
    King Sarkap my coming will rue,
    His head in four pieces I'll hew;
    Then forth as a bridegroom I'll ride,
    With you, little maid, as my bride!'

Now when Rasâlu replied so gallantly, the maiden looked in his face, and seeing how fair he was, and how brave and strong, she straightway fell in love with him, and would gladly have followed him through the world.

But the other sixty-nine maidens, being jealous, laughed scornfully at her, saying, 'Not so fast, O gallant warrior! If you would marry our sister you must first do our bidding, for you will be our younger brother.'

'Fair sisters!' quoth Rasâlu gaily, 'give me my task and I will perform it.'

So the sixty-nine maidens mixed a hundredweight of millet seed with a hundredweight of sand, and giving it to Rasâlu, bade him separate the seed from the sand.

Then he bethought him of the cricket, and

drawing the feeler from his pocket, thrust it into
the fire. And immediately there was a whirring
noise in the air, and a great flight of crickets alighted
beside him, and among them the cricket whose life
he had saved.

Then Rasâlu said, 'Separate the millet seed from
the sand.'

'Is that all?' quoth the cricket; 'had I known
how small a job you wanted me to do, I would not
have assembled so many of my brethren.'

With that the flight of crickets set to work, and in
one night they separated the seed from the sand.

Now when the sixty-nine fair maidens, daughters
of the King, saw that Rasâlu had performed his task,
they set him another, bidding him swing them all, one
by one, in their swings, until they were tired.

Whereupon he laughed, saying, ' There are seventy
of you, counting my little bride yonder, and I am not
going to spend my life in swinging girls ; yet, by the
time I have given each of you a swing, the first will
be wanting another !   No! if you want to swing, get
in, all seventy of you, into one swing, and then I will
see what I can compass.'

So the seventy maidens, merry and careless, full
of smiles and laughter, climbed into the one swing,
and Raja Rasâlu, standing in his shining armour,
fastened the ropes to his mighty bow, and drew it up
to its fullest bent.   Then he let go, and like an arrow
the swing shot into the air, with its burden of seventy
fair maidens, merry and careless, full of smiles and
laughter.

But as it swung back again, Rasâlu, standing
there in his shining armour, drew his sharp sword and

severed the ropes.   Then the seventy fair maidens
fell to the ground headlong ; and some were bruised
and some broken, but the only one who escaped
unhurt was the maiden who loved Rasâlu, for she fell
out last, on the top of the others, and so came to no
harm.

After this, Rasâlu strode on fifteen paces, till he
came to the seventy drums, that every one who came
to play *chaupur* with the King had to beat in turn ;
and he beat them so loudly that he broke them all.
Then he came to the seventy gongs, all in a row,
and he hammered them so hard that they cracked
to pieces.

Seeing this, the youngest Princess, who was the
only one who could run, fled to her father the King
in a great fright, saying—

'A mighty Prince, Sarkap! making havoc, rides
　　along,
　He swung us, seventy maidens fair, and threw us
　　out headlong ;
　He broke the drums you placed there and the gongs
　　too in his pride,
　Sure, he will kill thee, father mine, and take me for
　　his bride !'

But King Sarkap replied scornfully—

'Silly maiden, thy words make a lot
　　Of a very small matter ;
For fear of my valour, I wot,
　　His armour will clatter.
As soon as I've eaten my bread
I'll go forth and cut off his head !'

Notwithstanding these brave and boastful words

he was in reality very much afraid, having heard of Rasâlu's renown. And learning that he was stopping at the house of an old woman in the city, till the hour for playing *chaupur* arrived, Sarkap sent slaves to him with trays of sweetmeats and fruit, as to an honoured guest. But the food was poisoned.

Now when the slaves brought the trays to Raja Rasâlu, he rose up haughtily, saying, 'Go, tell your master I have nought to do with him in friendship. I am his sworn enemy, and I eat not of his salt!'

So saying, he threw the sweetmeats to Raja Sarkap's dog, which had followed the slaves, and lo! the dog died.

Then Rasâlu was very wroth, and said bitterly, 'Go back to Sarkap, slaves! and tell him that Rasâlu deems it no act of bravery to kill even an enemy by treachery.'

HOW RAJA RASÂLU PLAYED CHAUPUR
WITH KING SARKAP

NOW, when evening came, Raja Rasâlu went forth
to play *chaupur* with King Sarkap, and as he passed
some potters' kilns he saw a cat wandering about
restlessly ; so he asked what ailed her that she never
stood still, and she replied, ' My kittens are in an unbaked pot in the kiln yonder.   It has just been set
alight, and my children will be baked alive ; therefore
I cannot rest ! '

Her words moved the heart of Raja Rasâlu, and,
going to the potter, he asked him to sell the kiln as
it was ; but the potter replied that he could not settle
a fair price till the pots were burnt, as he could not
tell how many would come out whole.   Nevertheless,
after some bargaining, he consented at last to sell the
kiln, and Rasâlu, having searched through all the pots,
restored the kittens to their mother, and she, in gratitude for his mercy, gave him one of them, saying,
' Put it in your pocket, for it will help you when you
are in difficulties.'

So Raja Rasâlu put the kitten in his pocket, and
went to play *chaupur* with the King.

Now, before they sat down to play, Raja Sarkap
fixed his stakes.   On the first game, his kingdom ; on

the second, the wealth of the whole world ; and on
the third, his own head. So, likewise, Raja Rasâlu
fixed his stakes. On the first game, his arms ; on
the second, his horse ; and on the third, his own
head.

Then they began to play, and it fell to Rasâlu's
lot to make the first move. Now he, forgetful of
the dead man's warning, played with the dice given
him by Raja Sarkap ; then, in addition, Sarkap let
loose his famous rat, Dhol Raja, and it ran about the
board, upsetting the *chaupur* pieces on the sly, so that
Rasâlu lost the first game, and gave up his shining
armour.

So the second game began, and once more Dhol
Raja, the rat, upset the pieces ; and Rasâlu, losing
the game, gave up his faithful steed. Then Bhaunr
Irâqi, who stood by, found voice, and cried to his
master—

‘ I am born of the sea and of gold ;
  Dear Prince ! trust me now as of old.
    I'll carry you far from these wiles—
My flight, all unspurr'd, will be swift as a bird,
    For thousands and thousands of miles !
Or if needs you must stay ; ere the next game you play,
    Place hand in your pocket, I pray ! ’

Hearing this, Raja Sarkap frowned, and bade his
slaves remove Bhaunr Irâqi, since he gave his master
advice in the game. Now when the slaves came to
lead the faithful steed away, Rasâlu could not refrain
from tears, thinking over the long years during which
Bhaunr Irâqi had been his companion. But the horse
cried out again —

'Weep not, dear Prince! I shall not eat my bread
Of stranger hands, nor to strange stall be led.
Take thy right hand, and place it as I said.'

These words roused some recollection in Rasâlu's
mind, and when, just at this moment, the kitten in
his pocket began to struggle, he remembered the
warning which the corpse had given him about the
dice made from dead men's bones. Then his heart
rose up once more, and he called boldly to Raja
Sarkap, 'Leave my horse and arms here for the
present. Time enough to take them away when
you have won my head!'

Now, Raja Sarkap, seeing Rasâlu's confident bearing, began to be afraid, and ordered all the women of
his palace to come forth in their gayest attire and
stand before Rasâlu, so as to distract his attention
from the game. But he never even looked at them;
and drawing the dice from his pocket, said to Sarkap,
'We have played with your dice all this time; now
we will play with mine.'

Then the kitten went and sat at the window through
which the rat Dhol Raja used to come, and the game
began.

After a while, Sarkap, seeing Raja Rasâlu was
winning, called to his rat, but when Dhol Raja
saw the kitten he was afraid, and would not go
farther. So Rasâlu won, and took back his arms.
Next he played for his horse, and once more
Raja Sarkap called for his rat; but Dhol Raja,
seeing the kitten keeping watch, was afraid. So
Rasâlu won the second stake, and took back Bhaunr
Irâqi.

Then Sarkap brought all his skill to bear on the
third and last game, saying—

> 'O moulded pieces, favour me to-day!
> For sooth this is a man with whom I play.
> No paltry risk—but life and death at stake;
> As Sarkap does, so do, for Sarkap's sake!'

But Rasâlu answered back—

> 'O moulded pieces, favour me to-day!
> For sooth it is a man with whom I play.
> No paltry risk—but life and death at stake;
> As Heaven does, so do, for Heaven's sake!'

So they began to play, whilst the women stood
round in a circle, and the kitten watched Dhol Raja
from the window. Then Sarkap lost, first his
kingdom, then the wealth of the whole world, and
lastly his head.

Just then, a servant came in to announce the birth
of a daughter to Raja Sarkap, and he, overcome by
misfortunes, said, 'Kill her at once! for she has been
born in an evil moment, and has brought her father
ill luck!'

But Rasâlu rose up in his shining armour, tender-
hearted and strong, saying, 'Not so, O king! She
has done no evil. Give me this child to wife; and
if you will vow, by all you hold sacred, never again
to play *chaupur* for another's head, I will spare yours
now!'

Then Sarkap vowed a solemn vow never to play
for another's head; and after that he took a fresh
mango branch, and the new-born babe, and placing
them on a golden dish, gave them to the Prince.

Now, as Rasâlu left the palace, carrying with him the new-born babe and the mango branch, he met a band of prisoners, and they called out to him—

' A royal hawk art thou, O King! the rest
But timid wild-fowl. Grant us our request—
Unloose these chains, and live for ever blest!'

And Raja Rasâlu hearkened to them, and bade King Sarkap set them at liberty.

Then he went to the Mûrti Hills, and placed the new-born babe, Kokilân, in an underground palace, and planted the mango branch at the door, saying, ' In twelve years the mango tree will blossom; then will I return and marry Kokilân.'

And after twelve years, the mango tree began to flower, and Raja Rasâlu married the Princess Kokilân, whom he won from Sarkap when he played *chaupur* with the King.

THE KING WHO WAS FRIED

NCE upon a time, a very long time ago indeed, there lived a King who had made a vow never to eat bread or break his fast until he had given away a hundredweight of gold in charity.

So, every day, before King Karan—for that was his name—had his breakfast, the palace servants would come out with baskets and baskets of gold pieces to scatter amongst the crowds of poor folk, who, you may be sure, never forgot to be there to receive the alms.

How they used to hustle and bustle and struggle and scramble! Then, when the last golden piece had been fought for, King Karan would sit down to his breakfast, and enjoy it as a man who has kept his word should do.

Now, when people saw the King lavishing his gold in this fashion, they naturally thought that sooner or later the royal treasuries must give out, the gold come to an end, and the King—who was evidently a man of his word—die of starvation. But, though months and years passed by, every day, just a quarter of an hour before breakfast-time, the servants came out of the palace with baskets and baskets of gold; and as the crowds dispersed they could see the King sitting down to his breakfast in the royal banqueting hall, as jolly, and fat, and hungry, as could be.

Now, of course, there was some secret in all this, and this secret I shall now tell you. King Karan had made a compact with a holy and very hungry old *faqîr* who lived at the top of the hill; and the compact was this: on condition of King Karan allowing himself to be fried and eaten for breakfast every day, the *faqîr* gave him a hundredweight of pure gold.

Of course, had the *faqîr* been an ordinary sort of person, the compact would not have lasted long, for once King Karan had been fried and eaten, there would have been an end of the matter. But the *faqîr* was a very remarkable *faqîr* indeed, and when he had eaten the King, and picked the bones quite quite clean, he just put them together, said a charm or two, and, hey presto! there was King Karan as fat and jolly as ever, ready for the next morning's breakfast. In fact, the *faqîr* made *no bones at all* over the affair, which, it must be confessed, was very convenient both for the breakfast and the breakfast eater. Nevertheless, it was of course not pleasant to be popped alive every morning into a great frying-pan of boiling oil; and for my part I think King Karan earned his hundredweight of gold handsomely. But after a time he got accustomed to the process, and would go up quite cheerfully to the holy and hungry one's house, where the biggest frying-pan was spitting and sputtering over the sacred fire. Then he would just pass the time of day to the *faqîr*, to

make sure he was punctual, and step gracefully into
his hot oil bath.   My goodness! how he sizzled and
fizzled!   When he was crisp and brown, the *faqîr*
ate him, picked the bones, set them together, sang
a charm, and finished the business by bringing out
his dirty, old ragged coat, which he shook and shook,
while the bright golden pieces came tumbling out of
the pockets on to the floor.

So that was the way King Karan got his gold,
and if you think it very extraordinary, so do I!

Now, in the great Mânsarobar Lake, where, as of
course you know, all the wild swans live when they
leave us, and feed upon seed pearls, there was a
great famine.   Pearls were so scarce that one pair
of swans determined to go out into the world and
seek for food.   So they flew into King Bikramâjît's
garden, at Ujjayin.   Now, when the gardener saw
the beautiful birds, he was delighted, and, hoping to
induce them to stay, he threw them grain to eat.
But they would not touch it, nor any other food he
offered them; so he went to his master, and told
him there were a pair of swans in the garden who
refused to eat anything.

Then King Bikramâjît went out, and asked them
in birds' language (for, as every one knows, Bikramâjît understood both beasts and birds) why it was
that they ate nothing.

'We don't eat grain!' said they, 'nor fruit, nor
anything but fresh unpierced pearls!'

Whereupon King Bikramâjît, being very kind-
hearted, sent for a basket of pearls; and every day,
when he came into the garden, he fed the swans with
his own hand.

But one day, when he was feeding them as usual, one of the pearls happened to be pierced. The dainty swans found it out at once, and coming to the conclusion that King Bikramâjît's supply of pearls was running short, they made up their minds to go farther afield. So, despite his entreaties, they spread their broad white wings, and flew up into the blue sky, their outstretched necks pointing straight towards home on the great Mânsarobar Lake. Yet they were not ungrateful, for as they flew they sang the praises of Bikramâjît.

Now, King Karan was watching his servants bring out the baskets of gold, when the wild swans came flying over his head; and when he heard them singing, 'Glory to Bikramâjît! Glory to Bikramâjît!' he said to himself, 'Who is this whom even the birds praise? I let myself be fried and eaten every day in order that I may be able to give away a hundred-weight of gold in charity, yet no swan sings *my* song!'

So, being jealous, he sent for a bird-catcher, who snared the poor swans with lime, and put them in a cage.

Then Karan hung the cage in the palace, and ordered his servants to bring every kind of birds' food; but the proud swans only curved their white necks in scorn, saying, 'Glory to Bikramâjît!—he gave us pearls to eat!'

Then King Karan, determined not to be outdone, sent for pearls; but still the scornful swans would not touch anything.

'Why will ye not eat?' quoth King Karan wrathfully; 'am I not as generous as Bikramâjît?'

Then the swan's wife answered, and said, 'Kings do not imprison the innocent. Kings do not war against women. If Bikramâjît were here, he would at any rate let me go!'

So Karan, not to be outdone in generosity, let the swan's wife go, and she spread her broad white wings and flew southwards to Bikramâjît, and told him how her husband lay a prisoner at the court of King Karan.

Of course Bikramâjît, who was, as every one knows, the most generous of kings, determined to release the poor captive; and bidding the swan fly back and rejoin her mate, he put on the garb of a servant, and taking the name of Bikrû, journeyed northwards till he came to King Karan's kingdom. Then he took service with the King, and helped every day to carry out the baskets of golden pieces. He soon saw there was some secret in King Karan's endless wealth, and never rested until he had found it out. So, one day, hidden close by, he saw King Karan enter the *faqîr's* house and pop into the boiling oil. He saw him frizzle and sizzle, he saw him come out crisp and brown, he saw the hungry and holy *faqîr* pick the bones, and, finally, he saw King Karan, fat and jolly as ever, go down the mountain side with his hundredweight of gold!

Then Bikrû knew what to do! So the very next day he rose very early, and taking a carving-knife, he slashed himself all over. Next he took some pepper and salt, spices, pounded pomegranate seeds, and pea-flour; these he mixed together into a beautiful curry-stuff, and rubbed himself all over with it—right into the cuts in spite of the smarting. When he thought he was quite ready for cooking, he just went up the hill to the *faqîr's* house, and popped into the frying-pan. The *faqîr* was still asleep, but he soon awoke with the sizzling and the fizzling, and said to himself, ' Dear me! how uncommonly nice the King smells this morning ! '

Indeed, so appetising was the smell, that he could hardly wait until the King was crisp and brown, but then——oh, my goodness ! how he gobbled him up !

You see, he had been eating plain fried so long that a devilled king was quite a change. He picked the bones ever so clean, and it is my belief would have eaten them too, if he had not been afraid of killing the goose that laid the golden eggs.

Then, when it was all over, he put the King together again, and said, with tears in his eyes, ' What a breakfast that was, to be sure ! Tell me how you managed to taste so nice, and I'll give you anything you ask.'

Whereupon Bikrû told him the way it was done, and promised to devil himself every morning, if he might have the old coat in return. ' For,' said he, ' it is not pleasant to be fried ! and I don't see why I should in addition have the trouble of carrying a hundredweight of gold to the palace every day. Now, if *I* keep the coat, I can shake it down there.'

To this the *faqîr* agreed, and off went Bikrû with the coat.

Meanwhile, King Karan came toiling up the hill, and was surprised, when he entered the *faqîr's* house, to find the fire out, the frying-pan put away, and the *faqîr* himself as holy as ever, but not in the least hungry.

'Why, what is the matter?' faltered the King.

'Who are you?' asked the *faqîr*, who, to begin with, was somewhat short-sighted, and in addition felt drowsy after his heavy meal.

'Who! Why, I'm King Karan, come to be fried! Don't you want your breakfast?'

'I've. had my breakfast!' sighed the *faqîr* regretfully. 'You tasted very nice when you were devilled, I can assure you!'

'I never was devilled in my life!' shouted the King; 'you must have eaten somebody else!'

'That's just what I was saying to myself!' returned the *faqîr* sleepily; 'I thought—it couldn't—be only —the spices—that——'— —Snore, snore, snore!

'Look here!' cried King Karan, in a rage, shaking the *faqîr*, 'you must eat me too!'

'Couldn't!' nodded the holy but satisfied *faqîr*, 'really—not another morsel—no, thanks!'

'Then give me my gold!' shrieked King Karan; 'you're bound to do that, for I'm ready to fulfil my part of the contract!'

'Sorry I can't oblige, but the devil—I mean the other person—went off with the coat!' nodded the *faqîr*.

Hearing this, King Karan returned home in despair and ordered the royal treasurer to send him gold; so that day he ate his breakfast in peace.

And the next day also, by ransacking all the private treasuries, a hundredweight of gold was forthcoming; so King Karan ate his breakfast as usual, though his heart was gloomy.

But the third day, the royal treasurer arrived with empty hands, and, casting himself on the ground,

T

exclaimed, 'May it please your majesty! there is not any more gold in your majesty's domains!'

Then King Karan went solemnly to bed, without any breakfast, and the crowd, after waiting for hours expecting to see the palace doors open and the servants come out with the baskets of gold, melted away, saying it was a great shame to deceive poor folk in that way!

By dinner-time poor King Karan was visibly thinner; but he was a man of his word, and though the wily Bikrû came and tried to persuade him to eat, by saying he could not possibly be blamed, he shook his head, and turned his face to the wall.

Then Bikrû, or Bikramâjît, took the *faqîr's* old coat, and shaking it before the King, said, 'Take the money, my friend; and what is more, if you will set the wild swans you have in that cage at liberty, I will give you the coat into the bargain!'

So King Karan set the wild swans at liberty, and as the pair of them flew away to the great Mânsarobar Lake, they sang as they went, 'Glory to Bikramâjît! the generous Bikramâjît!'

Then King Karan hung his head, and said to himself, 'The swans' song is true!—Bikramâjît is more generous than I; for if I was fried for the sake of a hundredweight of gold and my breakfast, he was devilled in order to set a bird at liberty!'

ONCE upon a time there was a King who had no children, and this disappointment preyed so dreadfully upon his mind that he chose the dirtiest and most broken-down old bed he could find, and lay down on it in the beautiful palace gardens. There he lay, amid the flowers and the fruit trees, the butterflies and the birds, quite regardless of the beauties around him ;—that was his way of showing grief.

Now, as he lay thus, a holy *faqîr* passed through the garden, and seeing the King in this pitiful plight, asked him what the sorrow was which drove him to such a very dirty old bed.

'What is the use of asking?' returned the King ; but when the *faqîr* asked for the third time what the sorrow was, the King took heart of grace, and answered gloomily, 'I have no children!'

'Is that all?' said the *faqîr;* 'that is easily remedied. Here! take this stick of mine, and throw it twice into yonder mango tree. At the first throw five mangoes will fall, at the second two. So many sons you shall have, if you give each of your seven Queens a mango apiece.'

Then the King, greatly delighted, took the *faqîr's* stick and went off to the mango tree. Sure enough, at the first throw five mangoes fell, at the second, two. Still the King was not satisfied, and, determining to make the most of the opportunity, he threw the stick into the tree a third time, hoping to get more children.   But, to his surprise and consternation, the

stick remained in the tree, and the seven fallen mangoes flew back to their places, where they hung temptingly just out of reach.

There was nothing to be done but to go back to the *faqîr*, and tell him what had happened.

' That comes of being greedy ! ' retorted the *faqîr* ; ' surely seven sons are enough for anybody, and yet you were not content !   However, I will give you one more chance.   Go back to the tree ; you will find the stick upon the ground ; throw it as I bade you, and beware of disobedience, for if you do not heed me this time, you may lie on your dirty old bed till doomsday for all I care ! '

Then the King returned to the mango tree, and when the seven mangoes had fallen—the first time five, the second time two—he carried them straight into the palace, and gave them to his Queens, so as to be out of the way of temptation.

Now, as luck would have it, the youngest Queen was not in the house, so the King put her mango away in a tiny cupboard in the wall, against her return, and while it lay there a greedy little mouse came and nibbled away one half of it. Shortly afterwards, the seventh Queen came in, and seeing the other Queens just wiping their mouths, asked them what they had been eating.

'The King gave us each a mango,' they replied, 'and he put yours in the cupboard yonder.'

But, lo ! when the youngest Queen ran in haste to find her mango, half of it was gone ; nevertheless she ate the remaining half with great relish.

Now the result of this was, that when, some months afterwards, the six elder Queens each bore a son, the youngest Queen had only half-a-son—and that was what they called him at once,—just half-a-son, nothing more : he had one eye, one ear, one arm, one leg ; in fact, looked at sideways, he was as handsome a young prince as you would wish to see, but frontways it was as plain as a pikestaff that he was only half-a-prince. Still he throve and grew strong, so that when his brothers went out shooting he begged to be allowed to go out also.

'How can *you* go a-shooting?' wept his mother, who did nothing but fret because her son was but half-a-son; 'you are only half-a-boy; how can you hold your crossbow?'

'Then let me go and play at shooting,' replied

the prince, nothing daunted. 'Only give me some sweets to take with me, dear mother, as the other boys have, and I shall get on well enough.'

'How can I make sweets for half-a-son?' wept his mother; 'go and ask the other Queens to give you some.'

So he asked the other Queens, and they, to make

fun of the poor lad, who was the butt of the palace,
gave him sweets full of ashes.

Then the six whole princes, and little Half-a-son,
set off a-shooting, and when they grew tired and
hungry, they sat down to eat the sweets they had
brought with them. Now when Prince Half-a-son
put his into his half-a-mouth, lo and behold ! though
they were sweet enough outside, there was nothing
but ashes and grit inside. He was a simple-hearted
young prince, and imagining it must be a mistake,
he went to his brothers and asked for some of theirs ;
but they jeered and laughed at him.

By and by they came to a field of melons, so carefully fenced in with thorns that only one tiny gap
remained in one corner, and that was too small for
any one to creep through, except half-a-boy ; so
while the six whole princes remained outside, little
Half-a-son was feasting on the delicious melons inside, and though they begged and prayed him to
throw a few over the hedge, he only laughed, saying,
‘ Remember the sweets !—it is my turn now ! ’

When they became very importunate, he threw
over a few of the unripe and sour melons ; whereupon
his brothers became so enraged that they ran to the
owner of the field and told him that half-a-boy was
making sad havoc amongst his fruit. Then they
watched him catch poor Prince Half-a-son, who of
course could not run very fast, and tie him to a tree,
after which they went away laughing.

But Prince Half-a-son had some compensation for
being only half-a-boy, in that he possessed the
magical power of making a rope do anything he bade
it. Therefore, when he saw his brothers leaving him

in the lurch, he called out, 'Break, rope, break! my companions have gone on,' and the rope obeyed at once, leaving him free to join his brothers.

By and by they came to a plum tree, where the fruit grew far out on slender branches that would only bear the weight of half-a-boy.

'Throw us down some!' cried the whole brothers, as they saw Half-a-son with his half-mouth full.

'Remember the sweets!' retorted the prince.

This made his brothers so angry that they ran off to the owner of the tree, and telling him how half-a-boy was feasting on his plums, watched while he caught the offender and tied him to the tree. Then they ran away laughing; but Prince Half-a-son called out, 'Break, rope, break! my companions have gone on,' and before they had gone out of sight he rejoined his brothers, who could not understand how this miserable half-a-boy outwitted them.

Being determined to be revenged on him, they waited until he began to draw water from a well, where they stopped to drink, and then they pushed him in.

'That is an end of little Half-a-son!' they said to themselves, and ran away laughing.

Now in the well there lived a one-eyed demon, a pigeon, and a serpent, and when it was dark these three returned home and began to talk amongst themselves, while Prince Half-a-son, who clung to the wall like a limpet, and took up no room at all, listened and held his breath.

'What is your power, my friend?' asked the demon of the serpent. Whereupon the serpent replied, 'I have the treasures of seven kings underneath me! What is yours, my friend?'

Then the demon said conceitedly, 'The King's daughter is possessed of me. She is always ill; some day I shall kill her.'

'Ah!' said the pigeon, 'I could cure her, for no matter what the disease is, any one who eats my droppings will become well instantly.'

When dawn came, the demon, the serpent, and the pigeon each went off to his own haunt without noticing Prince Half-a-son.

Soon afterwards, a camel-driver came to draw water from the well, and let down the bucket; whereupon Prince Half-a-son caught hold of the rope and held on.

The camel-driver, feeling a heavy weight, looked down to see what it was, and when he beheld half-a-boy clinging to the rope he was so frightened that he ran clean away. But all Half-a-son had to do was to say, 'Pull, rope, pull!' and the rope wound itself up immediately.

No sooner had he reached the surface once more than he set off to the neighbouring city, and proclaimed that he was a physician come to heal the King's daughter of her dreadful disease.

'Have a care! have a care!' cried the watchmen at the gate. 'If you fail, your head will be the forfeit. Many men have tried, and what can *you* do that are but half-a-man?'

Nevertheless, Prince Half-a-son, who had some of the pigeon's droppings in his pocket, was not in the least afraid, but boldly proclaimed he was ready to accept the terms; that is to say, if he failed to cure the princess his head was to be cut off, but if he succeeded, then her hand in marriage and half the kingdom should be his reward.

'Half the kingdom will just suit me,' he said, 'see-ing that I am but half-a-man!'

And, sure enough, no sooner had the princess taken her first dose, than she immediately became quite well—her cheeks grew rosy, her eyes bright; and the King was so delighted that he gave immediate orders for the marriage. Now amongst the wedding guests were Prince Half-a-son's wicked brothers, who were ready to die of spite and envy when they discovered that the happy bridegroom was none other than their despised half-a-boy. So they went to the King, and said, 'We know this lad: he is a sweeper's son, and quite unfit to be the husband of so charming a princess!'

The king at first believed this wicked story, and ordered the poor prince to be turned out of the king-dom; but Half-a-son asked for a train of mules, and one day's respite, in order to prove who and what he was. Then he went to the well, dug up the treasures of seven kings during the serpent's absence, loaded the mules, and came back glittering with gold and jewels. He laid the treasures at the King's feet, and told the whole story,—how, through no fault of his own, he was only half-a-son, and how unkindly his brothers had behaved to him.

Then the marriage festivities went on, and the wicked brothers crept away in disgrace.

They went to the well, full of envy and covetous-ness. 'Half-a-son got rich by falling in,' they said; 'let us try if we too cannot find some treasure.' So they threw themselves into the well.

As soon as it was dark, the demon, the serpent, and the pigeon came home together. 'Some thief

has been here !' cried the pigeon, 'for my droppings
are gone ! Let us feel round, and see if he is here
still.'

So they felt round, and when they came upon the
six brothers, the demon ate them up one after another.

So that was an end of them, and Prince Half-a-
son had the best of it, in spite of his only being half-
a-boy.

THE MOTHER AND DAUGHTER WHO
WORSHIPPED THE SUN

NCE upon a time there lived a mother and a daughter who worshipped the Sun. Though they were very poor they never forgot to honour the Sun, giving everything they earned to it except two meal cakes, one of which the mother ate, while the other was the daughter's share, —every day one cake apiece ; that was all.

Now it so happened that one day, when the mother was out at work, the daughter grew hungry, and ate her cake before dinner-time. Just as she had finished it a priest came by, and begged for some bread, but there was none in the house save the mother's cake. So the daughter broke off half of it and gave it to the priest in the name of the Sun.

By and by the mother returned, very hungry, to dinner, and, lo and behold ! there was only half a cake in the house.

'Where is the remainder of the bread?' she asked.

'I ate my share, because I was hungry,' said the daughter, 'and just as I finished, a priest came a-begging, so I was obliged to give him half your cake.'

'A pretty story!' quoth the mother, in a rage. 'It is easy to be pious with other people's property! How am I to know you had eaten your cake first? I believe you gave mine in order to save your own!'

In vain the daughter protested that she really had finished her cake before the priest came a-begging,— in vain she promised to give the mother half her share on the morrow,—in vain she pleaded for forgiveness for the sake of the Sun, in whose honour she had given alms. Words were of no avail; the mother sternly bade her go about her business, saying, 'I will have no gluttons, who grudge their own meal to the great Sun, in my house!'

So the daughter wandered away homeless into the wilds, sobbing bitterly. When she had travelled a long long way, she became so tired that she could walk no longer; therefore she climbed into a big *pîpal* tree, in order to be secure from wild beasts, and rested amongst the branches.

After a time a handsome young prince, who had been chasing deer in the forest, came to the big *pîpal* tree, and, allured by its tempting shade, lay down to sleep away his fatigues. Now, as he lay there, with his face turned to the sky, he looked so beautiful that the daughter could not choose but keep her eyes upon him, and so the tears which flowed from them like a summer shower dropped soft and warm upon the young man's face, waking him with a start. Thinking it was raining, he rose to look at the sky, and see whence this sudden storm had come; but far and near not a cloud was to be seen. Still, when he returned

to his place, the drops fell faster than before, and one
of them upon his lip tasted salt as tears. So he swung
himself into the tree, to see whence the salt rain
came, and, lo and behold ! a beauteous maiden sat in
the tree, weeping.

'Whence come you, fair stranger ? ' said he ; and
she, with tears, told him she was homeless, houseless,
motherless.   Then he fell in love with her sweet face
and soft words ; so he asked her to be his bride, and
she went with him to the palace, her heart full of
gratitude to the Sun, who had sent her such good luck.

Everything she could desire was hers ; only when
the other women talked of their homes and their
mothers she held her tongue, for she was ashamed of
hers.

Every one thought she must be some great princess,
she was so lovely and magnificent, but in her heart
of hearts she knew she was nothing of the kind ; so
every day she prayed to the Sun that her mother
might not find her out.

But one day, when she was sitting alone in her
beautiful palace, her mother appeared, ragged and
poor as ever.   She had heard of her daughter's good
fortune, and had come to share it.

'And you *shall* share it,' pleaded her daughter ;
' I will give you back far more than I ever took from
you, if only you will go away and not disgrace me
before my prince.'

' Ungrateful creature ! ' stormed the mother, ' do
you forget how it was through my act that your good
fortune came to you ? If I had not sent you into
the world, where would you have found so fine a
husband ? '

'I might have starved!' wept the daughter; 'and now you come to destroy me again. O great Sun, help me now!'

Just then the prince came to the door, and the poor daughter was ready to die of shame and vexation; but when she turned to where her mother had sat, there was nothing to be seen but a golden stool, the like of which had never been seen on earth before.

'My princess,' asked the prince, astonished, 'whence comes that golden stool?'

'From my mother's house,' replied the daughter, full of gratitude to the great Sun, who had saved her from disgrace.

'Nay! if there are such wondrous things to be seen in your mother's house,' quoth the prince gaily, 'I must needs go and see it. To-morrow we will set out on our journey, and you shall show me all it contains.'

In vain the daughter put forward one pretext and another: the prince's curiosity had been aroused by the sight of the marvellous golden stool, and he was not to be gainsaid.

Then the daughter cried once more to the Sun, in her distress, saying, 'O gracious Sun, help me now!'

But no answer came, and with a heavy heart she set out next day to show the prince her mother's house. A goodly procession they made, with horsemen and footmen clothed in royal liveries surrounding the bride's palanquin, where sat the daughter, her heart sinking at every step.

And when they came within sight of where her mother's hut used to stand, lo! on the horizon showed a shining, flaming golden palace, that glittered and

glanced like solid sunshine.   Within and without all
was gold,—golden servants and a golden mother!

There they stopped, admiring the countless marvels
of the Sun palace, for three days, and when the third
was completed, the prince, more enamoured of his
bride than ever, set his face homewards ; but when he
came to the spot where he had first seen the glittering
golden palace from afar, he thought he would just
take one look more at the wondrous sight, and, lo!
there was nothing to be seen save a low thatched
hovel!

Then he turned to his bride, full of wrath, and said,
' You are a witch, and have deceived me by your detestable arts !   Confess, if you would not have me strike
you dead ! '

But the daughter fell on her knees, saying, ' My
gracious prince, I have done nothing !   I am but a
poor homeless girl.   It was the Sun that did it.'

Then she told the whole story from beginning to
end, and the prince was so well satisfied that from
that day he too worshipped the Sun.

NCE upon a time a poor Brâhman was walking along a dusty road, when he saw something sparkling on the ground. On picking it up, it turned out to be a small red stone, so, thinking it somewhat curious, the Brâhman put it into his pocket and went on his way. By and by he came to a corn-merchant's shop, at the side of the road, and being hungry he bethought himself of the red stone, and taking it out, offered it to the corn-dealer in exchange for a bite and sup, as he had no money in his pocket.

Now, for a wonder, the shopkeeper was an honest man, so, after looking at the stone, he bade the Brâhman take it to the king, for, said he, 'all the goods in my shop are not its equal in value!'

Then the Brâhman carried the stone to the king's palace, and asked to be shown into his presence. But the prime minister refused at first to admit him ; nevertheless, when the Brâhman persisted that he had something beyond price to show, he was allowed to see the king.

U

Now the snake-stone was just like a ruby, red and fiery; therefore, when the king saw it he said, 'What dost thou want for this ruby, O Brâhman?'

Then the Brâhman replied, 'Only a pound of meal to make a girdle cake, for I am hungry!'

'Nay,' said the king, 'it is worth more than that!'

So he sent for a *lâkh* of rupees from his treasury, and counted it over to the Brâhman, who went on his way rejoicing.

Then the king called his queen, and gave the jewel into her custody, with many instructions for its safe keeping, for, said he, there was not its like in the whole world. The queen, determined to be careful, wrapped it in cotton-wool, and put it away in an empty chest, locking the chest with double locks.

So there the ruby snake-stone lay for twelve long years. At the end of that time the king sent for his queen, and said, 'Bring me the ruby; I wish to satisfy myself that it is safe.'

The queen took her keys, and going to her room, opened the chest, and, lo! the ruby was gone, and in its place was a handsome stripling! She shut down the box again in a great hurry, and thought and thought what she had better do to break the news to the king.

Now as she thought, the king became impatient, and sent a servant to ask what the delay was. Then the queen bade the servant carry the box to the audience chamber, and going thither with her keys, she unlocked the chest before the king.

Out stepped the handsome stripling, to everybody's astonishment.

'Who are you?' quoth the king, 'and where is my jewel?'

'I am Ruby Prince,' returned the boy; 'more than that you cannot know.'

Then the king was angry, and drove him from the palace, but, being a just man, he first gave the boy a horse and arms, so that he might fight his way in the world.

Now, as Prince Ruby journeyed on his steed, he came to the outskirts of the town, and saw an old woman making bread, and as she mixed the flour she laughed, and as she kneaded it she cried.

'Why do you laugh and cry, mother?' quoth Prince Ruby.

'Because my son must die to-day,' returned the woman. 'There is an ogre in this town, which every day eats a young man. It is my son's turn to provide the dinner, and that is why I weep.'

Then Prince Ruby laughed at her fears, and said he would kill the ogre and set the town free; only the old woman must let him sleep a while in her house, and promise to wake him when the time came to go forth and meet the ogre.

'What good will that do to me?' quoth the old woman; 'you will only be killed, and then my son will have to go to-morrow. Sleep on, stranger, if you will, but I will not wake you!'

Then Prince Ruby laughed again. 'It is of no use, mother!' he said, 'fight the ogre I will; and as you will not wake me I must even go to the place of meeting and sleep there.'

So he rode off on his steed beyond the gates of the city, and, tying his horse to a tree he lay down to sleep peacefully.   By and by the ogre came for its dinner, but hearing no noise, and seeing no one, it thought the townspeople had failed in their bargain, and prepared to revenge itself.   But Ruby Prince jumped up, refreshed by slumber, and falling on the ogre, cut off its head and hands in a trice.   These he stuck on the gate of the town, and returning to the old woman's house, told her he had killed the ogre, and lay down to sleep again.

Now when the townspeople saw the ogre's head and hands peering over the city gate, they thought the dreadful creature had come to revenge itself for some slight.   Therefore they ran to the king in a great fright, and he, thinking the old woman, whose son was to have formed the ogre's dinner, must have played some trick, went with his officers to the place where she lived, and found her laughing and singing.

'Why do you laugh?' he asked sternly.

'I laugh because the ogre is killed!' she replied, 'and because the prince who killed it is sleeping in my house.'

Great was the astonishment at these words, yet, sure enough, when they came to examine more closely, they saw that the ogre's head and hands were those of a dead thing.

Then the king said, 'Show me this valiant prince who sleeps so soundly.'

And when he saw the handsome young stripling, he recognised him as the lad whom he had driven from the palace.   Then . he turned to his prime minister, and said, 'What reward should this youth have?'

And the prime minister answered at once, 'Your

daughter in marriage, and half your kingdom, is not
too high a reward for the service he has rendered!'

So Ruby Prince was married in great state to the
king's fair daughter, and half the kingdom was given
him to rule.

But the young bride, much as she loved her gallant
husband, was vexed because she knew not who he was,
and because the other women in the palace twitted
her with having married a stranger, a man come from
No-man's-land, whom none called brother.

So, day after day, she would ask her husband to
tell her who he was and whence he came, and every
day Ruby Prince would reply, 'Dear heart, ask me
anything but that; for that you must not know!'

Yet still the princess begged, and prayed, and wept,
and coaxed, until one day, when they were standing
by the river side, she whispered, 'If you love me, tell
me of what race you are!'

Now Ruby Prince's foot touched the water as he
replied, 'Dear heart, anything but that; for that you
must not know!'

Still the princess, imagining she saw signs of yielding in his face, said again, 'If you love me, tell me
of what race you are!'

Then Ruby Prince stood knee-deep in the water,
and his face was sad as he replied, 'Dear heart, anything but that; for that you must not know!'

Once again the wilful bride put her question, and
Ruby Prince was waist-deep in the stream.

'Dear heart, anything but that!'

'Tell me! tell me!' cried the princess, and, lo! as
she spoke, a jewelled snake with a golden crown and
ruby star reared itself from the water, and with a

sorrowful look towards her, disappeared beneath the wave.

Then the princess went home and wept bitterly, cursing her own curiosity, which had driven away her handsome, gallant young husband. She offered a reward of a bushel of gold to any one who would bring her any information about him ; yet day after day passed, and still no news came, so that the princess grew pale with weeping salt tears. At last a dancing-woman, one of those who attend the women's festivals, came to the princess, and said, ' Last night I saw a strange thing. When I was out gathering sticks, I lay down to rest under a tree, and fell asleep. When I awoke it was light, neither daylight nor moonlight ; and while I wondered, a sweeper came out from a snake-hole at the foot of the tree, and swept the ground with his broom ; then followed a water-carrier, who sprinkled the ground with water ; and after that two carpet-bearers, who spread costly rugs, and then disappeared. Even as I wondered what these preparations meant, a noise of music fell upon my ear, and from the snake-hole came forth a goodly procession of young men, glittering with jewels, and one in the midst, who seemed to be the king. Then, while the musicians played, one by one the young men rose and danced before the king. But one, who wore a red star on his forehead, danced but ill, and looked pale and wan. That is all I have to say.'

So the next night the princess went with the dancing-girl to the tree, where, hiding themselves behind the trunk, they waited to see what might happen.

Sure enough, after a while it became light that was

neither sunlight nor moonlight; then the sweeper
came forth and swept the ground, the water-carrier
sprinkled it, the carpet-bearers placed the rugs, and
last of all, to the sound of music the glittering procession swept out. How the princess's heart beat
when, in the young prince with the red star, she
recognised her dearest husband; and how it ached
when she saw how pale he was, and how little he
seemed to care to dance.

Then, when all had performed before the king,
the light went out, and the princess crept home.
Every night she would go to the tree and watch;
but all day she would weep, because she seemed no
nearer getting back her lover.

At last, one day, the dancing-girl said to her,
'O princess, I have hit upon a plan. The Snake-
king is passionately fond of dancing, and yet it is
only men who dance before him. Now, if a woman
were to do so, who knows but he might be so pleased
that he would grant her anything she asked? Let
me try!'

'Nay,' replied the princess, 'I will learn of you
and try myself.'

So the princess learnt to dance, and in an incredibly short time she far surpassed her teacher.
Never before or since was such a graceful, charming,
elegant dancer seen. Everything about her was
perfection. Then she dressed herself in finest muslins
and silver brocades, with diamonds on her veil, till
she shone and sparkled like a star.

With beating heart she hid behind the tree and
waited. The sweeper, the water-carrier, the carpet-
bearers, came forth in turn, and then the glittering

procession. Ruby Prince looked paler and sadder than ever, and when his turn came to dance, he hesitated, as if sick at heart ; but from behind the tree stepped a veiled woman, clad in white, with jewels flashing, and danced before the king. Never was there such a dance !—everybody held their breath till it was done, and then the king cried aloud, 'O unknown dancer, ask what you will, and it shall be yours !'

'Give me the man for whom I danced !' replied the princess.

The Snake-king looked very fierce, and his eyes glittered, as he said, 'You have asked something you had no right to ask, and I should kill you were it not for my promise. Take him, and begone !'

Quick as thought, the princess seized Ruby Prince by the hand, dragged him beyond the circle, and fled.

After that they lived very happily, and though the women still taunted her, the princess held her tongue, and never again asked her husband of what race he came.

NOTES TO TALES

SIR BUZZ

Sir Buzz, p. 1.—In the vernacular Mîyân Bhûngâ, which is Pânjabî for Sir Beetle or Sir Bee. The word is clearly connected with the common Aryan roots *frem, bhran, bhan, bhin*, to buzz as a bee or beetle.

Tigress, p. 2.—Not otherwise described by the narrators than as a *bhût*, which is usually a malignant ghost, but here she is rather a bene-volent fairy.

Span, p. 3, etc.—The word in the vernacular was *hâth*, the arm below the elbow, or conventionally half-a-yard, or 18 inches.

Hundredweight, p. 4, etc.—The word here is *man*, an Indian weight of about 80 lbs.

Princess Blossom, p. 6.—Bâdshâhzâdî Phûlî, Princess Flower, or Phûlâzâdî, Born-of-a-flower.

One-eyed Chief Constable, p. 9.—*Kotwâl* is the word used in the original; he is a very familiar figure in all oriental tales of Musalmân origin, and must have been one in actual medieval oriental life, as he was the chief police (if such a term can be used with propriety) officer in all cities. The expression 'one-eyed' is introduced to show his evil nature, according to the well-known saying and universal belief—

> *Kânâ, kâchrâ, hoch-gardanâ : yeh tînon kamzât !*
> *Jablag bas apnâ chale, to koî na pûchhe bat.*

> Wall-eyed, blear-eyed, wry-necked : these three are evil.
> While his own resources last none asketh them for help.

Vampire, p. 10, etc.—The word used was the Arabic *ghûl* (in English usually ghowl or ghoul), the vampire, man-devouring demon, which corresponds to the *bhût* and *pret*, the malignant ghosts of the Hindus. It may be noted here that the Persian *ghol* is the *loup-garou* of Europe, the man-devouring demon of the woods.

King Indar or Indra, p. 11.—Was originally the beneficent god of heaven, giver of rain, etc., but in the later Hindu mythology he took only second rank as ruler of the celestial beings who form the Court of Indra (*Indar kâ akhârâ* or *Indrâsan Sabhâ*), synonymous with gaiety of life and licentiousness.

THE RAT'S WEDDING

Pipkin, p. 14.—*Ghará*, the common round earthen pot of India, known to Anglo-Indians as 'chatty' (*châtí*).

Quarts of milk, p. 18.—The vernacular word was *ser*, a weight of 2 lbs. ; natives always measure liquids by weight, not by capacity.

Wild plum-tree, p. 19.—*Ber*, several trees go by this name, but the species usually meant are (1) the *Zizyphus jujuba*, which is generally a garden tree bearing large plum-like fruit : this is the *Pomum adami* of Marco Polo ; (2) the *Zizyphus nummularia*, often confounded with the camel-thorn, a valuable bush used for hedges, bearing a small edible fruit. The former is probably meant here.—See Stewart's *Punjab Plants*, pp. 43-44.

Millet, p. 20.—*Pennisetum italicum*, a very small grain.

Green plums I sell, etc., p. 20.—The words are—

> *Gaderî gader ! gaderî gader !*
> *Râjâ dî bett châhâ le giâ gher.*
>
> Green fruit ! green fruit !
> The rat has encompassed the Râjâ's daughter.

Stool, p. 21.—*Pîrhî*, a small, low, square stool with a straight upright back, used by native women.

Stewpan-lid, p. 21.—*Sarposh*, usually the iron or copper cover used to cover *degchîs* or cooking-pots.

THE FAITHFUL PRINCE

Bahrâmgor, p. 23.—This tale is a variant in a way of a popular story published in the Panjab in various forms in the vernacular, under the title of the *Story of Bahrâmgor and the Fairy Hasan Bâno*. The person meant is no doubt Bahrâmgor, the Sassanian King of Persia, known to the Greeks as Varanes V., who reigned 420-438 A.D. The modern stories, highly coloured with local folklore, represent the well-known tale in India—through the Persian—of *Bahrâmgor and Dilârâm*. Bahrâmgor was said to have been killed while hunting the wild ass (*gor*), by jumping into a pool after it, when both quarry and huntsman disappeared for ever. He is said to be the father of Persian poetry.

Demons: Demonsland, p. 24 ff.—The words used are *deo* or *dev* and *deostân*; here the *deo* is a malicious spirit by nature.

Jasdrûl, p. 25.—It is difficult to say who this can be, unless the name be a corruption of Jasrat Râî, through Râwal (*rûl*) = Râo = Râî; thus Jasrat Râî = Jasrat Râwal = Jasad Râwal = Jasadrûl. If this be the case, it stands for Daśaratha, the father of Râma Chandra, and so vicariously a great personage in Hindu story. It is obvious that in giving names to demons or fairies the name of any legendary or fabulous personage of fame will be brought under contribution.

Shâhpasand, p. 25.—This is obviously a fancy name, like its proto-type Dilârâm (Heart's Ease), and means King's Delight. The variant Hasan Bâno means the Lady of Beauty. In the Pushto version of probably the original story the name is Gulandâma = Rosa, a variant probably of the Flower Princess. See Plowden's *Translation of the Kalîd-i-Afghânî*, p. 209 ff.

Chief Constable, p. 28.—See note to Sir Buzz, *ante*.

Emerald Mountain, p. 29.—Koh-i-Zamurrad in the original. The whole story of Bahrâmgor is mixed up with the 'King of China,' and so it is possible that the legendary fame of the celebrated Green Mount in the Winter Palace at Pekin is referred to here (see Yule's *Marco Polo*, vol. i. pp. 326-327 and 330). It is much more probable, however, that the legends which are echoed here are local variants or memories of the tale of the Old Man of the Mountain and the Assassins, so famous in many a story in Europe and Asia in the Middle Ages, *e.g. The Romans of Bauduin de Sebourg*, where the lovely Ivorine is the heroine of the Red Mountain, and which has a general family likeness to this tale worth observing (see on this point generally Yule's *Marco Polo*, vol. i. pp. cxliv-cli and 132-140, and the notes to *Ind. Ant.* vol. xi. p. 285 ff.; which last, though treated as superseded here, may serve to throw light on the subject). It is evident that we are here treading on very interesting ground, alive with many memories of the East, which it would be well worth while to investigate.

Nânak Chand, p. 30.—Judging by the analogy of the name Nânaksâ (*sic*) in *Indian Fairy Tales*, pp. 114 ff. and 276, where Nânaksâ, obviously Nânak Shâh or Bâbâ Nânak, the founder of the Sikh religion, *ob.* 1538 A.D., is turned into a wonder-working *faqîr* of the ordinary sort, it is a fair guess to say that this name is meant for him too.

Safed, p. 31.—On the whole it is worth while hazarding that this name is a corruption, or rather, an adaptation to a common word—*safed*, white—of the name Saifûr for the demon in the older legends of Bahrâmgor. If so, it occurs there in connection with the universal oriental name Faghfûr, for the Emperor of China. Yule, *Marco Polo*, vol. ii. p. 110, points out that Faghfûr = Baghbûr = Bagh Pûr, a

Persian translation of the Chinese title Tien-tse, Son of Heaven, just as the name or title Shâh Pûr = the Son of the King. Perhaps this Saifûr in the same way = Shâh Pûr. But see note in *Ind. Ant.* vol. xi. p. 288.

Antimony, p. 31.—Black sulphuret of antimony, used for pencilling the eyes and beautifying them. There are two preparations for darkening the eyes—*surma* and *kâjal*. *Kâjal* is fine lamp-black, but the difference between its use and that of *surma* is that the former is used for making a blot to avoid the evil eye (*nazar*) and the latter merely as a beautifier.

Yech-cap, p. 31.—For a detailed account of the *yech* or *yâch* of Kashmîr see *Ind. Ant.* vol. xi. pp. 260-261 and footnotes. Shortly, it is a humorous though powerful sprite in the shape of an animal smaller than a cat, of a dark colour, with a white cap on its head. The feet are so small as to be almost invisible. When in this shape it has a peculiar cry—*chot, chot, chû-û-ot, chot*. All this probably refers to some night animal of the squirrel (? civet cat) tribe. It can assume any shape, and, if its white cap can be got possession of, it becomes the servant of the possessor. The cap renders the human wearer invisible. Mythologically speaking, the *yech* is the descendant of the classical Hindu *yaksha*, usually described as an inoffensive, harmless sprite, but also as a malignant imp.

The farther you climb the higher it grows, p. 32.—This is evidently borrowed from the common phenomenon of ridge beyond ridge, each in turn deceiving the climber into the belief that he has reached the top.

THE BEAR'S BAD BARGAIN

Khichrî, p. 36.—A dish of rice and pulse (*dâl*).

The weights the bear carries.—These are palpable exaggerations; thus in India the regulation camel-load is under 3 cwts., but they will carry up to 5 cwts. A strong hill-man in the Himâlayas will carry ½ cwt., and on occasion almost a whole cwt. up the hill.

PRINCE LIONHEART

Lionheart, p. 42.—The full vernacular title of this Prince was Sherdil Shahryâr Shahrâbâd, Lionheart, the Friend and Restorer of the City. All these names are common titles of oriental monarchs.

Knifegrinder, Blacksmith, Carpenter, p. 43.—In the vernacular *sânwâlâ, lohâr, tarkhân*. The first in the East, like his brother in the West, is an itinerant journeyman, who wanders about with a wheel for grinding.

Demon, p. 43.—Here *bhût*, a malignant ghost or vampire, but as his doings in the tale correspond more to those of a *deo*, demon, than of a *bhût*, the word has been translated by 'demon.'

Pipal, p. 44.—Constantly occurring in folk-tales, is the *Ficus religiosa* of botanists, and a large fig-tree much valued for its shade. It is sacred to Hindus, and never cut by them. One reason perhaps may be that its shade is very valuable and its wood valueless. Its leaves are used in divination to find out witches, thieves, liars, etc., and it is the chosen haunt of ghosts and hobgoblins of all sorts—hence its frequent appearance in folk-lore.

Mannikin, p. 44.—The word used was the ordinary expression *maddhrâ*, Panjâbî for a dwarf or pigmy.

Ghost, p. 47.—*Chuṛel*, properly the ghost of a woman who dies in childbirth. The belief in these malignant spirits is universal, and a source of much terror to natives by night. Their personal appearance is fairly described in the text : very ugly and black, breastless, protruding in stomach and navel, and feet turned back. This last is the real test of a *chuṛel*, even in her beautiful transformation. A detailed account of the *chuṛel* and beliefs in her and the methods of exorcism will be found in the *Calcutta Review*, No. cliii. p. 180 ff.

Jinn, p. 51.—A Muhammadan spirit, properly neither man, angel, nor devil, but superhuman. According to correct Muhammadan tradition, there are five classes of *Jinns* worth noting here for information—Jânn, Jinn, Shaitân, 'Ifrît, and Mârid. They are all mentioned in Musalmân folk-tales, and but seldom distinguished in annotations. In genuine Indian folk-tales, however, the character ascribed to the Jinn, as here, has been borrowed from the Râkshasa, which is Hindu in origin, and an ogre in every sense of the European word.

Smell of a man, p. 51.—The expression used is always in the vernacular *mânushgandh*, *i.e.* man-smell. The direct Sanskrit descent of the compound is worthy of remark.

Starling, p. 52.—*Mainâ :* the *Gracula religiosa*, a talking bird, much valued, and held sacred. It very frequently appears in folk-tales, like the parrot, probably from being so often domesticated by people of means and position for its talking qualities.

Cup, p. 54.—*Donâ*, a cup made of leaves, used by the very poor as a receptacle for food.

Wise woman, p. 54.—*Kuṭnî* and *paphe-kuṭnî* were the words used, of which perhaps 'wise woman' is the best rendering. *Kuṭnî* is always a term of abuse and reproach, and is used in the sense of witch or wise woman, but the bearers do not seem to possess, as a rule, any supernatural powers. Hag, harridan, or any similar term will usually correctly render the word.

Flying palanquin, p. 59.—The words used for this were indifferently *ḍolâ*, a bridal palanquin, and *burj*, a common word for a balloon.

THE LAMBIKIN

Lambikin, p. 61.—The words used were Panjâbî, *lelâ*, *leṛâ*, *lekṛâ*, and *lelkaṛâ*, a small or young lamb.

Lambikin's Songs, pp. 61, 63.—Of the first the words were Panjâbî—

> *Nânî kol jâwângâ :*
> *Moṭâ tâjâ âwângâ*
> *Pher tûṅ main nûṅ khâwângâ.*

Of the second song—

> *Waṅ piâ lelkaṛâ : waṅ pî tû.*
> *Chal ḍhamkiriâ ! Ḍham ! Kâ ! Ḍhû !*

These the rhymes render exactly. The words *ḍham*, *kâ*, *ḍhû* are pronounced sharply, so as to imitate the beats on a drum.

Drumikin, p. 62.—The *ḍhamkîriâ* or *ḍhamkîrî* in Panjâbî is a small drum made by stretching leather across a wide-mouthed earthen cup (*piyâlâ*). The Jaṭṭs make it of a piece of hollow wood, 6 inches by 3 inches, with its ends covered with leather.

BOPOLUCHI

Bopolûchî, p. 65.—Means Trickster.

Uncle: uncle-in-law, p. 65.—The words used were *mâmû*, mother's brother, and *patiauhrâ*, husband's (or father-in-law's) younger brother.

Pedlar, p. 65.—*Wanjârâ* or *banjârâ* (from *wanaj* or *banaj*, a bargain), a class of wandering pedlars who sell spices, etc.

Robber, p. 66.—The word used was *thag*, *lit.* a deceiver. The *Thags* are a class but too well known in India as those who make their living by deceiving and strangling travellers. Meadows Taylor's somewhat sensational book, *The Confessions of a Thug*, has made their doings familiar enough, too, in England. In the Indian Penal Code a *thag* is defined as a person habitually associated with others for the purpose of committing robbery or child-stealing by means of murder.

Crow's, etc., verses, pp. 66, 67.—The original words were—

> *Bopo Lûchî !*
> *Aqloṅ ghuṭhî,*
> *Thag nâl thagî gaî.*

> Bopo Lûchî !
> You have lost your wits,
> And have been deceived by a *thag*.

Bridal scarlet, p. 68.—Every Panjâbî bride, however poor, wears a dress of scarlet and gold for six months, and if rich, for two years.

PRINCESS AUBERGINE

Princess Aubergine, p. 71.—The vernacular name for the story is *Baingan Bâdshâhzâdî*. The *Baingan, baigan, begun,* or *bhântâ* is the *Solanum melongena, i.e.* the egg-plant, or *aubergine*. Europeans in India know it by the name of *brinjâl;* it is a very common and popular vegetable in the rains.

Exchanging veils, p. 73.—To exchange veils among women, and to exchange turbans among men, is a common way of swearing friendship among Panjâbîs. The women also drink milk out of the same cup on such occasions.

Nine-lakh necklace, p. 75.—The introduction of the *Nau-lakkhâ hâr*, or nine-*lakh* necklace, is a favourite incident in Indian folk-tales. *Nau-lakkhâ* means worth nine lâkhs, or nine hundred thousand rupees. Frequently magic powers are ascribed to this necklace, but the term *nau-lakkhâ* has come also to be often used conventionally for 'very valuable,' and so is applied to gardens, palaces, etc. Probably all rich Râjâs have a hankering to really possess such a necklace, and the last Mahârâjâ of Patiâlâ, about fifteen years ago, bought a real one of huge diamonds, including the Sansy, for Rupees 900,000. It is on show always at the palace in the fort at Patiâlâ.

VALIANT VICKY

Valiant Vicky, the Brave Weaver, pp. 80, 81.—In the original the title is 'Fatteh Khân, the valiant weaver.' Victor Prince is a very fair translation of the name Fatteh Khân. The original says his nickname or familiar name was Fattû, which would answer exactly to Vicky for Victor. Fattû is a familiar (diminutive form) of the full name Fatteh Khân. See *Proper Names of Panjâbîs, passim,* for the explanation of this.

THE SON OF SEVEN MOTHERS

For a long and interesting variant of this tale see *Indian Antiquary*, vol. x. p. 151 ff.

Fakîr, p. 89.—Properly *faqîr*, is a Muhammadan devotee, but in modern India the term is used for any kind of holy man, whatever be his religion. For instance, the 'Salvation Army' were styled at Lahore, at a meeting of natives, by a Sikh gentleman of standing, as *Vilâyatî fuqrâ*, European *faqîrs*. The power of granting children to barren women is ascribed in story to all saints and holy personages of fame.

Witch, p. 94.—The word used was *ḍâyan*. In the Panjâb a woman with the evil eye (which by the way is not necessarily in India possessed by the wicked only, see *Panjab Notes and Queries*, 1883-84, *passim*), who knows the *ḍâyan kâ mantar*, or charm for destroying life by taking out the heart. The word in its various modern forms is derived from the classical *ḍâkinî*, the female demon attendant on Kâlî, the goddess of destruction.

Jôgi's wonderful cow, p. 96.—The *jôgi* is a Hindu ascetic, but like the word *faqîr*, *jôgi* is often used for any kind of holy man, as here. Supernatural powers are very commonly ascribed to them, as well as the universal attribute of granting sons. Classically the *yôgi* is the devotee seeking *yoga*, the union of the living with the sublime soul. The wonderful cow is the modern fabulously productive cow *Kâmdhain*, representing the classical *Kâmdhenu*, the cow of Indra that granted all desires. Hence, probably, the dragging in here of Indra for the master of the *jôgi* of the tale. *Kâmdhain* and *Kâmdhenu* are both common terms to the present day for cows that give a large quantity of milk.

Eighteen thousand demons, p. 96.—No doubt the modern representatives—the specific number given being, as is often the case, merely conventionally—of the guards of Indra, who were in ancient days the *Maruts* or Winds, and are in modern times his Court. See note on p. 300 *ante*.

THE SPARROW AND THE CROW

The Song, p. 102 ff.—The form of words in the original is important. The following gives the variants and the strict translation—

> *Tû Chhappaṛ Dâs,*
> *Main Kâng Dâs,*
> *Deo paneriyâ,*
> *Dhoven chucheriyâ,*
> *Khâwen khijeriyâ,*
> *Dekh chiṛiyâ kâ chûchlâ,*
> *Main kâng sapariyâ.*

> You are Mr. Tank,
> I am Mr. Crow,
> Give me water,
> That I may wash my beak,
> And eat my *khichṛî*,
> See the bird's playfulness,
> I am a clean crow.

Tû Lohâr Dâs,
Main Kâng Dâs,
Tû deo phaṛwâ,
Main khodûn ghasarwâ,
Khilâwen bhainsarwâ,
Chowen dûdharwâ,
Pilâwen hirnarwâ,
Toṛen singarwâ,
Khôden chalarwâ,
Nikâlen panarwâ,
Dhoven chunjarwâ,
Khâwen khijarwâ,
Dehk chiṛiyâ kâ chûchlâ,
Main kâng saparwâ.

You are Mr. Blacksmith,
I am Mr. Crow,
You give me a spade,
And I will dig the grass,
That I may give it the buffalo to eat,
And take her milk, ·
And give it the deer to drink,
And break his horn,
And dig the hole,
And take out the water,
And wash my beak,
And eat my *khichṛi*,
See the bird's playfulness,
I am a clean crow.

THE BRAHMAN AND THE TIGER

The Tiger, the Brâhman, and the Jackal, p. 107 ff.—A very common and popular Indian tale. Under various forms it is to be found in most collections. Variants exist in the *Bhâgavata Purâṇa* and the *Gul Bakâolî,* and in the *Amvâr-i-Suhelî.* A variant is also given in the *Indian Antiquary,* vol. xii. p. 177.

Buffalo's complaint, p. 108.—The work of the buffalo in the oil-press is the synonym all India over—and with good reason—for hard and thankless toil for another's benefit.

As miserable as a fish out of water, p. 109.—In the original the allusion is to a well-known proverb—*mandâ hâl wâng Jaṭṭ jhaṛî de*—as miserable as a Jaṭṭ in a shower. Any one who has seen the appearance of the Panjâbî cultivator attempting to go to his fields on a wet, bleak February morning, with his scant clothing sticking to his limp and shivering figure, while the biting wind blows through him, will well understand the force of the proverb.

THE KING OF THE CROCODILES

King of the Crocodiles, p. 111.—In the original the title is *Bâdshâh Ghariâl.*

Lying amid the crops, p. 111.—It is commonly said in the Panjâb that crocodiles do so.

Demons of crocodiles, p. 112.—The word used for *demon* here was *jinn*, which is remarkable in this connection.

Henna, p. 113.—*Mehndî* or *hinâ* is the *Lawsonia alba*, used for staining the finger and toe nails of the bride red. The ceremony of *sanchit*, or conveying the *henna* to the bride by a party of the bride's friends, is the one alluded to.

LITTLE ANKLEBONE

Little Anklebone, p. 118 ff.—This tale appears to be unique among Indian folk-tales, and is comparable with Grimm's Singing Bone. It is current in the *Bâr* or wilds of the Gujrânwâlâ District, among the cattle-drovers' children. Wolves are very common there, and the story seems to point to a belief in some invisible shepherd, a sort of Spirit of the Bâr, whose pipe may be heard. The word used for 'Little Anklebone' was *Gîrî*, a diminutive form of the common word *giṭṭâ*. In the course of the story in the original, Little Anklebone calls himself Giṭeṭâ Râm, an interesting instance of the process of the formation of Panjâbî proper names.

Auntie, p. 118.—*Mâsî*, maternal aunt.

Tree that weeps over yonder pond, p. 119.—*Ban, i.e. Salvadora oleoides*, a common tree of the Panjâb forests.

Jackal howled, p. 119.—A common evil omen.

Marble basins, p. 120.—The word used was *daurâ*, a wide-mouthed earthen vessel, and also in palaces a marble drinking-trough for animals.

The verses, p. 122.—The original and literal translation are as follows—

> *Kyûṅ garjâe badalâ garkanâe ?*
> *Gaj karak sâre des ;*
> *Ohnâṅ hirnîâṅ de than pasmâe :*
> *Giṭeṭâ Râm gîâ pardes !*

Why echo, O thundering clouds?
Roar and echo through all the land ;
The teats of the does yonder are full of milk :
Giṭeṭâ Râm has gone abroad !

THE CLOSE ALLIANCE

Providence, p. 123.—*Khudâ* and *Allah* were the words for Providence or God in this tale, it being a Muhammadan one.

Kabâbs, p. 124.—Small pieces of meat roasted or fried on skewers with onions and eggs : a favourite Muhammadan dish throughout the East.

His own jackal, p. 127.—From time immemorial the tiger has been supposed to be accompanied by a jackal who shows him his game and gets the leavings as his wages. Hence the Sanskrit title of *vyâghra-nâyaka* or tiger-leader for the jackal.

Pigtail, p. 127.—The Kashmîrî woman's hair is drawn to the back of the head and finely braided. The braids are then gathered together and, being mixed with coarse woollen thread, are worked into a very long plait terminated by a thick tassel, which reaches almost down to the ankles. It is highly suggestive of the Chinese pigtail, but it is far more graceful.

THE TWO BROTHERS

Barley meal instead of wheaten cakes, p. 129.—*Jau kî rofi*, barley bread, is the poor man's food, as opposed to *gihûn kî rofi*, wheaten bread, the rich man's food. Barley bread is apt to produce flatulence.

With empty stomachs, etc., p. 130.—The saying is well known and runs thus—

> *Kahîn mat jâo khâlî pef.*
> *Hove mâgh yâ hove jefh.*

Go nowhere on an empty stomach,
Be it winter or be it summer.

Very necessary and salutary advice in a feverish country like India.

If any man eats me, etc., p. 130.—Apparent allusion to the saying rendered in the following verse—

> *Jo nar totâ mârkar khâve per ke heth,*
> *Kuchh sansâ man na dhare, woh hogâ râjâ jefh.*
> *Jo mainâ ko mâr khâ, man men rakhe dhîr ;*
> *Kuchh chintâ man na kare, woh sadâ rahegâ wazîr.*

Who kills a parrot and eats him under a tree,
Should have no doubt in his mind, he will be a great king.
Who kills and eats a starling, let him be patient :
Let him not be troubled in his mind, he will be minister for life.

Snake-demon, p. 131.—The word was *isdâr*, which represents the Persian *izhdahâ*, *izhdâr*, or *izhdar*, a large serpent, python.

Sacred elephant, p. 131.—The reference here is to the legend of the *safed hâthî* or *dhaulâ gaj*, the white elephant. He is the elephant-headed God Ganeśa, and as such is, or rather was formerly, kept by Râjâs as a pet, and fed to surfeit every Tuesday (*Mangalwâr*) with sweet cakes (*chûrîs*). After which he was taught to go down on his knees to the Râjâ and swing his trunk to and fro, and this was taken as sign that he acknowledged his royalty. He was never ridden except occasionally by the Râjâ himself. Two sayings, common to the present day, illustrate these ideas—' *Woh to Mahârâjâ hai, dhaule gaj par sowâr:* he is indeed king, for he rides the white elephant.' And ' *Mahârâjâ dhaulâ gajpati ki dohâî:* (I claim the) protection of the great king, the lord of the white elephant.' The idea appears to be a very old one, for Ælian (*Hist. Anim.* vol. iii. p. 46), quoting Megasthenes, mentions the white elephant. See M'Crindle, *India as described by Megasthenes and Arrian*, pp. 118, 119; *Indian Antiquary*, vol. vi. p. 333 and footnote.

Brass drinking bowl, p. 133.—The *lotâ*, universal throughout India.

Ogre, p. 135 ff.—In the original *râkhas* = the Sanskṛit *râkshasa*, translated ogre advisedly for the following reasons:—The *râkshasa* (*râkshas*, an injury) is universal in Hindu mythology as a superhuman malignant fiend inimical to man, on whom he preys, and that is his character, too, throughout Indian folk-tales. He is elaborately described in many an orthodox legend, but very little reading between the lines in these shows him to have been an alien enemy on the borders of Aryan tribes. The really human character of the *râkshasa* is abundantly evident from the stories about him and his doings. He occupies almost exactly the position in Indian tales that the ogre does in European story, and for the same reason, as he represents the memory of the savage tribes along the old Aryan borders. The ogre, no doubt, is the Uighur Tâtar magnified by fear into a malignant demon. For the *râkshasa* see the *Dictionaries* of Dowson, Garrett, and Monier Williams, *in verbo;* Muir's *Sanskrit Texts*, vol. ii. p. 420, etc. : and for the ogre see *Panjab Notes and Queries*, vol. i., *in verbo*.

Goat, p. 135.—The ogre's eating a goat is curious : *cf.* the Sanskṛit name *ajagara*, goat-eater, for the python (nowadays *ajgar*), which corresponds to the *izhdahâ* or serpent-demon on p. 131.

THE JACKAL AND THE LIZARD.

The verses, p. 144 ff.—In the original they are—

> *Chândî dâ merâ chauntrâ, kot sonâ lipâî!*
> *Kâne men merâ gâkrû, shâhzâdâ baithâ hai!*

My platform is of silver, plastered with gold !
Jewels are in my ears, I sit here a prince !

The verses, p. 146.—In the original they are —

Hadt dâ terâ chauntrâ, kot gobar lipât !
Kâne men tert jûtt ; kot gîdar baithâ hai !

Thy platform is of bones, plastered with cow-dung !
Shoes are in thy ears ; some jackal sits there !

THE SPARROW'S MISFORTUNE

Verses, p. 149.—In the original these are—

Saukan rangan men charhf,
Main bht rangan men part,

My co-wife got dyed,
I too fell into the vat.

Verses, p. 150.—In the original—

Ik sart, ik balt ;
Ik hinak mode charhf,

One is vexed and one grieved ;
And one is carried laughing on the shoulder.

The allusion here is to a common tale. The story goes that a man
who had two wives wanted to cross a river. Both wives wanted to go
across first with him, so in the end, leaving the elder to walk, he took the
younger on his shoulder, who mocked the elder with the words—

Ik sart, dût balt ;
Dût jât mûnde charhf.

First she was vexed, next she grieved ;
While the other went across on the shoulder.

Hence the sting of the old sparrow's taunt.

Verses, p. 157.—In the original—

Ik chamkhat hût ;
Chirt rangan charhf ;
Chirâ bedan kart ;
Pípal patte jhart ;
Mahtn sing jhart ;
Natn baht khârt ;
Koïl hût kânt ;
Bhagtû dîwânt ;

Bandî padnî ;
Rânî nâchnî ;
Putr dholkî bajânî ;
Râjâ sargî bajânî ;

One hen painted,
And the other was dyed,
And the cock loved her,
So the *pîpal* shed its leaves,
And the buffalo her horns,
So the river became salt,
And the cuckoo lost an eye,
So Bhagtû went mad,
And the maid took to swearing,
So the Queen took to dancing,
And the Prince took to drumming,
And the King took to thrumming.

THE PRINCESS PEPPERINA

Princess Pepperina, p. 159.—In the original *Shâhzâdî Mirchâ* or *Filfil Shâhzâdî : mirch* is the *Capsicum annuum* or common chilli, green and red.

Sheldrakes, p. 165.—The *chakwâ*, male, and *chakwî*, female, is the ruddy goose or sheldrake, known to Europeans as the Brâhmanî duck, *Anas casarca* or *Casarca rutila*. It is found all over India in the winter, and its plaintive night cry has given rise to a very pretty legend. Two lovers are said to have been for some indiscretion turned into Brâhmanî ducks, and condemned to pass the night apart from each other, on the opposite sides of a river. All night long each asks the other in turn if it shall join its mate, and the answer is always 'no.' The words supposed to be said are—

Chakwâ, main âwân?   Nâ, Chakwî !
Chakwî, main âwân?   Nâ, Chakwâ !

Chakwâ, shall I come?   No, Chakwî !
Chakwî, shall I come?   No, Chakwâ !

PEASIE AND BEANSIE

Peasie and Beansie, p. 167.—In the original Moṭho and Mûngo. *Moṭho* is a vetch, *Phaseolus aconitifolius ;* and *mûng* is a variety of pulse, *Phaseolus mungo.* Peasie and Beansie are very fair translations of the above.

Plum-tree, p. 167.—*Ber, Zizyphus jujuba.*

THE SNAKE-WOMAN

King' Ali Mardân, p. 178.—'Ali Mardân Khân belongs to modern history, having been Governor (not King, as the tale has it) of Kashmîr, under the Emperor Shâh Jahân, about A.D. 1650, and very famous in India in many ways. He was one of the most magnificent governors Kashmîr ever had, and is now the best-remembered.

Snake-Woman, p. 178.—In the original *Lamiâ*, said in Kashmîr to be a snake 200 years old, and to possess the power of becoming a woman. In India, especially in the hill districts, it is called *Yahawwâ*. In this tale the *Lamiâ* is described as being a *Wâsdeo*, a mythical serpent. *Wâsdeo* is the same as Vâsudeva, a descendant of Vasudeva. Vasudeva was the earthly father of Krishṇa and of his elder brother Balarâma, so Balarâma was a Vâsudeva. Balarâma in the classics is constantly mixed up with Sêsha (now Sesh Nâg), a king of serpents, and with Vâsuki (Bâsak Nâg), also a king of serpents ; while Ananta, the infinite, the serpent whose legend combines that of Vâsuki and Sêsha, is mixed not only with Balarâma, but also with Krishṇa. Hence the name Wâsdeo for a serpent. The Lamiâ is not only known in India from ancient times to the present day, but also in Tibet and Central Asia generally, and in Europe from ancient to mediæval times, and always as a malignant supernatural being. For discussions on her, see notes to the above in the *Indian Antiquary*, vol. xi. pp. 230-232, and the discussion following, entitled 'Lamiâ or Λάμια,' pp. 232-235. Also Comparetti's *Researches into the Book of Sindibâd*, Folklore Society's ed., *passim*.

Dal Lake, p. 178.—The celebrated lake at Srinagar in Kashmîr.

Emperor of China's Handmaiden, p. 178.—A common way of explaining the origin of unknown girls in Musalmân tales. Kashmîr is essentially a Musalmân country.

Shâlimâr gardens, p. 178.—At Srinagar, made by the Emperor Jahângîr, who preceded 'Ali Mardân Khân by a generation, for Nûr Mahal. Moore, *Lalla Rookh*, transcribes in describing them the well-known Persian verses in the Dîwân-i-Khâs (Hall of Private Audience) at Delhî and elsewhere—

'And oh ! if there be an Elysium on earth,
It is this, it is this.'

The verses run really thus—

Agar firdûs ba rû-e-zamîn ast,
Hamîn ast o hamîn ast o hamîn ast !

If there be an Elysium on the face of the earth,
It is here, and it is here, and it is here !

Shâh Jahân built the Shâlimâr gardens at Lahor, in imitation of those at Srinagar, and afterwards Ranjît Singh restored them.   They are on the Amritsar Road.

Gangâbal, p. 179.—A holy lake on the top of Mount Harâmukh, 16,905 feet, in the north of Kashmîr.   It is one of the sources of the Jhelam River, and the scene of an annual fair about 20th August.

Khichṛî, p. 181.—Sweet *khichṛî* consists of rice, sugar, cocoa-nut, raisins, cardamoms, and aniseed ; salt *khichṛî* of pulse and rice.

The stone in the ashes, p. 184.—The *pâras,* in Saṅskṛit *sparśamani,* the stone that turns what it touches into gold.

Attock, p. 184.—In the original it is the Aṭak River (the Indus) near Hotî Mardân, which place is near Aṭak or Attock.   The similarity in the names 'Ali Mardân and Hotî Mardân probably gave rise to this statement.   They have no connection whatever.

THE WONDERFUL RING

The Wonderful Ring, p. 185.—In the vernacular *'ajab mundrâ :* a variant of the inexhaustible box.

Holy place, p. 188.—*Chaunkâ,* a square place plastered with cow-dung, used by Hindus when cooking or worshipping.   The cow-dung sanctifies and purifies it.

Aunt, p. 191.—*Mâsî,* maternal aunt.

THE JACKAL AND THE PEA-HEN

Plums, p. 195.—*Ber, Zyziphus jujuba.*

THE GRAIN OF CORN

The verses, p. 201.—In the original they were—

> *Phir gîâ billî ke pâs,*
> *' Billî, rî billî, mûsâ khâogî ?*
> *Khâṭṭ khûṇḍ pâṛ nâ !*
> *Khûṇḍ chanâ de nâ !*
> *Râjâ khâṭṭ ḍaṇḍe nâ !*
> *Râjâ rânî russe nâ !*
> *Sapnâ rânî ḍase nâ !*
> *Lâṭhî sapnâ mâre nâ !*
> *Âg lâṭhî jalâve nâ !*
> *Samundar âg bujhâve nâ !*
> *Hâthî samundar sukhe nâ !*
> *Nâṛe hâṭhî bandhe nâ !*
> *Mûsâ nâṛe kâṭe nâ !*
> *Lûngâ phir choṛûn nâ !'*

He then went to the cat (saying),
' Cat, cat, eat mouse.
Woodman won't cut tree !
Tree won't give peas !
King won't beat woodman !
Queen won't storm at king !
Snake won't bite queen !
Stick won't beat snake !
Fire won't burn stick !
Sea won't quench fire !
Elephant won't drink up sea !
Thong won't bind elephant !
Mouse won't nip thong !
I'll take (the pea) yet, I won't let it go !'

It will be seen that in the text the order has been transposed for obvious literary convenience.

Verses, p. 202.—In the original these are—

Usne kahâ, ' Lap, lap, khâûngî !'

Phir gîâ mûsâ ke pâs, ' Mûsâ, re mûsâ, ab khâ jâoge ?' ' Ham bhî nâre katenge.'

Phir gîâ nâre ke pâs, ' Nâre, re nâre, ab kâte jâoge ?' 'Ham bhî hâthî bandhenge.'

Phir gîâ hâthî ke pâs, ' Hâthî, re hâthî, ab bandhe jâoge ?' ' Ham bhî samundar sûkhenge.'

Phir gîâ samundar ke pâs, ' Samundar, re samundar, ab sukhe jâoge ?' ' Ham bhî âg bujhâenge.'

Phir gîâ âg ke pâs, ' Âg, rî âg, ab bujhât jâogî ?' ' Ham bhî lâthî jalâvenge.'

Phir gîâ lâthî ke pâs, ' Lâthî, re lâthî, ab jal jâoge ?' ' Ham bhî sâmp mârenge.'

Phir gîâ samp ke pâs, ' Sâmp, re sâmp, ab mâre jâoge ?' ' Ham bhî rânî dasenge ?'

Phir gîâ rânî ke pâs, ' Rânî, rî rânî, ab dasî jâoge ?' ' Ham bhî râjâ rusenge.'

Phir gîâ râjâ ke pâs, ' Râjâ, re râjâ, ab rânî rus jâoge ?' ' Ham bhî khâtî dandenge.'

Phir gîâ khâtî ke pâs, ' Khâtî, re khâtî, ab dande jâoge ?' 'Ham bhî khund kâtenge.'

Phir gîâ khund ke pâs, ' Khund, re khund, ab kâte jâoge ?' ' Ham bhî chanâ denge.'

Phir woh chanâ lekar chalâ gîâ ?

The cat said, ' I will eat him up at once ! '

(So) he went to the mouse, 'Mouse, mouse, will you be eaten?' 'I will gnaw the thong.'

He went to the thong, 'Thong, thong, will you be gnawed?' 'I will bind the elephant.'

He went to the elephant, 'Elephant, elephant, will you be bound?' 'I will drink up the ocean.'

He went to the ocean, 'Ocean, ocean, will you be drunk up?' 'I will quench the fire.'

He went to the fire, 'Fire, fire, will you be quenched?' 'I will burn the stick.'

He went to the stick, 'Stick, stick, will you be burnt?' 'I will beat the snake.'

He went to the snake, 'Snake, snake, will you be beaten?' 'I will bite the queen.'

He went to the queen, 'Queen, queen, will you be bitten?' 'I will storm at the king.'

He went to the king, 'King, king, will you be stormed at by the queen?' 'I will beat the woodman.'

He went to the woodman, 'Woodman, woodman, will you be beaten?' 'I will cut down the trunk.'

He went to the trunk, 'Trunk, trunk, will you be cut down?' 'I will give you the pea.'

So he got the pea and went away.

THE FARMER AND THE MONEY-LENDER

Money-lender, p. 203.—*Lâlâ*, a disreputable tradesman, a sharp practitioner.

Râm, p. 203.—Râma Chandra, now 'God' *par excellence*.

Conch, p. 204.—*Sankh*, the shell used in Hindu worship for blowing upon.

THE LORD OF DEATH

Lord of Death, p. 207.—*Maliku'l-maut* is the Muhammadan form of the name, *Kâl* is the Hindu form. The belief is that every living being has attached to him a 'Lord of Death.' He is represented in the 'passion plays' so common at the Dasahrâ and other festivals by a hunchbacked dwarf, quite black, with scarlet lips, fastened to a 'keeper' by a black chain and twirling about a black wand. The idea is that until this chain is loosened or broken the life which he is to kill is safe. The notion is probably of Hindu origin. For a note on the subject see *Indian Antiquary*, vol. x. pp. 289, 290.

THE WRESTLERS

The Wrestlers, p. 211.—The story seems to be common all over India. In the *Indian Antiquary,* vol. x. p. 230, it is suggested that it represents some aboriginal account of the creation.

Ten thousand pounds weight, p. 211.—In the original 160 *mans,* which weigh over 13,000 lbs.

GWASHBRARI

Gwâshbrârî, etc., p. 216 ff.—The Westarwân range is the longest spur into the valley of Kashmîr. The remarkably clear tilt of the strata probably suggested this fanciful and poetical legend. All the mountains mentioned in the tale are prominent peaks in Kashmîr, and belong to what Cunningham (*Ladâk,* 1854, ch. iii.) calls the Pîr Panjâl and Mid-Himâlayan Range. Nangâ Parbat, 26,829 ft., is to the N.W. ; Harâ Mukh, 16,905 ft., to the N. ; Gwâshbrârî or Kolahoî, 17,839 ft., to the N.E. Westarwân is a long ridge running N.W. to S.E., between Khrû and Sotûr, right into the Kashmîr valley. Khrû is not far from Srinagar, to the S.E.

Lay at Gwâshbrârî's feet, his head upon her heart, p. 219.—As a matter of fact, Westarwân does not lay his head anywhere near Gwâshbrârî's feet, though he would appear to do so from Khrû, at which place the legend probably arose. An excellent account of the country between Khrû and Sesh Nâg, traversing most of that lying between Westarwân and Gwâshbrârî, by the late Colonel Cuppage, is to be found at pp. 206-221 of Ince's *Kashmîr Handbook,* 3rd ed., 1876.

THE BARBER'S CLEVER WIFE

Hornets' nest, p. 224.—Properly speaking, bees. This species makes a so-called nest, *i.e.* a honey-comb hanging from the branch of a tree, usually a *pîpal,* over which the insects crawl and jostle each other in myriads in the open air. When roused, and any accident may do this, they become dangerous enemies, and will attack and sting to death any animal near. They form a real danger in the Central Indian jungles, and authentic cases in which they have killed horses and men, even Europeans, are numerous.

Fairy, p. 228.—*Parî,* fairy, peri : the story indicates a very common notion.

THE JACKAL AND THE CROCODILE

Verses, p. 233.—In the original they are—

Gâdar, ghar kyâ lâyâ ?
Kyâ chîz kamâyâ ?
Ki merâ khâtir pâyâ.

Jackal, what hast thou brought home ?
What thing hast thou earned ?
That I may obtain my wants.

The story has a parallel in most Indian collections, and two in *Uncle Remus*, in the stories of 'The Rabbit and the Wolf' and of 'The Terrapin and the Rabbit.'

HOW RAJA RASALU WAS BORN

Râjâ Rasâlû, p. 234.—The chief legendary hero of the Panjâb, and probably a Scythian or non-Aryan king of great mark who fought both the Aryans to the east and the invading tribes (? Arabs) to the west. Popularly he is the son of the great Scythian hero Sâlivâhaṇa, who established the Sâka or Scythian era in 78 A.D. Really he, however, probably lived much later, and his date should be looked for at any period between A.D. 300 and A.D. 900. He most probably represented the typical Indian kings known to the Arab historians as flourishing between 697 and 870 A.D. by the synonymous names Zentil, Zenbil, Zenbyl, Zambil, Zantíl, Ranbal, Ratbyl, Reteil, Retpeil, Rantal, Ratpíl, Ratteil, Ratbal, Ratbil, Rútsal, Rúsal, Rasal, Rásil. These are all meant for the same word, having arisen from the uncertainty of the Arabic character and the ignorance of transcribers. The particular king meant is most likely the opponent of Ḥajjâj and Muḥammad Qâsim between 697 and 713 A.D. The whole subject is involved in the greatest obscurity, and in the Panjâb his story is almost hopelessly involved in pure folklore. It has often been discussed in learned journals. See *Indian Antiquary*, vol. xi. pp. 299 ff. 346-349, vol. xii. p. 303 ff., vol. xiii. p. 155 ff. ; *Journal Asiatic Society of Bengal* for 1854, pp. 123-163, etc. ; Elliot's *History of India*, vol. i. pp. 167, 168, vol. ii. pp. 178, 403-427.

Lonân, p. 234.—For a story of Lonân, see *Indian Antiquary*, vol. ix. p. 290.

Thrown into a deep well, p. 234.—Still shown on the road between Siâlkoṭ and Kallowâl.

Gurû Gorakhnâth, p. 234.—The ordinary *deux ex machinâ* of modern folk-tales. He is now supposed to be the reliever of all troubles, and possessed of most miraculous powers, especially over snakes. In life he seems to have been the Brâhmanical opponent of the mediæval reformers of the fifteenth century A.D.   By any computation Pûran Bhagat must have lived centuries before him.

Pûran Bhagat, p. 235.—Is in story Râjâ Rasâlû's elder brother. There are numerous poems written about his story, which is essentially that of Potiphar's wife.   The parallel between the tales of Râjâ Rasâlû and Pûran Bhagat and those of the Southern Aryan conqueror Vikramâditya and his (in legend) elder brother Bhatṛihari, the saint and philosopher, is worthy of remark.

HOW RAJA RASALU WENT OUT INTO THE WORLD

Bhaúnr'Irâqî, p. 238.—The name of Rasâlû's horse ; but the name probably should be Bhaúnrî Râkhî, kept in the underground cellar. 'Irâqî means Arabian.

Verses, p. 240.—In the original these are—

Main âiâ thâ salâm nûn, tûn baiṭhâ pîṭh maroṛ !
Main nahîn terâ râj waṇḍânundâ ; main nûn nahîn râj te loṛ.

I came to salute thee, and thou hast turned thy back on me !
I have no wish to share thy kingdom !   I have no desire for empire.

Mahlân de vich baiṭhîe, tûn ro ro na sunâ !
Je tûn merî mâtâ hain, koî mat batlâ !
Matte dendî hai mân tain nûn, putar : gin gin jholî ghat !
Châre Khûnṭân tûn râj kare, par changâ rakhîn sat !

O sitting in the palace, let me not hear thee weeping !
If thou be my mother give me some advice !
Thy mother doth advise thee, son : stow it carefully away in thy wallet !
Thou wilt reign in the Four Quarters, but keep thyself good and pure.

Verses, p. 241.—In the original these are—

Thoṛâ thoṛâ, beṭâ, tûn disîn, aur bahotî disî dhûṛ :
Putr jinân de ṭur chale, aur mâwân chiknâ chûṛ.

It is little I see of thee, my son, but I see much dust.
The mother, whose son goes away on a journey, becomes as a powder (reduced to great misery).

HOW RAJA RASALU'S FRIENDS FORSOOK HIM

Verses, p. 242.—Originals are—

Agge sowen lef nihâlîân, ajj sutâ suthrâ ghâs !
Sukh wasse yeh des, jâhan âeajj dî rât !

Before thou didst sleep on quilts, to-day thou has slept on clean grass !
Mayest thou live happy in this land whither thou hast come this night !

Snake, p. 242.—Most probably represents a man of the 'Serpent Race,' a Nâga, Taka, or Takshak.

Unspeakable horror, p. 243.—The undefined word *âfat*, horror, terror, was used throughout.

Verses, p. 244.—Originals are—

> *Sadâ na phûlan toriân, nafrâ: sadâ na Sâwan hoe:*
> *Sadâ na joban thir rahe: sadâ na jîve koe:*
> *Sadâ na râjiân ḥâkimî: sâda na râjiân des:*
> *Sadâ na hove ghar apnâ, nafrâ, bhaṭh piâ pardes.*

Teris (a mustard plant) do not always flower, my servant: it is not always the rainy season (time of joy).

Youth does not always last: no one lives for ever:

Kings are not always rulers: kings have not always lands:

They have not always homes, my servant: they fall into great troubles in strange lands.

These verses of rustic philosophy are universal favourites, and have been thus rendered in the *Calcutta Review*, No. clvi. pp. 281, 282—

> Youth will not always stay with us:
> We shall not always live:
> Rain doth not always fall for us:
> Nor flowers blossoms give.

> Great kings not always rulers are:
> They have not always lands:
> Nor have they always homes, but know
> Sharp grief at strangers' hands.

HOW RAJA RASALU KILLED THE GIANTS

Giants, p. 245.—*Râkshasa*, for which see previous notes.

Nîlâ city, p. 245.—Most probably Bâgh Nîlâb on the Indus to the south of Aṭak.

Verses, p. 246.—In the original these are—

> *Na ro, mata bholîe: na aswân ḍhalkâe:*
> *Tere beṭe ki 'tvaz main sir desân châe.*
> *Nîle-ghorewâliâ Râjâ, munh dhârî, sir pag,*
> *Woh jo dekhte âunde, jin khâiâ sârâ jag.*

Weep not, foolish mother, drop no tears:

I will give my head for thy son.

Gray-horsed Râjâ: bearded face and turban on head,

He whom you see coming is he who has destroyed my life!

Verses, pp. 247, 248.—In original—

> *Nasso, bhajo, bhâio ! Dekho koî galî !*
> *Tehrî agg dhonkdî, so sir te ân balî !*
> *Sûjhanhârî sûjh gae ; hun laihndî charhdî jâe !*
> *Jithe sânûn sûkh mile, so jhatpat kare upâe !*

Fly, fly, brethren ! look out for some road !
Such a fire is burning that it will come and burn our heads !
Our fate has come, we shall now be destroyed !
Make some plan at once for our relief.

Gandgari Mountains, p. 248.—Gandgarh Hills, to the north of Atak : for a detailed account of this legend see *Journal Asiatic Society of Bengal* for 1854, p. 150 ff.

HOW RAJA RASALU BECAME A JOGI

Hodînagarî, p. 250.—A veritable will-o'-the-wisp in the ancient Panjâb geography : Hodînagarî, Udenagar, Udaynagar, is the name of innumerable ruins all over the northern Panjâb, from Siâlkot to Jalâlâbâd in Afghânistân beyond the Khaibar Pass. Here it is more than probably some place in the Rawâl Pindi or Hazârâ Districts along the Indus.

Rânî Sundrân, p. 250.—The daughter of Hari Chand.

Alakh, p. 251 ff.—' In the Imperishable Name,' the cry of religious mendicants when begging.

Verses, p. 252.—In original—

> *Jâe bûhe te kilkiâ : lîa nâm Khudâ :*
> *Dûron chalke, Rânî Sundrân, terâ nâ :*
> *Je, Rânî, tû sakhî hain, kharî faqîrân pâ :*

Coming to the threshold I called out : I took the name of God :
Coming from afar, Rânî Sundrân, on account of thy name.
If thou art generous, Rânî, the beggar will obtain alms.

The *Musalmân* word *Khudâ,* God, here is noticeable, as Rasâlû was personating a *Hindû jogî.*

Verses, p. 252.

> *Kab kî pât mundran ? Kab kâ huâ faqîr ?*
> *Kis ghatâ mânion ? Kis kâ lâgâ tîr !*
> *Kete mâen mangiâ ? Mere ghar kî mangî bhîkh ?*
> *Kal kî pât mundrân ! Kal kâ huâ faqîr !*
> *Na ghat, mâîân, mâniân : kal kâ lâgâ tîr.*
> *Kuchh nahîn munh mangî : Kewal tere ghar ke bhîkh.*

When didst thou get thy earring?   When wast thou made a *faqîr*?
What is thy pretence?   Whose arrow of love hath struck thee?
From how many women hast thou begged?   What alms dost thou
    beg from me?
Yesterday I got my earring : yesterday I became a *faqîr*.
I make no pretence, mother : yesterday the arrow struck me.
I begged nothing : only from thy house do I beg.

Verses, p. 253.—In original—

> *Tarqas jaṛiâ tîr motîân ; lâlân jaṛî kumân ;*
> *Piṇḍe bhasham lagâiâ : yeh mainân aur rang ;*
> *Jis bhikhiâ kâ lâbhî hain, tû wohî bhikhiâ mang.*
> *Tarqas jaṛiâ merû motîân : lâlân jaṛî kumân.*
> *Lâl na jânâ bechke, motî be-waṭṭî.*
> *Motî apne phir lai ; sânûn pakkâ tâm diwâ.*

Thy quiver is full of pearly arrows : thy bow is set with rubies :
Thy body is covered with ashes : thy eyes and thy colour thus :
Ask for the alms thou dost desire.
My quiver is set with pearls : my bow is set with rubies.
I know not how to sell pearls and rubies without loss.
Take back thy pearls : give me some cooked food.

Verses, p. 253.—In original—

> *Kahân tumhârî nagarî? kahân tumhârâ ṭhâon?*
> *Kis râjâ kâ betrâ jogî? kyâ tumhârâ nâon?*
> *Siâlkoṭ hamârî nagarî ; wohi hamârâ ṭhâon.*
> *Râjâ Sâlivâhan kâ main beṭrâ : Lonâ parî merâ nâon.*
> *Piṇḍe bhasam lagâe, dekhan terî jâon.*
> *Tainûn dekhke chaliâ : Râjâ Rasâlû merâ nâon.*

Where is thy city?   Where is thy home?
What king's son art thou, *jôgi*?   What is thy name?
Siâlkoṭ is my city : that is my home.
I am Râjâ Sâlivâhan's son : the fairy Lonâ is my mother.
Ashes are on my body : (my desire was) to see thy abode.
Having seen thee I go away : Râjâ Rasâlû is my name.

Sati, p. 254.—The rite by which widows burn themselves with their
husbands.

HOW RAJA RASALU JOURNEYED TO THE CITY
OF KING SARKAP

Râjâ Sarkap, p. 255.—*Lit.* King Beheader is a universal hero of
fable, who has left many places behind him connected with his memory,
but who he was has not yet been ascertained.

Verses, p. 255.—In original—

Bâre andar piâ karanglâ, na is sâs, na pâs.
Je Maullâ is nûn zindâ kare, do bâtân kare hamâre sâth.
Laihndion charhî badalî, hâthân pâiâ zor :
Kehe 'amal kamâio, je jhaldi nahîn ghor ?

The corpse has fallen under the hedge, no breath in him, nor any one near.
If God grant him life he may talk a little with me.
The clouds rose in the west and the storm was very fierce ;
What hast thou done that the grave doth not hold thee?

Verses, p. 256.—In original—

Asîn bhî kadîn duniyân te inhân the ;
Râjâ nal degrîân pagân banhde,
Turde pabbân bhâr.
Âunde tara, nachâunde tara,
Hânke sawâr.
Zara na mitthî jhaldî Râjâ ;
Hun sau manân dâ bhâr.

I, too, was once on the earth thus ;
Fastening my turban like a king,
Walking erect.
Coming proudly, taunting proudly,
I drove off the horsemen.
The grave does not hold me at all, Râjâ :
Now I am a great sinner.

Chaupur, p. 256.—*Chaupur* is a game played by two players with 8 men each on a board in the shape of a cross, 4 men to each cross covered with squares. The moves of the men are decided by the throws of a long form of dice. The object of the game is to see which of the players can move all his men into the black centre square of the cross first. A detailed description of the game is given in *The Legends of the Panjâb*, vol. i. pp. 243, 245.

HOW RAJA RASALU SWUNG THE SEVENTY FAIR MAIDENS, DAUGHTERS OF THE KING

The daughters of Râjâ Sarkap, p. 257.—The scene of this and the following legend is probably meant to be Kot Bithaur on the Indus near Atak.

Verses, p. 258.—In original—

Nîle-ghorewâliâ Râjâ, niven neze âh !
Agge Râjâ Sarkap hai, sir laisî ulâh !

Bhalâ châhen jo apnâ, tân pichhe hî muṛ jâh !
Dûron bîṛâ chukiâ ithe pahutâ âh :
Sarkap dâ sir kaṭke ṭoṭe kassân châr.
Tainûn banâsân wohṭrî, main bansân mihrâj !

Grey-horsed Râjâ, come with lowered lance !
Before thee is Râjâ Sarkap, he will take thy head !
If thou seek thy own good, then turn thee back !
I have come from afar under a vow of victory :
I will cut off Sarkap's head and cut it into four pieces.
I will make thee my little bride, and will become thy bridegroom !

Hundredweight, p. 258. — *Man* in the original, or a little over 80 lbs.

Verses, p. 260.—In original—

Ik jo âiâ Rajpût kaṭdâ mâromâr,
Paske lârhân kapiân siṭṭîâ sîne bhâr.
Dharin dharin bheṛen bhaniân aur bhane ghariâl !
Tain nûn, Râjâ, marsî ate sânûn kharsî hâl.

A prince has come and is making havoc ;
He cut the long strings and threw us out headlong.
The drums placed are broken and broken are the gongs.
He will kill thee, Râjâ, and take me with him !

Verses, p. 260.—In original—

Chhoṭî nagarî dâ waskîn, Rânî waḍî karî pukâr.
Jân main niklân bâhar, tân merî tan nachâve dhâl.
Fajre roṭî tân khâsân, sir laisân utâr.

Princess, thou hast brought a great complaint about a dweller in a small city.
When I come out his shield will dance for fear of my valour.
In the morning I will eat my bread and cut off their heads.

HOW RAJA RASALU PLAYED *CHAUPUR* WITH RAJA SARKAP

Dhol Râjâ, p. 263.—It is not known why the rat was so called. The hero of a well-known popular love-tale bears the same name. Dhol or Dhaul (from Sanskrit *dhavala*, white) is in popular story the *cow* that supports the earth on its horns.

Verses, p. 263.—In original—

Sakhî samundar jamiân, Râjâ lîo rud gar thâe :
Âo to chaṛho merî pîṭh te, koṭ tudh kharân tarpâe.

Uṛde pankhī maiṅ na desāṅ, jo dauran lakh karoṛ.
Je tudh, Râjâ, pârâ khelsiâ, jeb hâth to pâe.

O my beloved, I was born in the ocean, and the Râjâ bought me with much gold.

Come and jump on my back and I will take thee off with thousands of bounds.

Wings of birds shall not catch me, though they go thousands of miles.

If thou wouldst gamble, Râjâ, keep thy hand on thy pocket.

Verses, p. 264.—In original—

Na ro, Râjiâ bholiâ ; nâ maiṅ charsâṅ ghâh,
Na maiṅ ṭursâṅ râh.
Dahnâ dast uṭhâeke jeb de vich pâh !

Weep not, foolish Râjâ, I shall not eat their grass,
Nor shall I go away.
Take thy right hand and put it in thy pocket !

Verses, p. 265.—In original—

Dhal, we pâsâ dhalwiṅ ithe basante lok !
Sarâṅ dharâṅ han bâziâṅ, jehṛî Sarkap kare so ho !
Dhal, we pâsâ dhalweṅ, ithe basantâ lok !
Sarâṅ dharâṅ te bâziâṅ ! Jehṛî Allah kare so ho !

O moulded pieces, favour me : a man is here !
Heads and bodies are at stake ! as Sarkap does so let it be.
O moulded pieces, favour me : a man is here !
Heads and bodies are at stake ! as God does so let it be !

Verses, p. 266.—In original—

Hor râje murghâbiâṅ, tu râjâ shâhbâz !
Bandî bânâṅ âe band khalâs kar ! umar terî drâz.

Other kings are wild-fowl, thou art a royal hawk !
Unbind the chains of the chain-bound and live for ever !

Mûrtî Hills, p. 266.—Near Râwal Piṇḍî to the south-west.

Kokilâṅ, p. 266.—Means 'a darling' : she was unfaithful and most dreadfully punished by being made to eat her lover's heart.

THE KING WHO WAS FRIED

The king who was fried, p. 267.—The story is told of the hill temple (*maṛhî*) on the top of Piṇḍî Point at the Murree (*Maṛhî*) Hill Sanitarium. Full details of the surroundings are given in the *Calcutta Review*, No. cl. p. 270 ff.

King Karan, p. 267.—This is for Karṇa, the half-brother of Pâṇḍu, and a great hero in the *Mahâbhârata* legends. Usually he appears in the very different character of a typical tyrant, like Herod among Christians, and for the same reason, viz. the slaughter of innocents.

Hundredweight, p. 268.—A *man* and a quarter in the original, or about 100 lbs.

Mânsarobar Lake, p. 269.—The Mânasaśarovara Lake (= Tsho-Mâphan) in the Kailâsa Range of the Himâlayas, for ages a centre of Indian fable. For descriptions see Cunningham's *Ladâk*, pp. 128-136.

Swan, p. 270.—*Hansa* in the original : a fabulous bird that lives on pearls only. Swan translates it better than any other word.

King Bikramâjît, p. 270.—The great Vikramâditya of Ujjayinî, popularly the founder of the present Saṁvat era in B.C. 57. Bikrû is a legitimately-formed diminutive of the name. Vikramâditya figures constantly in folklore as Bikram, Vikram, and Vichram, and also by a false analogy as Bik Râm and Vich Râm. He also goes by the name of Bîr Bikramâjît or Vîr Vikram, *i.e.* Vikramâditya, the warrior. In some tales, probably by the error of the translator, he then becomes two brothers, Vir and Vikram. See Postans' *Cutch*, p. 18 ff.

PRINCE HALF-A-SON

Half-a-son, p. 275.—*Adhiâ* in the original form ; *âdhâ*, a half. The natives, however, give the tale the title of 'Sat Bachiâṅ diâṅ Mâwâṅ,' *i.e.* the Mothers of Seven Sons.

THE MOTHER OF SEVEN SONS

Broken-down old bed, p. 275.—This, with scratching the ground with the fore-finger, is a recognised form of expressing grief in the Panjâb. The object is to attract *faqîrs* to help the sufferer.

THE RUBY PRINCE

Prince Ruby, p. 289.—*La'ljî*, Mr. Ruby, a common name : it can also mean 'beloved son' or 'cherished son.'

Snake-stone, p. 290.—*Mani*, the fabulous jewel in the cobra's hood, according to folklore all over India. See *Panjâb Notes and Queries*, vol. i. for 1883-84.

ANALYSIS OF THE TALES

ON THE PLAN ADOPTED BY THE FOLKLORE
SOCIETY OF ENGLAND

I

Number in collection, 1. *Reference to pages*, 1 to 12. *Specific name*, Sir Bumble. *Dramatis personæ:* soldier's son, tigress, one-span mannikin, princess weighing five flowers, one-eyed kotwal, tradesmen, vampire in form of Brâhman. *Thread of story*, soldier's widow's only son goes to seek his fortune with two rupees ;[1] meets tigress and takes thorn out of her foot ; tigress gives him a box to carry nine miles before opening ; carries it five miles and drops it, because it is heavy. One-span mannikin of prodigious strength appears from box, he has a beard of a span and a quarter. Mannikin can fly through the air like a beetle or bumble bee and fetches food by cheating the tradesmen of the neighbourhood.[2] Food is brought in enormous quantities,[3] mannikin gobbling up what soldier's son cannot eat. They meet Princess Blossom who weighs only five flowers. Mannikin brings about meeting between her and the soldier's son,[4] and mounts guard over them. Protects them against her father the king's people. Is then dismissed as useless any longer, but warns them of danger, and gives them a hair of his beard which they are to burn in case of need. They meet a vampire in the form of a Brâhman who shelters them and gives them the golden key of a cupboard which they are not to open. Soldier's son out of curiosity opens the cupboard which contains skeletons of vampire's victims. Vampire returns, but Princess Blossom burns hair, whereon mannikin appears and pursues and slays vampire.[5] Story ends. Mannikin disappears, and soldier's son and the princess live with his mother. *Incidental circumstances:* (1) 3 found in the father's coat, starts off to seek his fortune with 2, leaving the other for his mother's support ; (2) he shows them the soldier's son's Rs. 2 and flies off with the food without paying for it ;

(3) two *mans* of flour and one *man* of sweets; (4) by flying with the soldier's son through the air and dropping him on to her bed; (5) through a series of metamorphoses—(*a*) vampire changes into rain and mannikin into a storm-wind beating back the rain; (*b*) vampire into dove and mannikin into hawk; (*c*) vampire to a rose falling into Indra's lap from heaven and mannikin to a musician who demands and gets the rose; (*a*) vampire rose falls to the ground, mannikin picks it up, but one petal escapes and then vampire petal turns to mouse and mannikin to cat who eats the mouse. *Where published*, Indian Antiquary, vol. x. p. 40 ff. *Nature of collection:* (1) *Original or translation*, original, collected by F. A. Steel: (2) *Narrator's name*, from a Panjâbi Musalmân child, name not given; (3) *Other particulars*, nil.

II

Number in collection, 2. *Reference to pages*, 13 to 22. *Specific name*, Rat's Wedding. *Dramatis personæ:* rat, woodcutter, potter, neatherd, bride, bride's mother. *Thread of story*, rat on a wet day finds a dry root and takes it home; on his way meets a man trying to light a fire with damp wood, offers him his dry root out of compassion, but takes a morsel of dough in return; meets a potter trying to pacify some hungry children, gives him the dough and is given in exchange a pipkin (earthen pot); meets neatherds milking buffaloes into their shoes for want of a pail, offers pipkin and demands buffalo in return;[1] gets buffalo given as a joke; meets a bridal party carrying palanquin; bearers want meat for their food, offers buffalo; bearers kill buffalo and eat it and run away for fear of consequences; rat takes possession of bride, sets her to cry wild plums in the streets to sell for her food; her mother hears her and takes her back; rat claims his bride and is finally set on a red-hot stool by a trick[2] and so got rid off.[3] *Incidental circumstances:* (1) rat is now proud and considers himself a good hand at a bargain; (2) the stool is hollowed out in the centre, a red-hot stone is placed in the hollow covered over with a saucepan-lid and a cloth spread over all; (3) his tail is burnt off and half his hair and some of his skin, so he runs off. *Where published*, Indian Antiquary, vol. xi. p. 226 ff. *Nature of collection:* (1) *Original or translation*, original, collected by F. A. Steel; (2) *Narrator's name*, Nâmdâr, a boy at Muzaffargaṛh, Panjâb, of Purbîâ (*i.e.* N.-W. Provinces) origin; (3) *Other particulars*, nil.

III

Number in collection, 3. *Reference to pages*, 23 to 34. *Specific name*, Faithful Prince. *Dramatis personæ:* Bahrâmgor, golden deer, demon

Jasdrûl, fairy Shâhpasand, woodman, chief constable, demon Nânak Chand, demon Safed, Shâhpasand's maid. *Thread of story*, hero goes hunting in the west;[1] finds and catches golden deer, who flies with him to fairy[2] land; mannikin demon Jasdrûl[2a] gives him keys of 100 palaces and gardens;[3] fairy princess finds him asleep;[4] marries him;[5] hero pines for home and demon sends him and his wife, but gives them a hair to burn when they want help; they go to hero's home[6] and live with his former huntsman in his garret; chief constable sees heroine combing her hair,[7] tries to seize her, but she escapes to the emerald mountain as a pigeon; hero follows her[8] by calling Jasdrûl to his help by burning the hair; seeks princess by aid of magic wand[9] in demon Nânak Chand's possession, then by aid of *surma*[10] in demon Safed's possession, then by aid of invisible cap and the *surma* he reaches the emerald mountain and gets access to heroine,[11] discovers himself,[12] and dwells there for ever. *Incidental circumstances :* (1) in the 4th direction (west), in which he hunts ; (2) 7 days and 7 nights through the air ; (2a) who was the golden deer on earth ; (3) 100th palace mere hovel full of poisonous things in a lovely garden 7 miles square ; (4) she is a pigeon in the air and a girl on the ground ; she wakes him by kissing him ; (5) marriage is orthodox ; (6) find everything changed, a new king on the throne and a price on hero's head, so they have to hide ; (7) hair is golden and neck fair ; (8) finds out where she is gone by the blind old guardian of the girl saying a voice (the heroine's) had said, ' I go to the emerald mountain '; prince follows her with persistence and courage ; (9) to protect him from harm ; (10) to rub on his eyes ; it brings what is far near ; (11) heroine is locked up inside 7 prisons to prevent her escaping to hero and a maid brings her food every day ; hero with invisible cap on watches maid into a door ; follows her on to heroine ; (12) hero still invisible eats out of her dish, whereon she calls out and he takes off his cap. *Where published*, Indian Antiquary, vol. xi. p. 285 ff. *Nature of collection :* (1) *Original or translation*, original, collected by F. A. Steel ; (2) *Narrator's name*, Habîb, a Musalmân cooly in Kashmîr ; (3) *Other particulars*, nil.

IV

Number in collection, 4. *Reference to pages*, 35 to 41. *Specific name*, The Bear's Bad Bargain. *Dramatis personæ :* old woodman and wife, bear. *Thread of story*, old woodman and wife allowed to have fruit from rich neighbour's pear tree, provided the fruit fell into their yard. Old wife refuses to cook savoury dish for her husband unless he will first work for it by cutting a quantity of firewood. Woodman goes to work, bear comes by and offers to do the work if he may have a share of the dish. Woodman agrees for a huge quantity of wood : while bear is working out his dinner woodman and wife eat up all the dish leaving pot only. In their fear of consequences they hide in the garret ; bear comes, finds food gone and is furious and takes away pot ; sees pear tree, climbs into it and collects the fruit into the pot. Woman sneezes loudly, bear thinking this is a gun runs off dropping pot of pears into the yard, so the old couple get them, bear gets nothing but a stomach-ache. *Incidental circumstances :* (1) bear eats only the unripe fruit, filling the ripe fruit into the pot to sell his brother bears at a profit. *Where published*, Indian Antiquary, vol. xi. p. 340 ff. *Nature of collection :* (1) *Original or translation*, original, collected by F. A. Steel ; (2) *Narrator's name*, Habîb, a Musalmân cooly in Kashmîr ; (3) *Other particulars*, amid roars of laughter round a camp fire at the Tar Sar Lake in Liderwat, to the N. E. of Srînagar.

V

Number in collection, 5. *Reference to pages*, 42 to 60. *Specific name*, Prince Lionheart and his Three Friends. *Dramatis personæ :* Prince Lionheart ; knifegrinder, blacksmith, carpenter—companions to Prince ; mannikin demon, female malignant ghost, (sleeping) beauty, jinn, witch. *Thread of story*, hero is a miraculously born [1] only son, sets off on his travels with three companions—knifegrinder, blacksmith, and carpenter ; they reach a deserted city, [2] knifegrinder is set to cook, while the others explore ; mannikin demon frightens knifegrinder, [3] and eats up the dinner ; same incident happens to blacksmith and carpenter ; demon is finally killed by hero, [4] inhabitants return to city, and hero makes knifegrinder king ; hero gives knifegrinder a barley plant as his (hero's) life-index ; [5] hero with blacksmith and carpenter reach another deserted city ; [6] blacksmith set to cook, female malignant ghost frightens blacksmith [7] and then carpenter, is killed at last by hero ; [8] inhabitants return and blacksmith made king as before, and given a barley plant ; hero and carpenter reach a third city, carpenter made king by hero, [9] and hero goes on alone, sees rubies floating down a river, follows them up stream and finds a female head hanging in a basket on a tree over the stream ; [10] head belongs to (sleeping) beauty lying in the palace near, hero joins head to body and brings (sleeping) beauty to life. Finds beauty in the power of a jinn, [11] who cut off her head and hung it up whenever he went abroad. Beauty finds out the jinn's life-index, [12] and then hero kills jinn, and marries beauty. Beauty afterwards washes her golden hair and some of the hairs float down the river [13] to a king's palace ; king determines to possess the owner and sends witch [14] to find her ; she worms out of beauty the secret of hero's life-index, [15] kills

hero,[16] and carries her off by stratagem.[17]   The hero's life-index left
with his companions informs them of his fate,[18] they set off after him,
find him and bring him to life again.[19]   Carpenter then finds princess,[20]
restores her to hero by means of a flying palanquin;[21] hero and beauty
return to hero's father.[22]   *Incidental circumstances:* (1) father and
mother have no children and meet a *faqīr* who grants a son by
making mother eat a barleycorn; (2) because of the annoyances
caused by a demon; (3) mannikin demands the dinner, on knifegrinder's refusal shoots up into a tall demon, hangs knifegrinder on a
tree, but rope breaks and knifegrinder escapes shivering, hides himself
under a blanket and says he has fever and that a dog carried off the
dinner; (4) hero fights the demon and kills him by inducing him to 'fight
fair,' *i.e.* to assume size and strength equal to hero's; (5) as long as the
plant lived hero would be well, when it drooped he would be ill,
when it died he would be dead; (6) because of a murderous *churel*
(female malignant ghost); (7) by her appearance, an old woman, awful
and forbidding, with black wrinkled skin and feet turned backwards;
(8) to hero she appears a beautiful girl, but hero orders her to assume
her proper shape, and slays her there and then; even in this beautiful
form she has her feet turned back; (9) simply at carpenter's request
(probably an error on the part of the narrator); (10) the drops of blood
from it floating down the stream were the rubies the hero had seen;
(11) jinn used to cut off her head daily when he went out and put it on
again when he returned; this was from jealousy; she was a human
princess; (12) his life lay in a bumble bee living in the crop of a starling
kept in a golden cage on the top twig of a tree guarded by a savage
horse and dog; by changing their food (*i.e.* the grass was kept before
the dog and the bones before the horse to make them savage), hero gets
at bee, and when he kills it the jinn dies; (13) she did not like it floating on the water, so she made a cup of a leaf for it and floated that;
(14) he sends for three witches, the first can find her on the earth, the
second can tear open the sky to find her, the third can patch up the
hole in the sky—he chose the third; (15) his life lay in his sword, as he
used to go hunting daily, beauty in her fright, lest anything should
happen to it, changes it and tells witch so; (16) witch gets possession
of the sword and burns it, this throws hero into a fever and, when the
rivet of the handle comes out, hero's head falls off; (17) by inducing
beauty to get to a boat and floating her down stream; (18) the barley
plant suddenly snapped in half and the head fell to the ground; (19)
blacksmith fastens the handle on by forging a new rivet and knifegrinder
brightens it up, hero is alive and well again; (20) beauty had vowed
not to marry her new lover for twelve years, carpenter hawks wood about
at an exorbitant price and beauty sends for him and learns about hero;

(21) carpenter makes miraculous flying palanquin and shows it beauty to try, the new lover's sister and witch get into it also, carpenter throws them out at a height and kills them, palanquin flies straight to hero ; (22) hero's father at first thinks hero is an enemy. *Where published*, Indian Antiquary, vol. x. p. 228 ff. *Nature of collection :* (1) *Original or translation*, original, collected by F. A. Steel ; (2) *Narrator's name*, not given ; a boy, who sold eggs, born in the North-West Provinces, but residing at Firôzpûr ; (3) *Other particulars*, nil.

VI

Number in collection, 6. *Reference to pages*, 61 to 64. *Specific name*, Lambikin. *Dramatis personæ :* lambikin and his granny, jackal, vulture, tiger, wolf, dog, and eagle. *Thread of story*, lambikin meets successively jackal, vulture, tiger, wolf, dog, and eagle, and avoids them all by saying he is not fat yet, but is going to his granny to be fattened.[1] On his return fattened he trundles along in a drumikin made of his brother's skin, and avoids all but the jackal by saying lambikin had fallen into the fire, jackal recognises his voice, drags him out and eats him. *Incidental circumstances :* (1) granny puts him into a bin where he eats for seven days. *Where published*, Indian Antiquary, vol. xii. p. 175 ff. *Nature of collection :* (1) *Original or translation*, original, collected by F. A. Steel ; (2) *Narrator's name*, not given ; (3) *Other particulars*, it is a common nursery story all over the Panjâb.

VII

Number in collection, 7. *Reference to pages*, 65 to 70. *Specific name*, Bopolûchî. *Dramatis personæ :* heroine, robber, crow, peacock, jackal, robber's mother. *Thread of story*, village girls begin boasting about their future weddings ; heroine boasts that her uncle will come with fine dresses, food, and jewels ; robber[1] overhears her ; determines to marry her ; brings everything as she had boasted, saying he is her uncle and that she is wanted to marry his son ; carries her off ; on the road, a crow, peacock, and jackal all warn her of her danger ;[2] robber reaching home discloses himself ; leaves her in charge of his old mother and goes off to arrange wedding ; heroine kills the mother,[3] and in disguise escapes ;[4] robber follows her home,[5] and finally catches her and carries her off with the help of three men ; heroine kills these[6] and finally kills robber[7] and possesses herself of all his wealth. *Incidental circumstances :* (1) disguised as a pedlar, selling female trinkets ; (2) by a verse of warning which both hear and which robber explains satisfactorily ; (3) by a trick induces the old woman to let her pound her head with a pestle to make her hair grow ; (4) dresses up the corpse in her own bridal clothes and puts on the old woman's, meets robber outside carrying a stolen millstone, but he thinking she might be a witness of the theft slinks away ; (5) being sure the robber would follow she lives in her friends' houses till she is no longer welcome ; (6) they carry off her bed, she pretends to be asleep, but has bill-hook under the clothes which she whips out and cuts off their heads ; (7) he escapes up a tree, but she sets it on fire and burns him. *Where published*, Indian Antiquary, vol. ix. p. 205 ff. *Nature of collection :* (1) *Original or translation*, original, collected by F. A. Steel ; (2) *Narrator's name*, not given ; an old peasant from Kasûr in the Lahore district ; (3) *Other particulars*, nil.

VIII

Number in collection, 8. *Reference to pages*, 71 to 79. *Specific name*, Princess Aubergine. *Dramatis personæ :* poor Brâhman couple, heroine, wicked queen, king, heroine's son. *Thread of story*, a poor Brâhman couple find an aubergine,[1] which contains the heroine ; she is brought up by them as daughter of the house ; a queen in the neighbourhood hears of her, determining to kill her by magic out of jealousy, tries to find out her life-index, and in doing so kills her own seven sons ;[2] finds it eventually ;[3] kills heroine,[4] but she is laid out in the wilderness and neither buried nor burnt. King goes out hunting to allay his grief for the loss of his sons ;[5] finds heroine's body ;[6] watches beside it for days,[7] finds a boy beside the body after a year ;[8] finds out that the heroine is alive at night, but dead in the day-time, and the life-index ;[9] heroine marries him and the queen is punished.[10] *Incidental circumstances :* (1) it has only one fruit on it which is not plucked till the couple are actually starving ; (2) knows heroine to be a fairy, and so her first seven spells do not elicit a true answer as to the life-index which heroine says lies in the life of the seven sons successively ; (3) the eighth spell is strong enough to elicit the truth ; the life-index is the nine-lakh necklace in a box in a bee in a green and red fish ; (4) by the illness trick curable only by the possession of the life-index ; queen's husband finds it for her ; heroine knows she is to die and warns the Brâhman couple as to how to deal with her corpse, viz. to dress her in her best and carry her on her bed into the wilderness ; (5) goes hunting to the north, the direction forbidden him by the wicked queen ; (6) in an enclosure surrounded by a high wall heroine appears to be sleeping ; (7) it never decays ; (8) the child is heroine's son ; (9) as long as the queen is wearing the necklace heroine dies ; queen took it off at night, queen tries to poison child by offering it sweets, but the child will not take these until it gets possession of her necklace and it is then restored to the heroine ; (10) by being buried in a ditch filled with scorpions and serpents.

Where published, Indian Antiquary, vol. ix. p. 302 ff. *Nature of collection:* (1) *Original or translation*, original, collected by F. A. Steel; (2) *Narrator's name*, not given; an old woman at Kasûr in the Lahore district; (3) *Other particulars*, it is very common in the Panjâb. The narrator was not a Panjâbi, but of Pûrbiâ origin.

IX

Number in collection, 9. *Reference to pages*, 80 to 88. *Specific name*, Valiant Vicky, the Brave Weaver. *Dramatis personæ:* hero, elephant, tiger, king, king's daughter and hero's wife. *Thread of story*, hero who is very vain without reason, kills a mosquito with his shuttle and sets up for being a great man, sets off to seek his fortune, comes to city where a dreadful elephant eats up one of the people, offers to kill elephant, does so by accident,[1] is made commander-in-chief, tiger ravages the country, hero goes out to kill it,[2] kills it by accident,[3] marries king's daughter, foreign prince comes to ravage the country with his army, hero sent to oppose him, hero and his wife prepare for flight, and by accident[4] set the enemy fighting among themselves, and thus destroy the army, hero becomes a great man, and refusing to fight any more, lives and dies covered with honour. *Incidental circumstances:* (1) as he was running he dropped the poisoned cakes his wife made for him, elephant eats these up as he follows hero and is poisoned at once; (2) with an army, he runs up a tree as soon as tiger charges and army deserts him; (3) goaded by hunger he tries to creep down the tree while tiger is asleep, tiger gets up and, as he is swinging himself back into the tree, his knife falls into tiger's mouth and kills him; (4) hero and his wife try to slink through the army at night, hero's wife drops her bag of household utensils which wakes up the army, who, thinking they are attacked, begin fighting among themselves and destroying each other in the dark, hero takes advantage of this and returns home victorious. *Where published*, Indian Antiquary, vol. xi. p. 282 ff. *Nature of collection:* (1) *Original or translation*, original, collected by F. A. Steel; (2) *Narrator's name*, not given; a Muhammadan at Sopûr in Kashmîr; (3) *Other particulars*, nil.

X

Number in collection, 10. *Reference to pages*, 89 to 101. *Specific name*, The Son of Seven Mothers. *Dramatis personæ:* king, hero, white-hind witch, her mother, hero's wife. *Thread of story*, a king has seven wives and no children, saint grants them all a son each,[1] king goes hunting in forbidden direction,[2] and there meets the white hind,[3] which he follows up and recognises as the daughter of the house in cottage on the road,[4] marries her on his love being tested by first blinding the seven queens and imprisoning them, she is a witch and gives the eyes to her mother to wear as a necklace, the seven queens eat up their children from starvation except the youngest,[5] whose child thus becomes the son of seven mothers and hero, hero helps them to live,[6] hero shoots one of the white-hind queen's pigeons,[7] white hind recognises him and promises to show him where his mothers' eyes are, sends him to her mother with instructions[8] to kill him, on the road hero is forcibly married to a princess[9] who reads instructions and alters the contents into instructions to give him the seven queens' eyes,[10] gets the eyes, again shoots one of the white hind's pigeons who sends him off to her mother with instructions to kill him on pretence of getting him the wonderful cow,[11] he gets the cow,[12] shoots a third pigeon and the white hind sends him a third time to her mother on pretence of getting him the million-fold rice, gets the rice,[13] brings home his bride, who informs his father of the doings of the white hind,[14] white hind is killed,[15] and all goes well. *Incidental circumstances :* (1) by simple word of mouth ; (2) north, the seven queens had dreams that some evil would come of his hunting to the north ; (3) the golden horns and silver hoof ; (4) king follows her up till she disappears, he then goes into a hovel for a drink, and in the daughter of the house he recognises the white hind, she is white-skinned and golden-haired ; (5) she would not eat her share and so returned the others her share of their children and saved her own child ; (6) by going out of the prison and procuring sweets, etc. ; (7) and thus becomes introduced to the white hind ; (8) written on a potsherd ; (9) princess having power to choose a husband says she will only choose the 'son of seven mothers,' hero as a stranger is dragged into her presence and is chosen by her ; (10) he finds the old mother wearing the necklace of eyes, but she has eaten *one*, so the youngest queen, hero's own mother, gets only one back ; (11) the *jôgi's* wonderful cow's milk flows all day and makes a pond as big as a kingdom, it is guarded by 18,000 demons ; (12) he goes on the road to look up his princess, who again alters the instructions, and white hind's mother shows him how to get the cow, viz. by telling the *jôgi* that his skin was wanted for a new drum for the *jôgi's* master, Râjâ Indra, and taking the cow as a bribe to let the *jôgi* off ; he was not to look right or left while going there to the demons ; (13) in the same way the white hind's mother tells him how to get the rice guarded by 18,000,000 demons, he plucks it, and on his way back turns round, whereon he is reduced to ashes, the old mother finds him, makes them into a paste and the paste into his image, puts a drop of blood from her little finger into his mouth, blows on it and so restores him ; (14) she gets a palace built on the plan of the king's and invites king to see her husband, king does so and meets the seven blind queens and his son, the whole story is thus explained; (15) she is put to death and her grave ploughed over. *Where published*, Indian Antiquary, vol. x. p. 147 ff. *Nature of collection :* (1) *Original or translation ;* original, collected by F. A. Steel; (2) *Narrator's name*, not given ; a Purbiâ boy living at Firôzpûr ; *Other particulars*, nil.

XI

Number in collection, 11. *Reference to pages*, 102 to 106. *Specific name*, The Sparrow and the Crow. *Dramatis personæ :* sparrow, crow, pond, deer, cow, grass, blacksmith. *Thread of story*, sparrow makes some *khichrî* for herself and the crow, tells crow he is too dirty to eat it without washing. Crow goes to the pond and asks for water, who sends him to the deer for the use of his horn to dig a place for the water to flow into, who sends him to the cow for milk to console him for the pain of losing a horn, who sends him to the grass to get food in order to make milk, who sends him to the blacksmith for a sickle to cut the blades with, who tells him to light a fire that he may forge a sickle, and in doing so the crow falls into the fire and is killed, and the sparrow gets the *khichrî*. *Incidental circumstances*, nil. *Where published*, Indian Antiquary, vol. ix. p. 207 ff. *Nature of collection :* (1) *Original or translation*, original, collected by F. A. Steel ; (2) *Narrator's name*, not given ; (3) *Other particulars*, very common tale in the Firôzpûr, Siâlkôt, and Lahore districts.

XII

Number in collection, 12. *Reference to pages*, 107 to 110. *Specific name*, The Tiger, the Brâhman, and the Jackal. *Dramatis personæ :* tiger, Brâhman, *pîpal* tree, buffalo, the road, jackal. *Thread of story*, tiger caught in a trap, gets Brâhman to let him out, proceeds to eat him on being released, but gives Brâhman leave to ask three things if the tiger was just, he asks a *pîpal* tree,[1] a buffalo,[2] and the road,[3] who tell him that in their own cases ingratitude is shown in a very strong light, and that he cannot expect anything else, he then consults a jackal, who, by a trick,[4] releases him and shuts tiger up in the cage again. *Incidental circumstances :* (1) *pîpal* complains that in return for the shelter he gives to mankind they tear down his branches for food for their cattle ; (2) buffalo complains that while she gave milk she was well fed, but now that she is dry they yoke her to the oil-press ; (3) the road complains that in return for the ease it gives mankind they do nothing but trample on it, and leave it the refuse of their pipes and grain ; (4) he pretends he cannot comprehend the Brâhman's story, and the tiger from irritation at his denseness jumps into the cage to show him how matters were at the commencement, jackal shuts the door. *Where published*, Indian Antiquary, vol. xii. p. 170 ff. *Nature of collection:* (1) *Original or translation*, original, collected by F. A. Steel; (2) *Narrator's name*, not given, a Jaṭṭ boy of Chûhar-khâna in the Gujrânwâlâ district; (3) *Other particulars*, nil.

XIII

Number in collection, 13. *Reference to pages*, 111 to 117. *Specific name*, The King of the Crocodiles. *Dramatis personæ:* farmer, king of the crocodiles, farmer's wife and daughter (heroine). *Thread of story*, crocodiles destroy a farmer's cornfields, he throws stones at them, whereon they attack him and release him only on condition that he marries his daughter to the biggest, he agrees but his wife refuses, various misfortunes ensue in consequence,[1] so the daughter is married to the king of the crocodiles in ordinary fashion, and disappears beneath the stream with him,[2] her father after a while follows her,[3] finds her dwelling in splendour and comfort, and in time induces her mother to join them in their home beneath the waters. *Incidental circumstances:* (1) the girl's suitors die one after another and at last the girl falls and breaks her leg; (2) as soon as the bride's feet touch the river the waters divide and she walks to the crocodile's palace dry-shod, her husband gives the father a brick to throw into the river whenever he wants to visit them and the waters will divide for him; (3) by the use of the brick he finds that beneath the waters the crocodiles are in human form, being crocodiles only on shore and out of the waters. *Where published*, Indian Antiquary, vol. ix. p. 280 ff. *Nature of collection:* (1) *Original or translation*, original, collected by F. A. Steel; (2) *Narrator's name*, not given; (3) *Other particulars*, common story in the Panjâb among the women.

XIV

Number in collection, 14. *Reference to pages*, 118 to 122. *Specific name*, Little Anklebone. *Dramatis personæ:* shepherd boy, wolf, old woman, king. *Thread of story*, a small shepherd boy meets a wolf who eats him,[1] and at his request after eating him hangs his anklebone by a thread to a tree overhanging a pond, three robbers come underneath to divide their spoil when a jackal howls[2] and at the same moment the anklebone falls on one of their heads, they run away, whereon anklebone obtains their wealth, buys a pipe and plays on it to the female animal creation,[3] and he milks them and makes a pond of milk; an old woman comes for water and discovers it,[4] informs the king of the country who chases anklebone, and when he catches him finds him to be a mere anklebone and so lets him go ; his piping, however, is still to be heard in the wilds. *Incidental circumstances:* (1) anklebone has an aunt, and his aunt decides that the wolf is to eat the shepherd instead of the sheep, the child always piped while tending the sheep ; (2) a bad omen, and hence the robbers' fright ; (3) does, tigresses, and she-wolves come together to hear him play and he milks them ; (4) she asks for water and anklebone directs her to the milken pond. *Where published*, Indian Antiquary, vol. xii. p. 103 ff. *Nature of collection: Original or translation*, original, collected by F. A. Steel ; (2) *Narrator's name*, not given, told by a small boy of the *Bâr* (wilds) of the Gujrânwâlâ district ; (3) *Other particulars*, nil.

XV

Number in collection, 15. *Reference to pages*, 123 to 128. *Specific name*, The Close Alliance. *Dramatis personæ:* farmer, tiger, farmer's wife, jackal. *Thread of story*, a farmer is ploughing with bullocks, tiger proposes to eat the bullocks, but agrees to take the farmer's wife's milch cow instead, she refuses to give her up, and frightens tiger by a trick,[1] and so saves the cow ; tiger meets his jackal,[2] who persuades the tiger to return, as it was only a woman that frightened him, tiger won't go until they tie their tails together ; farmer's wife again frightens tiger,[3] who runs off with the jackal tied to his tail, jackal is bumped to death in the flight.[4] *Incidental circumstances:* (1) she dresses herself up as a horseman and shouts out that she is glad the tiger is there, as she has not had any food for three days, when she had eaten three tigers ; tiger is frightened and runs off; (2) who used to find him prey and took the leavings as his wages; jackal is determined not to be done out of his bones by tiger's cowardice, and so eggs him on to return ; (3) she calls out to the jackal that it was kind of him to bring such a fat tiger for dinner ; (4) there is a moral attached to the story, 'Don't trust cowards.' *Where published*, Indian Antiquary, vol. xi. p. 319 ff. *Nature of collection:* (1) *Original or translation*, original, collected by F. A. Steel ; (2) *Narrator's name*, Habîb, a Musalmân cooly in Kashmîr ; (3) *Other particulars*, a common village tale in Kashmîr.

XVI

Number in collection, 16. *Reference to pages*, 139 to 143. *Specific name*, The Two Brothers. *Dramatis personæ:* stepmother, her two stepsons, snake-demon, magician, old woman, scavenger, minister's daughter. *Thread of story*, the two heroes' stepmother ill-treats them,[1] and they run away to seek fortune riding on one pony, halt under a tree, a starling and a parrot are talking in the tree,[2] eldest son eats parrot and is thus destined to be a king, the younger eats the starling and is destined to be a minister. They journey on but miss their whip, elder goes on on foot, younger goes back with pony to find whip under the tree, the snake-demon of the tree bites and kills him, elder reaches a city and is proclaimed king,[3] and hearing nothing of his brother appoints another minister; magician finds younger hero under the tree and restores him to life,[4] he journeys on but reaches a different city, finds an old woman herding goats, gives her his pony for his board and lodging, finds that an ogre devours daily an inhabitant of the city in turn, offers himself for the old woman when her turn comes,[5] attacks ogre and kills him, cuts off his head and goes to sleep; a scavenger comes to clean up the place and finding the ogre dead and the hero asleep, buries the hero alive and takes the head of the ogre to the king, obtains half the kingdom, but not the princess promised in reward;[6] some potters find the hero and take him, and finding himself supplanted the hero joins them and becomes a very skilful potter; the annual fleet of ships to the city cannot get away owing to foul winds, so hero is chosen for the human sacrifice necessary for a fair wind, he however makes the ships sail,[7] and goes off with the merchants, who take him to his brother's kingdom, there he meets and marries the minister's daughter,[8] and finally is recognised by his brother who makes him minister;[9] but the scavenger king is put to death.[10] *Incidental circumstances:* (1) she starves and beats them and then tells their father they are peevish and so he ill-treats them too; (2) they are quarrelling, starling says whoever eats him will become a minister, and parrot that whoever eats him will become a king, thereupon the brothers kill and eat them; (3) the king had died and the sacred elephant is to choose his successor by saluting him, he will choose none of the inhabitants and so hero as a stranger is dragged before him, elephant salutes him at once; (4) magician's wife taunts her husband till he agrees to arrange the boy's restoration to life, he directs her to put her water-pot into the stream near the tree, whereon *all* the water flows into the pot and it dries up, snakes cannot bear the thirst thus created and agree to restore the boy to life as the price of recovering their water, the water is restored by emptying the pot back into the stream; (5) the ogre got daily a human being, a goat, and a cake, he generally ate the human being first, but hero takes a very fat goat and a very large cake, so demon goes at them first, and while he is eating, hero attacks him; (6) the marriage is delayed for a year, as the king was sure the scavenger was not the real hero; (7) by cutting his little finger; with the third drop of blood the ships float down the wind; (8) he makes a model of his palace in clay for amusement, the minister's daughter sees it and swears she will marry no one else; when she marries him her father gets the merchants to take them out to sea and drop the hero overboard, but he climbs in by a rope to his wife's cabin, who brings him home disguised as a maid ; (9) he personates the gardener's daughter and makes up a bouquet for his brother the king in the fashion in vogue in their own country, king recognises this, goes to see the gardener's daughter and finally is sure of his brother by the latter's relation of his story ; (10) the princess that was to have married him marries the elder hero, the younger already having a wife. *Where published,* Indian Antiquary, vol. xi. p. 342 ff. *Nature of Collection :* (1) *Original or translation,* original, collected by F. A. Steel ; (2) *Narrator's name,* not given ; (3) *Other particulars,* collected in Kashmîr.

XVII

Number in collection, 17. *Reference to pages,* 144 to 147. *Specific name,* The Jackal and the Iguana. *Dramatis personæ :* jackal, iguana. *Thread of story,* a half-starved jackal finding a pair of slippers in a gutter wears them as earrings, builds a mud platform by a tank and sets himself up for somebody. He insists on all the animals who go there to drink first saluting him,[1] a tiger out of jest does so and so do others, this makes jackal very proud ; an iguana, however, tricks him, and jeers at him, and finally escapes him by a trick.[2] *Incidental circumstances :* (1) by repeating some verses in his honour ; (2) iguana pretends he is so hoarse that he cannot unless he drinks first, so he is allowed to do so, he then repeats verses in parody of those insisted on, jackal pursues him, catches his tail just outside his hole, but iguana induces him to let go by saying if he will do so he will come out and repeat the verses properly. *Where published,* new. *Nature of collection :* (1) *Original or translation,* original, collected by F. A. Steel ; (2) *Narrator's name,* not given, a Muhammadan girl of Muzaffargarh ; (3) *Other particulars,* daughter of a Police Inspector, native of Chûniân in the Lahore district.

XVIII

Number in collection, 18. *Reference to pages,* 148 to 158. *Specific name,* Death and Burial of Poor Hen-sparrow. *Dramatis personæ :* cock-sparrow, old and young hen-sparrows, *pîpal* tree, buffalo, cuckoo, Bhagtû the tradesman, maid, queen, prince, king. *Thread of story,* old cock-sparrow marries a young hen, old hen sitting disconsolate on a branch in the rain is dyed in gay hues by the colours that run from a crow's nest above her ;[1] young sparrow sees it and is informed by the old hen that the way to be dyed is to pop into the dyer's vat, young hen does so and is scalded ; is found there by her husband who picks her up

and takes her home in his beak, on arrival at the nest old hen jeers and
the sparrow in his wrath opens his mouth to abuse her and so drops the
young hen who is drowned in the stream beneath him, he then mourns
her by losing his feathers and is joined in the mourning in a comic
way successively by a *pīpal* tree, a buffalo, a cuckoo, a tradesman, a
maid, the queen, the prince, and the king. *Incidental circumstances:*
(1) the crow had used scraps of dyed cloth for his nest. *Where
published*, Indian Antiquary, vol. xi. p. 169 ff. *Nature of collection:*
(1) *Original or translation*, original, collected by F. A. Steel; (2)
Narrator's name, Hajjan, a Pathân girl at Muzaffargarh; (3) *Other
particulars*, nil.

XIX

Number in collection, 19. *Reference to pages*, 159 to 166. *Specific
name*, Princess Pepperina. *Dramatis personæ:* bulbul and his mate,
jinn, heroine, hero, heroine's enemies, pair of sheldrakes. *Thread of
story*, bulbul wants a green pepper to eat, her mate goes for it, finds it
in jinn's deserted palace,[1] they eat it,[2] bulbul lays an egg[3] beside it
which jinn finds and takes charge of, out of the egg comes heroine,[4] jinn
befriends her, she meets hero,[5] and marries him,[6] leaves her home for
his,[7] her enemies then calumniate her by ostensibly proving her to be
an ogress,[8] so she is turned out of the palace,[9] and becomes a garden
and her soul goes into two sheldrakes,[10] here her husband finds her[11]
and lives with her for the rest of their days in happiness.[12] *Incidental
circumstances:* (1) there is no sign of animal life in it, not even birds
and insects; (2) he finds one pepper plant with one green pepper on it,
the jinn is undergoing a twelve years' sleep and while he is waking they
eat it and fly away; (3) of a glittering emerald-green colour; (4) the
jinn had carefully put it away, it turned into a little maiden dressed in
emerald green with a talisman in the shape of an emerald round her
neck like a green pepper; (5) hero (a king) comes hunting, finds heroine
and they fall in love; (6) jinn smells him, but heroine protects and
hides him, and as the jinn's time for sleeping had come again, she persuades him into letting her marry a person as beautiful as herself and
produces hero; (7) jinn follows them as a dove, a hawk, and an eagle
till he is satisfied that she goes to her new home safely and then goes to
his sleep; (8) Pepperina's talisman always speaks the truth on hearing
a lie and while she wears it no one can harm her, one day she left it at
her bathing-place, her enemies tell a lie, and so ascertain she has it off
her neck, go to her, kill her child in bed and put the blood on her lips as
she sleeps, tell her husband that she is therefore an ogress; (9) scourged
out; (10) her body is the marble wall, her eyes the pool, her green
mantle the grass, her hair the creepers, her mouth and teeth the roses

and narcissus, her soul a sheldrake and his mate; (11) her husband arrives out hunting, overhears sheldrake say that if he will kill them both at one blow he will recover his wife, he does so, and Pepperina appears in her garden; (12) jinn, having awakened, joins them, builds them a palace and lives with him, then Pepperina never leaves the palace again. *Where published*, Indian Antiquary, vol. x. p. 80 ff. *Nature of collection:* (1) *Original or translation*, original, collected by F. A. Steel; (2) *Narrator's name*, not given, a Muhammadan woman from Kasûr; (3) *Other particulars*, nil.

XX

Number in collection, 20. *Reference to pages*, 167 to 172. *Specific name*, Peasie and Beansie. *Dramatis personæ:* Peasie, Beansie, a plum-tree, a *pîpal*, a stream, Peasie's father, brother, and sister-in-law. *Thread of story*, the younger sister Peasie is a pleasant girl, the elder Beansie is disagreeable. Peasie goes to see her father and on her way benefits a plum-tree,[1] a *pîpal*,[2] a stream,[3] and a fire,[4] and delights her father. They all reward her,[5] on her way home. Beansie is very jealous, and next day Beansie goes to see what she can get out of her father, but on the way will help nothing, and so when she reaches her father she gets a beating from her brother and his wife,[6] and is played tricks by the plum-tree and so on. *Incidental circumstances:* (1) she tidies up the plum-tree's thorns for him; (2) binds up a broken branch for the *pîpal;* (3) clears the stream's channel; (4) takes away the ashes that are choking the fire; (5) her father gives her a spinning-wheel, a buffalo, a brass pot, a bed, and other things, as if she were a bride going to her husband, the stream gives a fine cloth, the *pîpal* a string of pearls, the fire a nice hot cake, the plum-tree ripe yellow fruit; (6) they say that the day previous Peasie had got great presents out of the father, and that as Beansie had turned up the next day the sisters evidently were trying to see what they could get out of him. *Where published*, new. *Nature of collection:* (1) *Original or translation*, original, collected by F. A. Steel; (2) *Narrator's name*, not given, a Jatt boy in Farmânâ, in the Rohtak district; (3) *Other particulars*, common all over the Rohtak district.

XXI

Number in collection, 21. *Reference to pages*, 173 to 177. *Specific name*, The Jackal and the Partridge. *Dramatis personæ:* jackal, partridge, crocodile. *Thread of story*, jackal sets partridge to—(1) make him laugh, (2) make him cry, (3) give him a dinner, (4) save his life—as proofs of her friendship; partridge (1) sets two travellers fighting,[1] and so makes him laugh ; (2) sets a hunter and his dogs to worry the jackal,[2] and so makes him cry ; (3) gets some women to chase her,[3] while the jackal eats the dinner ; (4) prevents a crocodile from drowning the jackal, and so saves his life.[4] *Incidental circumstances:* one is going in front of the other, she settles gently on the former's stick over his shoulder, the hindmost then throws his shoe at her and knocks off the foremost's turban, and there is a fight ; (2) she induces jackal to enter a tree and while there by fluttering about attracts a hunter and his pack, who spy out the jackal and worry him ; (3) she pretends to be wounded, and so the women drop their food to chase her ; (4) induces a crocodile to carry them across a river and *en route* suggests he should upset the jackal, but at last dissuades him by saying that the jackal had left his life behind him on the other shore. *Where published*, new. *Nature of collection:* (1) *Original or translation*, original, collected by F. A. Steel ; (2) *Narrator's name*, not given ; (3) *Other particulars*, nil.

XXII

Number in collection, 22. *Reference to pages*, 178 to 184. *Specific name*, The Snake-woman and King Ali Mardan. *Dramatis personæ:* Ali Mardan, snake-woman, *jôgi*. *Thread of story*, hero goes out hunting and meets heroine,[1] takes her to live with him, comes across *jôgi's* servant with enchanted ointment[2] box, and sends for *jôgi*, *jôgi* comes, and shows him how to prove her to be snake-woman,[3] and finally how to kill her,[4] her ashes contain the philosopher's stone.[5] *Incidental circumstances:* (1) she is a *lamia*, and says she is a slave of the king of China who has lost herself ; (2) it enables its possessor to annihilate distance, *jôgi's* servant is on his way to fetch sacred water for his master and strays into hero's garden ; (3) a serpent being obliged to assume its own form at night, hero gives the snake-woman some salt food to eat, which obliges her to change her form and go out for water, hero following her ; (4) she is induced to play at cooking food with hero and while putting bread into the oven is tipped in by hero and burnt ; (5) the essence of the snake-woman is found in her ashes, and is a stone which will turn anything it touches into gold, hero will not keep it, but throws it into a river. *Where published*, Indian Antiquary, vol. xi. p. 230 ff. *Nature of collection:* (1) *Original or translation*, original, collected by F. A. Steel ; (2) *Narrator's name*, Pandit Nânâ Beo, at Khrû, near Srînagar. *Other particulars*, nil.

XXIII

Number in collection, 23. *Reference to pages*, 185 to 194. *Specific name*, The Wonderful Ring. *Dramatis personæ:* spendthrift hero, cat, parrot, snake, princess, witch. *Thread of story*, spendthrift hero starts with four rupees,[1] spends one each on a cat, a dog, a parrot, and a snake, and then starves, on this the snake in gratitude[2] obtains for him the wonderful ring,[3] which will procure whatever is wanted instantly for its possessor,[4] by means of this ring hero builds a golden palace in the sea and marries a princess,[5] turns her into gold at her request, heroine washing by the sea puts her golden hair into a cup of leaves which are floated to a king's palace, his son sees them and determines to marry the owner, a witch is sent to find her,[6] does so, and by a trick gets possession of the ring,[7] takes princess to her master,[8] princess refuses to marry him for six months in hopes her husband will turn up, meanwhile hero returns, the cat and parrot explain to him what had happened, and parrot flies off to heroine,[9] parrot and cat then get possession of the wonderful ring from the witch, and by it she is restored to the hero. *Incidental circumstances:* (1) finding him wasting all the property his brother divides it with him, he soon wastes his share and at last borrows the four rupees from his wife; (2) having by the hero been released from the thraldom of his master, a *jôgi;* (3) the snake takes him to his father who offers him anything he wishes, hero chooses by snake's advice the father's enchanted signet ring; (4) food or any wish whatever: it is to be put into a cooking-place and sprinkled with curds; (5) the king of a city has issued a proclamation that whoever will build a golden palace in the sea in a single night shall marry his daughter; (6) she is rowed in a boat to the palace, when she raises her thumb the men are to row, when she puts it down they are to stop; (7) persuades heroine to get hero to leave it with her in case any accidents happened to him when hunting, and persuades them both that she is heroine's aunt; (8) persuades her to take a sail in the boat and then rows off with her, recognising her by her golden hair; (9) the cat and parrot tell the princess to strew some rice about while the witch sleeps, this brings rats, whereon the cat catches one and puts its tail up the witch's nose, which makes her sneeze violently and throw the ring out of her mouth, where she always kept it, on which the parrot seizes it and takes it to his master. *Where published*, Indian Antiquary, vol. x. p. 347 ff. *Nature of collection:* (1) *Original or translation*, original, collected by R. C. Temple; (2) *Narrator's name*, not given; (3) *Other particulars*, small boy at Firozpûr.

XXIV

Number in collection, 24. *Reference to pages*, 195 to 197. *Specific name*, The Jackal and the Pea-hen. *Dramatis personæ:* jackal, pea-hen. *Thread of story*, jackal and the pea-hen swear friendship, pea-hen eats plums, and jackal a kid. Pea-hen buries the stones and explains that they will grow into trees, whereon jackal buries his bones, pea-hen's stones come and jackal's do not, whereon pea-hen jeers at him and he in his anger eats her. Moral, 'Don't be wiser than your friends.' *Incidental circumstances*, nil. *Where published*, new. *Nature of collection*: (1) *Original or translation*, original, collected by F. A. Steel; (2) *Narrator's name*, not given; (3) *Other particulars*, common everywhere in the Panjâb.

XXV

Number in collection, 25. *Reference to pages*, 198 to 202. *Specific name*, The Grain of Corn. *Dramatis personæ*: farmer's wife, crow. *Thread of story*, a crow swoops off with a grain of corn while a farmer's wife is winnowing, she throws a stone at the crow and knocks him over, but agrees to let him off if he will recover the grain. It has fallen into a crack in a tree, whereon he tries to get a woodman to cut the tree down, he refuses, so he goes successively to the king, queen, snake, stick, fire, water, ox, rope, mouse, and lastly, a cat. The cat goes at once for the mouse and so the train is fired, and the crow gets the grain of corn. *Incidental circumstances*, nil. *Where published*, new. *Nature of collection*: (1) *Original or translation*, original, collected by F. A. Steel; (2) *Narrator's name*, not given. (3) *Other particulars*, common story everywhere in the Panjâb.

XXVI

Number in collection, 26. *Reference to pages*, 203 to 206. *Specific name*, The Farmer and the Money-lender. *Dramatis personæ*: farmer, money-lender, Râm. *Thread of story*, farmer asks the money-lender how he got so rich, the money-lender says from Râm (God), and sets the farmer to find him, the farmer sets out and finds a man who calls himself Râm, who gives him a conch to blow whenever he wants anything, but he must blow it in a particular way. The money-lender worms the secret out of him except the way in which the conch is to be blown, but steals it, and gives it him back on the understanding that he gets double of whatever it brings the farmer, farmer in his wrath and mortification wishes he lost an eye, on which the money-lender loses both, and being blind falls into a well and is killed. *Incidental circumstances*: (1) He starts with three cakes, gives one to a *jôgi*, and one to a Brâhman, and asks the way to Râm (God), neither helps him, and then he gives his third and last to the man who says he is Râm. *Where published*, new. *Nature of collection*: (1) *Original or translation*, original, collected by F. A. Steel; (2) *Narrator's name*, not given, a Jaṭṭ boy in Rohtak; (3) *Other particulars*, common everywhere.

XXVII

Number in collection, 27.   *Reference to pages*, 207 to 210.   *Specific name*, The Lord of Death.   *Dramatis personæ:* old man, Lord of Death in his metamorphosed forms of scorpion, snake, buffalo, ox, maiden, old man.   *Thread of story*, every traveller on a certain road dies, an old man travels it, sees a scorpion changed into a snake and follows it up, watches it kill one person after another,[1] a river crosses the road, snake changes into a buffalo, and offers to ferry some travellers over, drops them in the stream, old man crosses in a boat and finds buffalo has become an ox which a peasant leads home, in the night it becomes a snake and kills the whole household and live-stock, another river crosses the road and the snake becomes a beautiful girl over whom two brothers quarrel and kill each other,[2] the creature again becomes a snake, then becomes an old man, whom the traveller seizes and asks who he is, the reply is 'I am the Lord of Death,' on which the old man demands death, but is told his hour is not yet come.   *Incidental circumstances :* (1) it kills all the travellers in an inn, then the king in his house, then goes up the waterspout and takes the king's eldest daughter ; (2) the snake-girl agrees to marry the elder brother, sends him off on the pretext of making him fetch a glass of water from a well, while he is away she offers to run off with the younger, who refuses ; on the elder's return she charges the younger with attempt at seduction, on this they fight and kill each other.   *Where published*, Indian Antiquary, vol. ix. p. 209 ff.   *Nature of collection* : (1) *Original or translation*, original, collected by F. A. Steel ; (2) *Narrator's name*, not given, a boy from the North-West Provinces ; (3) *Other particulars*, nil.

XXVIII

Number in collection, 28.   *Reference to pages*, 211 to 215.   *Specific name*, The Wrestlers (a tale of heroes).   *Dramatis personæ* : 1st wrestler, 2nd wrestler's daughter, 2nd wrestler, an old woman and her daughter.   *Thread of story*, a wrestler hears of another and comes to test his skill with him, the wrestler possesses miraculous ways proved by various incidents,[1] finds the rival out when he reaches his house, shows his strength, but is astonished at that displayed by the rival's daughter,[2] meets rival in the woods and they try strength,[3] meet an old woman whom they ask to be umpire, she takes them up and they wrestle on her hand ; the old woman is after her daughter who has been stealing her camels, the girl on seeing her walks off with 160 camels in her blanket and performs other marvellous feats ending in populating a mud-bank with the contents of her blanket.[4]   *Incidental circumstances :* (1)

he takes 10,000 lbs. of flour, mixes it in a pond as gruel, and eats up the
result as a meal ; an elephant comes to drink, finds no water and tries
to kill the wrestler, but he takes the elephant up by the trunk, flings
him over his shoulder and goes on ; (2) he chucks the elephant over the
house wall, but the rival's daughter sweeps it over the wall back again
as a mouse ; (3) finds him dragging along 160 carts laden, pulls at the .
other end and the party comes to a standstill ; (4) her blanket contains
successively 160 camels, two or three trees for them to eat, a farmer who
tries to stop her, and all his fields, oxen, and house, a town bodily, and
everything she met.   By a river she stops and eats a water-melon and
puts the whole lot into its rind and floats it down the river, when it lands
on a mudbank, upsets, and thus populates it.   *Where published*, Indian
Antiquary, vol. xi. p. 229 ff.   *Nature of collection:* (1) *Original or
translation*, original, collected by F. A. Steel ; (2) *Narrator's name*, not
given, a Musalmân cook at Muzaffargaṛh ; (3) *Other particulars*, narrator
came from Bândâ.

XXIX

Number in collection, 29.   *Reference to pages*, 216 to 219.   *Specific
name*, The Legend of Gwâshbrârî, the Glacier-hearted Queen.   *Dramatis
personæ* : Mount Westarwân, Mount Gwâshbrârî.   *Thread of story*,
Mount Westarwân (male) is the tallest mountain in Kashmîr, and the
others are jealous, and induce Mount Gwâshbrârî (female) to make him
fall in love.   When the full beauty of the evening glow falls over her he
calls out to her to kiss him, but she says he is too tall, so he lays his
great length across the plains of Kashmîr in order to reach her, but she
makes him lie at her feet for ever, and that is why he stretches all across
the Kashmîr plains.   *Incidental circumstances*, nil.   *Where published*,
Indian Antiquary, vol. xi. p. 259 ff.   *Nature of collection :* (1) *Original
or translation*, original, collected by F. A. Steel ; (2) *Narrator's name*,
Paṇḍit Nânâ Beo of Khrû, Kashmîr ; (3) *Other particulars*, nil.

XXX

Number in collection, 30.   *Reference to pages*, 220 to 229.   *Specific
name*, The Barber's Clever Wife.   *Dramatis personæ:* barber, barber's
wife, thieves, the leading thief.   *Thread of story*, stupid barber loses all
his money, clever wife tells him to beg of the king, who gives him a
piece of waste land,[1] wife by a trick gets thieves to dig it up for her,[2]
she has a fine harvest which she sells for a crock of gold pieces, thieves
attempt several times to get possession of this, first time get a crock of
goats' droppings instead,[3] second time they are stung by hornets,[4] third

time get their noses cut off,[5] fourth time the chief gets his tongue bitten off,[6] fifth time lose their suit in court,[7] all by the sharpness of the barber's wife. *Incidental circumstances :* (1) the man though starving is such a fool that he accepts anything offered ; (2) she and her husband go looking about the field all day as if something was there, and she confides to the thieves that a pot of gold is buried somewhere in it, at night they plough it up to find it ; (3) she sees one of the thieves hiding in the house and says to her husband that the crock is in the niche by the door loud enough for the thief to hear, he carries off the crock, but it is full of droppings ; (4) another thief hides, she sees him and says to her husband that she has hung up the gold in a bag to a tree outside, the 'bag' is a hornets' nest, and when the thieves go for it they are thoroughly stung ; (5) she slices off each man's nose just as it appears through the window as they try to get in, except the leader's ; (6) they carry her off, bed and all, while asleep and pass under a banyan tree into which she swings herself, they rest under it, she then pretends to be a fairy in the tree in love with the leading thief, he climbs into the tree and she tells him the way to catch a fairy is to touch her tongue with the tip of his, he puts out his tongue and she bites off the end, which causes him to fall down on the thieves and they all run away, she goes home again ; (7) by sheer force of argument she wins her suit. *Where published,* new. *Nature of collection :* (1) *Original or translation,* original, collected by F. A. Steel ; (2) *Narrator's name,* not given ; (3) *Other particulars,* a very common tale all over the Panjâb.

XXXI

Number in collection, 31. *Reference to pages,* 230 to 233. *Specific name,* The Jackal and Crocodile. *Dramatis personæ :* Mr. Jackal, Miss Crocodile. *Thread of story,* jackal makes love to the crocodile, and induces her to swim him across a stream to some fruit he wants to eat under promise of marriage, and back again, when he says he thinks it may be a *long* time before he can make arrangements for the marriage, crocodile in revenge watches till he comes to drink and seizes him by the leg, by a trick he escapes,[1] crocodile then goes to his den, but he makes her show involuntarily where she is,[2] and so escapes her. *Incidental circumstances :* (1) she seizes him by the leg, but he cries out that if she will only get hold of his leg *instead* of a root it will be all right, she leaves go in order to do so and he escapes ; (2) he says when he finds her there shamming dead that the dead always wag their tails and she does so, showing her to be alive. *Where published,* new. *Nature of collection :* (1) *Original or translation,* original, collected by F. A. Steel ; (2) *Narrator's name,* not given ; (3) *Other particulars,* a very common story.

XXXII

Number in collection, 32. *Reference to pages*, 234 to 237. *Specific name*, How Râjâ Rasâlu was born. *Dramatis personæ:* Râjâ Sâlbâhan, Rânî Lonân, Pûran Bhagat, Gurû Gorakhnâth. *Thread of story*, king has two wives, has a son by the elder with whom the younger falls in love and accuses to the father from jealousy,[1] he cuts off his hands and feet and throws him down a well, a saint sees him and restores his hands and feet to him and rescues him, the prince turns saint and visits his old home,[2] he restores his mother's sight,[3] and procures a son for his stepmother,[4] who is to be Râjâ Rasâlu, a great man, but who will desert his mother.[5] *Incidental circumstances:* (1) she accuses him of attempt at rape; (2) finds the garden where he was brought up neglected, makes it green again by sprinkling water over it; (3) she had gone blind weeping for him; (4) by giving her a grain of rice to eat; (5) the father is told that he must not see the child's face for twelve years, so the hero is shut up with a colt born at the same hour as himself in a cellar. *Where published*, Legends of the Panjâb, vol. i. p. 1. *Nature of collection:* (1) *Original or translation*, translation by R. C. Temple; (2) *Narrator's name*, not given, a village accountant from Râwal Pindî; (3) *Other particulars*, translated from original MSS. in possession of Mr. J. G. Delmerick.

XXXIII

Number of collection, 33. *Reference to pages*, 238 to 241. *Specific name*, How Râjâ Rasâlu went out into the world. *Dramatis personæ:* Râjâ Rasâlu, Râjâ Sâlbâhan. *Thread of story*, at eleven years old hero leaves his home,[1] meets some women drawing water at a well, breaks all their pitchers,[2] they complain to king, who is afraid to see him, as twelve years have not expired, so he gives the women iron pitchers, hero breaks these,[3] still king will not send for him, so he goes to see him, but king turns his back on him, so hero goes to seek fortune.[4] *Incidental circumstances:* (1) On his favourite horse; (2) by throwing stones; (3) by shooting them with arrows; (4) but he first gets his mother's blessing. *Where published*, Legends of the Panjâb, vol. i. p. 4. *Nature of collection:* (1) *Original or translation*, translated by R. C. Temple; (2) *Narrator's name*, not given, a village accountant from Râwal Pindî; (3) *Other particulars*, translated from the original MSS. in possession of Mr. J. G. Delmerick.

XXXIV

Number in collection, 34. *Reference to pages*, 242 to 244. *Specific name*, How Râjâ Rasâlu's friends forsook him. *Dramatis personæ:*

Râjâ Rasâlu, carpenter, goldsmith. *Thread of story*, hero starts with two friends[1] to seek fortune, first night he and his friends keep watch, friends kill serpents, hero kills a horror which so frightened the friends that they turn back, hero goes on alone. *Incidental circumstances:* (1) They are a goldsmith and a carpenter. *Where published*, Legends of the Panjâb, vol. i. p. 8. *Nature of collection:* (1) *Original or translation,* translated by R. C. Temple; (2) *Narrator's name,* not given, a village accountant of Râwal Pindî; (3) *Other particulars,* translated from original MSS. in possession of Mr. J. G. Delmerick.

XXXV

Number in collection, 35. *Reference to pages*, 245 to 249. *Specific name*, How Râjâ Rasâlu killed the Giants. *Dramatis personæ:* Râjâ Rasâlu, old woman, giants, giantess. *Thread of story*, hero comes to a city, finds an old woman,[1] whose last son is to be given up to the giants,[2] offers himself in his place,[3] goes off to the giants,[4] proves himself to be the expected hero,[5] kills them all except one giantess whom he imprisons in a cave for ever.[6] *Incidental circumstances:* (1) she is baking and sometimes laughing and sometimes crying; (2) she explains that a giant takes one inhabitant, a buffalo, and a loaf a day, six of her sons have gone, the seventh's turn has come; (3) the city officials try to prevent him; (4) meets one on the road and cuts off his hand, he runs off and tells the others; (5) proofs, his heel ropes bind the giants and his sword cuts them into pieces of their own accord, his arrow pierces seven iron plates and the seven last giants placed one behind the other; (6) she flies to a cave, and he places a figure of himself in full armour mounted at the door, which always frightens her back when she tries to come out. *Where published*, Legends of the Panjâb, vol. i. p. 17. *Nature of collection:* (1) *Original or translation,* translated by R. C. Temple; (2) *Narrator's name,* not given, a village accountant from Râwal Pindî; (3) *Other particulars,* translated from original MSS. in possession of Mr. J. G. Delmerick.

XXXVI

Number in collection, 36. *Reference to pages*, 250 to 254. *Specific name*, How Râjâ Rasâlu become a Jôgi. *Dramatis personæ:* Râja Rasâlu, Rânî Sundrân, *jôgi*. *Thread of story*, hero finds an old *jôgi* sitting outside a Rânî's gate trying to see her,[1] becomes his disciple, sees her,[2] tells her who he is, she falls in love with him, he runs away,[3] she goes to *jôgi* to inquire, he tells her he has eaten the hero,[4] so she burns herself to death. *Incidental circumstances:* (1) he has been there twenty-two years; (2) she sends maids out first, but they faint at his beauty, so she goes to see him herself; (3) for fear he should be found out and killed now that he has told his name; (4) out of revenge for her showing herself to hero, though she would never see him. *Where published*, Legends of the Panjâb, vol. i. p. 31. *Nature of collection:* (1) *Original or translation*, translated by R. C. Temple; (2) *Narrator's name*, not given, a village accountant from Râwal Pindî; (3) *Other particulars*, translated from original MSS. in possession of Mr. J. G. Delmerick.

XXXVII

Number in collection, 37. *Reference to pages*, 255 to 256. *Specific name*, How Râjâ Rasâlu journeyed to the City of King Sarkap. *Dramatis personæ:* Râjâ Rasâlu, headless corpse. *Thread of story*, hero finds a headless corpse whom he resuscitates,[1] tells him he is going to play the king at dice, corpse tells him his own story,[2] and shows him how to circumvent the king.[3] *Incidental circumstances:* (1) by merely praying to God; (2) he was the king's brother, king killed a man every day before breakfast, got no convenient victim one day so he killed his brother; (3) he is to make his dice from the bones in the graveyard where he finds the corpse. *Where published*, Legends of the Panjâb, vol. i. p. 39. *Nature of collection:* (1) *Original or translation*, translated by R. C. Temple; (2) *Narrator's name*, not given, a village accountant from Râwal Pindî; (3) *Other particulars*, translated from original MSS. in possession of Mr. J. G. Delmerick.

XXXVIII

Number in collection, 38. *Reference to pages*, 257 to 261. *Specific name*, How Râjâ Rasâlu swung the Seventy Fair Maidens, Daughters of the King. *Dramatis personæ:* Râjâ Rasâlu, cricket, seventy maidens, Râjâ Sarkap. *Thread of story*, hero is proceeding to play dice with the king, meets a cricket burning in a forest fire, saves it, it gives him a hair[1] which he is to burn when he is in trouble, meets the king's seventy daughters, the youngest falls in love with him, the others demand impossible tasks of him before he can marry her, crickets help him;[2] next task to swing them all, he swings them all in one swing and cuts the ropes and all are killed or hurt except his bride, who runs off to tell her father, meanwhile hero announces his arrival,[3] king tries to poison him, but hero saves himself.[4] *Incidental circumstances:* (1) one of its feelers; (2) he is to separate a hundredweight of millet seed from a hundredweight of sand, he burns the feeler and crickets come to perform the task; (3) by beating and breaking seventy gongs for announcing visitors; (4) he gives the food to dogs that die. *Where published*, Legends of the Panjâb, vol. i. p. 43. *Nature of collection :* (1) *Original or translation*, translated by R. C. Temple; (2) *Narrator's name*, not given, a village accountant from Râwal Pindî; (3) *Other particulars*, translated from original MSS. in possession of Mr. J. G. Delmerick.

XXXIX

Number in collection, 39. *Reference to pages*, 262 to 266. *Specific name*, How Râjâ Rasâlu played *chaupur* with Râjâ Sarkap. *Dramatis personæ ;* Râjâ Rasâlu, cat, kitten, Râjâ Sarkap. *Thread of story*, hero on his way to play dice with the king, meets a cat whose kittens he saves,[1] she gives him one in gratitude to help him in difficulties, hero goes on and plays his enemy,[2] loses the first two games,[3] but kitten befriends him,[4] and he wins his enemy's head,[5] and that moment his enemy has a daughter born whom he wishes to kill, as she was born in an unlucky time, hero saves the child who is given to him to be his wife when she grows old enough,[6] he carries off and finally marries her. *Incidental circumstances :* (1) the kittens are in an unburnt pot in a kiln about to be fired, hero buys up the kiln as it stands and saves them ; (2) stakes are—hero : first game his arms, second his horse, third his head ; enemy : first game his kingdom, second his wealth, third his head ; (3) enemy employs a rat, Dhol Râjâ, to upset hero's pieces so that enemy always wins ; (4) horse sees this and warns hero who lets loose his kitten, kitten watches over rat's hole ; (5) hero remembers the corpse's advice and changes dice with enemy and so wins ; (6) the child is given him with a mango branch and he is to marry the girl when the mango tree blossoms, *i.e.* in 12 years ; he meets some prisoners who ask him to release them and he makes his enemy do so before he finally goes away. *Where published*, Legends of the Panjâb, vol. i. p. 47. *Nature of collection :* (1) *Original or translation*, translated by R. C. Temple ; (2) *Narrator's name*, not given, a village accountant from Râwâl Pindî; (3) *Other particulars*, translated from original MSS. in possession of Mr. J. G. Delmerick.

XL

Number in collection, 40. *Reference to pages*, 267 to 274. *Specific name*, The King who was fried. *Dramatis personæ ;* Râjâ Karan, *faqîr*, swans, Râjâ Bikramâjît. *Thread of story*, king gives away a hundredweight of gold every day in charity before his breakfast, procures this supply by allowing himself to be fried and eaten by a *faqîr* daily and restored to life,[1] some swans go to the hero's garden,[2] he feeds them on pearls, when the pearls fail swans fly home again singing his praises, king hears them and imprisons them,[3] female swan escapes back to hero,[4] tells him what has happened, hero comes to king as his servant, finds out the secret,[5] and gets himself fried, eaten, and restored, and gets hold of the gold-producing garment,[6] king goes to *faqír*, but it is of no use, as *faqír* will not eat him, having had his meal, king's supply of gold fails, and so he commences to starve himself to death, but hero eventually gives him gold and saves him.[7] *Incidental circumstances:* (1) as a reward for this the *faqír* shakes the gold required daily out of his ragged old coat, the restoration to life is by merely collecting the bones and repeating charms over them ; (2) the swans live at Mânsarobar lake and feed only on unpierced pearls, a famine of pearls drives them away for food ; (3) for singing another man's praises ; (4) she refuses to eat even pearls, because the king has done so wicked a thing as to imprison a female, so he lets her go ; (5) by dogging the king's footsteps and seeing what he does ; (6) he rubs himself all over with spices and the *faqír* is so pleased with the meal that he hands him over the gold-producing coat to keep, he supplants the king by going before the appointed time to be cooked ; (7) by giving up the coat on condition that the swans are released. *Where published*, Calcutta Review, No. cl. p. 270 ff. *Nature of collection:* (1) *Original or translation*, original, collected by R. C. Temple ; (2) *Narrator's name*, not given, a Brâhman who performed at the shrine commemorating the events narrated in the tale ; (3) *Other particulars*, told as having occurred at the hill temple on the top of Pindî Point at Murree.

XLI

Number in collection, 41. *Reference to pages*, 275 to 283. *Specific name*, Prince Half-a-son. *Dramatis personæ:* faqír, hero, his brothers, princess. *Thread of story*, faqír grants hero's father seven sons, but the youngest (hero) is only half-a-boy,[1] goes shooting with his brothers, is bullied by them, they come to a melon field into which only hero can get,[2] so he pays them out,[3] they peach on him and he is imprisoned but releases himself,[4] so with some fruit on a plum tree into which hero only can climb,[5] eventually they push him into a well, there he finds means for making himself wealthy by curing princess of possession by a devil,[6] he does so and marries her,[7] proves himself to be a prince,[8] the brothers go into the well and are all killed.[9] *Incidental circumstances:* (1) his attention is attracted to the father by his lying on a dirty bed, he gives each wife a mango to eat, the youngest wife's is half eaten by a rat, so she has only half-a-boy ; (2) only half-a-boy could get through the thorn hedge round it ; (3) so he gorges the melons and throws the brothers

the unripe and sour ones ; (4) hero has the miraculous power of making
a rope do as he pleases, so when he is tied up he tells the rope to untie
itself; (5) only hero is light enough to climb into the tree and get the
plums ; (6) in the well are a demon, a pigeon, a serpent, hero overhears
their conversation, pigeon's dung will cure the princess of possession by
the demon, and the serpent sits over vast wealth, a camel driver comes
to draw water, whereon hero tells the rope to draw him out of the well ;
(7) hero proclaims himself a physician and cures the princess with the
pigeon's dung ; (8) his brothers traduce him, but he gets the serpent's
wealth and proves himself a prince ; (9) pigeon discovers that her dung
has been disturbed, so she and the serpent and the demon look for the
thieves, finding the brothers the demon kills them. *Where published*,
Indian Antiquary, vol. x. p. 151 ff. *Nature of collection:* (1) *Original
or translation*, original, collected by R. C. Temple; (2) *Narrator's
name*, not given, a boy at Firôzpûr ; *Other particulars*, nil.

XLII

Number in collection, 42. *Reference to pages*, 284 to 288. *Specific
name*, The Mother and Daughter who worshipped the Sun. *Dramatis
personæ:* heroine's mother, heroine, hero, the sun. *Thread of story*,
heroine and her mother worship[1] the sun and lay aside everything for it
except their own food, a meal cake each, heroine has eaten cake and
gives half her mother's to a passing beggar, on which her mother turns
her adrift, she wanders in the jungle and meets hero, a prince hunting
in the jungle,[2] he marries her, her mother comes to visit her,[3] which
makes hero determined to visit her home, he does so and finds it a
magnificent palace, but on leaving it he finds it only a hovel, so he
accuses his wife of being a witch, but is pacified on its being explained
that the sun did it all. *Incidental circumstances:* (1) they are very poor
people living in a hovel ; (2) she has climbed into a tree for safety, and
her tears drop on to his face as he sleeps; (3) heroine is very much
afraid of this owing to her lowly birth and appearance, while the mother
is there hero comes up, on which she is instantly turned into a golden
stool, and seeing this makes hero determined to visit heroine's home.
Where published, new. *Nature of collection:* (1) *Original or translation*,
original, collected by F. A. Steel; (2) *Narrator's name*, not given,
a Jatt boy in Ridhânâ, Gohânâ tahsîl, Rohtak district ; (3) *Other
particulars*, common everywhere in the Panjâb in many versions.

XLIII

Number in collection, 43. *Reference to pages*, 289 to 297. *Specific
name*, The Ruby Prince. *Dramatis personæ :* Brâhman, king, queen,

hero, ogre, princess, dancing girl. *Thread of story*, a Brâhman finds a ruby and takes it to a merchant, who tells him it is valuable, so Brâhman takes it to the king, who gives him a lakh of rupees for it, and gives it to his wife to take care of, wife locks it up in a box, in twelve years the box is opened, and the ruby, being a snake-stone, has turned into hero, king turns him out and hero saves city from ravages of the ogre infesting it,[1] so he marries the king's daughter, but her curiosity sends him into snake-land again,[2] and there he remains until a dancing-girl sees him,[3] princess then recovers him with dancing-girl's help.[4] *Incidental circumstances:* (1) he meets an old woman, whose son is to be given up to the ogre that day, offers himself in his place and kills the ogre ; (2) she is piqued by not knowing who her husband is, and insists on her telling him who he is, on the third time she repeats the question he vanishes into the river into the power of a jewelled-hooded serpent ; (3) she sees the snake-king and his suite including hero come out of the snake's hole and hold festival, hero has to dance to the king ; (4) princess learns how to dance, and when it comes to the hero's turn he is too ill to do so, so she dances for him, and in reward demands 'the man she danced for,' and carries him off. *Where published*, new. *Nature of collection:* (1) *Original or translation*, original, collected by F. A. Steel ; (2) *Narrator's name*, not given, a Jaṭṭ boy of Dobuldan in Rhotak district ; (3) *Other particulars*, current in different forms.

A SURVEY OF THE INCIDENTS IN MODERN INDIAN FOLK-TALES

PRELIMINARY

EVERY tale must consist of two parts, the theme and its working up, for no story can be generally acceptable and so live until the bare bones of its plot are duly clothed with a padding of incident. Again, neither plot nor padding has any chance of survival in the struggle for existence alone, being essential to each other. Incidents, however interesting in themselves, are a mere confused jumble unless held acceptably together by a reasonable plot, and a plot unaccompanied by suitable incidents is a skeleton without flesh—a dead thing with which no one cares to have any concern. Therefore in examining a tale one meets with two distinct features more or less inseparably mixed up according to the skill of the narrator, but still distinct in history and origin, and capable of complete separation ; for it is obvious that the padding of plot A, or at any rate *parts* of it, can be made to fit into plot B, and that this habitually occurs in actual practice no one who has any acquaintance with story-tellers will be inclined to deny. It is well known that wherever these congregate certain of them have a greater reputation than others, and the real meaning of this is that these individuals possess a greater natural aptitude than the rest for interchanging plot and padding, for serving up the same old dishes with fresh relishes as it were. To carry the argument further, it is clear that in any given tale, plot and incidents may well have a perfectly separable history, or rather the plot may have one history and the parts of the padding as many distinct histories as there are incidents.

Writing under correction and away from books, it would seem that the investigators of folk-tales have hitherto mainly confined themselves to the comparison of the themes or general machinery of the stories, and have only noticed the various incidents in a casual kind of way—have, in fact, assumed too much that the same theme is always worked out in the same manner.   Now let us think out how a bright-witted village boy, famous for his tales, and rather tired of constantly repeating them, but still anxious to please his audience and proud of his skill, will proceed, remembering that in him is no spark of that scientific fervour that would preserve the tale intact for the sake of its history and analogies.   He has stored away in his memory many a theme and many an incident, he has an imagination sufficiently brilliant to see where certain stock incidents that he wots of will come in effectively, and he has—what really gives him his superiority—the skill to attract the attention of his hearers to the various portions of his plot, as he develops it by means of ever-varying incidents, each suited to its place.   The consequence is that as a matter of fact he does not always tack on the same incidents to the same plot every time he narrates it, and he is encouraged in varying the machinery of his narratives by the reputation that his skill in doing this gives him of having an inexhaustible repertory.   The moral of this is that if one only compares tales as a whole one is investigating but half the subject, and, as will be shown below, the least important half.

It should be remembered that the narrator of folk-tales never writes —memory is his only guide aided by what imagination he possesses, and that the power of sustained mental effort is not to be expected in the uncultured.   Now in framing the plot of a tale imagination comes prominently into play, and helped on by memory there is no sustained mental effort, but unless the incidents which imagination allows to crowd in on to the theme as it is developed are shaped almost entirely according to memory, the mental efforts of the story-teller become both sustained and severe.   Consequently it will be found that the plots of folk-tales as actually told by village crones and children are much more liable to variation from the standard than are the incidents with which they are enriched and rendered acceptable.   Consequently, also, since the incidents are more apt to retain their stock forms than the plots, they make up the most important portion of a tale from the investigator's point of view.   However, as it would not do to ignore for this reason the comparison of themes, an analysis of the tales on the Folklore Society's plan has been added to this work, as well as a survey of the incidents occurring in it and in modern Indian folklore generally.   One more point is worthy of remark here : a mere incident in a long tale is often the theme of a shorter one with incidents of its own, so that a tale may have incidents and sub-incidents, but for the practical purposes of investigation no distinction need be made between them.

Probably the best method of investigating the incidents of Indian folk-tales would be the historical plan of comparing those occurring in all the known collections of fixed eras : *e.g.* suppose separate compared

collections were made of those now current, of those current in the
middle ages, the *Purânas*, the Plays, and so on, of those current in
earlier times as in the *Mahâbhârata, Râmâyana*, etc., and, lastly, of
those in the earliest known Indian literature as the *Jâtakas;* would not
thus be established data on which a conclusive history of the various
notions could be based, and by which the first appearance of each
would be detected?   Of course, very great care would have to be
exercised in ascertaining the true era to which any particular collection
under investigation really belonged, especially when the oriental habits
of imitating MSS. and of interpolation be considered.   In all likelihood,
as the life of a tale in any given form is a long one, four or five such
eras would be sufficient for all practical purposes, and the object of the
present survey is to make a commencement at collecting together under
their various heads the incidents of the folk-tales told in our own times.
It does not aim at being anything more than a commencement, and
makes no pretensions to completeness, as only such books have been
examined as profess to be collections of folk-tales, and no attempt has
been made to collate the many tales scattered up and down modern
books of travel and oriental research.   However, it will be seen that
what books have been examined have afforded data enough to enable a
tentative grouping of the incidents under appropriate heads and sub-
heads.   Of course, before the method of investigation above shadowed
forth can be systematically taken up, the question of what heads and
sub-heads are the most appropriate for grouping will have to be
definitely settled.   The books now under examination are *Wide-awake
Stories*, 1884 (*W.A.S.*), *Indian Fairy Tales*, 1880 (*I.F.T.*), *Old Deccan
Days*, 3rd ed., 1881 (*O.D.D.*), *Folktales of Bengal*, 1883 (*F.T.B.*),
Legends of the Panjâb, vol. i. 1883-84 (*L.P.*), and the tales from Bengal
by the late Mr. Damant in the *Indian Antiquary*, 1872-78 (*I.A.*).   It
is to be regretted that Mr. Swynnerton's *Râjâ Rasâlû*, though advertised,
is not in time to be included in the category.   In this collection of books
are found about 200 tales, all Aryan, and covering an immense tract of
country, as it consists of tales told in Kashmîr and the Panjâb, in Oudh
and the North-West Provinces, in Bengal and in Bombay.   Our European
readers should bear in mind the immense distances which separate these
different parts of India, and their complete isolation from each other
until quite recent times.   It is barely forty years ago, and easily within
the memory of living persons, since a Kashmîrî meditating a journey
even into the neighbouring Panjâb had the funeral ceremonies of his race
performed over him, so small was his chance of returning home again.
We are apt to look upon India, with the help especially of native
'reformers,' who speechify to us sheer nonsense about 'united India'
and the 'Indian nation,' as one country, but to the natives Bombay,

Bengal Proper, Oudh, the Panjâb, and even *parts* of these, are as different 'countries,' as France and England, and as Norway and Germany are to us Europeans. So that in comparing the tales of these collections we are investigating the common heritage of peoples who have now very little sympathy one with the other, and are obtaining a fair notion of what modern Indian Aryan folk-tales, as a whole, really are.

The incidents have been divided into four classes:—(I.) into those connected with the *Actors;* (II.) with the *Progress* of the tale; (III.) with the *Means* necessary to ensure the progress of the tale; and (IV.) *Miscellaneous* incidents. Each class is divided into major and minor heads and sub-heads. Thus, in Class I., Actors, the major heads are— (1) the stepmother, (2) saints and holy personages, (3) witches, (4) ogres, (5) calumniated persons, (6) substituted persons, (7) the son of seven mothers, (8) the sleeping beauty, (9) the egg hero, (10) minor actors, (11) the hero's companions, and (12) special points in the personal appearance of the heroine. Class II., Progress, is thus divided—(1) seeking fortune, (2) dreams, (3) the life-index, (4) tricks, (5) living in animals' bellies. In Class III. the major heads are—(1) *deus ex machinâ*, (2) devices for summoning the absent, (3) forbidden things, (4) story-telling to explain the situation, (5) proofs of identity, (6) temporary death, (7) enchantments, (8) metamorphosis, (9) disguises, (10) invisibility, (11) the inexhaustible pot, (12) the snake-jewel (*mani*), (13) Solomon's judgment, (14) miraculous vehicle. Class IV., Miscellaneous, has the following divisions—(1) Miscellaneous points, (2) points in marriages, (3) modes of vengeance, (4) numbers. So that the four classes of incidents are divisible into 35 major heads.

But it is not until these 35 major heads are further divided into their minor and sub-heads, that the drift of the argument becomes clearly visible. Thus—

Class I., Actors: major head—(1) The stepmother, minor heads— (*a*) ill-treats her stepchildren; sub-heads—(i) sons, (ii) daughters, (iii) children: (*b*) miscellaneous: (*c*) falls in love with her stepson. (2) Saints and holy personages: (*a*) *faqîrs:* (*b*) celebrated miracles; (i) of Sakhî Sarwar, (ii) of Guggâ, (iii) of Nâmdev, (iv) of Dhannâ, the Bhagat. (3) Witches: (*a*) powers: (*b*) appearance: (*c*) doings. (4) Ogres: (*a*) their attributes; (i) eating human flesh, (ii) power of meta- morphosis, (iii) miscellaneous: (*b*) their doings; (i) ogress marries hero, (ii) ogre has possession of sleeping beauty, (iii) befriend human beings, (iv) do domestic service, (v) bring malicious charges, (vi) other malicious actions: (*c*) their death: (*d*) human beings suspected of being ogres; (i) consequences: (*e*) ogre varied as jinn. (5) Calumniated persons: (*a*) persons who suffer: (*b*) special calumniators: (*c*) calumniated wife;

(i) ill-treated daughter, (ii) Potiphar's wife. (6) Substituted persons :
(a) persons who suffer : (b) persons or articles substituted : (c) miscellaneous exchanges. (7) The son of seven mothers. (8) (a) Sleeping beauty :
(b) beauty : (c) sleeping hero. (9) (a) Egg hero : (b) fruit hero. (10)
Minor actors : (a) chief constable and his son : (b) fairies : (c) fates : (a)
demons : (e) ghosts ; (i) malignant female, (ii) friendly, (iii) malignant,
(iv) attributes : (f) mannikin : (g) magicians : (h) vampires : (i) serpents.
(11) Companions of the hero : (a) human ; (i) attributes : (b) non-human.
(12) Special points in the personal appearance of the heroine : (a) complexion ; (i) fair, (ii) white : (b) hair ; (i) golden, (ii) black, (iii) very
abundant : (c) eyes ; (i) blue, (ii) brown, (iii) black.

Class II., Progress : (1) Seeking fortune : (a) (i) hero alone, (ii)
metamorphosed : (b) hero and companions : (c) by companies : (d)
variants. (2) Dreams : (a) warning : (b) prophetic : (c) effects. (3)
The life-index : (a) a bird : (b) an insect : (c) a plant : (d) a necklace :
(e) other objects : (f) survival in a custom. (4) Tricks : (a) humorous ;
(i) bounce, (ii) biter bit, (iii) success by mere accident : (b) malicious ;
(i) of witch to kill hero, (ii) of heroine's enemies, (iii) pretended illness,
(iv) impossible task, (v) letter to murder bearer, (vi) cheating, (vii) lies,
(viii) miscellaneous : (c) to escape enemy : (d) to punish enemy. (5) (a)
Living in animals' bellies : (b) extraordinary voracity : (c) extraordinary
strength.

Class III., Means : (1) *Deus ex machinâ* : (a) a god ; (i) a spirit :
(b) a talking animal ; (i) showing the way to fortune, (ii) warning of
danger, (iii) other objects, (iv) explaining the situation, (v) aiding in
reward for services rendered, (vi) the thorn in the tiger's foot, (vii) the
thorn in the serpent's throat, (viii) punishing for refusal to help, (ix)
aiding out of mere friendship : (c) a talking plant : (d) talking inanimate
objects : (e) understanding animals' speech : (f) hair ; (i) its miraculous
powers : (g) a ship. (2) Devices for summoning the absent : (a) enchanted articles ; (i) supernatural objects : (b) street crying ; (i) answering a proclamation : (c) unintelligible request : (d) other devices. (3)
Forbidden things : (a) cupboard ; (i) room : (b) direction : (c) looking
behind : (d) breach of silence. (4) Story-telling to explain the situation : (a) animals as narrators : (b) rectification of mistakes. (5) (a)
Proofs of identity ; (i) of hero, (ii) of heroine, (iii) of other persons : (b)
signs of the coming hero. (6) Temporary death : (a) persons most
affected : (b) long sleep : (c) methods of killing ; (i) Lord of Death : (d)
methods of restoration to life ; (i) by effigy, (ii) by granting extension of
life, (iii) by working through others, (iv) by miscellaneous means, (v)
miraculous cures generally : (e) revivifying and healing powers of blood ;
(i) drops of blood becoming rubies : (f) restoration of beauty ; (i) of
eyesight. (7) Enchantments : (a) things ; (i) palace : (b) creatures. (8)

Metamorphosis : (*a*) of the dead ; (i) metempsychosis, (ii) into inanimate objects : (*b*) of the deity ; (i) *avatâras* or incarnations, (ii) into inanimate objects : (*c*) of superhuman personages ; (i) ogres, (ii) angels, (iii) jinns, (iv) vampires, (v) mannikin, (vi) fairies, (vii) ghosts, (viii) Lord of Death, (ix) demons : (*d*) of living things ; (i) one into another, (ii) into inanimate things : (*e*) of inanimate things, (i) one into another : (*f*) temporary metamorphosis ; (i) change of skin, (ii) beauty and the beast, (iii) variants. (9) Disguises : (*a*) of hero : (*b*) of hero's companions : (*c*) of heroine : (*d*) of heroine's enemies : (*e*) of superhuman beings ; (i) ogress. (10) Invisibility : (*a*) invisible cap ; (i) ring : (*b*) by other means : (*c*) natural invisibility. (11) Inexhaustible pot : (*a*) box : (*b*) melon : (*c*) basket : (*d*) shells : (*e*) leaf or platter : (*f*) branch : (*g*) bag : (*h*) bowl : (*i*) cow : (*j*) rice : (*k*) ring : (*l*) conch : (*m*) mat. (12) Snake-jewel : (*a*) in heroine : (*b*) moon and star hero. (13) Solomon's judgment. (14) Miraculous vehicle : (*a*) animals : (*b*) inanimate objects : (*c*) flying through the air : (*d*) charms.

Class IV., Miscellaneous : (1) Miscellaneous points : (*a*) the cat's nine lives : (*b*) alchemy : (*c*) dropping jewels : (*d*) being one-eyed : (*e*) symbolism : (*f*) the king chosen by the sacred elephant : (*g*) deserted city ; (i) palace, (ii) land, (iii) garden : (*h*) choice : (*i*) riverside waif : (*j*) little slipper : (*k*) gambling extraordinary : (*l*) the evil eye : (*m*) human sacrifice : (*n*) wolf children : (*o*) bargain with animals : (*p*) delicate heroine ; (i) five-flower princess, (ii) one-flower princess, (iii) delicate hero : (*q*) nostrum for procuring sons ; (i) children granted by saints : (*r*) ordeal ; (i) to prove chastity, (ii) to prove truth. (2) Points in marriages : (*a*) without ceremony : (*b*) postponement : (*c*) extraordinary : (*d*) condition of impossible task ; (i) general impossibilities : (*e*) public choice or *swayamvara*. (3) Modes of vengeance : (*a*) on hero's enemies : (*b*) on heroine's enemies : (*c*) on murderers : (*d*) miscellaneous punishments. (4) Numbers : (*a*) one ; (i) only children : (*b*) two : (*c*) three ; (i) third, (ii) three days : (*d*) four : (*e*) five : (*f*) six ; (i) half twelve : (*g*) seven ; (ii) seventh : (*h*) nine : (*i*) twelve ; (i) twelve years : (*j*) eighteen : (i) multiple of twelve : (*k*) twenty-four ; (i) multiple of twelve : (*l*) miscellaneous ; (i) nineteen, (ii) thirteen, (iii) eight, (iv) twenty-two, (v) twenty-one, (vi) fourteen, twice seven, (vii) thirty-six, (viii) sixteen, (ix) thirty-two : (*m*) large numbers ; (i) one hundred and one, (ii) one thousand and one : (*n*) miscellaneous large numbers ; (i) one thousand, (ii) one hundred and sixty, (iii) seventy, (iv) sixty, (v) three hundred and sixty, (vi) one hundred, (vii) fifty-two, (viii) eighty-four : (*o*) fractions—aliquot parts of five ; (i) one and a quarter, (ii) two and a half, (iii) one and a half.

The above sub-heads and minor heads number 304, so that the incidents in the collections under review may be divided in 4 classes with

35 major heads and 304 minor and sub-heads. It is not improbable that the incidents in folk-tales generally will fall under one or other of these, so that they very likely will not require much adding to as research proceeds. In the following pages the details on which the above grouping is based are given categorically, and every statement referred chapter and verse to the place whence they came.

CLASS I.—ACTORS

(I.) Stepmother

(a) *Ill-treats her stepchildren* : (1) *Sons:* kills her stepson and gives his body as a dish to his father ; hates her stepson older than herself. (2) *Daughters:* gives up her stepdaughter to be married to the voracious fish, *i.e.* apparently to death ; substitutes her own daughter for stepdaughter. (3) *Children:* pays a soldier to kill her stepchildren ; demands their lives to cure her of imaginary disease. (*O.D.D.* 3, 197, 219, 220, 223.—*I.F.T.* 7-10.—*F.T.B.* 97.—*W.A.S.* 138.—*I.A.* IV., 261.)

(b) *Miscellaneous:* is younger than elder stepson's wife, and so hates her. (*F.T.B.* 96.)

(c) *Falls in love with her stepson:* and then ill-treats him. (*L.P.* 2.)

(II.) Saints and Holy Persons

(a) *Faqîrs:* are fed before breaking fast; grant sons to the barren ; are magicians ; can restore to life ; can transform ; grant sons and daughters ; restore hands and feet that have been cut off; restore sight ; have second sight; can destroy life ; can turn a parched-up garden into a green one; can make fruit fresh at the wrong season ; turn blood into water ; are proved by miracles, handling a red-hot nail, turning sugar into ashes, ashes into sugar, clay bricks into gold, bringing the dead to life ; eat human flesh : if the body of one be eaten by followers they will all obtain his powers. (*I.F.T.* 68, 227, 92 ff.—*W.A.S.* 282 ff., 290, 248, 267, 281, 47, 98, 247.—*O.D.D.* 8, 9, 15, 554.—*I.A.* I., 118, 171 ; IV., 57.—*F.T.B.* 1, 117, 187.—*L.P.* 3, 2, 74, 76, 77, 79, 97, 139, 142, 222, 233, 504.)

(b) *Celebrated miracles:* (1) *Of Sakhî Sarwar:* restoring a dead child to life, restoring a dead horse to life, curing a camel's broken leg, making a blind man see, restoring a eunuch to full manhood, curing leprosy. (*L.P.* 81, 85, 213, 214, 215, 222, 223.) (2) *Of Gurû Guggâ:* speaking from his mother's womb. (*L.P.* 153, 157.) (3) *Of Nâmdev:*

restoring a dead cow to life. (*L.P.* 80.) (4) *Of Dhannâ the Bhagat:* making the god come out of the stone (idol). (*L.P.* 80, 87 ff.)

(III.) WITCHES

(*a*) *Powers:* can find anything on earth ; can open the sky ; can patch up the sky ; possess second sight ; can restore to life ; can set fire to water ; can turn stone into wax ; can separate lovers ; turns hero into a sheep, monkey. (*W.A.S.* 61 ff., 109.—*L.P.* 258, 259.—*I.A.* I., 117, 118.)

(*b*) *Appearance:* old woman in trouble (see also *metamorphosis*) ; white hind with golden horns ; is a queen. (*W.A.S.* 62, 100, 84.)

(*c*) *Doings:* undertakes to find (and succeeds by tricks [*variant,* fails]) heroine for her enemy ; gets possession of hero's life-index and kills him ; demands the eyes of her lover's seven wives as the price of marriage, and when obtained gives them to her mother as a garland ; attempts to destroy hero by letter of destruction. (*W.A.S.* 62 ff., 100 ff., 202 ff.—*L.P.* 259 ff.)

(IV.) OGRES

(*a*) *Their attributes*—(1) *Eating flesh:* ogress gorges animals raw ; eats up her own husband and co-wife ; eats up all the servants and animals ; eats living things wholesale ; requires a hundred times more food than human beings ; gorges on live animals at night ; to guard heroine swallows up her suitors ; ogre eats carrion ; feeds on human flesh ; is of a gigantic size. (*F.T.B.* 72, 79, 120, 272.—*O.D.D.* 27, 198.—*I.F.T.* 5, 51, 99, 175.—*W.A.S.* 171.—*I.A.* I., 171 ; IV., 55.) (2) *Power of metamorphosis:* ogre changes to an old woman with a shining robe ; to a vampire, etc. ; jinn changes to a dove, hawk, eagle to watch heroine ; ogress becomes a lovely girl ; a wounded deer ; a goat. (*O.D.D.* 27, 40.—*I.F.T.* 175.—*W.A.S.* 13 ff., 173.—*F.T.B.* 190, 193, 270.—*I.A.* I., 170.) (3) *Miscellaneous:* ogre's breath is a great rushing wind ; can lengthen their arms 80 miles ; possess great wealth ; can fly through the air ; know human beings by smell. (*I.F.T.* 185, 50.—*F.T.B.* 274, 67, 270, 76, 83.—*O.D.D.* 199, 58, 198.—*W.A.S.* 59, 58, 172.—*I.A.* IV., 50, 58.)

(*b*) *Their doings*—(1) *Ogress marries hero:* lives with him and her human co-wife ; has children, but destroys them in the end ; marries hero's father ; temporarily marries hero and his friends. (*F.T.B.* 67 ff., 118, 270.—*I.F.T.* 51, 175.—*I.A.* I., 70 ; IV., 56.) (2) *Ogre has possession of sleeping beauty* ; jinn has possession of egg-heroine ; ogress befriends sleeping beauty. (*W.A.S.* 60, 170.—*F.T.B.* 82.—*I.F.T.*

54.—I.A. I., 116.) (3) *Befriends human beings:* because they are
called aunt and uncle. (*I.F.T.* 54 ff.—*F.T.B.* 249, 250.—*O.D.D.* 40.)
(4) *Do domestic service:* ogress is a maid. (*F.T.B.* 79.) (5) *Bring
malicious charges :* ogress charges human co-wives with being cannibals.
(*I.F.T.* 175-176, 51.) (6) *Other malignant actions :* ogress is a witch and
deceives heroine by 'tricks ; has her seven human co-wives blinded ;
tries to destroy her stepson by tricks ; tries to drag hero into the
glittering well ; ogress gambles with hero and first wins his companions,
his hawk, and himself, but subsequently loses her dog, her hawk, and
hero to hero's brother; [*variant* told in *Legends of the Panjâb*]. (*F.T.B.*,
88, 118, 190-194.—*I.F.T.* 53, 190.) *Tale :* ogre eats up one inhabitant
of the city daily with a cake and a goat (*variant*, a basket of bread and
a buffalo), hero offers himself in place of an old woman who has befriended him, fights and kills ogre ; *variant tale*, ogress eats up a victim
daily placed in a temple for her by night, taking one of each family in
turn, heroes stand proxy for family that shelter them and kill her, a
woodcutter sets up a false claim to the feat, but heroes triumphantly
prove they did it ; *variant*, ogress swallows one of seven companions
every night. (*W.A.S.* 143-144 ff., 306 ff., 258 ff.—*F.T.B.* 74 ff.—*I.F.T.*
178, 65, 269.—*L.P.* 17 ff.—*I.A.* I., 170.)

(*c*) *Their death :* killed by hero ; ogress killed by her own son ; by
her stepson ; by spilling charmed water over them. (*O.D.D.* 63.—
W.A.S. 70.—*F.T.B.* 73, 277.—*I.F.T.* 62.)

(*d*) *Human beings suspected of being ogres :* heroine when in fish's
stomach ; heroine. (1) *Consequences :* heroine killed ; deserted by
husband and friends; driven from her home and whipped and murdered.
(*I.F.T.* 75, 78, 5.—*F.T.B.* 276.—*W.A.S.* 175.)

(*e*) *Ogre varied as jinn :* with all the characteristics of an ogre.
(*W.A.S.* 170 ff.)

(V.) CALUMNIATED PERSONS

(*a*) *Persons who suffer from calumny :* hero, heroine, wife, nurse,
sister-in-law, co-wives, husband, stepson. (*F.T.B.* 79, 179.—*L.P.* 1.
—*O.D.D.* 55 ff., 86 ff., 220 ff.—*I.F.T.* 51.—*W.A.S.* 143, 247, 296.)

(*b*) *Special calumniators :* ogress, a woodcutter, a scavenger, jealous
sister-in-law, co-wife, wife, stepmother, brothers. (*I.F.T.* 51.—*F.T.B.*
79, 179.—*W.A.S.* 143, 247, 296.—*L.P.* 21, 149.—*I.A.* IX., 5.)

(*c*) *Calumniated wife ; tale :* a gardener's daughter playing with
seven (*variant*, three) poor girls is seen and married by the king, has a
son with a moon on his forehead and stars on his hands (*variant*, also a
daughter); king goes away and tells her to beat a magic drum to call
him, she does so too often out of joke, and so when she is in real danger
he won't come to help her, her enemies then substitute a stone (*variant*,

puppies) for her wonderful child and she is degraded and made into a servant, but finally is restored to her place by her child. *Variant tale* · has to ring a bell, does so too often, has a hundred boys and one girl, they are thrown to rats by her enemies and exchanged for stones, she is imprisoned and finally restored by her daughter, who marries hero. *Tale*: heroine's child is killed and her mouth sprinkled with its blood by her co-wives and she is then charged with being an ogress, whipped and turned out of the palace, heroine is charged with adultery with the saint that granted her a son, wife turned away with her son (hero), because soothsayer has said father will die if he ever sees his son. (*I.F.T.* 119 ff.—*O.D.D.* 53 ff.—*F.T.B.* 236 ff.—*W.A.S.* 175.—*L.P.* 149.— *I.A.* IV., 54.) (1) *Variant*: ill-treated daughter. *Tale*: seventh daughter of king displeases him and is sent into the desert, where she is miraculously supplied with food and marries hero eventually. *Variant tale*: in the desert procures rice and strews it on the ground, peacocks come to eat it and she makes her fortune out of fans made of their feathers, and finally saves her father, the merchant, when he fails in business, and marries hero. (2) *Varied as the tale of Potiphar's wife.* (*I.F.T.* 164 ff., 193 ff.—*F.T.B.* 124 ff.—*W.A.S.* 247, 299.—*L.P.* 1.)

(VI.) SUBSTITUTED PERSONS

(*a*) *Persons who suffer by substitution*: children, wives, hero's companions, hero's enemy. (*O.D.D.* 55, 223 ff.—*F.T.B.* 35 ff., 196, 242.— *I.F.T.* 3, 80, 121.)

(*b*) *Persons or articles substituted*: stones, pups for children, wife's sister, a ghost, a common woman, an old woman, the wife's servant for life, a fool for the companion, hero for hero's enemy. (*O.D.D.* 55, 223 ff.—*F.T.B.* 242, 35 ff., 296.—*I.F.T.* 3, 80, 121, 143, 166.— *W.A.S.* 287.)

(*c*) *Miscellaneous exchanges*: the queen changes her own dead baby for the heroine's, chief constable does. (*O.D.D.* 143.—*F.T.B.* 105.)

(VII.) SON OF SEVEN MOTHERS

(*a*) *Tale*: the king's seven queens are blinded by the enmity of the enemy and rival, and then imprisoned; they have one son each, and eat their children from starvation, except the seventh, who refuses; this child supports the seven blind queens in various ways and becomes thus '*the son of seven mothers*'; he then recovers their eyes, finds them wealth, and kills their enemy. *Variant*: is the son of the seventh queen, the rest being barren, and so is heir to all the queens, and is thus '*the son of seven mothers*'; all their husbands are lost, and he seeks and after many adventures finds and restores them. *Variant:* is the son of discarded queen only. (*W.A.S.* 98 ff. —*I.F.T.* 52 ff., 178 ff.— *O.D.D.* 8 ff.—*F.T.B.* 117 ff.—*I.A* I., 170 ff.)

(VIII.) Sleeping Beauty

(*a*) *Tales:* is in an enchanted palace in an ogre's power, is awakened by a golden stick and put to sleep by a silver one, is befriended by an ogress and found eventually and carried off by hero. *Variants of details:* is in an enchanted palace under the waters and uses the snake-jewel to view the world; is awakened and put to sleep by sticks at her head and feet; palace is at the bottom of a well. (*F.T.B.* 251 ff., 21 ff., 81 ff.—*I.F.T.* 186 ff., 54 ff.—*W.A.S.* 85 ff.—*I.A.* I., 116.) *Variants of tale:* found beheaded in an enchanted palace in the power of an ogre, her head is in a golden basket in a tree overhanging a stream, dripping drops of blood transformed into rubies, which float down stream, she is brought to life merely by joining the head to the body, the ogre beheads her daily when he goes out from jealousy, she is found and carried off by hero: found beheaded in an enchanted palace in a whirlpool, the drops of blood floating away as rubies, she is brought to life by a golden rod. (*W.A.S.* 56 ff.—*F.T.B.* 224 ff.)

(*b*) *Variants of idea: beauty* is found in a palace under the waters swinging under a silver jewelled tree, is under the power of a serpent, gives heroine a golden flute to play when she is in trouble and ring to find ogres' land : is found by hero reading a holy book in a palace made out of her own body : farmer's daughter marries a crocodile and is found in her palace under the waters by her father, the way thither being by means of an enchanted brick which parted the waters. (*O.D.D.* 35 ff.—*W.A.S.* 120 ff.)

(*c*) *Sleeping hero:* is found in a palace made of his own body: is found killed in effigy by heroine in a palace in a deserted jungle: is found by heroine in the hundredth enchanted palace and awakened by a kiss—*mere variant of sleeping beauty.* (*I.F.T.* 165 ff., 166.—*W.A.S.* 30.—*I.A.* I., 219.)

(IX.) Egg Hero

(*a*) *Heroine:* comes out of an *egg* deposited in a cupboard, marries hero, has two boys and dies; *heroine is found in an egg:* a bulbul lays an egg beside a pepper plant with single pepper on it, jinn keeps the egg and from it comes the heroine with the pepper for a charmed amulet round her neck. (*F.T.B.* 73-76.—*I.F.T.* 81.—*W.A.S.* 169 ff.)

(*b*) *Variants; fruit: hero's dead children* found in the magic fruit which grew out of their bodies; *heroine* found in a *belfruit; heroine* born in an *egg-plant*, becomes the child of a poor Brâhman, gets into her enemy's power and is killed by her, and finally becomes a *sleeping beauty ; heroine and her maids* sleep in a *pomegranate* each, the fruit is plucked by hero metamorphosed into a parrot and heroine is restored to ordinary life for him. *Tale:* snake-stone ruby is put into a box for twelve years and turns into hero. (*I.F.T.* 11, 143-146, 81.—*W.A.S.* 79-85, 303.—*O.D.D.* 95-101.)

(X.) Minor Actors

(*a*) *Chief constable and his son:* the son is hero's friend and guardian from danger, opposes hero's taking away heroine : falls in love with heroine and wants to take her from the hero : replaces heroine's sleeping infant by his own dead one, claims heroine. (*I.F.T.* 212 ff.—*W.A.S.* 12, 33.—*F.T.B.* 104, 105.)

(*b*) *Fairies:* the king of the fairies (Indra) ; the fairy's skin is white, but her clothes, etc., are all red ; fairy dolls are found in the sun-jewel box. (*I.F.T.* 1, 168, 169.)

(*c*) *Fates:* the home of the *fates* is a land of stones, each of which is a fate ; *fate* marries hero's sister's daughter. (*I.F.T.* 64.—*F.T.B.* 9 ff.)

(*d*) *Demons:* devastate deserted city (see *ghost, ogre,* and *mannikin.*) (*W.A.S.* 48.)

(*e*) *Ghosts:* (1) *Malignant female ghost,* devastates deserted city, has an enormous appetite, in appearance an old woman awful and forbidding with black wrinkled skin and feet turned backward. (2) *Friendly ghosts:* befriend a poor Brâhman by threshing his corn and procuring him a feast, befriend a barber by bringing him money and filling his granary. (3) *Malignant ghosts:* destroy human beings. (4) *Attributes of ghosts:* activity, power to lengthen limbs (see *ogres*), insensibility to pain, speaking through the nose, can enter a bag, accompanied by a blast of cold air, wander at midnight. (*W.A.S.* 52, 53 ff.—*F.T.B.* 182 ff., 198 ff., 203 ff., 258 ff., 260, 263.)

(*f*) *Mannikin:* is one span high and has a beard a span and a quarter long, is of prodigious strength and can fly through the air, has an enormous appetite, helps hero and heroine, devastates the deserted city, is killed by hero. (*W.A.S.* 7 ff., 49 ff., 52.)

(*g*) *Magicians:* restore hero's companion to life. (*W.A.S.* 141.—*L.P.* 504.)

(*h*) *Vampire:* is hero and heroine's enemy, befriends hero and heroine for future evil purpose. (*W.A.S.* 12 ff.)

(*i*) *Serpents:* first kill and then restore to life hero's companion, show hero how to get serpent out of his throat, destroy a family leaving only sleeping beauty, kill and restore to life hero, also heroine's bullocks, also heroine, aids hero, must resume their shape at night if they travel, possess power of metamorphosis, can fly through the air, is guardian of a tree, can scorch and burn by their breath, can put on wings; a palace of glass surrounded by a ditch, and a wall of needles sprinkled with salt and water will keep them out. *Tale:* serpent issuing from queen's nostril as thin as a thread, kills the king (elected daily) every night, is killed by hero. (*W.A.S.* 139 ff., 193 ff.—*O.D.D.* 121.—*F.T.B.* 21, 18 ff., 100.—*L.P.* 47 ff., 154-155, 177, 179 ff., 180, 181, 183, 189, 416, 481, 487 ff., 488, 495, 498, 502, 520 ff.)

(XI.) THE COMPANIONS OF THE HERO

(*a*) *Human:* his two wives, his three friends, viz. sons of the prime minister, chief constable, and richest merchant (*varied* as barber); his three friends—knifegrinder, blacksmith, carpenter; his half-brother by ogress stepmother; his three friends—a goldsmith, a carpenter and his parrot; one friend: of *heroine*, two girls. (*O.D.D.* 24, 95.—*F.T.B.* 261, 69.—*W.A.S.* 48, 254.—*L.P.* 7.—*I.A.* I., 285; III., 9.)

(*b*) *Their attributes:* born on the same day at the same hour as hero, is his faithful friend through all his difficulties. *Tale:* hero being enraged with him desires him to be killed and demands his eyes as proof of his death, but the companion is saved by a stratagem, and eventually interprets a dream for the hero. *Tale:* saves hero successively from a falling tree, a falling doorway, and a serpent, but is turned into a stone for eight years for licking the blood of the serpent from heroine's breast, and is eventually restored to life by hero's child. *Variant:* hero's friend saves him from riding on a dangerous elephant, from passing under a ruinous gateway, eating the head of a poisonous fish, a serpent bite while asleep, and is himself turned into a marble statue by hero by mistake and brought to life by the blood of hero's infant. *Varied as hero's servant* who is turned out for licking the blood from his master's wife's breast whom he has saved from a serpent. *Tale:* the three companions save him from temporary death and restore him to his wife, ogre half-brother kills his own mother (ogress) in order to save hero: hero's younger brother saves him from ogress: heroine's two girl-companions never leave her, sleeping with her in pomegranates. (*O.D.D.* 66, 68-70, 75 ff., 95.—*W.A.S.* 65 ff.—*F.T.B.* 69-73, 192 ff., 93 ff.—*L.P.* 9 ff., 63.—*I.A.* I., 285.)

(*c*) *Non-human:* eaglets, old war-horse, cat and dog, dog, hawk, parrot, *mainá*; a cat, a dog, a parrot, and a snake. *Tale:* hero leaves *mainá* and parrot as guard over his wife in his absence, when his enemy seduces her the *mainá* remonstrates and is killed, but the parrot manages to escape and lets hero know what she has been doing. (*O.D.D.* 14, 70, 80.—*F.T.B.* 189, 192.—*L.P.* 9 ff., 63.—*W.A.S.* 197.)

(XII.) Special Points in the Personal Appearance
of Heroine

(*a*) *Complexion of heroine:* (1) *Fair:* fair as a rosy pomegranate,
fair as a lotus. (*O.D.D.* 23, 201, 205, 95, 102.—*W.A.S.* 3.—*F.T.B.*
21, 44, 282.—*I.F.T.* 62.) (2) *White:* white as a marble. *Variant:*
complexion of red fairy is white, but her clothes, etc., are all red.
(*W.A.S.* 100.—*O.D.D.* 102.—*F.T.B.* 168.)

(*b*) *Hair of Heroine:* (1) *Golden:* of pure gold, of gold with teeth
of gold; of red gold but eyelashes black; *varied* as hero's golden, as
sleeping beauty's golden. (*W.A.S.* 33, 60, 100, 201 ff.—*I.F.T.* 43,
62, 98, 1, 54, 93, 50.—*O.D.D.* 35.) (2) *Black:* jet black; *varied* as
ogress princess's black. (*O.D.D.* 95, 206, 40.—*F.T.B.* 282.—*I.F.T.*
73.) (3) *Very abundant:* falls to her ankles. (*F.T.B.* 82.—*W.A.S.*
76.)

(*c*) *Eyes of Heroine:* (1) *Blue.* (*I.F.T.* 62, 98.) (2) *Brown.* (*I.F.T.*
73.) (3) *Black.* (*I.F.T.* 96.)

CLASS II.—PROGRESS

(I.) Seeking Fortune

(*a*) A very common *motif* in the tales; (1) *By hero alone.* (*W.A.S.*
196, 251.—*O.D.D.* 10, 62, 126, 132.—*I.F.T.* 63.—*F.T.B.* 65, 182.)
(2) *By hero metamorphosed* into a parrot. (*O.D.D.* 102.)

(*b*) *By hero and companions:* with heroine, with three companions, with
two wives, with one companion and old war-horse, with one companion.
(*W.A.S.* 13, 47.—*O.D.D.* 24, 70.—*I.A.* I., 171, 344.)

(*c*) *By companies:* seven men start together, two heroes together.
(*I.F.T.* 173.—*W.A.S.* 138.—*F.T.B.* 17, 261.—*I.A.* I., 218.)

(*d*) *Variants of idea:* hero starts to seek heroine, heroines run away
owing to ill-treatment at home, hero starts to find 'touchstone' (*variant*
of the impossible task trick). (*I.F.T.* 154.—*O.D.D.* 197.—*I.A.* II.,
357.) *Variant as tale:* heroine goes to seek Mahâdev (God) with two
companions, crosses river of fire alone and finds Mahâdev as a *faqîr*
who grants her desires, viz. a son; hero goes to seek Râm. (*O.D.D.*
229, 253.—*W.A.S.* 215 ff.)

(II.) Dreams

(*a*) *Warning dreams:* the king's seven queens are warned of his
danger if he hunt in the north by each having a dream to the same
effect, heroine's dream warns her of her danger, shows heroine the real
character of her husband, doe has a dream that her husband the buck

will be killed by a hunter. (*W.A.S.* 98.—*O.D.D.* 266.—*I.A.* IX., 7. —*L.P.* 462.)

(*b*) *Prophetic dreams:* heroine's husband dreams he has become a *faqír*, does so afterwards; king dreams of a miraculous tree and hero finds it; hero dreams of a glass palace containing a princess white as marble, finds it; hero dreams that he is directed by a god to cross over a hedge of seven bayonets to the inside of his temple, does so miraculously; heroine dreams of her future husband the hero, will marry no one else, finally marries him; direct hero to wealth; hero dreams of his future bride; king sees a tree with silver stem, golden branches, diamond leaves, pearly fruits, and peacocks playing in it, this sends him blind, and he dreams that until he can see them in reality, he will not recover sight, his dame goes for them; king dreams of sleeping beauty, from whose mouth a flower of flame issues and recedes as she breathes, hero goes to find her. (*O.D.D.* 25, 33, 68, 97-98, 119.—*I.A.* IX., 5; I:, 115; IV., 55.—*L.P.* 233.)

(*c*) *Effect of dreams:* hero by guidance of dreams learns infinite wisdom; a poor woodcutter's dreams that he is a rich man get him into great trouble; hero's dreams of success in hunting lead him to go where he comes to great grief; dreamer goes blind. (*O.D.D.* 99.—*L.P.* 419 ff.—*I.A.* I., 115.)

(III.) LIFE-INDEX

Outside a person's life is an object which faithfully reflects the conditions of his life: this life-index is always very difficult of access.

(*a*) *Life-index is a bird;* kept in a cage on the head of a snake on the top of a tree, guarded by wild beasts and ogres; when the bird is killed the ogre it indicated dies; when the bird dies ogre whose life it indicated dies; of hero's ogress stepmother is a green parrot in a cage under six pitchers of water in the centre of a circle of palm-trees in a thick forest in a far country guarded by 1000 ogres; when the parrot dies the magician whose life it indicated dies; is a cockatoo, when it dies the ogress it indicated dies; is a *mainá* in its nest in a tree across the seas, when killed so as not a drop of its blood is spilt the ogre it indicated dies. (*I.F.T.* 58 ff., 62, 187-188.—*F.T.B.* 121 ff.—*O.D.D.* 13 ff.—*I.A.* I., 171.)

(*b*) *Is an insect:* a bumble bee in the crop of a *mainá* on the topmost twig of a solitary tree guarded by a savage horse and dog, when the bee is killed the indicated ogre dies; two bees on the top of crystal pillar in deep water, to be dived for and killed without losing a drop of blood, when these are killed over ashes indicated ogre dies; male and female bee in a wooden box in a deep water to be crushed to death by hero without losing a drop of blood, when hero kills them indicated ogres die. (*F. T. B.* 85 ff., 253.—*W. A. S.* 59-60.—*I. A.* I., 117.)

(*c*) *Is a plant:* a barley plant given by hero to his three friends, when it droops he is ill, when it snaps in half he is dead ; a tree planted by hero on his departure indicates his fortunes : a flower while gathered heroine lives, while torn up by the roots she is dead ; a lemon containing the hero's mother's eyes. (*F. T. B.* 189 ff., 192.—*I. F. T.* 41, 145.—*W. A. S.* 52 ff., 64.—*I. A.* I., 116, 171.)

(*d*) *Is a necklace:* in a box in a bee in a red and green fish, while worn by another heroine is dead, when recovered she lives ; golden necklace in a wooden box in a fish's heart, when worn by another heroine dies, when recovered she lives ; a golden necklace, as above, indicating heroine's life ; a sandalwood necklace, as above, indicating hero's life. (*W. A. S.* 83-87.—*F. T. B.* 2 ff.—*O. D. D.* 240 ff., 233 ff.)

(*e*) *Other objects:* falsely said to be in the seven sons of heroine's enemy ; in the milk of hero's wife put into a pot and given him, when it turns red his father is dead, when blood-red his mother is killed and his own life in danger ; in the hero's sword, when heated he has fever, when the rivet of the handle comes out his head falls off, when rivet fastened in his head joins his body, and when it is reburnished he lives again ; is a bull which feeds on *ikop*, and if sacrificed will prolong king's life ; is a lamp under a tree in the mountains and will restore magician's life. (*W. A. S.* 82, 62 ff.—*F. T. B.* 71 ff.—*I. A.* VI., 222.—*L. P.* 503.)

(*f*) *Survival in a custom:* hero is handed over his bride on the day she is born, and with her is given him a young mango tree, which flowers in twelve years ; when it flowers she is to be his wife. (*L. P.* 50.—*W. A. S.* 280.)

(IV.) TRICKS

(*a*) *Humorous:* heroine's mother puts her daughter's rat-husband on to a red-hot stool and so gets rid of him. *Tale:* lambikin tricks jackal, vulture, tiger, wolf, dog, and eagle by pretending that he is not fat enough to be eaten yet, gets fattened but gets into drumikin, and so escapes all except jackal, who finds him out and eats him up ; sparrow circumvents the crow by sending it to clean itself before it can share the sparrow's dinner ; jackal serves the generous Brâhman by inducing the tiger to get into the cage from which the Brâhman had released him, and then locking him into it ; jackal tells a tiger the best way to eat a man is to get into a bag and have the man thrown in to him, tiger does so and is shut up and killed ; jackal to save himself tells tiger that another also wants to eat him, and then shows him his reflection in a well, tiger jumps down to get at his rival and is killed ; jackal finds a pair of shoes, puts them on his ears, and proclaims himself a great personage, all animals do homage except the iguana, who jeers at him, jackal pursues and catches him by the tail near his hole, but is induced by a trick to let him go, and so iguana escapes ; hero keeps the dresses of girls bathing and so secures a wife ; hero shoots an arrow in a certain direction for three mendicants to race for, while they are running he carries off their miraculous property ; a conceited husband with awk-ward habits is set to find a 'cleverer man than himself,' and so got rid of ; hero washes off heroine's disguise by throwing water over her ; heroine's sister drops pearls along the road, and so lets heroine find her ; jackal tricks a princess into marrying his friend the poor weaver ; old hen-sparrow induces her jealous co-wife to go into a scalding dyer's vat to dye herself into gay colours, then when the cock picks her up in his beak to carry her home jeers at him, so that he opens his beak to abuse her and so drops and kills the co-wife ; partridge has to induce jackal to laugh and cry, get him his dinner, and save his life, so she sets two men fighting, sets a hunter and dogs on him, sets women chasing her, while jackal eats their food, and finally prevents a crocodile from drowning him.   *Tale :* the minister has been boasting of his wife's chastity, so king sends him away on duty and goes to his wife's house, gets admittance by a stratagem, apologises, but leaves his signet ring, the minister finds and thinks his wife unchaste until the king explains ; cat to get hero's enchanted ring from witch's mouth gets heroine to scatter rice about, which brings rats, so the cat catches one and puts its tail up the witch's nose while she sleeps, she sneezes out the ring ; crow, after trying many ways to induce a man to cut a grain of corn out of a tree, sets a cat to catch a rat which sets the whole train of events in motion till he gets his grain ; to recover touchstone from robber, bag of sham touchstone is deposited with him, and he gives back the real one ; hero, who has been cheated by the market people, exacts heavy tolls as the queen's wife's brother.   *Tale :* the faithful wife deceives her lovers by inducing them to visit her all together, she then locks them up to escape from each other and goes away, and lets them discover themselves [found in *Alif Laila*].   *Tale :* idiot son is saved by his mother thus : having committed murder and thrown the body down the well, she throws in a sheep, and so when he confesses the murder he is acquitted, because he pulls out the sheep in place of the body. *Variant :* he steals royal camel carrying gold, his mother hides the gold but scatters comfits about the house, so the idiot confesses the theft 'on the day that it rained comfits,' and is not believed.   *Tale :* jackal saves his foot from alligator by saying he has caught something else, escapes him by inducing him to show his bubbles above the stream, by inducing him to roll about under a heap of figs, by inducing him to call out from his house. *Tale:* barber's clever wife induces thieves to plough up her field by wandering about it in search for treasure she says her grandfather buried there, the harvest money she puts away,·induces thieves to think it is in a pot containing droppings from goats which they eat as sweets, cuts off their noses as they appear at her window, induces them to climb into a bees' nest at night as the bag containing her gold, finally frightens them when they carry her off into thinking she is a ghost, and bites off the leader's tongue by telling him that is the way to kiss a fairy, which she makes him believe she is. *Tale:* four friends unjustly treated by the king turn thieves, king's son tries to catch them, and they trick him into being shaved and turned naked into the streets, magician tries and they cut his hand, king tries and they tie him to a bull's tail and turn him adrift into the jungle. *Tale:* successful roguery to the end of life, barber's son who begins by selling his friend and ends by becoming a rich man. (1) *Bounce:* farmer's wife frightens a tiger by mere bounce, idiot hero accidentally frightens fairies into helping him by saying he will eat '*five*' (*i.e.* cakes), but which they take to mean fairies, hero saves himself from tigers by saying aloud that the king had sent him to catch tigers wholesale, hero bounces ghost by showing him his own face in the glass and telling him he has bagged many like him, their companions frighten and subdue demons by mere bounce, a blind and a deaf man first frighten an ogre and then try and cheat each other by mere bounce. (*I.A.* IX., 2 ff. ; I., 286, 345 ; II., 358-359 ; III., 10, 342 ; IV., 57.—*I.F.T.* 617, 27 ff., 34-35 ff., 201, 202, 208 ff.—*F.T.B.* 258, 226 ff.—*O.D.D.* 156 ff., 216 ff., 272, 273, 282 ff., 158-159, 184-185.— *W.A.S.* 69 ff., 111 ff., 134 ff., 118 ff., 25-26, 153 ff., 184 ff., 206, 209 ff., 234 ff., 243 ff.—*L.P.* 38 ff., 247 ff.) (2) *Biter bit: tale:* jackal persuades a barber that his fruit is ripening and eats it up, but the barber puts a sharp knife near the fruit and meanwhile the jackal is badly cut ; jackal tricks an old woman into bringing a pot of water as butter by covering it up as butter is usually covered, then begins to eat a bullock's carcass but the skin shrivels and imprisons him ; while inside he persuades the neighbouring yokels that he is a saint, so they feed him, and eventually wet the hide which enables him to escape, but is next bounced by a small kid, he then gets caught in a net but escapes by persuading an old woman to let him to drink. *Tale:* jackal induces a camel to swim him across a river on his back, but cheats the camel of his food when across, so on the way back the camel drops him in the river. *Tale:* pea-hen induces her friend the jackal to bury bones in order to breed young kids and then laughs at him, whereon he gets so angry that he eats her up. *Tale:* shopkeeper sets a farmer to find Râm to get rich, the farmer finds Râm and is told to blow a conch in a peculiar way, the shopkeeper worms part of the secret out of him, makes him promise to give him double of what he wishes for, at last the farmer wishes he had lost one eye, so shopkeeper goes blind, tumbles into a well, and is drowned. *Tale:* long series of tricks played by a farmer's wife on six thieves. (*I.A.* III., 11.—*O.D.D.* 163 ff., 178 ff.—*W.A.S.* 207 ff., 215 ff., 293 ff.) (3) *Success by mere accident:* potter defeats a tiger and then an army; tailor defeats a mosquito, then an elephant, then a tiger, and then an army, and so becomes a great man; old hen-sparrow sitting under a crow's nest on a wet day is gaily dyed with the drippings from a coloured cloth in the crow's nest. (*O.D.D.* 190 ff.—*W.A.S.* 89 ff., 157).

(*b*) *Malicious:* (1) *Of witch to catch heroine:* pretends to cry on account of hero's danger and so gets into her good graces, and pretends then to want to wash heroine's hair in a boat on the river near the palace, and so floats her down stream into her enemy's power; *ogress* sets heroine various tasks to detain her until ogre's return; induces her to set a line of rice by which she may be found after her departure. (2) *Of witch to kill hero:* gets heroine to worm his life-index out of him. (3) *Of heroine's enemies:* her enemy tells her he is her long-lost uncle and his son is to marry her, and so carries her off; pushes her into a river; ogress pretends to be her aunt; so does witch. (4) *Pretended illness trick:* heroine's enemy's illness can only be cured by the application of heroine's life-index (an egg-plant); stepmother's illness curable only by application of hero and heroine's livers; by death of heroine; by hero's performing impossible tasks; stepmother can only be cured by her stepchildren's life-index (a shaddock) and then by their blood. (5) *Impossible task trick:* witch sends hero to get the wonderful cow, then his mother's eyes, then the million-fold rice: hero is sent to procure tigress's milk, eagle's feathers, ogre's night-growing rice, water from dangerous glittering well: hero sent to fetch foam of the sea, rice from Ceylon, milk from Ceylon: (*W.A.S.* 63 ff., 64, 74 ff., 79, 103 ff., 202 ff., 295.—*L.P.* 262-263.—*I.F.T.* 10, 55 ff., 147, 181 ff.—*F.T.B.* 120 ff., 248 ff., 88.—*O.D.D.* 223, 6, 81-82.—*I.A.* I., 171; IV., 261). (6) *Letter containing instructions to kill bearer:* borne by hero and written on a potsherd, it is read and altered by his wife, who thus circumvents her husband's enemy; borne by hero and sent by ogress's mother: borne by hero and sent by various enemies; borne by fool and delivered by wrong person, who is killed instead. (*W.A.S.* 103 ff.—*F.T.B.* 120.—*I.F.T.* 53 ff., 184 ff.—*I.A.* XI., 85; III. 321.) (7) *Cheating:* jeweller sees that hero has a bangle like the one he has lost, and so raises hue and cry that he is the thief, the bangle not being the same one. (*O.D.D.* 264.) (8) *Lies:* wicked queen parts hero and his companion by ingenious lying; heroine tries to save herself by direct lies. (*O.D.D.* 68.—*L.P.* 285 ff.) (9) *Miscellaneous:* sham hero is detected

by eating coarse food which hero would not have eaten ; pretended
death by parrot to avoid being killed ; (metamorphosed) parrot saves
his own life by saying his value alive is very great and so induces a
merchant to buy him ; hero's enemies induce him to go hunting in the
wilds to kill him ; hero attempts to seduce heroine by pretending to be
her husband ; snake-woman detected by giving her salt food which
forces her out at night and thus to resume her real shape ; hero induces
snake-woman to bake bread at an oven and tips her in ; robber prays
publicly and worships vehemently, so hero thinks him a safe man and
gives him 'touchstone' to keep ; serpent lights a thousand lamps like
magician's life-index to prevent magician's followers from finding it and
restoring him to life ; deceptive invitation to a feast in order to kill
guests. (*O.D.D.* 103, 106, 113, 107.—*L.P.* 200 ff., 269 ff., 504, 512.
—*W.A.S.* 193, 194.—*I.A.* II., 358.)

(*c*) *To escape enemy :* heroine kills his old mother by inducing her to
let her pound her head in a mortar to make the hair grow ; by living
away from home ; by allowing her enemy to carry her off, apparently
asleep on a bed, while she has a bill-hook under the clothes with which
she kills him and his companions ; heroine sends her son to recover her
life-index, a necklace, from her enemy, the child cries for it and then
runs off to his mother with it. (*W.A.S.* 76, 77, 78, 87.)

(*d*) *To punish enemy :* heroine builds a palace exactly like hero's
father's, invites him there, and then tells him all that hero's enemy has
done ; heroine tips ogre into a well. (*W.A.S.* 110.—*O.D.D.* 199.)

(V.) Living in Animals' Bellies

(*a*) Hero lives four days and four nights in the alligator's belly ;
heroine stays twelve years in monster fish's belly while crow, jackal, and
snake go down into it to see what is there ; hero lives successively, for
a year, in a dog's, a cow's and a horse's belly and is vomited up at will.
(*I.F.T.* 66, 75 ff., 124 ff.) *Variant :* serpent lives in hero's throat.
(*O.D.D.* 118 ff.)

(*b*) *Variant of idea ; extraordinary voracity, tale :* a frog eats a rat's
dinner, then the rat, then the baker and his bread, then a man with
lemons and oranges, then a horse with its groom, finally a barber cuts
him open and they all escape alive. *Tale :* a monster fish is carrying
heroine alive, and at his own request snake cuts him open in order to
be relieved of her. *Tale :* heroine's suitors have all been swallowed alive
by an ogre, so saints cut them out alive. *Tale :* a man eats four cwts. of
bhang, meets a man who eats six, they fight, but are eventually brushed
away by the queen as *straws.* (*I.F.T.* 24-26, 76, 100.—*W.A.S.* 226-
227.—*I.A.* II., 271.)

(*c*) *Voracity varied as extraordinary strength, tale:* heroine packs 160 camels, their food, a farmer and his fields, crops, oxen, and house, a whole town, and *everything* she met, puts them in a melon rind, floats them down a river on to a sandbank, where they upset and populate the place. (*I.F.T.* 108 ff.—*W.A.S.* 223 ff.—*I.A.*, II., 271.)

CLASS III.—MEANS

(1) DEUS EX MACHINÂ

(*a*) (1) *Very rarely a god.* (*L.P.* 359 ff.—*I.A.* IX., 1, 2.—*F.T.B.* 51.—*O.D.D.* 97.) (2) *Sometimes a spirit:* ghosts in a well show hero to fortune. (*I.A.* III., 9.)

(*b*) *Ordinary form: a talking animal:* (1) *Showing the way to fortune:* tigress shows hero, parrot and *mainâ* show hero, camel, alligator, and tigress show hero from gratitude for services rendered, a parrot. *Tale:* two birds whose eggs will only hatch by application of a touchstone fish for one, catch fish and take out stone, as hero is seeking for one for his father they give it him. (*W.A.S.* 6, 139.—*I.F.T.*, 63 ff.—*F.T.B.*, 209 ff.—*L.P.* 233 ff.—*I.A.* II., 358; IV., 261.) (2) *Warning of danger:* crow, peacock, and jackal warn heroine; owls warn hero and heroine through his companion; (metamorphosed) parrot warns his parrot friends and shows them how to escape; birds warn hero's friend of hero's danger: calves warn hero's son that he is going to marry his own mother by mistake. (*W.A.S.* 74-75.—*O.D.D.* 74-75, 105.—*F.T.B.* 41 ff., 106.) (3) *Other objects:* doves show hero how to recover dead heroine in the magic palace made of her own body; bird (metamorphosed mother) asks after her children and husband and brings herself to their notice; alligator promises to take charge of hero's dead son; parrot leads hero to seek heroine; jackal shows heroine how to revive temporarily dead hero; parrot interprets hero's dream and shows him how to meet heroine; birds show heroine how to cure hero of his pain; parrot does so. (*I.F.T.* 6, 13, 14, 71, 153.— *O.D.D.* 131, 139.—*F.T.B.* 135, 218, 19.—*W.A.S.* 176.) (4) *Explaining the situation:* parrot and *mainâ* explain to hero the heroine's misfortunes; two birds do. (*I.F.T.* 149 ff.—*W.A.S.* 176.) (5) *Aiding in reward for services rendered:* ants help hero; tigers help hero; tiger by giving him a cub to guard him; cat by giving him a kitten; eagles by giving an eaglet; eagles show hero how to find the ogre's life-index; serpent saves heroine's life by improvising what she said she promised and was unable to procure; rat helps heroine and her children; seven-headed serpent befriends heroine and shows her how to restore her fish-husband to his human form; serpents show heroine how to get the serpent out of hero's throat, and discover to him treasures hidden by one of themselves ; parrot befriends poor fowler ; bull aids heroine ; miraculous birds aid hero, show heroine how to cure hero ; serpent aids hero ; parrot shows him the serpent in his shoe ; shows heroine how to find her lover and *vice versâ ;* hedgehog helps hero for being saved from drowning ; also cricket ; birds show hero how to get the tree that will restore his father's sight. (*I.F.T.* 153, 161, 156, 162, 180, 182.— *O.D.D.* 14, 21, 55-56, 220, 121.—*F.T.B.* 210, 281, 135, 219.—*W.A.S.* 198, 205, 271, 276.—*L.P.* 11, 12, 29, 41 ff., 42, 48 ff.—*I.A.* I., 116, 118 ; IV., 261.) (6) *Common variant of the idea : the thorn in the tiger's foot.* (7) *Varied further as a thorn in a serpent's throat.* (*I.F.T.* 17, 64, 165.—*O.D.D.* 21.—*F.T.B.* 218, 219.) (8) *The converse : punishment for refusal to render help.* (*W.A.S.* 181 ff.) (9) *Aiding out of mere friendship :* parrot helps hero. (*L.P.* 272 ff., 354 ff.— *W.A.S.* 205.)

(*c*) *Common form : a talking plant :* mango tree shows hero how the magic bird can be cut out of it ; heroine is blessed and aided by a plantain, cotton tree, and sweet basil ; heroine is rewarded by a plum tree, a *pîpal* tree for services rendered ; heroine's sister is punished for refusing help. (*I.F.T.* 202.—*F.T.B.* 281.—*W.A.S.* 179-180, 181-183.)

(*d*) *Other talking inanimate objects :* the bed's legs warn the king of danger ; heroine is rewarded by a fire and a stream for services rendered ; heroine's sister is punished for refusing help. (*I.F.T.* 204 ff.—*W.A.S.* 179-180, 181-183.)

(*e*) *Understanding non-human language :* goldsmith's wife hears jackal say that there is a diamond ring on the dead man's hand ; hears snake say where the gold and precious stones are ; fool understands what the cocks and hens say and shows king how to judge between in their disputes. (*F.T.B.* 150, 152.—*I.A.* III., 520.)

(*f*) *Hair, a common form :* a hair of the mannikin's beard when burnt protects hero and heroine from the ogre ; cricket's hair burnt protects hero. (*W.A.S.* 32, 34, 271.—*L.P.* 42-43.) *Variant :* the golden hairs of the heroine floating down stream are a source of wealth to the poor ; puts her into the power of her enemy : a single hair tied to a shell floats down the river and is found by her husband's brother, by her enemy. (*I.F.T.* 62.—*W.A.S.* 60 ff., 201 ff.—*F.T.B.* 87.) (1) *Miraculous powers of the hair : always used to help hero or heroine :* hero being obliged to cut down a tree with a wax hatchet as a condition of marriage to heroine, borrows a hair and stretches it along the edge and so succeeds ; the ogress's hair sets the forest on fire ; heroine's when torn burns up her enemies ; *burning a hair for protection.* (*I.F.T.* 163.—*W.A.S.* 13, 14, 271.—*O.D.D.* 63, 269.—*L.P.* 42-43.)

(*g*) *Sometimes a ship :* a ship takes hero and heroine home ; his wicked brothers throw him overboard, but heroine saves him by her forethought in providing mattresses (and a gourd) (and a pillow) to float him ; hero is taken off in a boat. (*I.F.T.* 47.—*F.T.B.* 269, 275.—*I.A.* II., 358 ; IV. 262-263.)

(II.) DEVICES FOR SUMMONING THE ABSENT

(*a*) *By enchanted articles:* a fan, a bell, a flower, a pin in a bird's beak, a drum, a horse, flowers floating on the water, a flute, a ring. (1) *Varied as supernatural objects : tale :* swans that only eat pearls fly about crying out the praises of their feeder (hero), jealous king hears and imprisons them, but releases female who flies off to hero, who comes and releases the pair. (*F.T.B.* 132, 238 ff., 136.—*I.F.T.* 4, 14, 120 ff., 125, 196, 145 ff., 169.—*W.A.S.* 206, 283 ff.)

(*b*) *By street crying :* heroine gets to hero (*variant,* hero gets to his enemy) by announcing that she will play any one at dice ; by crying milk in the streets ; heroine finds her mother by crying plums in the streets ; hero's companion finds heroine by crying wood in the streets at a fabulous price ; hero's friend gets to heroine by proclaiming himself able to cure diseases. (1) *Varied as answering a proclamation :* of impossible task. (*F.T.B.* 277.—*O.D.D.* 267.—*W.A.S.* 25, 66, 199, 296. —*L.P.* 49 ff., 188.—*I.A.* IX., 3 ; III., 9.)

(*c*) *By an unintelligible request :* hero sent by heroine to find the sun-jewel box ; heroine sends for *Sabr* (patience, that being the hero's name). (*I.F.T.* 167, 195.—*F.T.B.* 131 ff.)

(*d*) *Other devices :* hero sings to attract heroine ; hero's enemy (step-mother) mixes mud with his father's food under pretence of asking for fire and so gets to know him, eventually marries him ; the pigeons of hero fly into his enemy's window, and so introduce him ; a feast to the poor instituted to attract hero who is wandering about as a *faqir* [common device in the *Alif Laila*] ; hero's parrot with others eats up heroine's garden, which brings her out to see, whereon they all fly away except him, he pecks her cheek, and is so caught, when caught he explains about hero ; hero models his father's palace in mud and so attracts heroine ; by making a bouquet in the home fashion attracts the king his brother ; a deer chased by hero's enemy leads him to hero's wife ; hero does ·a lot of mischief to his father's people to get audience. (*I.F.T.* 127 ff.—*O.D.D.* 44, 2, 3.—*F.T.B.*—*W.A.S.* 148, 150, 252.—*L.P.* 52, 235.)

(III.) FORBIDDEN THINGS

(*a*) *Forbidden cupboard,* contains skulls of vampire's victims. (1) *Varied as forbidden room,* containing sleeping beauty. (*I.F.T.* 186.— *W.A.S.* 14.)

(*b*) *Idea varied as forbidden direction in hunting:* the north, the fourth side, the west; *under any circumstances,* the north; the south corner, the eastern corner, the western corner. (*F. T. B.* 190.—*W.A.S.* 85, 98, 27.—*I.F.T.* 153.—*I.A.* I., 117, 118.)

(*c*) *Looking behind forbidden:* punished by being turned into stone; by death; by destruction of the object looked at. (1) *Varied as* destruction to ashes for not fulfilling all the points of a charm. (*I.F.T.* 140 ff.—*W.A.S.* 109, 302.—*I.A.* IV., 57.)

(*d*) *Breach of silence:* as to miraculous events punished by death, by a flood, by disappearance of the subject. (*I.F.T.* 67, 90.—*W.A.S.* 309.)

(IV.) Story-telling to explain the Situation

Commonly brought in to explain and elucidate the difficulties of the tale when the *deus ex machinâ* is not employed, thus the murder by mistake of goldsmith's wife in place of ogress is explained in *F. T. B.* 150 ff., and hero is recognised by his relating his story (*I.F.T.* 191 ff.) The idea frequently occurs. (*O.D.D.* 90, 139, 145 ff., 231 ff.—*I.A.* IX., 8; IV., 59, 263.)

(*a*) *Animals are employed as narrators:* doves, birds, pigeons, serpents. (*I.F.T.* 5, 149.—*W.A.S.* 295.)

(*b*) *Mistakes rectified by story-telling:* case of horse that prevented king from drinking what was poison, but the king thought to be water, and was killed by him [occurs in the *Legends of the Panjâb*]; of parrot that was killed by mistake for presenting king with poisoned fruit. (*F.T.B.* 154, 157.)

(V.) Proofs of Identity

(*a*) (1) *Identity of hero* proved by a gold ring, by his reciting correctly the story of heroine, the story of his early life, by wound in his leg inflicted by heroine, by necklace, ring, and kerchief given on wedding day, by his signet ring. (2) *Of heroine* by a bangle, by possession of hero's ring, by her handiwork, by a wound in her leg (and stomach), by possession of hero's old cap, by her golden hair. (3) *Of other persons:* of hero's brothers by the scar of red-hot money, of hero's mother by her wearing his bride's jewel. (*O.D.D.* 11, 265, 269.—*F. T. B.* 92, 136.—*I.F.T.* 45, 131, 134, 199, 214, 223, 230.—*W.A.S.* 151, 205.—*I.A.* IX., 3; III., 10; IV., 59.—*L.P.* 290.)

(*b*) *Signs of the coming hero:* his heel-ropes will bind and sword kill his enemies of their own accord, his arrow will pierce seven frying-pans placed one behind the other, shooting two golden cups from off a tall standard, the falling of miraculous mangoes into his skirt. (*L. P.* 19, 23, 24.—*W. A. S.* 261 ff.)

(VI.) Temporary Death

Temporary death: body does not decay and comes to life at night, is restored to life in various ways, mostly miraculous. *Tale:* sages will not allow hero to be killed by lightning as fate had decreed, so fate bargains with them to strike his little finger, so that he might only be insensible for a while. (*O.D.D.* 231, 246, 270.—*F.T.B.* 9, 85.—*I.A.* I., 219.)

(*a*) *Persons most affected:* hero, heroine, sleeping beauty. (*O.D.D.* 265 ff., 83 ff., 136 ff.—*F.T.B.* 82, 253.—*W.A.S.* 57, 86, 140.—*L.P.* 362, 47.)

(*b*) *Variants of idea:* long sleep or loss of power; *faqîr* sleeps for six months and wakes for six months; *jinn* for twelve years; heroine is thrown into a comatose state for an indefinite period from a scratch of ogre's nail, revives on removal of nail; it takes the winged horse six months to recover virtue when it is lost. (*I.F.T.* 139.—*O.D.D.* 83 ff.—*F.T.B.* 214 ff.—*W.A.S.* 170.)

(*c*) *Methods of killing:* mendicant kills heroine by throwing a powder in her face: lord of death metamorphosed as bullock offers to swim travellers over a river, drops them in the middle; as a young girl sets two brothers at variance by making love to both till they kill each other: a flash from heroine's eyes kills a deer; hero is destroyed in effigy by having pins stuck through it, when pins are taken out he revives. (*I.F.T.* 77, 165 ff.—*W.A.S.* 220, 222.—*L.P.* 446.) (1) *Idea varied* as the 'Lord of Death.' (*W.A.S.* 219 ff.)

(*d*) *Methods of restoration to life:* (1) *By effigy:* ashes of the heroine are collected, cleaned, and mixed with clay and water, then made into her effigy and revivified; *bones* of a deer (and a man) collected are vivified by *faqîr*, of a tiger by hero and his companions, of the entire population, human and animal, of a deserted city by hero and companions; ashes of hero restored to life by application of life-giving herb. (*I.F.T.* 78.—*W.A.S.* 109, 283.—*F.T.B.* 266, 267, 277.—*L.P.* 492.) (2) *By granting extension of life:* hero granted twenty years' extension on condition of wearing a talisman. (*I.F.T.* 117-118.) (3) *By causing others to do it:* magician obliges serpents to restore hero's companion to life, hedgehog who befriends hero does. (*W.A.S.* 141-142.—*L.P.* 47.) (4) *Miscellaneous methods:* killing two birds at one blow restores heroine to life, by simple prayer, if knife that killed is dropped the victim is restored, by charms. (*W.A.S.* 177, 269.—*I.A.* I., 119.—*L.P.* 472, 474.) (5) *Miraculous cures generally:* hero by using dung of enchanted birds, serpent bite by the use of fresh *nîm* leaves, bathing in a sacred stream cures blindness and leprosy, a drop of sacred water brings to life, a sacrifice of a *man* of *ghî* and cat's milk cures of posses-

sion. (*F.T.B.* 135, 219.—*L.P.* 484, 155, 214, 215, 358, 415, 456.—
W.A.S. 247, 248, 295.—*I.A.* III., 9.)

(*e*) *Variants of idea: revivifying and healing powers of blood:* the
blood of heroine's little finger restores hero's head to his decapitated
body, from mendicant's little finger restores hero to life from his stone
state, the blood of hero's infant restores the marble statue to life, the
blood of (life-index) *mainá* if spilt will create 100 ogres, of bees will
create 1000 ogres. (1) *Varied:* blood from hero's little finger (also
mere touch) brings a fair wind. *Extension of this idea: the drops of
blood become rubies:* from head of sleeping beauty. (*I.F.T.* 84, 187,
141.—*W.A.S.* 109, 55-56, 147.—*F.T.B.* 85, 93 ff., 224-225.—*I.A.*
IV., 262.—*L.P.* 362, 447, 472.)

(*f*) *Restoration of beauty:* religious mendicant restores heroine's
beauty by setting her on fire; by bathing in enchanted tank *once.*
(1) *Varied as restoration to eyesight: restoration after metamorphosis* by
water. (*I.F.T.* 76, 77.—*O.D.D.* 62.—*F.T.B.* 283, 182, 123.)

(VII.) ENCHANTMENTS

(*a*) *Enchanted things: shaddock* grows out of the mother's grave to feed
her daughters starved by their stepmother, a pool is covered with *cream*
for their food, *box* contains a supernatural mannikin, *wand* protects hero
from danger as long as it is held, *eye-salve* brings what is far near, *horn*
when blown stops a famine, *rice* grows only at night, *necklace* retreats
into the wall when hung up, *plates* breed maggots in the food placed on
them, *echoing chamber* tells all that is going on about it, *the emerald city
and mountain* both find heroine and abduct her, *emerald necklace* always
tells the truth when any one near speaks a lie, *jôgi's* ointment-box anni-
hilates distance, *dice* made from dead men's bones that never lose, *conch*
that brings wealth, *wand* calls up the absent, *box* contains the *fan* which
will call up absent hero, *fruit* goes out of reach when hero wants to
pluck. (*O.D.D.* 4, 5, 62.—*F.T.B.* 88, 89.—*L.P.* 41.—*I.F.T.* 184,
229, 197, 226, 232.—*W.A.S.* 6, 31 ff., 36 ff., 174, 190, 216, 270.)
(1) *Enchanted palace:* usually belongs to ogre (see *Sleeping Beauty*);
is improvised for heroine by grateful serpent; contains a silver jewelled
tree, under which dwells (sleeping) beauty; leads hero to heroine;
under the waters occupied by the king of the crocodiles; is under the
waters of a tank. (*O.D.D.* 21 ff., 38.—*W.A.S.* 123 ff., 6.—*F.T.B.*
20, 81.)

(*b*) *Enchanted creatures: fish* jumps back into the water after being
cooked; *pigeons* fly away after being cooked; hero enchants *animals* in
the wilds by music; *hero* by enchantment is made to forget and desert
his wife and child; *cow* gives milk all day without bearing young, and

her dung is golden. (*I.F.T.* 71, 227, 228.—*W.A.S.* 129.—*O.D.D.* 143 ff.—*F.T.B.* 112.—*L.P.* 176.)

(VIII.) METAMORPHOSIS

(a) *Metamorphosis of the dead:* (1) *Metempscychosis of the dead into the living:* dead heroine princess becomes gardener's daughter, and as gardener's daughter marries her own husband the hero; dead hero's anklebone becomes himself, but reverts to the form of an anklebone when chased. In the future life heroine and mother become rich people, hero's father and mother poor wretches, heroine's unborn children fish, and hero is roasted eternally in a large pot by an ogre. (*I.F.T.* 4, 114 ff.—*W.A.S.* 124, 130.) Hero's dead wife becomes a bird; dead saint becomes a Brâhman. (*I.F.T.* 13.—*L.P.* 68.) (2) *Into inanimate objects:* dead dog-mother of human children becomes golden bejewelled image of dog; hero's dead children become a tree with two large flowers and fruits which cannot be plucked by hero's enemy but are easily plucked by hero; the various parts of heroine's dead body lying in the desert are formed into four palaces, a tank with a palace in the midst and doves flying about; dead heroine's eyes become a parrot and a starling, her heart a tank, her body a palace and garden, her arms and legs its pillars, her head its domes, herself into sleeping beauty whom hero finds; dead heroine becomes a lotus flower which cannot be caught except by hero, a tree bearing a fruit which contains herself and which cannot be plucked except by hero; drowned heroine becomes a sunflower which is burnt by her enemy, the ashes then become a mango tree with one fruit only, this falls into a poor milkwoman's can and turns into heroine; hero's friend becomes on being killed a tree with silver trunk, golden branches, diamond leaves, pearly fruit with peacocks playing in the branches. (*O.D.D.* 86-88.— *I.F.T.* 5, 10-11, 148 ff., 145, 146.—*W.A.S.* 175.—*I.A.* I., 19.)

(b) *Metamorphosis of deities:* (1) *Avatâras, incarnations:* deity into a boar which destroys hero's garden; Ganesa becomes an old woman and catches hero on the point of falling on the hedge of bayonets; goddesses become fortune-tellers to save hero; Râma becomes a wayfarer to help hero. (2) *Into inanimate objects:* goddess becomes a ball by being rubbed in the hands. (*I.F.T.* 68, 89.—*O.D.D.* 98, 261.—*W.A.S.* 216.)

(c) *Metamorphosis of superhuman personages:* (1) *Ogres:* ogress becomes a goat at night only; a beautiful girl; an old woman. (*I.F.T.* 173, 175, 51.—*O.D.D.* 27.—*I.A.* 170.) (2) *Angels:* angel becomes a religious mendicant. (3) *Jinns:* becomes a hawk, dove, and eagle to watch heroine. (*I.F.T.* 74, 77.—*W.A.S.* 173.) (4) *Vampires:*

vampire becomes a Brâhman, and afterwards rain, a dove, a rose falling
from heaven, a mouse to escape mannikin. (*W.A.S.* 13-15.) (5)
Mannikins: mannikin becomes storm-wind, a hawk, a musician, and a
cat to catch vampire; a huge demon. (*W.A.S.* 15, 49 ff.) (6) *Fairies:*
fairy princess is a pigeon while in the air, and becomes one to escape
her enemy. (*W.A.S.* 30, 33.) (7) *Ghosts:* hideous female malignant
ghost becomes a beautiful girl but with feet turned backwards; ghost
becomes a Brâhman; a Brâhman's wife; an insect which enters a phial
and bottled up in it for ever. (*W.A.S.* 54.—*F.T.B.* 183 ff., 197, 185-
186.) (8) *Lord of death:* tale: changes into a scorpion, snake, bullock,
ox, beautiful girl, old man. (*W.A.S.* 219 ff.) (9) *Demons:* into a merchant. (*I.A.* I., 345.)

(*d*) *Metamorphosis of living things:* (1) *one into another:* golden
deer becomes mannikin demon; white hind becomes white witch who
marries hero's father; crocodile becomes hero prince; hero's mother
becomes a black dog; hero becomes a parrot, hero's enemy becomes
hero, but only knowing half the spell, is unable to retransform himself
into any other human shape, finally becomes a ram and is killed; with
the object of gaining better fortune mouse becomes cat, dog, ape, wild-
bore, elephant, girl who becomes a queen the happiest of mortals, but
she falls into a well and is killed; heroine's hundred sons changed by
ogre into crows; hero becomes a fly to escape enemies; princess becomes
a kite to attract hero's attention; hero becomes a sheep, monkey, horse,
for going in forbidden direction; hero, a kingfisher and a parrot to do
impossible task; serpent becomes a Brâhman to attract heroine, goes
back again to serpent to kill hero, to Brâhman to cure her and to serpent
to bring hero to her; female Nâg becomes a serpent to save herself from
her too importunate lover and returns to her ordinary form to marry
him; serpent becomes a fish to kill hero, also a Brâhman. (*W.A.S.*
29, 100, 125.—*O.D.D.* 9, 101, 102, 117, 58.—*F.T.B.* 139 ff.—*I.F.T.* 56,
141.—*L.P.* 5, 180, 181, 183 ff., 416, 498, 499.—*I.A.* I., 117, 118, 171.)

(2) *Into inanimate things:* magician's victims become stones and
trees; heroine's hundred boys become a hundred mangoes and her girl
a rose bush, saved from the malice of their enemies by a flood and
restored to their own shapes in a strange land; hero's companion
changed into stone, and restored by hero's child; a thousand wooden
parrots made by hero become alive; serpent becomes a plum in order
to kill hero, a golden staff to kill magician; heroine's mother becomes
a golden stool. (*O.D.D.* 10, 57 ff., 75-78, 117.—*L.P.* 488, 502.—
W.A.S. 301.)

(*e*) *Metamorphosis of inanimate things:* all hero's property becomes
stone and charcoal as a punishment; heroine's hut becomes a gorgeous
palace. (*I.F.T.* 226.—*W.A.S.* 302.)

(*f*) *Temporary metamorphosis*: (1) *change of skin* [compare such instances as occur above and 'beauty and the beast' idea in Europe]. *Tale:* heroine becomes an old woman by putting on skin of a dead old beggar woman, she is given shelter as an old woman, but in the early morning she bathes in tank and takes off the skin, while she has it off she is a young girl ; king's son detects her by her habit of plucking the royal lotuses in the tank, marries her as an old woman, burns the skin and thus prevents her from becoming old any more. (*O.D.D.* 167 ff.) (2) *Variants:* hero as a jackal marries Brâhman's daughter, is a jackal as long as he has the skin on, is human when it is off ; monkey-son of the seventh queen can change his monkey's skin and become human and *vice versâ* at will. (*O.D.D.* 203 ff.)   *Variant of idea: tale:* hero is a fish, becomes a favourite of the queen, who determines to give him a wife, marries heroine, who restores him to his human shape by spells ; heroine becomes a white dog and can regain her human form only when she can manage to frighten hero ; hero's horse can be turned into a donkey by twisting his right ear and *vice versâ* by twisting the left ear ; snake-woman must resume her serpent form if she travel at night. (*O.D.D.* 203 ff., 167 ff., 218 ff.—*I.F.T.* 42 ff., 30 ff., 131.—*W.A.S.* 193.)

(IX.) Disguises

(*a*) *Of hero:* as a beggar to meet heroine, a religious mendicant to seek fortune, with companion as two old beggars to escape imprisonment, as a mendicant, with heroine as a pair of mendicants, as a madman to test virtue of his intended wife, as a religious mendicant in seeking broken-hearted his injured wife, as a prince to meet heroine, as a gardener's daughter to outwit magician, a female servant to be with heroine. (*O.D.D.* 119, 24, 72, 11.—*L.P.* 332 ff.—*I.F.T.* 226, 235, 2, 125.—*W.A.S.* 149.—*I.A.* IX., 6.)

(*b*) *Of hero's companions:* hero's brother as a lunatic to save hero. (*F.T.B.* 35 ff.)

(*c*) *Of heroine:* as old village woman to escape robbers, an old woman selling milk to find hero, old beggar woman to escape detection, as a female barber to procure hero's life-index (a necklace) from hero's enemy, as a cowherdess to marry hero (her own husband) now a merchant and stranger, as a male religious mendicant to save her husband and to find hero, as lost hero. *Tale:* becomes a chief minister, marries seven wives, recovers lost hero, remarries him with all the seven wives.—(*W.A.S.* 76.—*O.D.D.* 267, 199, 25 ff.—*F.T.B.* 14 ff., 134.— *I.F.T.* 222, 198 ff.)

(*d*) *Of heroine's enemies:* chief constable's son as a mendicant to catch heroine, robber as a pedlar to entrap heroine. (*I.F.T.* 214.— *W.A.S.* 73.

(*e*) *Of superhuman beings:* ogress as an old woman ; of saint's emissary (a god) as a Brâhman ; of dead saint as a Sayyid. (*O.D.D.* 58.—*L.P.* 76, 77.)

(X.) INVISIBILITY

(*a*) *Invisible cap,* called the *yech* cap, renders wearer invisible. (*W.A.S.* 37 ff.) (1) *Varied as invisible ring,* which renders wearer invisible. (*O.D.D.* 39 ff.)

(*b*) *Invisibility by other means:* holding a feather straight, blowing away enchanted sand. (*I.F.T.* 59, 139.)

(*c*) *Natural invisibility:* fairies invisible to adults but not to children. (*O.D.D.* 237.)

(XI.) INEXHAUSTIBLE POT

(*a*) *Inexhaustible pot: tale:* given to Brâhman in reward for prayer filled with comfits, is stolen by innkeeper, but he procures another filled with demons and chastises innkeeper. Procures a third filled with sweets with which he makes money and chastises his enemies. (*F.T.B.* 55-62.) *Variant: tale:* given by fairies to idiot hero to give him any dish he wants, is stolen by cooks. Idiot takes substituted pot to his mother who punishes him as a liar. He then gets an *inexhaustible box* filled with clothes which is also stolen as before. Eventually he gets a rope and stick which beat the cooks when wanted and so he recovers pot and box. (*I.F.T.* 32-34.)

(*b*) *Variant: tale: inexhaustible melons* given to Brâhman filled with jewels, who, not knowing their value, sells them. Then procures *inexhaustible pot* of food, which the king seizes. Eventually he recovers value of melons and pot by means of stick and rope which bind and beat the enemies. (*O.D.D.* 169-174 ff.)

(*c*) *Varied further into inexhaustible basket:* given by a saint filled with pearls and gold, renewable whenever finished.

(*d*) *Inexhaustible shell* from a Brâhmanî bull's neck filled with ornaments.

(*e*) *Inexhaustible leaf* (platted) filled with food of all sorts.

(*f*) *Inexhaustible cotton-branch* filled with clothes.

(*g*) *Inexhaustible bag and stone bowl.*

(*h*) *Inexhaustible cow.*

(*i*) *Inexhaustible rice.*

(*j*) *Inexhaustible ring* which produces what is asked for at once.

(*k*) *Inexhaustible conch* which brings wealth whenever blown.

(*l*) *Inexhaustible coat* that produces gold coins. (*F.T.B.* 282-283.— *I.F.T.* 156 ff.—*W.A.S.* 106, 108, 199 ff., 216 ff., 286 ff.)

(XII.) Snake Jewel: Mani

Typical tale: jewel in serpent's crest is equal in value to the treasure of seven kings, can be hidden only by cow-dung being thrown on it (or horse-dung), possession of jewel slays the serpent. *Typical tale:* jewel in serpent's crest lights the way into and out of enchanted palace beneath the waters, is possessed by sleeping beauty who on loss of it cannot return to the palace beneath the waters and loses hero till it is recovered for her. (*F. T. B.* 19 ff.—*W. A. S.* 140 ff.) *Variants:* diamond in serpent's mouth leads the way to the enchanted palace beneath the lake containing silver jewelled tree. (*O. D. D.* 33 ff.)

(*a*) *Variants of idea: jewel on the head of heroine:* has similar properties, hero's body shines dazzlingly, heroine shines as a star, the shining anklets on heroine perform wonders, heroine's face lights up the night, the snake-stone is a ruby found in the ground. (*O. D. D.* 88 ff., 136, 140, 255.—*I. F. T.* 158 ff.—*W. A. S.* 304.)

(*b*) *Variant: moon and star hero:* hero has a moon on his forehead, Indra the king of heaven has a sun on his head and moons on his hands and stars on his face, hero born of a snake-stone (ruby) has a red star on his forehead, seventh queen gives birth to a boy with a moon on his forehead and stars on his hands, heroine has a moon on her forehead and a star on her chin, hero and heroine have the sun on their heads, moons on their hands, and stars on their faces. (*F. T. B.* 236 ff., 242.—*I. F. T.* 1 ff., 119, 2.—*W. A. S.* 310.)

(XIII.) Solomon's Judgment

Variant of the idea: tiger judges between cat and dog as to their prowess, matter settled by cat running away; hero as (metamorphosed) parrot proves that the woman claiming the woodcutter's supposed wealth was never at the place where she said it had been given her by asking her to open a sealed bottle. (*I. F. T.* 13, 17.—*O. D. D.* 111, 112.) *Variant tale:* boys judge between ghost (in the form of a Brâhman) and a Brâhman as to the ownership of a house, the ghost being the false claimant. The judge decides that whichever of them shall enter a phial shall be adjudged the owner, the ghost immediately becomes an insect and enters phial and is thus proved to be a ghost and no Brâhman. (*F. T. B.* 185-186.) [A variant of this tale is told of one of the Hindû kings of Kashmîr in the *Râjâtaranginî.*] Shepherds judge between sham merchant (demon) and the real merchant by inducing demon to go into a hollow reed. (*I. A.* I., 345.)

(XIV.) Miraculous Vehicle

(*a*) *Animals:* horses, golden deer, birds, eaglets, parrots, snakes, seven-headed serpent, monster fish, alligator, winged horses, wind-winged camel ; *varied as* pony that jumps a river three miles broad, horse that jumps a sea surrounded by high spiked walls. (*O.D.D.* 14, 132, 142, 151, 30, 32.—*F.T.B.* 17, 73, 135, 214, 249.—*I.F.T.* 45, 53, 63, 75, 76.—*W.A.S.* 28.—*L.P.* 192, 238-291.)

(*b*) *Inanimate objects :* boat, paper boat, bed, palanquin (but in this case a balloon), enchanted club and rope, sword. (*F.T.B.* 88, 121.—*I.F.T.* 156 ff., 162, 187.—*W.A.S.* 66.—*I.A.* IV., 55.)

(*c*) *Idea varied as mere power to fly through the air :* hero's horse when his work in the tale is done, mannikin to help hero, to bring about meeting of hero and heroine and to protect both against their enemies, ogre to save his own life, saint to save hero. (*F.T.B.* 121, 217.—*I.F.T.* 45.—*W.A.S.* 8-12, 59.—*L.P.* 358, 495, 520 ff.—*I.A.* IV., 58.)

(*d*) *As possession of a charm :* the *jôgi's* ointment-box makes possessor traverse the earth at lightning speed. (*W.A.S.* 190.)

CLASS IV.—MISCELLANEOUS

(I.) Miscellaneous Points

(*a*) *Cat's nine lives :* story illustrating. (*I.F.T.* 18 ff.)

(*b*) *Alchemy :* making gold out of a stone, wealth by magic, heroine rubs balls of flour on her body which roll off in balls of gold, the stone from the ashes of the snake-woman will make gold. *Varied as* enchanted ring. (*I.F.T.* 59, 13.—*F.T.B.* 55 ff., 235.—*W.A.S.* 195, 200.)

(*c*) *Dropping jewels :* hero drops rubies when he laughs and pearls when he weeps, pearls and precious stones drop from heroine as she walks or speaks, whoever eats enchanted fish will drop jewels when he laughs and pearls when he weeps, when heroine laughs she fills a basket with flowers, when she weeps she fills a platter with pearls. (*I.F.T.* 13.—*O.D.D.* 239.—*F.T.B.* 97.—*L.P.* 233.)

(*d*) *Being one-eyed: sign of a wicked disposition :* hero's enemy is one-eyed, king of the tigers is, chief constable is, demon is. (*I.F.T.* 3, 36.—*W.A.S.* 12, 295.)

(*e*) *Symbolism :* heroine puts a rose to her teeth to let hero know that her father's name is *Dant* (tooth), then behind her ear that her country is *Karnâtak* (ear, Carnatic), then at her feet that her own name is Pânvpati (foot). (*I.F.T.* 7.)

(*f*) *King chosen by sacred elephant :* hero is chosen. (*W.A.S.* 141.—*F.T.B.* 100.—*I.A.* III., 11 ; IV., 261.)

(*g*) *Deserted city :* devastated by ogres, by ghosts, by demons, by a mannikin. *Variants :* (1) *deserted palace* of the ogre, of jinn ; (2)

deserted land; (3) *blighted garden* flourishing at the touch of the hero. (*W.A.S.* 49, 48, 52, 143, 169.—*F.T.B.* 65, 115, 74 ff., 169.—*I.F.T.* 178.—*O.D.D.* 197.)

(*h*) *Choice:* hero has the choice of riches, power, beauty, long life, health, happiness, and anything else he fancies, he chooses power of metamorphosis. (*O.D.D.* 100.)

(*i*) *Riverside waif:* heroine is put into a golden box as a baby and floated down stream, is found by a fisherman and adopted by a childless banker, hero is tossed ashore and befriended by washermen. (*O.D.D.* 256 ff.—*I.A.* IV., 263.)

(*j*) *Little slipper:* heroine's golden slipper will fit no one else, is found by hero. (*O.D.D.* 240.)

(*k*) *Gambling extraordinary:* hero loses first his companions (hawk and dog) and then himself to an ogress on a throw of dice, subsequently hero's brother wins them back; hero and his friends lose themselves to heroine; hero loses first his arms, then his horse, the third stake being his head, he then wins them back and finally wins last game, being his enemy's head. (*F.T.B.* 193-194, 277.—*L.P.* 48 ff.—*W.A.S.* 277 ff.)

(*l*) *Evil-eye: tale:* is the cause of general misfortune to hero and heroine, hero turned woodcutter works so well that the others drive him away, heroine cooks and weaves so well that she is turned out by the village women and carried off by boatmen, hero beats them at gambling and is thrown overboard. (*F.T.B.* 110 ff.)

(*m*) *Human-sacrifice:* for a fair wind. (*W.A.S.* 147.)

(*n*) *Wolf-children: variant tale:* a dog-mother has two girls instead of pups, but the queen has two pups in place of children. To avoid her girls being changed the dog hides them. They are subsequently found by two princes and married to them. The dog-mother seeks them. The elder daughter recognises and treats her kindly, but the younger ill-treats her till she dies. The elder then hides the corpse which turns into a golden bejewelled image of a dog. The elder girl is, as a reward, saved from death subsequently by a serpent, but the younger is killed. (*O.D.D.* 17, 22.) *Variant tale:* eagles carry off heroine and rear her. She subsequently meets hero and marries him, but is drowned by an enemy. She is however restored to life and to her human mother. (*O.D.D.* 84-90.)

(*o*) *Bargains with animals:* based on the supposition that they can talk, and so a variant consequent on the notion of the *deus ex machina*. *Moral tale:* ungrateful *mouse* seizes barber's razor for cutting his tail in taking out thorns; lends the razor to a grasscutter who breaks it, and the mouse takes his blanket instead; lends his blanket to a thresher to bind his sugar-canes, the blanket becomes torn and the mouse takes the canes; lends the canes to a confectioner to sweeten his wares, all of them being used he takes the confections ; lends them to feed the king's cows and takes the cows ; lends the cows for the king's feast on his daughter's wedding, takes the bride ; lends his wife to rope-dancers as a performer, she is killed and so he takes all their wives, and finally is killed himself by a trick. *Moral:* overreaching ambition. (*I.F.T.* 101, 107.) *Humorous tale:* a *rat* gives a dry root to a man who wants to light his fire for cooking on a wet day, gets some dough in return ; gives the dough to a potter for food, who gives him a pigskin in return ; gives the pigskin to a neatherd to milk his buffalo into, gets the buffalo given him as a joke ; meets a bridal party, offers them the buffalo for food, they take and eat it and run away to avoid the consequences and the rat takes possession of the bride, but finally loses her by a trick. (*W.A.S.* 18-23.) *Humorous tale:* a bear bargains to cut a quantity of wood for the hero in return for a savoury dish, cuts the wood, but finds that hero has eaten the food, so he takes the dish in revenge, and gets at hero's plums which he puts into the dish, at this point heroine sneezes which frightens the bear who drops the dish which hero and heroine pick up plums and all. (*W.A.S.* 40 ff.)

(*p*) *Delicate heroine:* (1) *ordinary form: five-flower princess:* heroine weighs five flowers only. (*W.A.S.* 10 ff.—*O.D.D.* 129 ff.) (2) *Varied* as one flower. (*I.F.T.* 1.) (3) *Variant: delicate heroine:* weighs only one flower ; Indra, the king of heaven, weighs but one flower. (*I.F.T.* 2.)

(*q*) *Nostrums for procuring sons:* pomegranate flower (and fruit) given to eat, mango fruit to eat, a drug to take, throwing a stick at mangoes and eating what falls, eating fruit (*lîchîs*). *Varied* as used to procure egg-heroine (*q.v.*), barley-corn to eat, grain of rice to eat, two flowers, bathing in a sacred well. *Variant:* half a mango produces half a son. (*F.T.B.* 1, 117, 187, 9.—*I.F.T.* 41, 91, 139.—*W.A.S.* 47, 249.—*L.P.* 2, 3, 139, 290, 291.—*I.A.* I., 219.) (1) *Children granted by saints and holy persons:* twin sons granted on condition that one is given up when adult to mendicant granting him. *Varied* as a son restored to life so claimed ; twin sons granted to the wrong queen by error, but the queen is to die at their birth for tricking the saint, and they are only to live twelve years ; the right queen is granted one son of extraordinary power. (*F.T.B.* 168.—*I.F.T.* 41, 91, 93, 98.—*W.A.S.* 47, 98, 249.—*L.P.* 3, 2, 77, 139, 142.)

(*r*) *Ordeal:* (1) *To prove chastity* hero and heroine have to spin a single thread of yarn (which has no cohesion) and to draw up with it water from a well in an unbaked pitcher ; heroine has to throw with dice a special number, bathe in boiling oil ; softening of a stone. (*L.P.* 39, 312, 315.—*I.A.* VI., 224.) (2) *To prove truth:* making a bamboo sprout. (*I.A.* VI., 224.)

(II.) Points in Marriages

(a) *Marriage without ceremony :* hero to sleeping beauty, hero to egg-heroine, hero to robber's daughter, by mere exchange of garlands between hero and heroine. (*W.A.S.* 70, 173.—*F.T.B.* 11, 22, 86.— *I.F.T.* 61.—*I.A.* II., 358.)

(b) *Enforced marriage postponed for a season :* by sleeping beauty to give her husband time to recover her, for one year, for six months, for six months to give winged horse time to rescue her, for twelve years to enable hero to find his mother, princess's marriage postponed for a year to give hero time to explain himself, for three years to enable heroine to avoid hero's enemy. (*W.A.S.* 64, 146, 204.—*F.T.B.* 29, 90, 217.—*O.D.D.* 44, 10.—*I.A.* I., 119; IV., 263.)

(c) *Marriage extraordinary :* hero to ogress, hero to his own mother in ignorance. (*F.T.B.* 67, 106.—*I.A.* IV., 56, 58.)

(d) *On condition of impossible task :* to crush the oil in 80 lbs. of mustard seed, to kill demon, to beat a drum in heaven, to cut down a tree with wax hatchet, to tame a vicious pony, jump over lofty spiked walls, to find silver tree with leaves of gold and flowers of pearl, to jump river round heroine's palace three times on old war-horse, to separate millet seed from sand, to solve inexplicable riddles. (1) *Expansion of idea : general impossibilities :* heroine is to marry a dead man, heroine is to get possession of unmatched robe. (*I.F.T.* 160 ff.—*O.D.D.* 30 32, 33, 73, 29, 229 ff.—*L.P.* 42, 43, 240.)

(e) *Public choice of a husband : Swayamvara.* (*O.D.D.* 29, 31, 33, 70, 95, 119, 240.—*W.A.S.* 104, 148, 172.—*I.F.T.* 163, 42 ff.—*L.P.* 240.—*I.A.* II., 263.)

(III.) Modes of Vengeance

(a) *On hero's enemies :* cutting to pieces and burying in the desert, burning in a wooden house and sending (female's) ashes to her mother as a present, burnt to ashes in a tower, killed and thrown into the desert, buried (female) to her head in a pit and shot to death with arrows, burying alive standing with thorns heaped around the body, burial alive and ploughing up the grave, simply put to death, boiling alive in caldrons. (*I.F.T.* 6, 11, 61, 192.—*F.T.B.* 16, 92, 107.—*W.A.S.* 110, 152.—*L.P.* 517.)

(b) *On heroine's enemies :* burning to death, imprisonment such as their calumnies had caused, hanging, imprisonment for life, tearing out the heart, killed by her husband's own hands, dashed to pieces, burial in a pit with scorpions and snakes, walking over the grave. (*O.D.D.* 65, 93, 238, 249, 269.—*I.F.T.* 137, 152.—*W.A.S.* 67, 88, 89.)

(c) *On murderers:* burnt alive. (*I.F.T.* 207.)

(d) *Miscellaneous punishments:* hero has to sell himself to a sexton and his wife to a merchant as slaves to pay a debt, hero induces his unchaste wife by a trick to eat her lover's heart, the queen who has tricked the saint into granting her twins in place of sister dies in childbirth, heroine is set to scare crows. (*I.F.T.* 69 ff.—*L.P.* 65, 142, 292.)

(IV.) NUMBERS

(a) *One:* priest says he eats *one* demon a day; *one* whip to winged horse is enough, more destroys his virtue; *one* dip in enchanted tank restores beauty. (1) Hero is *only* son of a widow, of a king, a merchant, *only* son, heroine is *only* daughter. (*O.D.D.* 277.—*W.A.S.* 5, 47.—*F.T.B.* 283-284, 214, 93.—*O.D.D.* 23, 239.)

(b) *Two:* hero has *two* wives, heroine has *two* companions, hero wanders *two* years as a parrot, jeweller has to make up *two* thousand rupees, worth of ornaments for the princess, king has *two* sons, *two* companions seek fortune, king gives every one what they want for *two* hours. (*O.D.D.* 24, 95, 116.—*L.P.* 25.—*W.A.S.* 196.—*I.A.* I., 345; II., 357.)

(c) *Three:* mendicant's disciple has *three* tasks set him, hero does *three* penances, mendicant laughs sardonically *three* times, Krishna has *three* wives, *three* women start to find Mahâdev, *three* companions outwit the demon, priest has a wife and *three* children, miraculous pony jumps a river *three* miles broad *three* times, horse jumps the high spiked wall of princess's sea-like bath *three* times, heroine and her companions sleep in *three* pomegranates, *three* pebbles restore metamorphosed fish to his human form. (1) *Third* son of king is hero, hero's *three* friends are chief actors in the tale, hero seeks fortune with *three* rupees, with *three* companions, tiger gives Brâhman leave to examine *three* things as to his rights, heroine has *three* sons, *three* vows are binding, hero *trebles* his capital miraculously, hero is given *three* lâkhs of rupees. (2) Hero sits as a stranger beside the king *three* days, heroine starves for *three* days, discarded body on metamorphosis lasts only *three* days, human co-wife discloses discovery of ogress co-wife on the *third* day, serpents go without water *three* days. (*F.T.B.* 71, 147, 261.—*W.A.S.* 5, 48, 116.—*L.P.* 65, 75, 126, 204, 223, 253, 423 ff.—*I.F.T.* 87, 115, 191.—*O.D.D.* 260, 252, 273 ff., 277, 30, 32, 80, 95, 104, 220.—*I.A.* IV., 263.)

(d) *Four:* hero's companions search *four* years for him, Brâhman has *four* children. *Varied* as hero's father, life on earth is described as of *four* days only, hero seeks fortune with *four* gold pieces and *four* companions, *four* companions start to seek fortune, hero has *four* wives.

(*O.D.D.* 147.—*F.T.B.* 53, 221.—*L.P.* 303.—*W.A.S.* 196-197.—*I.A.* I., 285 ; IV., 59.)

(*e*) *Five :* idiot meets *five* fairies, snake which kills eaglets is cut into *five* pieces, heroine weighs *five* flowers, the *five* arms, heroine's robe is of *five* colours, *five* girls live on the milk of *five* sacred cows, hero's enemy has *five* sons, ghost has *five mans* of gold, queen dies after *five* years. (*I.F.T.* 32 ff., 182.—*O.D.D.* 130.—*L.P.* 222, 342, 430.—*I.A.* II., 358 ; III., 10 ; IV., 260.)

(*f*) *Six :* hero plays in the desert *six* times, and *six* times *six* variations, hero eats *six mans* of *ganjâ* daily, farmer tricks *six* thieves. (1) As *half-twelve :* mendicant sleeps and wakes alternately for *six* months, heroine seeks her sister *six* months, marriage is postponed *six* months, hero has *six* months in which to find the 'touchstone.' (*I.F.T.* 139.'—*O.D.D.* 203.—*L.P.* 176.—*I.A.* II., 271, 357 ; III., 11.—*W.A.S.* 204.)

(*g*) *Seven :* a kite has *seven* chicks, makes a feast of *seven* dishes, hero has *seven* wives and *seven* children, *seven* country girls play together, enchanted box contains *seven* fairies, *seven* companions seek fortune, king has *seven* queens, *seven* thieves come to steal the king's daughter, *seven* fairies visit hero, hero's father has *seven* daughters, *seven* princes marry *seven* forlorn princesses, eagle's house has *seven* doors, heroine's abode is guarded by *seven* hedges of bayonets, and again by *seven* ditches and *seven* hedges of spears. *Varied* as tower of Ganesa's temple is so guarded, heroine's abode is across *seven* seas, Brâhman has *seven* daughters, *seven*-headed serpent helps heroine, hair of heroine is *seven* cubits long, prince is bathed *seven* times with *seven* jars of water and *seven* jars of milk, *seven* victims required to complete a human sacrifice, palace garden is *seven* miles square, heroine is locked up in *seven* prisons, lambikin is *seven* days fattening, heroine's enemy has *seven* sons, *seven* hundred ogres guard the miraculous flower, the wounded deer is hurled *seven* paces by the force of an arrow, *seven* thieves die of grief for each other, ogre kills off the old woman's *seven* sons, hero's arrow pierces *seven* frying-pans and *seven* ogres placed one behind the other, heroine's home is across *seven* rivers, hero has to cross *seven* rivers to reach heroine, when hero shoots a deer it falls *seven* paces towards him, heroine has *seven* companions, the *seven* lives in Hell, the *seven* climes of the world, heroine has to throw the *seven* to prove her virtue (the five and two), *seven* mangoes (five and two) produce *seven* sons, hero's wealth reaches *seven karors*, *seven* thieves attack the barber's clever wife, heroine is *seventh* daughter, *seventh* hedge cannot be crossed (*varied* as killing hero), *seventh* queen goes across *seven* oceans, *seventh* court of deserted palace contains the ogresses, *seventh* daughter is heroine, *seventh* queen is mother of hero, *seventh* son is hero, *seventh* daughter is the cleverest of all, *seventh* wife protects her sister-in-law, *seventh* queen has a monkey son, *seventh* son sets out to find heroine, has miraculous powers. (2) *Being seventh:* Hero's life-index is in a parrot under *six* pitchers. (3) Hero is *seven* days and *seven* nights on the back of the golden deer flying through the air, tiger watches hero *seven* days, hero is given *seven* days to arrange his marriage in. (*I.F.T.* 42 ff., 138, 21, 51, 119, 127, 169, 173, 175, 206.—*I.A.* I., 170, III., 342.—*O.D.D.* 237, 1, 7, 13, 79, 95, 96, 130, 131, 170, 136, 166, 220. —*F.T.B.* 87, 135, 194, 214, 270, 248, 124 ff., 7 ff., 236 ff.—*W.A.S.* 28, 29, 37, 70, 80-83, 95, 241, 290, 294 ff., 295.—*L.P.* 14, 17, 19, 51, 142, 171, 179, 181, 190, 204, 209, 237, 313, 336.)

(*h*) *Nine:* hero is to carry enchanted box *nine* miles, life-index is in the *nine-lâkh* necklace, garden, kerchief, the *nine* quarters of the world, hero is given *nine lâkhs* of rupees, the *nine* Nâgs, hero eats *nine mans* of *ganjâ* daily and fasts *nine* days. (*W.A.S.* 6, 83.—*L.P.* 209, 235, 287, 426, 438, 488.— *I.A.* I., 271.)

(*i*) *Twelve:* (1) idiot thinks he has been dead *twelve* years, camel has wandered *twelve* years, alligator has been ill *twelve* years, tiger has had a thorn *twelve* years in his foot, hero is impoverished for *twelve* years, heroine wanders for *twelve* years, hero serves a mendicant for *twelve* years, hero does penance for *twelve* years, saint grants *twelve* years further life, mendicant sleeps and wakes alternately for *twelve* years (*varied* as demon, jinn), famine lasts *twelve* years, heroine searches *twelve* years for Mahâdeo, marriage is postponed *twelve* years, dog-mother seeks her human children *twelve* years, heroine lives in disguise for *twelve* years, heroine is reared by eagles for *twelve* years, hero must not see his father and mother for *twelve* years after birth, is shut up in a cellar for *twelve* years, heroine's life-index (a mango tree) flowers after *twelve* years, barren heroine has a son after *twelve* years, the twins of the queen who has tricked the saint into granting them live only *twelve* years, the ace and *twelve* if thrown are to decide against heroine in the ordeal by dice of her virtue, maiden of *twelve* years must fetch water from golden well to cure leprosy. (2) Singer's voice can be heard a distance of *twelve* days off, hero has *twelve* children, priest's family eat *twelve* demons a day, hero has a box made which requires *twelve* men to open, wedding of hero (disguised heroine with ogress princess) lasts *twelve* days, marriage tents of heroine are *twelve* miles in circumference, hero has *twelve* children (*five* boys and *seven* girls), king has *twelve* wives, eagles leave *twelve* months' provisions when they go to find heroine's ring, melon to cure ogress must be *twelve* cubits long, serpent has destroyed everything within *twelve* miles of his lair, hero travels *twelve* miles per stage, hero is *twelve* months in his mother's womb. (*I.F.T.* 32, 35, 63, 64, 68, 74, 86, 87 ff., 98, 155, 167, 226.—*O.D.D*

252, 258, 277, 10, 18, 26, 34, 41, 44-45, 47, 50, 80, 122.—*F.T.B.* 120.
—*W.A.S.* 35, 64, 170, 305.—*L.P.* 3, 8, 12, 50, 74, 157, 313, 428, 438.
—*I.A.* I., 119.)

(*j*) *Eighteen: as multiple of twelve: eighteen* thousand demons watch the wonderful cow, *eighteen* million demons guard the million-fold rice. (*W.A.S.* 106, 108.)

(*k*) *Twenty-four: as multiple of twelve:* enchanted palace is *twenty-four* miles square, heroine must travel *twenty-four* miles without looking back, salary of heroine in disguise is *twenty-four lákhs* of rupees, heroine remains unmarried *twenty-four* years, serpent has destroyed everything within *twenty-four* miles of his lair. (*O.D.D.* 21, 22, 26, 70.—*L.P.* 9.)

(*l*) *Miscellaneous: nineteen* lines of houses are burnt down by heroine, *thirteenth* queen is heroine, melon to cure ogress has a stone *thirteen* cubits long, heroine lives across *thirteen* rivers, the *jôgi* has waited *twenty-two* years to see the heroine, *eight* charms cure of serpent-bite, hero's companion is turned into stone for *eight* years, heroine starts off with *twenty-one* gold pieces, hero is born on the *eighth* day of Bhâdoṅ, marriage is to be postponed only *eight* days, the *eight* families of Nâgs, heroine lives *fourteen* years in gardener's hut, heroine's home is *fourteen* (*twice seven*) hundred miles away, hero takes with him *twenty-two* hundred nobles, ogres eat *twenty-two mans* of rice and *twenty-two* buffaloes, hero plays *thirty-six* times in the desert to enchant the animals, music plays in *thirty-six* places at a marriage, heroine wears *sixteen* ornaments and *thirty-two* jewels, *thirty-six* bands accompany king in procession, serpent can change into *fifty-two* forms. (*O.D.D.* 269, 53, 77, 145.—*F.T.B.* 120, 214.—*L.P.* 31, 76, 155, 161, 176, 237, 300, 324, 342, 350, 426, 438, 515.—*I.A.* I., 117.)

(*m*) *Large numbers:* (1) *one hundred and one:* miraculous egg-plant has *one hundred and one* fruits on it, meaning that whoever marries the gardener's daughter will have *one hundred and one* children. (2) *One thousand and one:* hero's metamorphosed companions and himself number *one thousand and one*. (3) *Miscellaneous large numbers:* oven to kill serpent in consists of *one hundred* kinds of metal, wrestler eats *one hundred and sixty mans* of flour at a sitting, drags along *one hundred and sixty* carts, wrestler's daughter's wallet contains *one hundred and sixty* camels, buck has *three hundred and sixty* wives (does), *one thousand* crows circumvent hero and his companions, hero makes *one thousand* wooden parrots which come to life miraculously, hero has *one hundred and sixty* wives, hero wanders *seventy* years as a mendicant, heroine found in the *hundredth* enchanted palace, heroine has *sixty* maids, hero sports with *seventy* maidens, he announces himself by beating *seventy* gongs, *sixty* steps lead to hero's palace, the prayers of *three hundred and sixty* saints restore a flock of dead goats to life, hero seduces *three hundred and sixty* princesses, parrot has *three hundred and sixty* feathers. (*O.D.D.* 50, 51, 104, 105, 129.—*I.F.T.* 85, 91.—*W.A.S.* 29, 193, 223, 224, 226.—*L.P.* 20, 44, 63, 79, 241, 233, 466, 495.)

(*n*) *Fractions ; aliquot parts of five* : (1) *one and a quarter : one and a quarter lâkhs* of rupees are voted to a shrine, the gates of heroine's palace opened *one and a quarter* watches after sunrise, hero's accounts reach *one and a quarter lâkhs*, hero's ring is worth *one and a quarter lâkhs*, the stone over heroine's cellar (and over golden well) is *one and a quarter hundred mans*, king gives away *one and a quarter mans* of gold daily to the *faqîrs*, heroine prays *one and a quarter* watches before she begins her charming. (2) *Two and half* : hero gives *two and half karors* of rupees to his minister to buy the enchanted horses with, *two and a half* families only remain alive after vengeance on the Nâgs. (*L.P.* 212, 250, 253, 255, 282, 428, 447, 472, 518.—*W.A.S.* 281.)

.

THE END

.

Printed by R. & R. CLARK, *Edinburgh.*

www.ingramcontent.com/pod-product-compliance
Lightning Source LLC
Chambersburg PA
CBHW030820110726
47900CB00006B/1676